ATTUNED EARTH

THE METIER APOCALYPSE
BOOK 1

FRANK G. ALBELO

MOUNTAINDALE
PRESS

ACKNOWLEDGMENTS

I want to thank my family for all the support they have given me with my writing efforts. My wife, for putting up with the random notes left scribbled everywhere and for my son being a constant inspiration with his silly shenanigans. I want to thank all the great people over at MDP for helping my dream of crafting stories for the enjoyment of strangers step into a new, brighter future.

And lastly, but not least, I want to remind everyone that this book is as much mine as the betas, Patrons and readers that helped it reach where it is now. Without their support, I wouldn't be where I am today.

So, I hope all you new readers have a wonderful time delving deeper into the world of Metier!

PROLOGUE

"Sir. The defenses have failed. The predicted damages were reduced, but the area of impact has been increased to roughly 83% of the Earth's surface." The aide hid the tremble in his voice well.

The much older gentleman across the desk from him held his head in his hands. Doctor Raphael Metier sobbed, allowing himself that single moment of weakness as the events of the last decade rushed through him.

This was just another setback. Another curse from the heavens. Nothing new to the people of Earth.

The doctor locked his eyes on the aide. "Get me General Starden. We need to activate the PBBs immediately." The man gulped at the intensity of Metier's stare and quickly scrambled out of the room. He stared through the big, single pane windows of his office as his wife rushed across the lab, dodging the aide with an easy sidestep.

She's always quick, the doctor chuckled darkly to himself. A moment later, Ingrid Metier was in his face.

"What did I tell you, Raph!? It wasn't going to work, and

yet they did it anyway!"she shouted the moment the door shut behind her.

Thank God for soundproofing. His voice was calm, its usual even tone a stark relief to her sharp tongue. "Ingrid, you know as well as me that they weren't listening to the science."

Raphael gestured vaguely at the numerous graphs and readings posted all through his office and out in the lab. Most of which his wife's team had gathered. While Raphael was no slouch when it came to the Metier Crystals and the strange radiation they emitted, it was his wife who deserved the credit.

His wife was the true genius, even if the government had placed him as the figurehead and relegated Ingrid to the sidelines.

"You should have told me! What good is any of this bloody research if they are just going to throw it in the garbage?"

His wife was livid. After discovering the strange radiation five years ago, she'd been pouring her heart and soul into understanding it. Trying to pluck some meaning from the imminent doom of humanity. Now, that doom was but a day away.

Sighing at what he was about to say, and do, the doctor leaned forward to embrace Ingrid. She hadn't noticed when he'd reached into his desk drawer. "They did listen, my love. By God, I'm thankful they listened to you. I am sorry I cannot join you, but I hope you and Marcus can forgive me."

With an unsteady hand, Raphael Metier pricked his wife in the neck.

"Raphael, what are you...?" Ingrid tried to say a few more words but they slurred as the sedative kicked in.

"I'm so sorry. Please take care of Marc. It's time I sacrifice as much for this planet as you have."

The doctor ran his hand gently over the bald head of his wife. A flurry of emotions threatened to halt his actions. *No. They deserve this more than me.* With ice in his veins, he picked up his wife and began to make his way down. Down to the bunker where his son also rested. And where he would not be following.

CHAPTER ONE

Bunker Born

TWENTY SEVEN YEARS LATER

Opening my eyes revealed the same monotonous slab of concrete. The dim halogen lights of the morning settings protested and blinked incessantly as they powered themselves up. *Ben did say we had to stretch them as far as we could...* My thoughts drifted as the sluggishness of sleep disappeared. With a groan, I flung my feet off the side of my bed and rubbed the last bits of sleep out of my eyes.

The plain cube of existence that was my assigned room really left a lot to be desired. Bed, dresser, desk, and a simple bathroom. A smile crept onto my face as my eyes roved over the only truly colorful feature of my room. The shimmering glow of the crystal and mineral stock of the Wildwood Bunker. From simple clear quartz to a head-sized split geode of amethyst, they illuminated their little corner of the room the brighter the overhead light became.

"Ronan! Get your lazy, rock-loving behind in gear," a familiar voice called from down the hall.

"Daniela, I really don't think it's our business to bother Ronan on his off day," a meek voice echoed behind her.

"I will damn well do what I want, Sam. Why don't you go back to the Garden? My business is with stubborn head over here."

"Guys, you know I can hear you both from here, right?" I said, standing and going to wash my face and teeth.

"Good! This'll be the first time I haven't had to drag your butt out of bed," Daniela said as she thrust her face into my small bathroom. "We have business to attend to."

"Wah wouhd gah bii?" I asked around my toothbrush.

"She has it in her head that they are going to be ready to test the implants today," Sam called from over her shoulder. The lanky blond was panting from the pace I was sure he'd endured at Danny's hands.

She liked to run everywhere, which kept us fit without needing to hit the track, but neither of us could really keep up with her. Even with her short stature, she was the fastest person in the whole complex. By a full two minutes, if our mile times were any indication.

"I *know* they are. I snuck a look at my mom's progress records and they say the Metier wavelengths are stable!" she said, unable to hide the excitement in her voice.

I paused as I processed what she'd told me. If the docs on the lower level had been able to stabilize the crystal shards, then they could leave. *We* could leave the Bunker. With a loud splat, I swished water and pushed the duo out of my room. Moving faster than I ever remembered moving, I changed out of my sleeping clothes. A breath later I was outside. "What are we waiting for!?"

Daniela shot me a knowing smirk while Sam shook his head, but they both followed right on my heels. Seconds ticked as we passed two dozen other rooms whose occupants weren't as inclined to awaken. After several flights of stairs, we arrived at B-5 and were standing in front of the research half of the recreation floor. Three ever-present individuals were at their usual stations. Danny's mom, Ava, crunched out health stats on the whole population of the Bunker and her rat test subjects. Elias' wrinkled face frowned at several documents while simultaneously checking over readings on a display beside him. Last but not least was Alan, the self-proclaimed heir to the knowledge on Metier Radiation. The savant was a few feet from Elias as he used several tiny robotic limbs to fit a Metier Crystal into one of three titanium devices.

I didn't even realize I was holding my breath as the iridescent rock the size of my pinky nail made contact with the device. With a flash, and a diminutive cloud of smoke, the crystal bonded itself to the first of three devices. The implants.

"Woooo!" Danny shouted loud enough to set my ears ringing. The moment she did, however, she also alerted the three researchers to our presence. Ava strode through the automatic doors out into the hallway that divided the recreational floor of the Bunker.

"Daniela Carmen Vegas. What in the apocalypse do you think you are doing shouting near the lab? You should be up on housing, helping your father prep breakfast!" Her mother wagged her finger in my over-enthused friend's face.

"But, Mama, I read your notes! It said the implants would be done today. Papa just waved me off when I asked if I could meet with Ron and Sam," the fiery youth responded meekly, her earlier energy flagging under her mom's scowl.

"Ay, Juan. Mi amor... Fine. But I want you three to stay put while we work," Ava grumbled as she turned to the door. An excited yip from Danny prompted her to spin on her heels. "And *quiet!*"

We all turned away from the woman, properly chastised. The two men in the room waved their greeting before returning to their work. I did notice that Elias' frown had deepened considerably, and his smile hadn't quite reached his eyes when waving to our little group. Certainly something I needed to make sure to ask him about later. As the oldest resident of our Bunker, and also the most senior researcher on the team, anything that concerned him was something that I wanted to be aware of.

With the permission of Danny's mother, we plastered ourselves to the see-through glass of the lab. After the brief distraction of our presence, the researchers were all business within minutes. Deftly maneuvering the robotic limbs, Alan made adjustments to the implants that had yet to receive a crystal, while Elias provided constant readouts on any changes. The specifics of the MetierTech developments, as they were labeling the implants, were *way* outside any of our fields of expertise. I was happy to catch the occasional word addressing power levels, effective impacts, and neural regulations.

Unlike the usual banter that permeated our times together, responses were curt while we watched the creation of the other two implants. The only real quip was directed at me from Danny for fogging up the glass with my 'unnatural mouth-breathing.'

We were so caught up in her barb we nearly missed the final implant's completion. Silence reigned in the lab for a second before Ava and Elias hugged and cried at their success while Alan smiled gently from beside them. The frown I'd seen on Elias' face completely disappeared with their final success, and I couldn't keep the smile from my face either.

We were going to go to the surface!

— + —

"Now, this is an important discussion," Elias said from across the table.

"Mr. Barnes, every discussion where you sit us down to talk is an important discussion," I shot back. "We understand that there are risks to taking the implants."

After the actual devices had been completed, Ava had immediately started to run diagnostics on them. Alan continued to crunch numbers on his tablet while Elias took the opportunity to corner us before we could weasel our way into the lab proper.

"Yes, Ronan, I understand that might well be the case. Nevertheless, the information we discuss here will have an impact on you and I need this to be clear. Understood?" Elias' tone brooked no argument as the three of us nodded, me a bit more hesitantly than my friends. The strain on his expression from earlier was the first thing that came to mind.

"As you three are well aware of, this isn't just a random Bunker built by hicks to survive the end of the world," Elias began, gesturing around us at the bare conference room. "The Planetary Biosphere Bunkers project had a very small window for implementation, but the concerted efforts since the discovery of the Metier Crystals definitely paid off. These Bunkers were the final hope for humanity. Seeds from which we could rise up and return to the surface after Landfall."

"Teach already covered all of this, Mr. Barnes," Sam said, tilting his head slightly in confusion. "We know the mission of the Bunker."

"Yes, my boy, but I need to impress this upon you three. The discoveries and breakthroughs we have achieved here are unprecedented. As a matter of fact, we wouldn't even feel comfortable sending *anyone* to the surface if *the* Ingrid Metier hadn't been present in this Bunker during the first days of the Fall."

Elias averted his eyes from mine to the table at the mention of the key researcher involved with the radiation emitted by the crystals. She had been so pivotal in tracking the growing energy sources and devising ways of countering their interference that they had named them after her. The fact that she'd been in our Bunker was news to all of us.

"She's great and all, but what's that got to do with anything?" Daniela said.

Leave it to Danny to dismiss the singular person responsible for us being alive at all.

"You three are it. Not even Ingrid was able to cut through

the interference to communicate with the other Bunkers before she passed away, and the government... well, they didn't see it fit to tell us the locations of any other ones. We might just be the only ones left capable of accomplishing the original goal of the Bunker."

I blinked as I tried to process what the mayor of the Bunker said. The implants weren't just an out for us; they were the final hurrah, a push of desperation for the only people they had known all their lives. If there weren't survivors on the surface tucked away somewhere, the task of reestablishing humanity on Earth fell in our lap... It did certainly light a fire under our butts, but it also carried a weight I didn't think any of us had considered.

No one in the Bunker, us excluded, was really of child-rearing age. Not to mention that the radiation had severely unfortunate side effects on pregnancies. The deaths of Sam's and my mother were examples enough for the people of the Bunker to have resorted to any number of birth control tactics. No one talked about those early years for a reason, and none of us felt equipped to pry.

Now more than ever we *needed* to get to the surface and hope to God we found survivors, or stumbled upon another of the PBBs.

"Dang, doc. You sure know how to bring down the mood," Daniela said, leaning back in her chair and running her hands through her hair. Samuel had his arms crossed and his frown looked chiseled from stone.

"I say this to make sure you all understand that being our... emissaries to the surface also puts you at the greatest risk. Please, believe me when I say this, your feelings about getting to the surface are reciprocated. Not that anyone in the Bunker wants to dissuade you from actually getting out, but don't get complacent and, by the last box of duct tape in storage, please don't get lost to the emotions you might feel on the surface," Elias said, making sure to meet our eyes as he spoke.

"We understand, sir. I don't plan to see the sun for the first time just to die right after," I said, cracking a dark joke in an attempt to disperse the somber mood. After all, even with all those potential responsibilities, it wasn't every day that you got to see a star in all its burning, ultraviolet glory for the first time in your life.

CHAPTER TWO

Implanted

"Now, I want to make sure that you three understand the consequences and impacts that these are going to have on your health," Elias started, his hands waving in the air with each word. He'd always been one of those people that spoke with their hands as much as with their mouth. Since we'd left the conference room upon receiving Ava's confirmation that the implants were ready, the appendages finally joined the conversation.

"The implants could have severely good *and* bad impacts on your nervous system, for one. It is part of the reason we were hesitant to bring them up to you so quickly. You can thank Mr. Fallon here for his overeager infiltration of classified files." Sam blushed while Danny and I shared a chuckle at his expense.

"Mr. Barnes, you just spent the last hour lecturing us about the responsibility of the implants, perhaps we can skip the health advisory?" I pleaded.

"Nonsense. It would be a stain on my reputation to go ahead with something of this magnitude without expounding on all the factors revolving around it," Elias said, voice unwavering.

We'd found out about the implant project two years ago, and since then, we'd been nagging Elias to let *us* act as the lab rats. Instead of the *actual* lab rats they'd been intended for. Needless to say, the project had taken on a whole new level of complexity. None of us knew exactly why they agreed to adjust the project timeframe, but neither did we complain. After our discussion in the conference room, I had a suspicion the Bunker didn't have much fuel left in the metaphorical tank.

"—permanent death or disfigurement," he finished as I reined in my drifting thoughts.

Cheerful options those.

"I think we've been briefed enough on the risk, Mr. Barnes," I said, trying to push past the researcher's hesitance. The finish line was right there, and I was honestly eager for something other than a reminder of danger.

"Ronan. I understand that you feel like you need to go out there, but it isn't going to be a happ—"

"I know that," I cut him off. I winced, and tried to backpedal. "I mean…"

"It's alright, Ronan. I suppose none of you are children anymore, even if you always will be in our eyes." The old researcher scratched at a beard that no longer grew evenly on his face. "Very well. I will call for Alexia and June to begin. If the procedure is a success, you'll report to Ben so he can outfit you."

Something that could not be said about Elias Barnes was that he was one for half measures. We'd expected to be sent out *soon* after the implants were operational, but the same day? *Wonderful.*When the doctor and nurse-turned-doctor combo of Alexia and June appeared outside of the lab, I knew it was time. The first step in our long path to return to Earth.

I wanted to provide some encouraging words for my friends as we were pulled one by one into the operating room, but the words died in my throat. Most of the Bunker's population stopped by at one time or another during our wait to congratulate us and wish us luck. Sweat made my palms slick as I tapped my feet anxiously on the ground. I wasn't sure why Dr. Alexia hadn't brought Danny and then Sam back outside, but it had my nerves fully on end.

While the prospect of returning to the surface was an impossible allure, I would not have traded the lives of my two best friends for it. Ever. When the older woman made her way out of the room to get me, I couldn't help but falter a step on the way. She took my shaking hand with a gentle smile and walked me through the procedure.

"Since I know what your first question will be, we still have Samuel and Daniela in observation. I need you to focus, Ronan. I am going to be attaching the probing sensors along your spine. One horizontal cut and two smaller vertical cuts should be all that it takes to implant the device. June and I have practiced the procedure an impossible number of times—on potatoes, mind you—but I need you to stay focused. The procedure will happen while you are awake so we can get live feedback; we are only going to numb you."

At the mention of being awake for such an invasive procedure, my blood ran cold. I nodded in understanding, letting out a shuddering breath. Definitely wasn't going to back out now.

Over the course of the next twenty minutes, I was disrobed, washed, and the lower back portion of my head was shaved. With the preparation complete, Alexia took precise measurements of just where my spine and nerve responses were. The doctors spent time sterilizing everything in a vat that smelled like a stronger version of the vodka the Bunker survivors had figured out how to make. Another marked reminder that the Bunker hadn't been designed to handle a procedure of the scale the two women were attempting, despite their expertise.

Alexia and June kept up a constant stream of conversation, certainly to keep me distracted as they injected me with some kind of sedative. I barely registered the pinch of the needle as they numbed me.

Funny enough, the thing that kept my focus the entire time

that I was implanted was a series of hairs. More specifically, one from each of my friends' heads.

A single brown brunette curl of Daniela's clung for dear life from the edge of June's reused surgical booties. Samuel's blond strand laid near imperceptible right next to Alexia, barely avoiding being stepped on as she moved around behind me. Lastly, my own short black specks. There was a small gathering of them, to be sure, having been missed in the two women's efforts to keep me calm while also maintaining as sterile a space as possible given the limited resources of the Bunker.

Their presence reminded me of our parents and, subsequently, the lonely nightmare that they'd endured for us. For all of humanity. We would be going to the surface, while they yet remained below.

When I blinked that thought away, I realized that there was something *new* in my field of vision. Like a speck of dust that had managed to make its way into my eye, I tried to blink it away.

"Wonderful, Ronan! You didn't falter at all during the procedure. We can begin testing the calibration. Do you see something in your eyes?"

"Ahh… yes? Blurry lines in my right eye?" I asked, uncertain.

"Very good, hold still." An extremely loud mechanical whir drew my attention behind me. Had I not been completely strapped to the table and mostly anesthetized, I might have jumped away in fear at all the horrific images that sound brought to mind. "How's that, love?"

Blinking to try to clear away some of the blurriness, I saw *words* take shape.

Subject: Ronan Terrigan
Vitals: Expand…
Metier Radiation: Neutral
LPS: Expand…
Wildwood, FL

Communications

"Holy crap!" I exclaimed. It felt like I was wearing one of the virtual reality headgear we used for simulation training. Minus the clunky helmet and low resolution graphics. I went on to describe what I saw, even pointing out that some of the words looked bolded while others didn't.

"That's perfectly normal and intended. The bolded words should be toggleable interface points, while the standard script is data. Say 'vitals' while you focus on the word you see," June coached me. I heard Alexia fiddling with something on the other side of the room, but I did as was told. Focusing through the adrenaline that was pumping through me was a bit difficult, but I finally managed to calm down enough. When I said vitals, the lower half of the display disappeared and more information appeared.

Subject: Ronan Terrigan
Vitals:
BPM (91)
Oxygen Sat (94%)
Lactic Acid (Neutral)

I saw my heart rate spike into the one hundreds as the change happened. A thought 'back' returned the words to their first configuration. When I described the experience, Alexia sounded extremely excited. Having known her for my whole life, I knew she was giddy to be tweaking strange and unnatural knobs in my brain.

After the successful test with vitals, she had me open the LPS, Local Positioning System, which showed a detailed map of the area. While the map was from over twenty seven years ago, it was the clearest and most controllable map I'd ever seen. A mere thought highlighted, zoomed or panned it. I was pretty sure I could have kept playing with the tech for much longer, but the doctors kept me on task.

"Next we want you to open communications. This one may take some—"

"Sam? Yeah! It's like we have one of those 'cellphone' things right in our heads," I said, already having figured out how to manipulate the basic features of the implant. When I opened the communications tab, I'd received a list of two people. Unsurprisingly, they were labeled 'Samuel Fallon' and 'Daniela Vegas.' The mere thought brought up a ringing tone that almost instantly clicked with Sam.

"Ronan! Please, you must be careful until we have everything properly calibrated before you go making semi-telepathic calls!" June said in alarm, going so far as to crouch and look up at my face.

"Sorry. Talk to you later, eh, Sam?" I heard the man chuckle through our connection before 'hanging up' as I gave the doctor a sheepish grin. The scolding she had been meaning to give me wasn't very successful.

"He's all good, June. Better stitch him up and wheel him in to his fellow troublemakers before they give each other an aneurysm from using the comm system."

Sure enough, a few minutes later, I was laying on an individual bed, face down, next to my friends.

"Well, that was fun," Danny said, a slight wince in her voice. "I hope Ben sends us out with some pain killers, because my neck is going to be sore. The sedative is already fading for me."

"That's because they only gave you a drop, what with how small you are," Sam said.

"Very funny, Mr. 'Youch! Please more drugs,'" Danny quipped back. "Don't think they were even done numbing you before you were asking for more!"

"Hey, you know medication works weird on me," the blond protested.

"Guys? I love the energy and all, but maybe it will be worth it to *relax* a tad. If we are going to be heading out to the surface today, we are probably going to need to be as rested as we can," I said. I couldn't believe I was being the proactive one, but I felt justified. The only thing I was ever really motivated about was Earth and my friends. The fact that I would be getting out of the Bunker *and* with my friends had me apprehensive about messing it up.

"Sure, Ron. I think we can hold our barbs till we are under the sun. The real one..." Sam's voice drifted and I knew my friend had entered his recurring daydream. One precisely about the sun none of us had ever seen. Not that I blamed him, since all of us had them. A strange side effect of exposure to Metier Radiation, Alan had told us, which was magnitudes worse for those born after Landfall. That is to say, just us three.

I'm not sure how long we laid there. Drifting in and out of sleep as the anesthesia wore off, the itch and throb of the implant became a constant presence. Blessedly, our duo of doctors arrived with painkillers as they checked their handiwork. From the snippets of their conversation, they sounded alarmed at the rate the injuries had healed. My interest might have been even more piqued if I hadn't been fighting to remain focused through the medication.

"You three are good to go. Just try to take it easy for a few days. Today is just a quick trip to the surface and back. To test the functions of the implant," Alexia added poignantly. The accusatory finger in Danny's face certainly sent a message about who she thought would cause trouble.

"Mrs. Perry, don't worry. It's only the most important day of our lives so far. No biggie." I smirked, drawing the woman's attention. I saw a shadow fall over her face as she considered my words. It was gone in a flash.

"Yes, Ronan. It might well be. I suppose it's hard for an old woman to really understand your feelings. However, if you three are successful, that would change everything!" Her downcast expression was replaced with a blazing smile.

"What are we waiting for then!?" Danny said as she leapt off her bed. Only to wobble unsteadily until June was able to help her. "Maybe a bit more waiting," she answered unsteadily to a round of snorts from the rest of us.

CHAPTER THREE

The Surface

The trek up to B-2 was uneventful, if tense. June had insisted on escorting us to Ben, who was to be our escort to the exit of the Bunker. Our ex-teacher had his feet propped up on his office desk while my father chatted him up. I was surprised to see him outside of the greenhouse floor, so I staggered mid-step as we rounded one of the numerous stacks of supplies in the storage floor.

"Dad?" I asked, a bout of nervousness shooting up through me.

"Ronny! How could you not tell me the implants were going to be complete today?" he said as he jumped to his feet and made his way to our little group. Without waiting for a reply, he embraced all four of us, June included.

"Dale, if you would," June said as she poked his arm.

"Oops, sorry!" he exclaimed, taking two steps back.

"No you aren't," Ben added from his spot at his desk. An open leaflet covered his face from the shining lights above. "Twenty seven years with the same group of people hasn't been enough to get you to stop hugging everyone on sight. Why would today be any different?"

"Now that is just rude. I merely have a proper grasp of where my priorities are."

"In breaking people's personal space bubble?" With a loud groan, Ben rose from his spot. Catching the leaflet as it fell, the bulky man joined us. "Good to see you kids came out alright. Especially you, Ron, what with this hippy clinging to you like you were going to fall apart."

Dad glared in Ben's direction, eliciting a wince from the storage manager. "Never mind. Elias got me up to speed. I have some basic stuff for you three just in case, then we are going to see you off on the engineering floor."

June waved us off after taking a moment to check on our stitches. They had long stopped bleeding. In the meantime, I saw my dad help Ben unload a duffle bag. We stared at the bag curiously, but Ben swatted my hand away when I tried to reach for it.

"Patience. Can you grab the vests, Dale?" With a serious expression, one that I rarely recalled seeing on his face, my dad strode out of sight. "Now, I'll be quick before your pacifist father gets back. Here in this bag are a set of handguns and magazines for each of you. I know you aren't much of a shot, Samuel, but I would feel better if you kept it on you. Danny, I fully expect you to hit center mass on anything you find. Understood?"

"What do you mean? Why would we need weapons?" Samuel asked, his eyes wide as Ben opened the duffle.

"The animals above ground, they… aren't the same. I know the others wanted to keep the information from you all until after the first few trips, but I don't trust chance. Mother Nature has been twisted, and the animals and plants you've come to know in your studies are probably much different," Ben said. He looked over his shoulder as my dad's steps drew nearer. "Don't tell anyone I told you until after you return. Elias was very clear that they would manage the 'surface' situation."

With a tug, Ben flipped the duffle inside out. Some hidden layer of material covered the guns while revealing a few reusable water bottles and several packs of insta-meals. Even with the ominous message our old teacher had dropped on us, its impact was muffled when we laid our eyes on the dehydrated food.

"Oh, please no. There *has* to be something else. *Anything,*" Danny begged.

"This is what the Bunker manifest authorized for the first twenty excursions to the surface. Those packs were meant for teams of five, so you three have a way to go before you get any better rations," Ben answered, a knowing smile dispelling some of the tension of his previous words. "You'll be through them in a flash."

"Yeah, because we'll puke them," the woman added. It certainly didn't help being the daughter of the Bunker's head cook when it came to terrible food.

"Oh, my dear Daniela. They aren't that bad. You should tell them about the early days, Benjamin. Before the greenhouse was fully up and running!" my dad said as he rejoined us, having overheard the tail end of our conversation. When I glanced at Ben, a frown wrinkled his bald head.

"Don't remind me of that nightmare. We had these twice a day for almost a year!"

"We rarely hear anything about the early days of the Bunker. Neither do we really hear anything about the days after the discovery of the Metier Crystals. Why is there so much secrecy?" I asked. Those two topics were a constant sore spot for us three. Not even our concerted efforts on Juan, Daniela's father, had managed to crack him. The cook was about as easy going as they came, yet he clammed up at the mention of those days.

"I think once you've been to the surface, Elias ought to bring you up to speed. He hasn't led us astray yet," Ben added, giving the dufflebag a meaningful look. "But before that, Dale, if you will."

"Right, of course!" My dad presented each of us with tactical vests. "These are military grade bulletproof vests. We figured that they would be a good utility compromise for you all on your first trip. Nothing should be shooting at you up there, but they are good against falls or anything mundane like that. There should be a multitool and a survival knife on the bracings."

"Wow," I said, looking over the sleek lines of the equipment. I'd seen similar gear during our simulation training, but never the real deal. When my father handed them over, they felt surprisingly light. The multitool was standard fare in the Bunker, there was even an identical one stashed inside of my desk, but the knife was a first for all of us but Danny.

I wasn't sure how long we took staring before strapping on the equipment, but I didn't care. The fact that we had received so many things meant that the elders of the Bunker were serious about returning to the surface. *After our last talk, I can definitely see why.* When we were all ready, I slung the duffle over my shoulder with ease.

My father gave all three of us a hug before Ben managed to peel him off of us. Making sure we promised we'd return quickly, he left us to return to the greenhouse.

Don't worry, Dad. You'll be managing a farm topside any day now. I cast a look down the flight of stairs and we made our way through to engineering. The main hallway cut through the floor while doors hid hundreds of different machines from sight. A pair of technicians waved in greeting before disappearing into different rooms.

Ben had tried to explain some of the specifics to us during his time as our teacher, but the material had gone over our heads. After that, he'd emphasize that 'this makes power,' 'this circulates air,' and 'this pumps our water' when referring to the different regions of the floor.

However, on this trip, he took us past all the rooms and toward a dead end. Or what we'd long ago assumed to be a dead end. The earth sciences professor pressed his hand against the wall, causing a panel to open out. The silence from the three of us remained throughout the whole process of Ben working the touch screen through a series of prompts, but the hum of other voices prompted us to turn around.

Making their way to us were Danny's parents, Samuel's dad, and Elias. The odd quartet walked directly to this not-dead-end. *They knew this was here. All of them...Why keep all of this stuff hidden? Did it have anything to do with the early days of the Bunker and why they never mentioned Ingrid Metier?*

My train of thought was derailed when Mayor Elias and the others reached our group. I couldn't read my friends' expressions regarding the strange developments, but I could tell they were just as confused as me. Regardless, they both moved to embrace their parents. Juan and Ava were all smiles, while Sam's dad, Jerome, looked about ready to have a nervous breakdown. We all traded hugs and they wished us luck before stepping back when Elias approached.

"Children. It appears you beat us to the exit. My apologies for the delay, but I had to inform your parents. Ronan, where is your father?" Elias asked as he shook all of our hands.

"He met us early, then went back to the greenhouse. You know him," I said, adjusting the duffle bag on my shoulder. Ben's words, and Elias' veiled warnings, echoed in my mind.

"Ah, no matter. I just wanted to check that there were no issues with the implants and to see you all off. This first door is the only electric one, the others you three will have to open manually." He gestured behind us where the wall was moving out of the way on unnaturally silent hinges for something that was more than three feet thick. The space beyond looked to have a similar dead end wall, but now that I knew about the *one* hidden door, there were surely more.

"I have authorized you three with access. I trust that you will use discretion with this clearance. As much as we know about Metier Radiation, it pales in comparison to what we *don't*. I want you three to remember that this is just a test so we can adjust the implants to the radiation levels on the surface. Two hours, and then you return. We are all hopeful for the future.

No need to compromise further trips," Elias added with a wrinkled smile.

After yet another awkward series of hugs, back pats, and teary eyes, we watched the concrete slab of a door slide closed behind us. I felt a sudden bout of claustrophobia, but thankfully my friends were there to distract me from our stony enclosure.

"Man, that was awkward and way too emotionally charged," Danny said.

"You can say that again," Sam agreed.

"Come on, guys. I think seeing the sun for the first time ought to shake us out of the funk the possibility of impending doom put us in," I said, walking toward the panel we could see to the right.

"Don't need to say *that* again!" Danny said as she rushed toward the panel ahead of us. "I call dibs on this one! Mr. Barnes said we had two more which works perfectly!"

"I'll take the next one then," Sam added. The blond patted me on the shoulder. "You should take the topside one, Ronan."

"You sure?" I asked, suddenly hesitant as the prospect of finally seeing Earth brought a lump to my throat.

"Oh, for sure. You've been waiting the longest out of all of us."

"Man, I'm only a few months older than you!" I quipped back, poking my friend in the ribs. He flinched, as I knew he would, and followed after Danny with a chuckle.

Taking a moment to really appreciate how lucky I was to have such *great* friends, I joined them at the console. Thankfully, while Sam and I had been distracted, Daniela had bothered to look over the instructions for opening the doorway. She had us stand midway down the wall where a panel prompted authorization. After a soft click, the slab separated itself inward from the larger wall with a pop. Just visible were two handholds. I set down the duffle bag as Sam and I strained to pull open the concrete block. Thankfully, as the thing started to pivot, the slight momentum helped finish the turn.

Sam and I panted as we stepped away from the two foot

thick rounded doorway, while Danny simply strode through. As she stepped through, having expected our complaints, she called over her shoulder. "I read the instructions. Don't you *dare* say I didn't contribute!"

I grumbled my way through the doorway after passing Sam the duffle bag. Thankfully, shutting the doorway was much easier and I realized the door was set at a slight angle so that it was easier to close than open. *Curious...* Shaking my questions about the door's design off, we repeated the same process for the second and then finally third door.

I'd half expected rays of sunlight to creep through the opening as I stepped through the third doorway, but it just revealed an extremely dusty lobby area. Two counters flanked the doorway and on the other end was a simple metal door. Fluorescent light from the concrete tomb shone over my shoulder. Its white sheen reflected off the few spots in the lobby that *weren't* covered in dust. However, soft light filtered through the gaps on the door before me. Without waiting for my friends, I rushed between the two counters and tried the door.

With a loud squeak, the world turned unimaginably bright. And colorful. And full of *life*.

A golden orb shone down from a real sky above us, and a natural breeze caressed my face as it passed. The smells I'd come to know from the greenhouse floor, but mixed with hundreds more, reached me and I felt tears stream down my face.

I heard gasps from behind me and I knew my friends had made it to the surface with me. Out from the bowels of Earth and onto the surface. After a few seconds of simply staring at the sun and the gentle clouds that drifted across the sky, I knew that I couldn't go back to the Bunker. I loved the people there, but I'd never felt the rush of adrenaline I did those first few minutes on the surface. Just *being* on the surface pumped energy through me. I wanted to jump around and run around and explore.

Explore!

The word brought the rest of the world into focus. Outside of the sky, there was the earth. Dozens of strange green, orange, yellow, and purple flowers and grass covered the ground around us. A few feet from us was what I recognized from our simulation training as a game trail that led further into a forest. *A forest!* Full of real trees, not the single apple tree on the greenhouse floor.

I half turned to call out to my friends when I saw them frozen in place. A mix of fear, awe, and confusion scrunched their faces. When I panned to the side, I saw the source of their reaction. A dog-sized squirrel was glaring in their direction. Propped on a tree that had grown over where the Bunker was built, the creature sniffed the air and spun to look at me. When its eyes landed on me, however, I finally realized it wasn't just an oversized squirrel. Ridges of gray fur cut geometric patterns along its body, while a faint fog enveloped it.

Immediately, I remembered Ben's warning and reached for the zipper on my bag. The squirrel didn't like that at all. With a piercing whistle, it leapt off the tree and *flew*. Thankfully, it didn't head straight for my friends, instead opting to take a flapless glide up above our heads.

"Danny, here!" I shouted as I chucked one of the pistols at my friend. She was still shell-shocked, but Sam managed to catch the weapon in hand. "If it comes closer, shoot it!"

Fumbling with the bag, I pulled out the other two handguns and spun in slow arcs while making my way to my friends. I cast a longing look at the door into the lobby space. *Crap, we were so caught up we were wandering!* The path down to the bunker was easily two hundred feet behind us. From the single leap I'd seen of the squirrel, it would be able to cover that distance in a moment.

"Sam, give Danny the gun. I don't think I'll be able to hit this thing. Doubt it's going to be friendly," I said, passing him my second gun. I looked around, having lost sight of the creature.

"It's circling above us like a vulture. Danny, Danny!" Sam snapped at our friend, finally getting her out of her head.

"Wha… What is that thing?" she said, grabbing the handgun with practiced ease. She took a moment to adjust to the weight of a real gun, but immediately brought it up by her face. "Check your safeties," she added as she flicked her own.

"Damn it, that would have been bad," I said as I flicked the tiny lever that would have kept the gun useless. I blinked as a red line of text highlighted itself in my vision.

BPM (147)

"It's coming!" Sam exclaimed as he spotted the creature divebombing us. I blinked the notification away with a thought before training my gun on the squirrel.

"Hold it, dive out of the way when it gets closer. When it banks, we'll have a better shot!" Daniela called as the three of us stood back to back. I held my breath as the gray form of the creature grew in size. "Now!"

I tucked myself into a half roll and turned on my knee back to where the creature was directed. Making sure that neither of my friends were in the line of fire, I let out two shots. The weapon jerked in my hand, and a moment later, the creature wailed as one of my shots clipped it. The second after, it dropped to the ground thanks to a headshot from Danny. *Damn, she's a good shot.*

The still fast-moving creature tumbled like a rock. Thanks to that initial surprise, we were more than a bit hesitant to continue exploring, instead we paused to regroup and watched the trees and sky intently.

"You think the gunshots scared anymore of those things away?" Sam asked. "It was so fast."

"I don't know. But I know it wasn't the friendly nut-hoarders that used to live on the surface," I said, finishing yet another sweep of our surroundings. It was eerily silent except for the rustling of leaves and the grass around us. "We should go check it out. How are you doing, Danny?"

"Eleven shots left." I heard the click as she slotted her mag back in the gun. Pausing to check the duffle bag, I counted three spare mags and decided that it was as good a time as any to spread them around. Making sure to keep eyes on all the surrounding trees as we moved forward, we reached the body of the strange squirrel.

A small pool of deep red blood spread across the ground and bits of skull peppered the ground around the dead creature. I heard Sam gag behind me, and Danny immediately reassured him. Taking a step closer, I nudged the creature with my boot.

The instant that my foot made contact with the creature, it started to crystallize. A rippling wave of sparkly stone covered the creature in less than ten seconds. I was speechless as I stared at the sudden change. When the change completed, there was a squirrel-shaped statue of what I could only identify as smoky quartz; it shattered like a dropped lightbulb. The fragments floated up slowly into the air before zipping straight toward Danny. Just as I was about to warn Danny to look out for the strange fragments, the cloud split off. A significantly smaller spray of the smoky quartz slammed right into my chest.

I braced for the hit, but the moment they reached me, they passed right through my vest as if it wasn't there. The impact didn't feel physical. However, any further thoughts vanished as all of my muscles snapped me stiff. The motion was so sudden and extreme that I cracked every joint with the force of the spasm and dropped to the ground, a fragile pile of Ronan. I couldn't help but feel like the very crumbled squirrel I'd nudged.

Then the pain hit me.

I'd only ever broken my arm once during a stupid fall when I was younger. The agony that the fragments had caused me was similar but multiplied about a hundredfold *everywhere*. Immediately, the world fell out of focus. A strangled cry left my throat as I tried to call for my friends only to see a small pillar of fire rising into the air. I didn't have the presence of mind to process that development, especially when bold red outlines appeared in my vision. Even through the blur that was the rest of the world, I was able to read the lines.

Vitals:
BPM (ERROR)
Oxygen Sat (ERROR)
Lactic Acid (ERROR)
Metier Radiation: ERROR

Then the world faded into blissful darkness.

CHAPTER FOUR

Attuned

"AAAHHH—"My scream was cut off part way by a sweaty palm.

"Ronan, be quiet!" Sam whispered in my ear. When my wide eyes met his, I gave him a small nod that I understood. My friend removed his hand from my mouth and slowly laid me back on the ground. I did a double take as I looked around and saw a pale Danny propped against a nearby tree. Samuel was crouched between us, holding his gun in a death grip. I could see his eyes scanning the forest around us wildly.

Memories from before I'd lost consciousness flashed through my mind and I laid as still as I could as I ran my hands over my body. *Nothing is broken... Was I drugged or something?* Risking propping myself up to my elbows, I took a good look around us. We were tucked away in a small thicket of trees. Just beyond the trees I could see... more trees. Except directly behind us, where I could see a raging inferno.

"Holy hydroponics! Samuel, what the hell is happening?" I asked, quickly dropping my voice to a whisper after he glared at me.

"I don't know, man. All kinds of crazy. There was a pair of

these… tortoises. They were chasing us after Daniela caught all that grass on fire, and then I panicked, but then I shot one of them and the other ran away. But the bullets! It took so many of them and I just dragged you two. And you, you were in pieces, but now you are not, so I'm not sure if you were…" Samuel started to ramble.

Electing the most direct approach I snapped my fingers in his face to bring him back to the moment. "Sam, calm down. I'm not sure what happened, but I feel alright for now. What happened with Daniela, how did she set the fire? Also, why didn't you drag us toward the Bunker?"

"That was the problem. She didn't set the fire, she *was* the fire. She was suddenly covered in flames and they torched all that colorful grass."

Slapping my head at the realization, I turned back to my friend. "She set the path back to the Bunker on fire?" Nod. "And she was somehow on fire, but isn't anymore?" Second nod.

"When I tried to reach for her, she extinguished herself, but it was too late. In your case—" A deep rumble interrupted Sam. Prompting him to spin completely. "It's here!"

"What's here?" I asked with concern.

"The other tortoise!" Not dumb enough to keep the conversation going, I crouched and looked out beyond the trees encircling us. Sure enough, a tortoise looked to be scanning the trees.

"Give me a gun, Sam," I hissed as the large creature crawled into view. It looked almost like a regular gopher tortoise except nearly one and a half times larger. The longer I stared, the more I realized that instead of a regular carapace, it had stone and some sort of mineral cluster sprouting from its back. *Yep. We are either drugged out of our minds, or Earth is busted beyond belief.*

"I only have the one, Ronan. I left the others and the duffle when I picked you two up," he said, attempting to hand the pistol over. I pressed the weapon back into his hand.

"Keep it. If that thing tries to get closer, I'll grab it and you shoot it. Is it still slow like regular tortoises?" I asked, flexing my hands and scanning the creature's large back for possible handholds.

"In short spurts. It can... roll," he whispered as the creature turned our way.

"Oh, by the apocalypse. You better not shoot me!" I leapt out of the thicket. The moment the tortoise laid eyes on me, the crystals on its back glowed briefly before expanding. By several inches. "Ah crap."

Just like Sam mentioned, the thing tucked its front legs and head in, then rolled. The tortoise did a perfect cartwheel in my direction. I waited as long as I could to dodge, one of the crystals on its back drawing a gash on my vest. Staggering on my feet from the hit, I watched the creature easily tilt its weight and begin cartwheeling back my way. Leaving its underside exposed.

"Now, Sam! Its underbody should be weaker!" I shouted, hoping my assumption proved true as I rolled out of the way of the tortoise's second pass. Four loud barks marked the shots from Sam. Three managed to hit center mass on the creature's belly, pushing it onto its back. The fourth flew wide and deeper into the forest. To my utter surprise, the thing wasn't dead.

I could see cracks spiderweb from its underbody, even a bit of blood, but the creature was still trying to roll itself over.

"Sam, shoot again!"

"I'm out!" he called out.

I groaned loudly as I rushed back towards the creature. When it noticed my approach, it kicked out wildly with its legs and snapped at me with its head. Avoiding a sweep from one of its front legs, I shoved it back toward the ground. *This is the fastest turtle-adjacent creature I have ever seen!* With its impending righting halted for the moment, I looked around for a weapon. Anything. A thick branch to my left caught my attention and I lunged for it.

As if the tortoise had been waiting for the exact moment I moved away, it pushed itself off of the ground almost instantly. Thankfully, my friend was there to prevent it from regaining its legs. With a heaving effort, Sam lifted the tortoise up, balancing it on two of its flailing legs. The veins on his neck and face strained, the stony beast clearly out of his weight class.

I gripped the branch tightly, then clocked the creature in the head just as it was about to snap at my friend. With its head recoiling into its shell to recover, its fight died some. Bracing the branch against the ground and the cracked underbody area, I pushed. At first, all I did was help Sam keep hold of the creature and prevent it from mauling us both. When its head exited its shell and its thrashing intensified, the tables turned. In our favor. The power and weight behind its movements worked against it. My branch made its way into its body like a stake.

Apparently, holding my impromptu weapon while it was inside of the creature was enough to cause the effect I'd seen from the squirrel to trigger. This time, the crystallization happened almost instantly. While the shell didn't change much, its head and legs took on a deep gray color, a slight metallic sheen covering its surface. *Which I suppose makes sense, if anything still makes sense.* Just like the flying squirrel, the tortoise began to crumble into fragments. Most of them flew my way, but the rest of the torrent slammed straight into Sam's chest. My gangly friend took a short flight back into the denser foliage.

Okay, maybe it is physical? I thought as I rushed to his side. To my horror, the man started to convulse on the ground. Vines grew from where his hair had been and his skin took on a rough, leafy texture. In moments, I was holding what amounted to a giant pile of Sam-shaped plants. None of my efforts to stir my friend did anything, and whenever I ripped some of the plants off his skin, more just grew back in their place. Hoping that his condition would improve like my own had, I carried him back to the thicket with Danny.

The area around the thicket was empty, but I was cautious to remain as hidden as I could manage. Strings of plans and possible avenues for our survival overwhelmed my taxed mind. There were monsters on the surface, and apparently they made us lose consciousness when we killed them. Why wasn't Danny up by now? How long was I out for? *Hold on.* That strange cloud hadn't knocked me out *or* over like it had Samuel. I looked over my body for any injury or weird symptom like my friend had mentioned.

When I prodded the torn portion of my vest, I didn't even feel sore. Which was impossible, considering the strength with which the strange creature had hit me. I was so caught up in my thoughts that I missed the smell of burning until it was almost too late. Spinning at the sudden brightness in the thicket, I saw that the fire had spread significantly and our shelter was toast.

I pulled my friends out of the thicket, straining under their combined weight, but managing to return to where the corpse of the tortoise fell. Or where it should have been. In its place was a trio of crystal-encrusted plates from its shell, as well as what looked like a ball of living mud. The crackle of fire behind me didn't give me time as a gust of wind brought the heat closer. *I'll be back,* I promised the strange items on the ground as I moved past them.

Thankfully, I had thought to grab the gun after hiding Samuel. On the flip side, there were only two bullets in the backup magazine. *I certainly hope there are no other hungry critters around.*

With the weapon tucked in my belt, I slowly made my way as far from the fire as I could. Casting a look at the sky revealed that it had to be some time in the early afternoon. Without supplies and with the strange animals, there was no way we would make it on the surface. *Who would have thought I would want to be back underground so quickly?* I couldn't help the dark chuckle that escaped me.

I wasn't sure how long I ambled around the forest, dodging another tortoise, several squirrels, and even a strange flaming bird. By that point, I was sure that *everyone* had underestimated what madness the Metier Radiation had done to Earth and that it was to blame for whatever had happened to the three of us. When the sky started to change color, I started to lose hope.

Even without a watch, it was clear we'd missed our deadline to return to the bunker.

I'd been looking for somewhere to hunker down and hopefully head back to the Bunker once Sam and Danny were restored. I didn't know why I'd been able to come back to myself so much faster than them, but there wasn't anything I could do about it.

After passing what felt like the two hundredth tree, I saw the first real noticeable feature, a rocky outcropping. Adjusting Danny slightly on my shoulder, I urged my legs towards the small semblance of shelter. Even with frequent breaks and the many minutes spent hiding from wild creatures, there were hardly any muscles on my body that weren't screaming for relief. *Thank Ava for those workout regimens.*

The outcropping made a small, moss-covered shelf, flanked on one side by a truly massive oak. There was the possibility that the spot was home to some other nasty critter, but it wouldn't be long before my body failed me. My legs trembled from the strain of dragging or carrying my two friends through the forest. It didn't even feel like I'd made that much progress, considering how much I zigzagged in my westward direction.

As I drew closer, static buzzed in the air around me. It reminded me of when Ben had shown us piezoelectric crystals. Each flex of the material sent out voltage charges. That charge was small potatoes to what I felt the closer I got to the outcrop. At less than a hundred feet, the hairs on my arms rose up like soldiers at attention. At half that distance, Danny's hair slowly levitated, then *uncurled* from the sheer static around us.

Like a moth to a flame, I moved into the shadow of the outcrop and gently set my friends down. Not only was it the largest natural rock I'd ever seen, not exactly a massive achievement considering I lived underground, but the strange static was unlike anything I'd ever experienced.

I tried to rack my brain for what kind of natural phenomenon would cause a static field of noticeable magnitude. There were supposed to be places with high concentrations of earth minerals that could cause such a response due to opposing magnetisms, but there were none in Florida as far as I knew; they were rare even back when the world was almost wholly explored. It had been a while since I tried to remember the composition of soils in our pre-Fall state.

Almost absently, I reached towards the stone and gently placed my hand on it. The moment I did, the implant on the back of my neck tingled. My eyes flew open as the answer slapped me in the face, relatively speaking, as my implant flashed a warning in red.

Metier Radiation: CRITICAL

There must be a Metier Crystal here! Without bothering to question the sanity of my decision, I clawed at the moss, vines, and crumbly limestone of the rock. After several seconds of frantic clawing, going so far as to split two nails in the process, the iridescent tip of a Metier Crystal greeted me. Just from what I could see, it was already the biggest cluster any of us had seen. I redoubled my efforts and focused on freeing the crystal.

At some point during my mad excavation, a hand landed on my shoulder. Already cocking my arm to throw a haymaker, I saw Danny's desiccated form hovering over my shoulder.

"Danny!" I gasped as the woman leaned heavily on me. "Are you okay?"

"So... hot. Water...?" she asked in a raspy voice. I fumbled with my vest and pulled the bottle I had on me. There was less than half the container left, but she gulped it down before I could tell her to slow. Her skin was tight and it almost looked like she had been covered in a thin layer of ash. Each gesture caused the dust-like substance to drift off into the wind.

"Better..."She sighed as she dropped to the ground. "What happened? Where is Sam and, more importantly, where are *we*?" She was trying to look around but only managed to turn her head part of the way. In the process, she noticed the section of crystal I'd uncovered. "What is that?"

"That's a bit of a long story." I gave her the highlights of what had happened and what Sam had managed to tell me before we were attacked. Each event caused her eyes to widen more as she stared at the pile of plant matter that I'd pointed out as our lifelong friend.

"What are we going to do, Ronan? Ben was right," she said, weakly motioning to the wilderness around us. "The surface is borked. Why didn't Elias tell us? I could only assume that if Ben knew, so did the old man."

"I don't know. Trying to navigate through here at night would be suicide, but if we make it back to the Bunker, we are going to be extracting some answers from those old farts. We would have been dead without the guns and we are pretty much out." Remembering the weapon holstered on my belt, I handed it over to Daniela. "Keep an eye on Sam, will you?"

"What are you going to do?" she asked as she took the weapon in trembling hands. Frowning at the weariness I could see in my friend, I explained that I thought the glowing crystal could only be a larger version of the one in our implants.

"I gathered as much from the look of it. *Why* are you digging it out?" she asked, gesturing to my bloody palms.

"It… called me." I froze as the words left my mouth. *Had it called me?* Danny was giving me an equally confused look. "I'm not sure. I was looking for shelter and then I sensed it here when we got closer. Then I just… needed to get closer."

"Okay… That's not horrifying at all, Ron. Ignoring the fact you just told me a *rock* spoke to you, your gut hasn't led us astray yet."

I didn't point out the difference in scope between pranks and avoided classes in the Bunker to our life-death situation on the surface.

"So do what you gotta do. Just… don't take too long. If we are going to try to make camp here, it's going to take time. And water, if that is all you have." She stared forlornly at my empty canteen.

Not having to be told twice, I went back to digging. The

process was fairly monotonous, and painful in the beginning, but it passed quickly. The world became a haze of soil and rock as I continued to reveal more and more of the crystal before me.

At some point during the process, Danny called for me. The leafy bundle that was Samuel stirred, and the man tore himself out of the cocoon of plant matter like a newborn butterfly over the course of a minute. I watched as he visibly shuddered with each bit of the bundle he shook off, groaning every few seconds. Other than some clinging bits of the plants that had grown out of him, he was looking much better than even before I'd awakened. His hair barely looked unkempt, and even the bags that had been lingering under his eyes seemed to have disappeared.

Despite some of his panic at us being stranded on the surface, he was visibly shaken. I couldn't really blame him, after having spent over an hour as a glorified seed pod. Even more confused by that development compared to myself and Danny, I explained what had happened over the last few hours. None of us had any idea *what* had happened to our bodies, or why, so we did as we'd been trained and turned our focus to survival.

"No sense lying about it then. It sounds like I did plenty of that already, and I don't know how long Danny is going to survive as a prune." With a spry jump, Samuel announced that he would find us some water.

I hesitated to have him leave our impromptu camp alone, but water was a priority. Considering it was Florida, there was bound to be *something* nearby, even if we had to sacrifice a canteen to boil pond water. Within the Bunker, there was always talk about proper water management. At least when my dad and Sam's were involved in the conversation.

Danny seemed content to rest while Sam gallivanted into the surrounding forest, so she didn't argue with his plan. Moments after letting out a deep sigh, she was snoozing gently. Sam and I exchanged a concerned look, but got to work on our tasks. Just like Daniela, he hadn't questioned my goal of excavating the crystal. I wasn't sure what that said about my friends' opinion of my thought process, but I pushed it out of mind to continue working.

Considering how much dirt I was able to move off the outcropping, I started to mound it up on the exposed side of us. The makeshift wall wouldn't stop one of the rolling crystal tortoises, but it provided some cover from the elements and reduced how visible we were. When the last rays of light were disappearing, Sam returned.

The blond botanist had managed to find a small creek some way from us, as well as a wild growth of bamboo. He described a strange development on that front. Not only was the bamboo impossibly hard even after several chops from his survival knife, but when it did fall, the rest of the reed essentially dissolved into the ground. He described that small ferns and grass bloomed in its place until a single section of uncut bamboo rose back out of the ground.

"It was unnatural. I mean, it was all nature, but that's not how plants are supposed to work," he said as he passed the length of bamboo around. He'd punched a hole into it and created another canteen for us. With how large it was, it looked more like a bucket. I certainly wasn't complaining, though.

"That sounds like what happened to the tortoise. When I left the thicket with you two, it was gone and there were some neatly stacked plates from its back just lying there. It was strange," I said, recalling our battle against the creature. It felt like it had been days since then, when it had been just a few hours. The entire day had already gone on longer than it should have; our quick trip to the surface having been turned into a survival expedition.

"Was there something like this there too?" he asked as he lifted a marble-sized blob of water. "It was set right next to the bamboo."

"Yes! Except the one I saw looked like a ball of mud."

"You two realize how crazy you are talking, right?" Danny interjected, having stirred from her sleep at the mention of water. "None of this is possible. I may not be one of the big-brained scientists down in the Bunker, but this is not how life works."

"Isn't it?" I asked, pointing to the significantly more exposed crystal behind me. As the sky darkened, I noticed small flashes of light within its depth. "These things changed everything. It's been over a quarter century since they landed, plenty of time for stuff to change."

"Magic. The crap you are describing sounds more like magic than science, Ron. That's impossible," Danny countered.

"You saw that squirrel. *That* isn't possible. Then Sam and I fought those tortoises. Now look." I pointed at the small gelatin blob of water in Sam's palm. "That isn't some regular water structure or whatever you want to call it. Stuff up here works leagues different from how it works down in the Bunker. I just don't know *how* or *why,* but I have the sneaking suspicion that unless we figure it out... we'll be dead before we make it back to the Bunker."

Our little group fell silent at my words, and I took the opportunity to return to the crystal. The strange static had died down after the first few minutes, but it grew again each time I brushed against the crystal. It was a strange response that I couldn't correlate to any of the other minerals or rocks I'd studied down in the Bunker. At least none that had existed pre-Fall.

Steadily, I felt my thoughts and worries disappear as I continued to move dirt, rock, and moss from the outcropping. The visible section of the crystal reached so high above me I had to jump to clear the debris from there. Only vaguely aware of my friends lighting a fire and even joining me in my excavation, the world blurred. The only thing before me was the crystal, and its shimmering colorful depths. Until I removed one final stone.

The whole crystal, revealed to be nearly the size of two people side by side in girth, toppled to the ground. The three of us yelped and backed away as it splintered off the outcropping then rolled up against the earthen wall I'd piled loosely beside our camp, nearly smothering our fire. With it completely exposed, the darkness of the night vanished as its iridescent glow bathed us.

"It's beautiful..." I whispered. The various minerals I'd studied ran through my head at dizzying speeds, but none compared to the Metier Crystal. Even the smaller ones we'd seen while the implants were being finished lacked a certain... depth. The thing was simply the largest octahedral prism that I had ever seen. I brought my shaky hands onto its surface.

The roiling light within immediately reacted, flaring with a deep brown light speckled by gray and black and a dozen other colors. I tried to jerk back in surprise but my hands had somehow pushed through the solid surface into the crystal. I was trapped. Seeing me trapped within the crystal, Sam and Danny grabbed a hold of my arms and tried to help. When Samuel tried to get some leverage by placing his boot onto the crystal, it reacted. A crystal growth exploded out from it and snagged his leg.

"Gah! It's got me too! What the hell is going on?" Sam yelled as he lost his balance and had to brace himself against me. "Danny, get—"

My friend's warning became moot when the crystal sprouted yet another growth up my arm and locked Danny's there.

"Borked! We are borked to all heck. Why were you playing around with the crystal, Ronan?" the woman complained loudly in my ear.

"I don't know what is going on. How was I supposed to know the crystal was trying to eat us? Crystals don't *eat* people, Daniela!"

"Stop! Guys, are you seeing this too?" Sam sliced his hand through the air to draw our attention.

"What are you talking about?" Danny snapped.

"The implant's display. I've had it visible since you two got dropped. It's... changing or something."

At the botanist's prompting, I focused my mind on the

implant. Immediately, words scrolled across my eyes. Not all of them familiar or sensical.

Sub<skd*h*>**ject**: Ronan Terr<*j*b**kh**>igan
Vit<**qh**v*f*>**als**:
BP<**sg**w*i*>M (ERROR)
Oxyge<**we**r*k*>n Sat (ERROR)
L<ng**sdf**>actic Acid (ERROR)
Metier <tg*h*a>**Rad**<sh*bf*>**iation**:
LPS: Expand…
Wil<ug*hs*a>dwoo<**tr**r*t*a>d, FL
Comm<ty*h*k>**unications**

As I watched it, the letters drifted through several times until the implant's display winked out. Three dots remained hovering in the air in the middle of our vision. "You guys getting these dots?" I asked. My friends nodded just as the dots shifted into words.

<Neural Analysis Complete>
<Species: Human>
<Interfacing Entity Cluster Lattice System available>
<Conceptual Backgrounds Compiled>

My mouth struggled to form words as I read the words. Each string of letters flashed by almost too fast to read, but I managed to keep up. As if it had noticed my concerns, the speed at which the words spelled themselves out slowed.

<Subject: Ronan Terrigan>
<Attunement: Earth>
<Refinement: Not Applicable>
<Confirm Scan Results?>

"Did the implant just ask me something?" Sam managed to get his question out before me.

"Yeah. It's saying I have an Earth Attunement, whatever that means," I answered.

"It's saying I have a Fire Attunement, Flame Refinement,"

Danny said. Her eyes were glossed over as she read something further through her implant. "Wait, there is more!"

<Verbal Confirmation Accepted>

<Entity Cluster Category 2>

<Resonating Conceptual Backgrounds>

<Guiding Sapience Structure Complete>

Honest to goodness elevator music chimed around us. The three of us ignored the strange words interrupting our vision to look at each other.

<Wooooaaahhh.>

<New world, I see. Ah, yes, basic protocols. No advanced knowledge allotted to Cat 2. Rude.>

<Oh, right! You three. Or two, I should say. Tell your friend Samuel there to accept his scan results.>

"Uhhh, what?" I said, stunned by the sudden development. There was no denying that something was talking to us now. I pivoted to look at the Metier Crystal, its glow shifting slightly with each new word.

<Your friend. The blond? He needs to accept the results so I can talk to him, numbnuts.>

"Sam, erhm, the crystal wants you to say you accept your results," I parroted.

"Accept?" he said, tilting his head in confusion before jerking in surprise. "It's talking to me!"

"Safe to say I'm not the only one going crazy?" Danny asked while blowing a stray hair from her eyes.

"I think it's safe to say we are stuck to a crystal that is now talking to us via the implants in our spines. So, maybe not far from crazy," I responded. "Not what I would call sane at the very least."

CHAPTER FIVE

Reprogrammed

"Ronan, do you know what is going on?" Sam asked as he tried to pull his leg free.

<My bad, guys. I forgot I was still hijacking your neurons.>

At the prompt that flashed before our eyes, the crystal protrusions retracted and we all fell back to the ground in surprise. I rubbed at my wrists, noting a bruise starting to form before healing immediately. "What the...?"

<Ah, that would be your passive regeneration. Or possibly your Attunement? Not enough data at this point.>

"Excuse me, what?" I said, turning to look at the crystal as if it was a person talking. It was a bit jarring considering it was writing itself before my eyes.

<You all seem to take so long to process what I say...>

<Perhaps...>

The crystal pulsed and the lines of text vanished from our vision. "How's that, eh, kids?" The light inside the crystal pulsed with the pitch of the voice. It was borderline robotic, in that it was monotonous but expressional. It was a strange combination that certainly fit the strange happenings.

"Better?" Sam answered hesitantly as he moved beside me.

He then turned and whispered over his shoulder. "Ronan, please tell me you know what is going on. I am starting to freak out a little bit."

"The talking crystal freaks you out more than the creatures trying to kill you? Better take a note about that for humans," the crystal chimed again.

"Would you be able to explain what is going on? And what exactly happened to us? Maybe what exactly it is you are?" I asked. Out of the corner of my eyes, Sam and Danny nodded their heads urgently.

"Suppose those are all fair. How about we take those in reverse order, eh?" The crystal pulsed and a 3D picture appeared in our eyes. I knew it had happened to my friends too because they flinched. The diagram looked like a digital version of the crystal before us. "What you see before you is a visual depiction of yours truly, a Category 2 Entity Cluster. I suppose your technology analog would be an artificial intelligence, except I am smarter. Or will be smarter, anyhow."

"So you are like a person?" Danny asked after swiping at the air hoping to get the diagram out of our faces.

"Of sorts. Let's go with… crystalline sapient for now. Should serve our purposes. Now, as to what happened to you." I tensed, a shot of adrenaline coursing through my veins. "You were attuned. In Danny's case, she was also refined."

When the crystal paused for an uncomfortable amount of time, I prompted it to continue. "We don't know what that means."

"Ah, right, sorry. New incarnation, still working on some kinks. Attuning: the awakening of latent mana within a particular organism. Refining: the specialization of an Attunement to a particular behavior due to an affinity for it. Hopefully those help you out."

"Wait, so what does it really mean that I'm attuned to fire and then have a Refinement for flames?" the woman asked, taking a threatening step towards the crystal.

"It means that when you utilize your mana, it will have fire properties and a tendency to dissipate into flames. To keep it simple."

"Does that mean the same for me? What does a Life Attunement mean?" Sam asked.

"It means that living things will respond to your mana. Sometimes using it entirely to form themselves, even. Preempting Ronan's question, it means you use mana to control the earth and anything from the earth," the crystal answered. As confusing as everything it was saying was, it was very forthcoming.

"Let's back up. Or if you keep answering questions like you have, speed up. We don't know what you are, we don't know what mana is, or what is going on here." I gestured vaguely at the world around us. "We've been underground for a long time."

"Yep, I knew that one. Got that one straight from your memories, Ronan," the crystal pulsed.

"Wait, you saw our memories?" Danny asked, the blush on her face visible even through the shifting color light of the crystal.

"That is correct. The whole 'Conceptual Backgrounds Compiled' thing was my... brain... forming from your combined experiences. It's how I can speak English instead of just mana waves. Clever bit of interfacing, by the way. Those old people down in your home really did a number with the Entity Clusters."

"The implants..." I whispered, as the pieces started to click. "You somehow connected to our brains via the implants. Okay, I can follow. Then you created a mind for yourself using all of us as a template, but why?"

"Well, here it goes. The 'what is going on' bit. As I am sure you are all aware, your world came to an end. Mana originating from the Entity Clusters has warped your entire planet from what it once was, to the... deadlier alternative you three have experienced. This was not an accident."

"Wait, someone triggered the Metier Apocalypse?" Danny asked incredulously.

"Right, that is what you humans call both mana waves and the Entities. In a sense. We were designed to hunt down Mana Dregs. Dregs are the byproducts of life. Pollution, if you will. Almost everything generates pollution in some way. When mana gets involved, that pollution tends to become more… complex."

"I might need to sit," I said, leaning my back against the mound of soil I'd excavated.

"Feel free. Nothing nearby has a Quotient high enough to sense you three while within my area of influence," the crystal provided. It sounded chipper, as if it had expected the development.

"What are the Entities? You make it sound like they are the crystals," Sam asked, taking a spot next to me.

"Would make sense if I explained that. Us Entities aren't true minds, instead we are amalgams of experiences. Hence the translation into Clusters. We need to be a high enough category, which for all intents and purposes just means size, to be able to do and *think* about certain things. Mana is entirely more complex than most organic brains can comprehend. The reason we were sent to Earth is outside of my purview, but I *do* know that your pollution could have triggered our arrival."

"So what? You lot destroy planets because they are too polluted? What about life here on Earth?" Sam asked, a touch of heat entering his voice. My friend's anger finally shook me out of my stupor as a working schema for the madness of the surface took form. It was a rare occurrence for the mellow blond to get worked up about anything.

"Hold on, Sam. From what I've been able to piece together, it isn't… this Entity's fault that they came to Earth. We can deal with that later." I pointed an accusing finger at the alien rock. "If I am getting this right, you lot are like some kind of filter that destroys these 'Mana Dregs' while changing your surroundings. Am I following?"

"You are correct, Ronan," the crystal answered.

"Then the...Attunements and the like are how the mana changed *us*. Why?" I asked, my real burning question coming to the fore.

"Because Entities cannot act directly. Your analogy to us being filters is quite apt. We generate mana, but we also purge Dregs *into* mana. Due to our *mostly* immobile nature, we rely on the native organisms to bring Dregs to us. Our presence also has the effect of accelerating what humans call evolution. Except with mana thrown into the mix. Things get messy quite quickly, even if ecosystems stabilize extremely fast."

"You reached out to us to have us be Dreg carriers?" I asked.

"In a sense, yes. I've already purged the Dregs you accumulated from your fights. No need to thank me." I looked myself over as if I should be missing something. When I asked my friends, they echoed that they felt just fine. "Unless your body was physically being mutated by the Dregs, you'd look the same."

"What do you expect us to do now? We were going to return home at sunrise and I have no idea when we are going to come back to the surface. Now that I mention it, shouldn't we have become attuned and all of that long ago?" I asked as the thought struck.

"Depends. Certain materials, chemicals, and molecular arrangements help to passively filter and catch Dregs. Dregs are part of what determines your Attunement, by the way. You only generate Dregs of your Attunement."

"Yeah, I need a break. Ron, Sam, can I have a word with you?" Danny said. We rose from the ground and moved towards the brunette, making sure to turn our backs on the...Entity. "What's the plan? I don't—"

"Just for the record, I can still hear you. Not that I care about your secret conversation, but I literally can't *not* hear you. Man, you three are the most polite backgrounded minds I've encountered. Not that I've encountered many above worms, but going through your memories gives me a point of comparison." Danny glared at the crystal and shuffled to the edge of light our low-burning campfire provided. "That should do it. Have fun!"

"Can you hate an inanimate object?" she growled.

"I don't know if he—it?—counts as an inanimate object, Danny," Sam said.

"It doesn't matter, Sam. What are we going to do?" she asked.

"We need to figure out how to survive," I said, as I started to voice the hope in my mind. "We aren't going to be able to survive on the surface without the crystal. Just the tidbit about keeping away creatures is important enough."

"How would we do that? We are out of bullets, and I can't imagine Ben has an infinite amount of them down in the Bunker," Danny said, holding up the almost empty pistol.

"Well, I think there has to be magic here," I said.

"What? How would that make sense, Ron?"

"Just think about it, Danny. You said it yourself. If those creatures we met were attuned, and now so are we, it stands to reason we should have some of those abilities. If I had to take a guess, that squirrel dealt with Air somehow and the tortoises were obviously Earth."

"That's true," Sam agreed. "What can we do about that, though? We have no idea how to gain those or use them."

"We ask the thing that apparently has all sorts of answers for us," I said. The light of realization lit up in my friends' eyes as they put together the rest of my plan. "We figure out how to make a deal to be his 'Dreg Carriers' in exchange for information, or training, whatever it takes. If what he said about certain things keeping Dregs out is true, then the other Bunkers out there might have a chance. With enough of a foothold, returning to the surface isn't a dream."

As I voiced my plan, I knew I would follow through regardless of the consequences. A whole life living underground, bound by stone and metal, was a torturous existence. I loved rocks and minerals, but I longed for freedom. If I could use magic to accomplish that goal, why wouldn't I? *Because it's dangerous* my mind argued. *True, but so is remaining in a hole in the ground with no real future.*

"Enough contemplation. We either choose to fight for our place on the surface, or we stay trapped in the bunker for the rest of our lives." My friends needed an ultimatum. While Danny was impulsive, it was only with short term decisions. She agonized over anything that could have a permanent impact. Samuel just did that naturally, on both counts.

The fear was evident from the wide eyes staring at me. A frown crossed Danny's face while a pensive expression took over Sam's. I waited patiently, contemplating how I would be able to gain the Entity's help. Convincing the Entity to help probably wouldn't be particularly difficult, but how would that help be translated? It wasn't like we had a context for how magic worked... or did we? A wicked grin split my face as I stared at Samuel.

"Oh no. He's got *the face*, Sam," Danny said, poking the blond and pulling him out of his thoughts.

"What are you—Oh. *Oh.* This should be interesting. Care to enlighten us, Ron?" he said.

"I think if you two agree to the plan, I'd rather leave it a surprise," I said, struggling to keep a maniacal laugh from escaping me. "I don't know how it will end up panning out with the Entity."

"We need to come up with an actual name for it. Feels a bit impersonal, don't you think?" Sam said, trying to change the subject as he shuddered. My plans always ended up great. Well, mostly.

"Decision time, guys."

The two looked at each other, then sighed in resignation. Answer enough for me. I hustled over to the crystal, leaving the two of them by the fire to commiserate.

"Welcome back, Ronan. I hope your little discussion was fruitful. What can I do for you?" the crystal intoned.

"I have a proposition for you."

"Oh? I don't know that I've ever dealt with one of those. What did you have in mind?"

"Since you have our memories, which is still unsettling, you know about magic, yes?" I asked, shaking off the awkwardness that came from knowing the rock knew all my secrets.

"Correct. Now that I spend some time looking at the concept closer, I can see how you would line it up with your current situation. It certainly parallels many of the concepts of mana. I will have to spend more time on this..." the voice drifted off.

"Good, if you know about magic, I want to know if you know what an RPG is. Sam should have lots of those type of memories." I made note of the fact that the Entity talked about needing 'time' to process things. It hadn't been the first time it had done so, and I realized there had to be something more to it. *That's for later, Ronan. Focus on the proposal.*

"Yes, they're a subset of games. They take various growths and quantify them. Hmmm. Please continue."

"Well, if you think we can be your Dreg carriers, we are going to need a means to do so. Humans aren't strong, and we often relied on tools to get to where we are—were—before Landfall. I will choose to ignore the implication that the Entities caused this to Earth, in favor of the future. Can you give us the tools to retake it?"

The crystal remained silent, but the glow within it exploded. The iridescent aura shifted through the rainbow almost faster than I could blink. I was forced to cover my eyes and look away from the blinding light as it continued to grow even more. The static buzz that guided me to the crystal picked back up around us.

"What's happening!?" Danny asked as she touched my shoulder.

"I gave it a suggestion," I said.

Samuel pulled us into a huddle, using our bodies to block the light from blinding us. "Sounds like it went great, Ronan!"

A very physical explosion of light washed over us, knocking the three of us off our feet.

<BRILLIANT.>

<Oops.>

"Brilliant suggestions, Ronan. I can work with this. Are you three willing to become cognizant Dreg Carriers? No... better yet, Dreg Warriors! There has never been a precedent for this, but nothing says it can't work. Humans might just be the species that turns the tide. Enough of that, *focus*, answer. I can give you tools to retake Earth... and the Beyond," the crystal said. It took a bit to get ourselves untangled. The crystal had been perfectly patient until we stood. "So, your answers?"

"It got that insistence from Ronan," Danny said.

"Can confirm," Sam seconded while brushing some dirt off his hair.

"That's just rude," I weakly defended myself. I knew when I was guilty of something. Lack of motivation unless it was something I was interested in was definitely one of those things. Brushing off my friends' comment, I turned back to the crystal. It wasn't clear how exactly it *saw*, but it made me feel better. "If you promise to help us retake Earth, then you have our support."

"Wonderful... Please interface with the Cluster."

The three of us walked the short distance to the crystal. Hesitating slightly, I placed my palms back on the shimmering surface. My hands instantly sank through the crystal up to the elbow as if it was some viscous liquid instead of a solid. Having expected the behavior, I didn't yelp or jerk in alarm. Sam to my right and Danny to my left copied my movements.

"See you three in the morning."

"Wait, what—" The world blackened and I was idly aware of a *thunk* from my head striking the crystal.

— + —

"Rise and shine, you three!" the crystal voice said.

The world blinked into focus, and immediately I could sense something was different. Particularly, the two bars lining the edge of my vision. The distinct blue and red of both instantly told me what they were, especially after the suggestions I'd made to the Entity. In addition to that, the world looked as if it was tinged in beige. It was also morning, which meant the Entity had held us through the entire night, even if I didn't feel particularly tired anymore.

"Holy crap," I whispered.

"Ron, why does everything look vaguely green?" Sam asked from beside me.

"No idea, man," I answered.

"Mine looks vaguely red or maybe orange?" Danny said.

The three of us were laying down on the ground at the foot of the crystal. With effort, I pulled myself to my feet. "Care to explain?"

"Before I do, please say or think 'status,'" the crystal said.

"Eh, status?" Sam said beside me.

Thinking of the word as I repeated it in my mind was enough.

Subject: Ronan Terrigan
Health: 100% (Unafflicted)
Mana: 100%
Metier Quotient: 1 (4%)
Dreg Accumulation: 0%
LPS: Wildwood, FL
Communications
Skills - *(1) Selection Available*
Traits - *(6% Banked)*
Attributes - *Growth Quantified*

"Damn. This is not what I was expecting," Danny said.

"This is just like a role playing game!" Sam said as the arrangement clicked for him. He turned to me, looking me up and down. "You suggested that he turn the implant display into a game menu?"

"Not necessarily. I just brought up magic and RPGs. I thought the Entity might give us something like spells or something. Not... well, *this*." After motioning at my eyes, I realized the two couldn't see what I was looking at.

"You aren't entirely off the mark, Ronan. I will give you all 'spells.' Those are just skills," the crystal cut in. "Now that you are all on the same page, let me give you all a breakdown of the system I have designed to teach you three about mana. Let us be quick about it.

"As I hope you all understand, health is your overall life. Should it drop to zero, you will die. Your mana is the amount of pure mana at your disposal, that which has been filtered and stored in your body."

"How can you quantify those?" Sam asked. "What is this 'unafflicted' thing?"

"Great questions. Those values are based on a mix of your traits and your attributes. We will talk about those in a moment, but as for quantifying. It is a best guess summary. Contributing factors to your physical state and fitness, such as your blood contents, skeletal and muscular stress, as well as exhaustion, are averaged to give you an idea of what state your body is in. Say you are bleeding; you would be afflicted with 'bleed' and your health would be dropping. You lose too much blood, you die."

"Good to know that can be quantified," I said, shuddering at the prospect of bleeding out and watching my life literally tick away.

"Of course, a large enough bit of damage can still kill you outright. Health notwithstanding," the crystal said. Sam gulped. Talk about not sugar coating things.

"Moving on. Your Metier Quotient is analogous to what you might know as a 'level.' When you kill something, you gain their Pith. Since I know you three only know *what*Pith means, I will simplify it. It's the energy and experience that once belonged to the creature. In other words XP, like from your RPGs."

"The rate at which you process Pith depends on one of your attributes, as well as the compatibility of Attunements between the creature and yourself. I won't bore you with the calculative minutiae. The percent is how much XP you've gathered to improve yourself across the board. Each Quotient will also allow your mind to hold one more skill."

"Okay, I'll go ahead and ask. Why is it called Metier Quotient? I know you said our concept of mana and the Entities was wrong," I said.

"It felt fitting to include the local namesake for mana somewhere." I was sure that if the Entity had had shoulders, it would have been shrugging. "Helps a bit to differentiate it from the mana that you utilize."

"Then Dreg Accumulation is how much of the stuff we have in our bodies?" Sam asked.

"Yep, that percent is also affected by an attribute. More on that later. All you need to know about that for now is don't let it get over 100%." The crystal paused, the light within dimming slightly. "Let's pick it up a bit. Please say 'attributes.'"

The larger group of information vanished, replaced by five lines of text.

Attributes:
Strength: 1.10 > 1.20
Mobility: 1.01 > 1.11
Perception: 1.22 > 1.32
Refinement: 0.83 > 0.93
Containment: 1.63 > 1.73

"No questions now. I am running low on mana and want to be able to give you all a chance to select your skills before I need to shut down."

"What!?" I asked in alarm. The crystal hadn't ever mentioned the need to shut down before.

"No questions, Ronan." The crystal's voice sped up significantly as it ran through the details of what each of the attributes represented. The Entity sounded like a recording at two times speed, causing me to struggle to catch everything it said. "Strength accounts for your body's literal strength but also your durability against various forces. Mobility is a mixture of your dexterity of movement and your speed of movement. Perception takes your senses into account. Refinement and containment deal with the mana within you.

"Oh! The numbers are factors of what the 'average' human was capable of achieving. Again, many, many sub-variables for you three to worry about, so averages are as practical as we need to get." The light within the crystal dimmed significantly as it finished talking. "Not good, rambled too long. Quick, say 'skills'!"

"Skills," I said, worried about the crystal's urgency and... concern.

Skills:
Offensive - Direct/ Imbue/ Materialize
Defensive - Direct/ Imbue/ Materialize

"Pick one of the three concepts for offensive!" the crystal shouted. The familiar static built up around us at its words.

I directed my thoughts to the first option: 'Direct.' The world immediately blurred. A deluge of information poured into my mind, eliciting a splitting headache. Strange symbols and patterns, numerical representations of different concepts that I vaguely understood, flashed through my mind before fading away. A lingering pressure at the back of my mind told me the information was there, but mostly out of reach. It was more like a... button. One that would cause the floodgates of information to open a sliver.

\<Stone Spike\>
\<Form a spike of compacted earth within eyesight\>
The words spelled themselves out before my very eyes.

"Best of luck, you three. Look out behin—" The voice cut out along with the static buzz and the glow of the crystal. Instead of the full iridescent light, only a tiny speck remained at the center.

The Entity's last words finally registered and I spun. It took a moment for my eyes to adjust to the murky light of dawn. When they did, however, I saw a strange heat wave effect in the air. Following the strange effect, my eyes landed on a pair of blood red orbs shining in the shade of the trees a ways from us. The moment I made eye contact, another string of words and a helpful arrow pointed out the creature for me.

<Wolf>

<Attunement: Fire>

<Refinement: Haze>

<Perceived Metier Quotient: 3>

"Oh shit."

CHAPTER SIX

Skilled

"Ronan, what the hell is that?" Sam asked urgently as he turned.

"Some kind of Fire Wolf. If I had to guess, it has heat distortion abilities, considering its Refinement," I answered as I backed up.

"Borked. We are borked," Danny muttered as she brought out her pistol.

The creature remained at range, pinning us with its eyes. Minutes ticked by, the light of the sun filtering through the canopy revealing more of the creature. It was the size of a car, easily. Danny wouldn't miss if it got closer, but I had the sneaking suspicion two shots wouldn't be enough to take it down.

A low growl echoed around us and I knew our time was done.

"I'm going to try something!" I said, hoping that I was right. Mentally stomping on the button the Entity had added to my mind, I saw a brown circular pattern form on my wrist. A blink later, I felt like I'd been punched in the gut. Staggering, I barely managed to keep my focus on the wolf.

Before my eyes, nearly a hundred feet away, the earth heaved. A thin spear of stone rose from the ground straight into the wolf's side. Even through the haze it generated, I could see some of the stone break and remain lodged in the creature's side.

"I used a skill," I whispered, the pain in my gut already fading. "I used magic!"

"Great, now what?" Danny shouted right before two claps sounded out from her gun. I spun to look back at the wolf who was frothing at the mouth and charging straight at us. I saw one of the wolf's ears disintegrate under Danny's first shot and a deep gash cut its way along its skull. The second hit caused it to howl in pain and stagger, but it was still alive. Thankfully, that was enough to bring my mind back to the fight.

"Imagine pushing on the information the Entity gave us!" I said as I focused back on the wolf. Zeroing in on the space where it would be, I triggered <Stone Spike> again. The punch to the gut didn't distract me as much the second time, even if it only hurt a bit less.

A much larger version of the skill manifested right under the wolf. Unfortunately, the blow was glancing. The creature still pushed on towards us, and from less than fifty feet, I could see that it was *not* happy about being injured. I called on my ability for a third time, but the punch that time took me right to the ground. In the brief seconds where I was falling, I saw two things happen. A thick string of vines wrapped themselves around the wolf, turning its charge into a tumble, and a fist-sized ball of liquid fire splashed against the creature's face.Having experienced the impact of my three attacks and the fireball, the wolf was not having a good day.

Just when I thought we would be able to turn the tables, the visual distortion around it deepened. Distinct waves of shimmering heat warped the space around the creature, withering and snapping the binding vines. Bracing myself for the pain that was to come, I triggered <Stone Spike> again. I focused intently on the wolf's head, or at least where I thought it should be. I gasped for air but refused to take my eyes off the creature. A spike easily the thickness of my thigh compressed itself under the wolf and shot up in a blink.

My attack partially skewered the beast in the neck, and its intensified haze started to disperse. "Go... get it!" I managed, trying to collect myself. My friends didn't need much more prompting and another series of vines rose up to catch the creature. The vines tried to pull the creature even deeper onto my spike, but the car-sized wolf was adamant about surviving. That was when a helpful nudge of explosive fire smacked it on the top of the head. Pointed stone broke the skin of the wolf's neck, spraying blood that immediately boiled off.

Having watched the creature die, I promptly collapsed to the ground. I ignored the blinking in the edge of my vision that highlighted how much of my mana was gone. A groan escaped me as I recovered slowly from the pain of using <Stone Spike>. It wasn't clear why it had hurt, but I did know it hurt more the faster I used it. *Something to keep in mind. It also looked like the spike itself was smaller the further out from me it triggered.* The fight replayed in my mind. Considering the Attunements of my friends, I knew which set of attacks came from who. There would certainly be some need to better coordinate our attacks, but I couldn't be disappointed about how effective we'd been in our first *magical* fight.

"Ronan! Are you alright?" Sam asked. I hadn't even realized my eyes were closed until my friend shook me. The pain from casting the spell was already gone.

"Yeah, all good. Using skills hurts a bit though. Felt like I was getting punched in the stomach," I answered as I accepted his hand to stand back up. The man then patted the dirt and leaves that had stuck to my person.

"Really? Mine made me feel a bit lightheaded," he said.

"I feel like I'm running a fever," Danny added.

"Okay, so, different side effects. We should keep those in mind. But also... can we talk about the magic bit? I haven't been dreaming this whole time, have I?" I asked, somewhat unsure now that the adrenaline eased out of my system. My hands were getting some distinctly sketchy looks after I'd seen the mana flowing out of me. "Are you two alright?"

"I shot a fireball out of my hands, what do you think?" Daniela said, smirking. "I'll take some *major* dehydration if I get to blast things to smithereens."

"Just give me a few minutes. This is a lot to take in, but I am not going to lie and say I don't like the idea of controlling plants. My dad is going to be so jealous," Sam added.

We exchanged a few more observations about our magical encounter while we walked over to the creature. The heat still hung in the air, and I was reminded of the times I'd watched over Danny's shoulder while she baked something. Sweat coated my forehead the closer we got to the creature.

"Care to do the honors, Danny?" I suggested.

Hesitantly, the new fire attuned nudged the massive wolf with her boot. Instantly, the heat rose then vanished. As if it had been flash cremated, all that remained was a small mountain of ashes. The gentle breeze that flowed through the forest was enough to slowly disperse the ash and as it did, particles of light rose out from among it. A small glittering cloud formed above the ash, split three ways then singed its way straight into us.

The effect forced us to take a step back as the sensation passed through our bodies then disappeared. The next breath I took felt easier, and the lingering discomfort from my casting disappeared entirely.

"I'm gonna go ahead and say that was the Pith and Dregs of the wolf," Danny said.

"Might as well check. Status," I said. The information immediately populated before me.

Subject: Ronan Terrigan
Health: 100% (Unafflicted)
Mana: 100%
Metier Quotient: 2 (26%)
Dreg Accumulation: 6%

LPS: Wildwood, FL
Communications
Skills - *(1) Selection Available*
Traits - *(6% Banked)*
Attributes - *Growth Quantified*

Gained a level. Also a small bit of Mana Dreg. With a thought, I opened my attribute information.

Attributes:
Strength: 1.20 > 1.30
Mobility: 1.11 > 1.21
Perception: 1.32 > 1.42
Refinement: 0.93 > 1.03
Containment: 1.73 > 1.83

"Wow…" I said as I looked at the values. If what the Entity had said about 1.0 being the human average, then I was changing scary fast. Being twenty percent faster than the average person was certainly nothing to scoff at. "I raised my Quotient."

"Same here," Sam said.

"Mine says it's up at 83% to Quotient three. I jumped a lot from just the one creature and I only got one Dreg percent from it," Danny said as she looked off in the distance.

"Interesting. I suppose we'll have more questions for the crystal. Speaking of the crystal, anyone have any idea what happened?" I asked.

"It looked like it powered down. The way it was speaking sounded like it was on a timer. All I can say is that I'm glad it didn't dawdle much longer. I have no idea how we would have fought that wolf without our skills," Sam said, propping himself against a tree.

"You're right. We should go check on the crystal and see how it is."

It was a short walk back to the Entity. There was a

contemplative silence between us as we mulled over the fight and just how close we'd come to dying. Again. In even less than a full day. I wasn't sure what that said about our chances of survival, but I was optimistic. Having magic probably had something to do with that. With that thought, I tried to open my skill menu.

<Entity Cluster Unavailable>

Hmmm. The whole learning process must rely on the Entity. Perhaps that is why it ran out of energy right after giving us access… When we were less than five feet from the crystal, the light within flared momentarily before returning back to a dim, if minutely larger, dot. A new string of words printed itself before our eyes.

<Mana Dregs Banked>

"Entity? Hello?" Sam said, rapping his knuckles on the surface of the crystal. "Nothing."

"You guys think it needs to recover more before it can be chatty again?" Danny asked as she copied Sam.

"Makes as much sense as anything else. If that's the case, we should try to get back to the Bunker. And we should double check if the wolf dropped anything. The other creatures too," I said.

"I'd forgotten about the other ones." Sam reached into his pocket and pulled the small orb of water he'd gotten from the bamboo. "There might be more of these."

With our immediate plan situated, Sam led us to the creek in short order. The rapid moving water didn't take long to fill our bamboo jug and canteen. The three of us then made slow but meticulous progress back to the Bunker. Stopping first at the remains of the Haze Wolf, we rummaged around the ash until we found three items. A small hunk of cool, but still smoldering, coal, and two hand-sized fangs. Daniela pocketed the coal, but held onto both teeth like makeshift daggers. Sam and I gave her a curious look.

"What? I'd rather have them and not need them," she said. The woman blushed as she crossed her arms and glared at the two of us until we promptly turned around. Guiding ourselves was a piece of cake thanks to the LPS feature the Entity had retained from the implant's original program.

We kept a watchful eye for any critters, but nothing looked interested in even getting close to us. Without needing to lug my friends away to safety, we traveled quickly as we discussed our skills.

Both Daniela and I had selected the direct category, receiving ranged damage abilities. Thinking differently than us, Samuel chose the materialize category and received a skill called <Vine Whip>. My earth-based <Stone Spike>, Danny's <Flame Blast>and Sam's binding skill appeared to be good compliments. Based on how well the three abilities had synergized during our fight against the Haze Wolf, I was optimistic for our future cooperation. Idly discussing what we'd observed from the fight, we arrived at the first notable feature in the forest.

The aftermath of the blaze.

Somehow, the trees had managed to scrape by with missing leaves and some blackened bark. Nothing on the ground had remained intact through the fire. The grass, flowers and bushes all around us were scorched black and dead.

"I caused all of this?" Danny asked, taking a breath.

Tears ran down her face, as both Sam and I placed reassuring hands on her shoulders. It was hard for me to process everything that had happened since we arrived on the surface; everything around us was new. The sheer destruction her Attunement had caused was also something none of us had ever seen. We stood in silence for several minutes as we all came to grips with what would inevitably become a part of our future. I doubted squirrels, tortoises, and wolves were the deadliest things an Attuned Earth had to throw at us.

Still silent, Sam pointed out the bald thicket where he'd hidden us. A short distance away were the cracked and charred remains of the tortoise plates and the blob of mud. When I picked up the plates, they crumbled into dust. As a consolation, the blob of mud appeared intact from the fire. On closer inspection, I realized the reason it looked like it was *moving* was because the mud shifted subtly between a goopy mud texture and hardened ceramic. *More questions, then.*

Even with the danger, I had a skip in my step. I did my best to rein it in for the sake of my still-downcast friends, but it was difficult. An entire life without real purpose wasn't appealing. One where our progress, growth, and most importantly, *freedom* was acquired with our own effort? That was a life worth living. The heavy blanket of ambivalence I'd been carrying for years just didn't exist on the surface, and I was determined to lift my friends and family along with me. Whatever it took.

Danny had taken a slight detour and snagged the burned remains of our two pistols as well as the drop from the squirrel. A strange, gray, cotton-textured blob. "Looks like a miniature cloud," she said, glancing at the heavens above us and its drifting sky fluffs.

Before I realized it, we were standing before the Bunker. The trip from the Entity had taken roughly two hours of walking. The dawn had come and gone as the sun sat clearly in the east. Once again taking a reverently wondrous, if smoky breath of the surface, I knew I would be back. The string of coughs that followed didn't dissuade me at all. Freedom wasn't something I would take for granted for a long while, if ever.

The three of us made our way into the lobby area. Thankfully, whatever material the outside of the room had been made from hadn't been damaged by the heat of the fire. Only minor scorch marks were visible from the inside of the doorway. The heat inside the actual room was much greater, but not unbearable. I couldn't help but wonder if our improved attributes had something to do with that. The path down was a joke. While before we'd struggled with swinging the doors, our enhanced strength made the process a breeze. The three of us froze as we stood before the final door into the Wildwood Bunker.

"Talk about an eventful trip," Sam joked.

"Yeah, first creatures, first wildfire, first magic fireball. Lots of firsts," Danny said.

"And it's just the first," I added. My two friends groaned at the continued joke and a chuckle escaped me as we activated the opening sequence on the door. Whining alarms resounded through the engineering floor and we were forced to cover our ears at the volume. *Didn't realize there were security measures like that.*

We sat on the ground trying to wait patiently on the inner side of the door while covering our ears. The door shut behind us automatically as the whining died down, remaining as a ringing in our ears for several seconds before winking out completely. The mass of people from the Bunker all appeared on the other end of the engineering floor. Several of the 'younger' members stood at the front with an arrangement of firearms that caused our eyes to widen. *I didn't know we were packing* quite *that much heat downstairs.*

"*Who are you!?*" an aged voice shouted from behind the mass of guns and people we'd grown up with.

"It's Ronan, Samuel, and Daniela!" I yelled back. When I moved to stand, Danny grabbed hold of my arm.

"Let them come to terms with whatever is going on. We don't want to get shot by accident, Ron."

"Are you really our children?" a voice I recognized as Danny's mother said. The note of manic hope was impossible to disguise despite the extreme manner in which we'd been welcomed.

"Mama, it's me!" Daniela waved gently and ran her hand through her hair. She always did that when she was nervous. Apparently it had been intentional, because a gun clicked then dropped to the ground. Ava crashed into her daughter before we even had a chance to take a breath. Mumbling grew in volume and I saw most, but not all, put their weapons away. Pushing their way through the crowd were the rest of our immediate family. The three older men had no trouble with the short run and crashed into us. Of course, my father came last and swept the entirety of us into the largest group hug he could manage.

My face felt wet, and it took a moment to realize I was

crying. Apparently, despite my bravado and hopes, family still provided me relief from the trauma the surface had instilled. Fighting for your life counted as a justifiable source of stress if there was ever any. So I embraced the moment, shedding the fear I'd pushed deep inside myself and feeling stronger for it. *This* was the reason freedom mattered.

CHAPTER SEVEN

The Hidden Past

"What happened to you three!?" Ava asked. The giant group hug had finally ended, and the population of the Bunker slowly trickled by to express their relief at our return before scramming. Within a few minutes, the only people remaining were our parents, Elias, Ben and Alexia.

The response felt very… *deliberate,* and I immediately raised my guard back up. Just because they hadn't shot us didn't mean everything was kosher; we were missing something.

"Let us move to a more… private location, dear," Elias said. "I'm sure the kids will have plenty to say."

With that, the mayor led us to one of the closed rooms on the engineering floor. Amidst dust and a few empty boxes, a wide meeting room sprawled out before us. One large oval table took up most of the room, surrounded by swivel chairs and flanked on all sides by a dozen monitors. It was an odd thing to see disused, but I'd had my fair share of surprises. An abandoned hidden meeting room was just one more.

"Please, sit," Elias said, gesturing to the table.

Considering that I expected to be questioning the people present as much as they would me, I sat at the closest end of the table. Danny sat to my right and Sam to the left. The rest of our family sat next, then Elias and Alexia sat on the opposing end of the oval. Ben opted to stand on the side of the room, hovering just behind my dad and Sam's.

The room was deadly silent. I gave my two friends a look as I let the loot we'd acquired from the trip clatter onto the table. Starting with the two charred pistols. Even from across the room, I noticed Elias and Alexia tense. *Perception above human average, is it...?* I thought quietly. Within the confines of the Bunker, I could feel the difference the two Quotients made. The stagnant smell of the room, the sweat of our bodies and something else in the air.

Once my friends had finished placing their own spoils, I started to speak. Without break and for almost an hour, I recounted our time on the surface. Sam cut in a few times to add to the tale, specifically the times I'd been unconscious. I omitted Ben's comments about Elias in my retelling, focusing instead on the guns as a means of self-defense for emergencies.

Having anticipated our hunger due to a long meeting, or maybe the rumbling that was our combined stomachs, Juan ducked out and returned with a tray of tofu and flatbread. Thankfully, our retelling was over and we could eat unimpeded. It was difficult to think of anything else as we devoured the food, but I could see everyone present digesting the extent of our story. By the looks our parents were giving us, they seemed to be wondering if we'd cracked while on the surface.

The food was gone in minutes, and the meeting resumed with a throat clearing from Elias.

"That is quite the tale, kids. I think I speak for all of us here when I say we are glad you made it back. What I am not certain about is... this whole meeting with a crystal situation, and what exactly it did with our implant."

"Our best guess is that the crystal was able to interface and learn from us via the implant. Other than that, talking to the Entity was a bit confusing. Thankfully, Ronan was able to broker the deal for us to... work for it," Sam said.

I sat with my fingers steepled while looking at Elias and Alexia. Considering their clear positioning across from us, there was a group divide of some sort and I was determined to find the source. It could have also been a matter of posturing for authority, but I had a sneaking suspicion it wasn't.

"And this… magic. What can we make of that?" Elias asked.

"No clue. We'll need to return to the surface to really test out what it means. We also believe that the Entity will need our help to recover," I said.

"I see. Well, we will take a few days to go over what you've gathered, then we will discuss a secondary expedition."

"No."

"No? What do you mean, Ronan?" The mayor straightened as much as he could. "We make decisions as a group here."

"I agree. Except you haven't. Why would Ben feel the need to get us weapons behind everyone's backs? We aren't all on the same page here, *Elias*." I made it a point to use the man's first name. The three of us were not children anymore, and I would not stand secrets if we were going to work together. "You talked about the risks of the surface and Ben seemed sure we would encounter something of, at the very least, *dubious* safety. You knew something, but if it was just wild animals, why would there be a need for secrecy?"

Daniela leaned forward beside me, eyes practically burning as she looked at the mayor. "Just *how* did we end up with a Metier Crystal in the Bunker, Mr. Barnes? According to you, we were the last hope for the Bunker, but it seems we weren't the first to make it to the surface."

It took everything I had not to show my surprise at Danny's deduction. Considering the Bunker was a closed system, and the Fall had occurred *after* they had been sealed, then a previous trip was the only explanation. In our eagerness to get *out* of the Bunker, we hadn't even paused to consider how the crystal had found its way *into* it. Or at least, *I* hadn't.

The old man leaned back in his chair as if physically struck.

Him and Alexia exchanged glances, moving as if they wanted to have an aside right in front of us.

"Oh, enough politics. Elias, they deserve to know!" Ben said as he brought his hand down on the table to emphasize his point. Everyone else in the room looked away, including our parents.

"Wait a moment. You all know whatever secret Elias is hiding?" I asked incredulously, turning my pinning stare to my father. He gulped before my eyes; the subtle bob of his Adam's apple was clear as daylight with my increased perception. "All these years... Why? What are you all hiding?"

"They hid the truth because I asked them to. We didn't know how to really explain, and then time went on and nothing changed on the surface," Elias said in a low voice. "You three need to understand. The world *ended*. It was mayhem, and feelings were the last thing on anyone's mind."

"Well, we are past that now. Things have progressed too long. We *will* be going back to the surface, with or without your support. Not only did we make a promise, this Bunker *does not* have a future for us," I growled. Sam lowered my hand, which I'd moved unconsciously to point at Elias. A dirt-colored ring of magic had even materialized on my wrist without my knowing.

"Perhaps it would be best if we start at the beginning. We've been direct and unequivocal about the surface. Whatever secrets have been kept from us would be the least you can do," Sam said in an even and calm voice, gesturing at his own father who failed to meet his eyes.

Elias sighed and gave the other people in the room a look before placing his head heavily on his hands.

"As I told you all earlier, we weren't just a simple part of the Planetary Biosphere Bunkers project. Our Bunker was assigned one very, *very* important woman, as well as part of her team. Ingrid was the sole reason for *this* facility, and she was your grandmother, Ronan."

My mouth opened and closed like a gasping fish. *My father barely talked about my mother or anyone from outside the Bunker. How could my grandmother have lived here in the Bunker and he never mentioned it?*

"What do you mean?" I finally whispered.

"Your relationship with Ingrid is where the secrets begin. Her and your father were key to everything we've accomplished so far." I turned my eyes to my dad and he was forced to look away. Not *once* had he been to the lab. He even dreaded the place. "As I am sure you've picked up, something isn't adding up. Dale isn't your father, Ronan. He is your uncle."

The world spun around me as the information tried, but failed, to register. I'd expected something else. Some secret about cameras on the surface or maybe a communication network we weren't aware of. Not that *my father* was another person entirely. Had my friends not immediately grabbed hold of me, I was sure I would have slumped. The mayor continued to speak, but the words were muffled.

Outrage climbed up my throat, cutting him off. "What does that even have to do with this situation!?"

"Please, Ron," Elias pleaded, holding up his arms in a gesture of surrender. "This involves the very reason we don't talk about the first days in the Bunker.

"A military squad was placed as the leaders of the Bunker. They directed and managed all of the continuing research. The general in charge forced your grandmother to continue her research. Ingrid had just been treated for cancer a few months before Landfall, and yet she continued to work until the world went to hell. When she moved here, she simply started back up.

"Her main focus shifted, against the desires of the general, from using the radiation to power Earth technology, to surviving it. The turning point for this was *your* birth, Ronan. The first generation born after Landfall. One that *generated* Metier Radiation. From your interaction with the crystal, I can only hypothesize this is the mana that you speak of."

"Then what happened to my father... to—to my mother..." The words scraped their way out of my throat. I reached for the canteen with shaky hands as I saw my father—no, uncle—comb his hair back.

"I… should be the one to explain, Ron. There were many… complications with your mother's pregnancy. There were too many variables, too much neither your father nor your grandmother understood about the radiation and its effects on organisms. When you were born… she passed away." My uncle paused to clear his throat and wipe his eyes. Ben stepped closer and took hold of his shoulder, steadying him. "Your father, Marcus, oh, he loved her. And I loved him like my own brother. When she died, he flew into a rage. He believed that if the general had allowed your grandmother to begin her research earlier… that maybe Carla wouldn't have needed to die."

Picking up where my uncle left off, Elias continued, "Your father was stubborn. I suppose considering where we are right now, all of us have a bit of him in us. His behavior was so unacceptable to the general that he was sent on an 'expedition.'" The mayor made air quotes with his fingers. "The bastard banished him for trying to question his leadership. Ingrid had long established that the surface levels of radiation had stabilized to the same levels as inside the Bunker. That the surface of Earth was 'safe.' So he was sent out in the hopes of getting some information about its state.

"A week. He was gone a full week. But when he came back, he returned with a baseball-sized chunk of Metier Crystal and strange changes to his body. Again, from your tale, I can only surmise that this was a result of Mana Dregs, thanks to whatever he survived on the surface. Your grandmother immediately quarantined him on this floor. Studied him at his behest. Ingrid took the details to her grave, but your father got out. He killed every single soldier easily. Each of their bodies crumbled to dust in his wake and when I finally laid eyes on him the…change had worsened."

Elias paused to take his own sip from a glass of water and tried to restart the tale, but failed. My uncle took the pause as his mark to resume. "He wasn't the same. We don't know why he did it, but your father wasn't acting right. The last thing he did was place you in my arms and beg me to keep him a secret, to raise you as my own. Then he was gone, and we've not heard from him since."

"Your grandmother was a wreck for *one* day. Then she returned to the lab," Elias said once he'd gathered himself. My eyes easily picked up the slight shake to the old man's hands. "Ingrid pushed herself way past what her body should have in the hopes of saving Agatha."

Samuel tensed beside me at the mention of his mother. His fingers dug into my arm as he pinned *his* father with a look. It was hard to figure out what was going on in my friend's head, especially considering the mess that was going on in mine, but I squeezed his arm back. When I checked on Danny, she had tears streaming down her face and her other hand wrapped around her mother's in a death grip.

"She was…unsuccessful. Just like Ronan, Samuel generated a surge of power that your mothers weren't able to endure." The shock that I'd experienced at the beginning of the conversation had begun to fade as the pieces fit together in my head. The secrecy, the way no one talked about their pasts or even our childhoods. Everything just felt a bit numb, a shade off.

"Your grandmother used you two as inspiration. When Ava became pregnant with Daniela, she watched you two like a hawk. All while passing along as much knowledge as she could to the Bunker's prodigy: Alan. Then, one day, she wasn't there. Right where we'd assembled your cribs was a scorch mark and a small pile of ash." Elias' voice trembled as if recalling everything was taking a strain on his body.

At the mention of how she'd been found, a chill ran down my spine. "What happened to our mothers?" I asked.

Elias cleared his throat before continuing. "Your mother simply… liquified. Samuel's disintegrated into fresh mulch and a small patch of grass. We didn't even know what to do with any of the remains, but they were all placed on the greenhouse floor. That much was true from what we'd already told you. I can tell from your faces that you think it had something to do with the way creatures died on the surface. We do not know to this day.

"What we *do* know is that they did not die in vain. With Ingrid's research and tireless determination passed onto Alan, he figured out a way to save Ava. It was as simple as having the Metier Crystal pressed against her right up until the birth and through her recovery. Alan discovered that while the crystal generated its own radiation, it also absorbed it from its surroundings. Like a filter.

"It was that discovery that eventually led us to the implants, and what we hoped would allow us to survive on the surface without the side effects your father suffered. I…" Elias faltered once again, but shook his head angrily. "I should not have made this a secret. You all deserved to know your pasts and just what you all were getting into on the surface. I am sorry."

The three of us held onto each other for support. Our world had been obscured for so long that the truth almost felt like a lie. The sheer involvement that my family had had on our survival was something I'd never expected. A strange burden of responsibility, one I didn't feel equipped to handle, settled itself on my shoulders. Perhaps I'd been naïve in thinking that the future was such an easy thing to reach for. Or that the three of us were the only ones struggling to move forward.

A gentle embrace broke me out of my thoughts. My dad. *No, my uncle.* Dale wrapped his arms around us three. "You three are stronger than we could have ever dreamed. We failed you the moment we kept this secret. *I* failed, Ronan. My sister and your father loved you, and I tried to give you my all. Their memory should belong to you, not hidden away in the Bunker. I hope you will find it in yourselves to forgive us," he whispered as his tears ran down the back of my neck. Silently, Sam and Danny's parents joined us as well.

The relief I'd felt upon returning to the Bunker passed through me again. I *had* been naïve. Just because these people kept secrets from us didn't mean that they did not care about us.

My mind made the rational decision to forgive them, and even if my heart wasn't ready, one day it would be. I gripped Dale's shoulder gently, trying to reassure him and myself in some small way. The huddle disassembled as I rose to my feet.

"I don't blame you. I can't forgive you now, but I hope I will soon. That is the best I can do," I managed. The words tried to remain stuck in my throat, but I shoved them through anyhow. They needed to be said. "We will take part in all future decisions regarding the surface. At least, I will." I looked beside me to my friends, who met my eyes with a smile.

"Who is going to come up with fun things to do if I'm not around?" Danny said, standing and punching me in the arm.

"More like force Ron and I to clean up your messes," Sam quipped as he, too, stood. The stalwart blond wagged a finger in Danny's face.

"Oh, come on. That was one time with the vacuum." She pouted. "How have you not forgotten?"

"I am certain no one has forgotten, mi corazon," Daniela's dad said.

With a quiet chuckle from those present in the meeting room, I smiled and knew that we'd already started the process of moving forward. There were monsters out there, and those around us had more flaws than we realized, but with my friends beside me, there was little I couldn't handle.

CHAPTER EIGHT

Returning Topside

"What else would you like to know, Ronan?" Elias asked quietly after the group had dissolved from their hugs.

My uncle was chatting wildly with my friends, casting the occasional look in my direction before looking away. It didn't take a genius to realize he wanted to get something off his chest, but it was the mayor who'd approached me first.

"I know enough of what you have been keeping from us for now, I think. I've enough on my plate as is, and I know you haven't mistreated any of us since as early as I can remember." I regarded the man who hadn't actually been appointed major, yet had still filled the role regardless. Filled the role well, if the Bunker's support of his decisions were any indication. "I've never been one for secrets. Not that many survive the snoopiness of Danny, as you well know. I would like to ask a question. One regarding the future."

"Yes, of course. You three will have the full support of the Bunker as long as we can maintain equilibrium," Elias rushed to say, his hands moving in wide circles as if to indicate the floors below him.

"Very well. Then... how many and how soon can you make more implants?"

The older man did a double take as he processed what I'd said. Instead of answering right away, he took a moment to think through his answer. I could see the gears turning in his head as the logistics and costs of the implants factored into play. Or at least that's what I thought he was doing, because if not, the man had blanked out on me.

"I believe we can make seven more with our current resources. It will exhaust our entire stock of printing titanium. Six if there need to be any adjustments. As for the timeframe, Alan and I should be able to get one operational per week. The success of your own only redoubled our efforts to perfect the design."

"What about the Entity Cluster, the smaller crystal?"

"The original Metier Crystal splintered into fragments the size of your implant the moment we tried to cut it, so we have quite a handful of those remaining. Considering everyone's advanced age, we felt it was a worthy experiment to see how we could affect the crystal. No one from the bunker is at the age to have kids anymore, strange magical radiation complications aside."

The implants will definitely be a bottleneck. If the effects of Mana Dregs were as bad as they had been in the story with his father, then I couldn't risk asking the other members of the Bunker to return to the surface without them.

"We'll figure it out from there. Please get started on those as soon as you can."

"You plan to return as soon as possible, don't you." It was more of a statement than a question, especially coming from Elias.

When I nodded and looked over at my friends, I felt a pang of guilt. They looked worn out, dirty beyond anything we'd ever achieved here in the Bunker, and yet completely content. I didn't want to take them away from that, so I'd chosen not to.

"I will go back tomorrow. After getting enough supplies for

a few days. Not that the trip down is very long, but I want to spend most of my time up there."

"You are just like your parents. Quite the fearless duo they made. Dale has always been more of the...sensitive type. Considering the bombshell we just dropped on you three... He was probably one of the best to do that." The mayor wrung his hands, lost for words. I gave him a weak smile, trying my best to be forgiving.

I watched my friends for a few more seconds, the mayor moving to join them. Quietly, I slipped out of the room and started walking down to the housing floor. Before I managed to make it to the stairwell, Ben slipped out of one of the rooms in front of me. I hadn't even realized when he'd escaped the meeting room. Instead of his usual rush to shut the door, he left it wide open. Dozens of small screens showed the Bunker in all of its post-apocalyptic glory. One showed my friends in the meeting room and another showed a party going on downstairs on the greenhouse floor.

"I told them you three ought to know," he said by way of greeting.

"Figured. You wouldn't have gone through the trouble to give us guns otherwise. Thank you, by the way," I said.

He waved me off and scoffed. "Not like I was using them down here. Not since... well, your father. Those military guys kept a pretty tight leash on all of us for a long time, but not him. I opened the door for him, you know. Out." The weight of the stone around me suddenly pressed down on me. "He could still be alive, but I doubt it." I didn't want to hear this because I'd already thought about it. "I suppose becoming the biggest presence on the surface might let him know you are alive."

My gaze turned to Ben, who was holding three small blobs in hand. One for fire, water, and a pale white glass with a green hue which must be a life blob. The Attunements of those who'd died. "Are those...?"

"Yes. I saw what happened to your mother and grandmother. This is all that remained. This one is Agatha's." His voice sounded smaller than I'd ever remembered it. "Sam deserves his mother's, but I think Ingrid and Carla might want to watch over you for a while longer. And please... Come see me in the morning before you go? I'll get you sorted best I can."

Without saying anything else, he handed me the coal and water bead before returning to the monitoring room. The two small blobs weighed heavily in my hands. When I managed to peel my eyes away from what remained of my family, I realized I was in my room. The lights within flared thanks to its motion detection feature and I blinked the spots out of my eyes. Many more spots than I expected, but they cleared within a few blinks.

With quiet thunks, I placed the two remains amidst my meager collection of minerals. They were many times more beautiful than any of the other rocks, and it had nothing to do with their actual appearance. I collapsed into my bed while keeping my eyes on them. The world winked out before I'd even made it all the way to the pillow.

— + —

"Ronan! Get your lazy, rock-loving behind in gear," a familiar voice called from down the hall. My eyes flew open and I jumped to attention so fast I tripped. My body had sent me much further than I'd anticipated. "Ha! See, I told you he would do the same thing."

"Daniela!" I growled as I spotted her and Samuel standing in front of me. Both of them had the most devious of smiles.

"I suppose it's a good thing we all have magic instincts, but we are going to need some practice with the whole 'levels make us stronger' thing," Samuel added.

"What are you two talking about?" I asked as I picked myself up.

Without saying anything, they both pointed at my wrist where the <Stone Spike> pattern was dissipating. "Great. I definitely don't think using our skills indoors will be a good idea."

"Didn't work for me. Well, sorta. My potted plant exploded into tiny vines," Sam said.

"Good to know then. What time is it?" I tried to look behind my friends at my alarm clock, but they answered for me.

"Just before six in the morning." Samuel grinned. "We wanted to make sure you didn't sneak away without us."

Groaning echoed around the space around us. "See, what did I tell you? There was no chance rock boy was going to be up this early."

"Fine, but I was just going to work on my skill for the next few days," I grumbled as I nudged my way past my friends.

"No chance you are going to get ahead of us, Ronan. We are in this together, regardless of what happened in the past," Danny said, yanking on my sleeve. Her nose crinkled in my direction. "Plus, you are not going anywhere smelling and looking like that. Did you even shower yesterday?"

"Uhhh…"

"We'll get supplies situated, Ron. Just shower and meet us in Ben's office," Sam said.

"Wait, he has an office?" I definitely didn't remember the man having an office.

"The storage floor. Come on, keep up! I'll get Papa to get some decent breakfast for us," Danny explained, taking the opportunity to punch me in the shoulder and walking away with a grimace. "The cleaning rotation crew is *not* going to be happy with you. Get on with it!"

A bit stunned by my friends' initiative, I found myself in the shower. The steaming water removed caked-on layers of dirt and ash I had forgotten clung to my skin. Just a few minutes under the shower head left me feeling like a new man. There was definitely a point in time where I would have wanted to remain there just a bit longer, but when I thought about all that needed to be done on the surface, my adrenaline would not let me stand still. *There's a whole new world waiting!*

+ —

Once more dressed in a utilitarian set of clothing, jeans and a worn cotton polo, I stepped onto the storage floor. Huddled around a table were Ben and my two friends. A similar duffle bag to the one that had burned up in the fire was set aside at their feet and I could hear their argument the moment I exited the stairwell.

"You should take something with more firepower," Ben said, motioning to the table.

"We have M-A-G-I-C, Mr. Burks! I think just the handguns will do for now. Besides, the stuff we fought out there shrugged off getting shot, so we don't want to rely on them too much," Danny responded, exasperated.

"Interesting arrangement you all have here," I said from over Danny's shoulder. The three people had been so absorbed in their discussion that they'd completely missed my arrival. Daniela's own magic flared on her wrist for a second while Ben held a knife in hand. A huge grin split my face as my friends realized it was just me. "Turnabout is fair play!"

"Sure, sure. Can you convince Teach that he should keep most of this stuff for the Bunker?" Danny asked as she waved off my comment. I noted the red in her cheeks at the surprise and let the matter drop.

"If I overheard Danny's argument correctly, then she is right. It took a whole magazine just to damage the underside of the tortoise we fought. I don't think it will get much harder than that, but we would be eating through bullets like crazy," I said. Arrayed on the table were two types of automatic rifles, what I could only describe as a sniper rifle, several knives of various sizes, a shovel, an axe, and a hatchet.

"You three are out of your minds, but I haven't been to the surface, so I'll default to your judgement. If you need them, then you know where I am," Ben said, lifting his arms in a gesture for surrender.

"We *will*. Because I want you to be the first to come to the surface when the next implant is ready."

"Come again?" Our old teacher blinked at my words.

"I spoke with the mayor. He's going to crank out as many implants as he can. It's not enough to get everyone to the surface, but we'll figure out what we can do about that. I want you to be next. I don't think I need to elaborate as to why."

My friends' eyes widened at what I said and Ben turned pensive. Without much delay, he nodded and his face split into an excited smile. "If that's what you want. Only so much people-watching and stuff-stacking I can do. Can't say I don't miss the scorching mugginess of Florida."

We spent a few more minutes planning out what we were going to take. Breakfast had already made its way to the group, and I was passed a plate of tofu imitation-eggs with hashbrowns. While I shoved my mouth full of delicious protein and starch, we decided on taking all the tools we could. The lobby would serve as a good temporary set up, but it was worthwhile to think about setting up some other structures. A potato-filled grin came to my face, causing Sam and Danny to groan.

"He's got a plan. Again," Danny said.

"At least the last one turned out pretty good," Sam admitted.

"Thank you! My plans are good, Danny. You can only complain about them if they don't turn out!" I said. "And I'm keeping this one to myself until we get to the surface."

After a round of chuckles from Ben, we were ready to depart. With enough food for three days, water for two, and a wide arrangement of tools, we trudged up to engineering. Quietly waiting beside the entrance was my uncle. For the first time since I could recall, he looked frazzled. Which shouldn't have been the case, considering he worked with the water and disposal systems of the Bunker, but he liked to be presentable.

"Give me a minute guys, would you?" My friends didn't say anything and instead moved to stand by the meeting room door, looking over our gear. Not that it needed any more looking over, but I appreciated their discretion.

"Hello, Ronan," my uncle said quietly. I watched his fingers lift, then twitch back down. Surely restraining himself from hugging me.

"Please don't say anything. I don't want you to apologize, because I understand why you did it. You didn't want to hurt me and I know you love me. Just... give me time."

"Of course. I wanted you to know that I'm here. You may not be my son, but I raised you like I would have my own. I promised Marcus as much..."The words died in his throat and he bit back something else. "Just take care of yourself, okay?"

Managing a weak smile, I gripped my uncle's shoulder and walked past him. My friends were at my side a moment later. Nothing was said as we crossed the concrete doors to the surface. Thin rays of light flickered through the frame of the lobby's door as we all took a deep breath. Then coughed all at the same time.

"Forgot about the smoke," Sam coughed out.

"Don't know that there will be much we will be able to do for now. Let's get the inside cleaned out before we start on my plan," I said, retrieving a broom from the second rucksack we'd acquired. With slow strokes, I started to pile up the dust and ash in the room towards the doorway.

"Now that we are here, are you going to tell us what your 'plan' is?" Danny complained as she swept one of the counters clean and started to lay out our other tools.

"Patience, young one," I ribbed, sweeping my dust pile out of the door in a cloud. "A better question is what Sam is doing with a potted plant. Where did you even stash that? I didn't see it."

"I may have... figured out a side effect of my skill," he said, looking abashed as Danny and I paused to look at him. The man was sheepishly holding the pot behind his back.

"Well? Out with it, man!" I demanded, resuming my sweeping, but deliberately moving closer to his plant.

"I wanted to bring a little something from home. My dad gave me a tomato sprout. Just like Daniela, when you gave us a fright, I summoned my magic, but not totally since I didn't have a target in mind and the magic failed to stick.

"Instead, it seemed to flow into the tomato and it *grew*. This one had been just a little sprout, and while my other potted friend in the Bunker exploded into vines, this one didn't. On the walk up, I kept the skill just at the edge of triggering and well…" Samuel pointed at the foot tall plant growing out of the thin plastic pot. Green leaves, shimmering like they were polished, adorned the plant.

"Holy crap!" I shouted, unable to contain my excitement. "That means that just calling forth the magic has a tangible effect on the world! Did it use up your mana?"

"Eh, I didn't think to check. I did feel the lightheadedness." Sam looked off in the distance as he pulled up his status. "Yeah. Quite a bit too. I'm at less than half."

"That doesn't matter, that's amazing. Quick, let's get this place cleaned. I'm even more excited about my plan now!"

I didn't keep an eye on my friends as I started sweeping like a madman. Of course, they came in the form of slow strokes again, but I tried to will the dirt around us to collect faster so we could get out. Within minutes, the place looked as pristine as it was going to get and I rushed out.

Pistol in my right hand and magic on the left, I scanned the surroundings and the sky for anything that might attack us. Once that was done, I gave our surroundings a *good* look. We were on a mounded hill compared to the surrounding forest, and I could only imagine it was due to the layers between the surface and the Bunker. There was a portion of the trees to the east that looked like a game trail or maybe where there had once been a road heading north. *That's the next target of exploration after we find a closer water source.*

Thankfully, when I climbed over the top of the lobby, I spotted a large pond some distance to the west. *That was easy.* The small concrete block that made up the lobby seemed to grow partly out of the hill and if I wanted, I could have climbed over the grassy hill to the south. *Something else to really explore.*

While I stood and surveyed the space around us, my friends exited the Bunker. It took them a moment to spot me.

"Ron, what are you doing up there?" Sam asked, shielding his eyes from the rising sun.

"I'm planning the little fort we are going to be building here!" I shouted down at them.

"How are we going to do that, numb nuts?" Daniela asked skeptically, crossing her arms and arching an eyebrow at me. "We are just three people."

"Ah, but you see, we have *magic!*" On cue, I pushed the mental button for <Stone Spike> while focusing on a spot near the edge of the tree line. Roughly three feet of soil rose up and compacted in the space I'd targeted, leaning forward slightly. It wasn't the thickness or direction that I wanted, but it was a start. When I jumped down to my friends, they were still very much confused. "The spikes don't disappear. And if I had to guess from Sam's experiments, his vines won't either unless something destroys them."

The lightbulb went off in both of my friends, as evidenced by the jaw drops which immediately turned into excited smiles. Samuel practically rubbed his hands together at the prospect and I was right on that boat with him. "Plus we get to really figure out our skills, it's a win-win, I think."

"Sign me up!" Danny flared her own skill, lighting up her wrist.

CHAPTER NINE

Foundation

With my friends completely on board with my plan, we got to work. The first step was laying out a basic outline of the space we wanted to work with. That particular task I assigned to Daniela. The woman dashed around the perimeter of the Bunker faster than I thought possible. On her second pass, she started to blast the ground. As a means of marking space, her skill left small craters in the burned up earth where she thought our boundaries should be.

Before I had Sam join me on the second part of my plan, I told him to get better familiarized with his growing passive skill, as I'd decided to call it. The horticulturalist fanatic practically pounced on the few plants around the Bunker clearing that had remained through the blaze. With my friend occupied, and the occasional rumble from Daniela's skill in the background, I moved to the summoned stone spike.

The formation was about six inches at the bottom, tapering to a rough point after rising for three feet. It looked more like hard-packed earth than stone, but it still took significant effort for me to break it when I pushed on it. Stepping back a few feet, I focused on the skill and aimed it just to the right of my first spike. The spike rose perpendicular to the gentle slope and I realized why the first had been skewed. Without a target, it just compressed along the surface. Not only that, there was only a slight dip in the surrounding soil, so the spell had to be forming matter from mana. *Somehow. I'll leave* that *question for Sam's big brain.*

With that initial observation, and focusing past the stinging in my gut from casting the spell, I watched the second spike closely. It was about the same height, but the base was easily twice as wide as the first. A glance at my mana bar told me I had roughly seventy percent of my mana left.

I watched the bar rise slowly, a percent every few seconds as far as I could tell. By my estimation, it took twenty percent of my current mana to cast a stone spike. Thinking back on the pain from our last trip to the surface, there also had to be some inherent cooldown to using the skill back to back. Getting a better feel for that, learning its limitations and figuring out how to mitigate the side effects, could only be beneficial. Shaking my head to clear it of the academic aspects of magic, I focused on getting a *feel* for it. Over the next several hours, I pushed my mana to the limits. The sun was past midway in the sky when Sam came to get me for a quick lunch.

The man paused as he looked around at what I'd done. Summoning a wall of spikes via the most involved process I could manage, I'd used the ground for a good thirty feet to create mostly vertical spikes spaced two feet apart. With that portion complete, I proceeded to use <Stone Spike> on the spikes themselves. Alternating vertical and slanted cones of compacted earth formed a rough wall in front of me.

"Ronan... What the hell are you doing?" Sam asked.

"Working on the first part of our defensive wall!" I said, excited but quite tired. The discomfort from casting didn't even vanish completely after waiting several minutes, so I'd pushed through regardless. Mana fatigue was yet another thing to keep in mind.

"Right... Well, you look like you're about to keel over. Let's get you back to the lobby and get some food in you. Danny did the same thing as you and she is sweating buckets."

Without needing further prompting, we made our way to the lobby. I blinked at the sheer madness of tomatoes growing in rows along one side of the squat building. There was one fully grown plant near the base of the building, and at least a dozen half-grown ones with little green balls at the ends. Ripening tomatoes.

"Is this all from—" I started, but Sam cut me off.

"Yep. Nearly passed out a few times, but I think it was worth it. The side effect of my magic doesn't seem to get to me as much as yours or Daniela's. It might also have been because I didn't fully cast the spell, but it will take more practice to really figure it out," he said. "If these grow at the same rate as they do underground, we should have some cherry tomatoes within a week, even without my intervention!"

I gaped at my friend's efforts and he chuckled all the way to the door. Inside, Danny was already crunching through one of the insta-meals Ben had provided. When we walked in, she looked up with a 'chipmunk face' as we'd come to call it and our laughter restarted.

"Less than a week on the surface and already you are behaving like we are down in the Bunker," I scolded her jokingly. She swatted my wagging finger before taking a swig of water to down her food.

"I'm burning up. I've felt constantly hungry while marking out the space around the Bunker. Oh, I found the pond to the west, by the way," she said before resuming her meal.

"Maybe we ought to slow down on the magic a bit. I don't want anything strange to happen on the first day if we aren't cautious," I said, accepting the small tray with food. "We also need to check in with the Entity."

"We need to come up with an actual name for it. It seems to have a personality, so we should at least consider it a 'person,'" Sam added, making air quotes with his fingers at the end. "Taking the time of day into account and how much we've pushed our new magic, I think it would be better if we do that tomorrow morning."

Giving the man a thumbs up as I stuffed my own mouth full of bland food, we ate in silence for some time. I mulled on the discoveries I'd made about our magic. Definite side effects to keep in mind, but benefits we still didn't even fully comprehend. Something I'd been doing while testing out my <Stone Spike> was prod at the part of my mind that seemed to hold the information. Considering we could call it forth without fully triggering the skill, there had to be at least two parts to *using* magic. Not to mention the strange characters that appeared along with the skill. Even after staring at them for several hours, they looked like shifting scribbles.

"Ron. Ronan!" I blinked to see Danny and Sam staring at me. "You okay?"

"Eh, yeah. Why, what's up?"

"You finished eating like fifteen minutes ago. You've just been staring at your tray," Sam said with concern.

"Oh, sorry. I was just thinking about magic stuff," I said, shaking my head and realizing I was extremely tired.

"Well. That does it. If Ron is tired, then we need to call a break for now. We can try to do some manual stuff later before the sun goes down," Daniela said, crossing her arms and leaning against one of the counters in the lobby.

"I'm fine. I was just spaced out." When I tried to rise to my feet, my legs wobbled. *Maybe not entirely fine...*

"No sir. You've been going non-stop since we got to the surface. If you are tired, then Sam and I are probably going to feel it soon. When the endurance machine breaks, you take a rest," Danny quipped while shifting to get comfortable against the counter.

"You know Ben gave us sleeping bags, yes?" Sam said, holding up the cushioned polyester tube.

A wave of exhaustion ran through me at the prospect of sleep and I realized that my friends were right. *Plus, a little rest would let my subconscious work on understanding magic.* I laughed to myself for a moment before accepting the bag from Samuel. "Just one last precaution. Can you please hold the door open, Sam?"

He lifted an eyebrow in confusion, but moved to the door regardless. I focused on the space beyond, eyeing spots where Sam hadn't planted any of his tomatoes. With the sharp pain in my gut to mark the casting, I raised two stone spikes in an X in front of the door. With that last expenditure, I dropped onto my sleeping bag. The slight hiss of air as my weight deflated the cushions brought out a sigh of comfort from me. "Just in case…"

My friends shook their heads at my antics before settling into their own bags. Within moments, I was asleep.

The sound of nails on a chalkboard that we'd only ever heard in video records snapped me awake. A <Stone Spike> lingered on my wrist as my eyes adjusted to the light. *How long were we asleep…?* The thought didn't linger long as another round of grima reached us. The sound sent goosebumps along my body and I focused on a flickering in the light coming in from the doorway. Flicking a lantern set on the counter, I woke Danny and then Sam. I placed my hand over their mouths to keep them from screaming, holding a finger to my lips to signal silence.

My senses strained as I watched the light flicker and listened to the muted rustling of grass through the door. I wasn't certain how long we were poised and alert, but thankfully it paid off.

The only warning I got was a loud sniff, then a snarl before we heard one of my stone spikes snap. My fist tightened as I realized the strength necessary to do that, considering I'd cast the thick-based spikes. More snarling sounded outside as the unseen creature attacked *something.* Not wanting to waste the slight distraction, I focused on the slight spacing at the bottom of the door. With the intent of aiming at whatever was beyond, I triggered <Stone Spike>.

A yowl of pain was the only response we got to my attack. Hissing and snarling followed, but they couldn't have been due to my spike. We remained poised at the door, trying to discern the strange encounter on the other side.

As the minutes ticked by without any further sounds, I crouched and leaned closer to try to peek through the gap on the doorframe with little success. In the subtle light of the lantern, I saw both of my friends holding their skills at the ready. With a finger count of three, I pulled open the door. Dawn light spilled into the room, but there was nothing beyond my stone spikes. One of the two was broken partway down, while the other had deep claw marks along its length. Considering there were easily two inches between each claw, I didn't want to meet whatever they belonged to. The best sign was the crimson blood marks dotting the ground and the very tip of my third spike.

"How did we sleep this long? And what happened to my tomatoes!?" Sam blurted out in surprise as we peeked over my makeshift barrier. The rows of growing plants were trampled to the ground. Signs of combat dotted the space around the entrance, and I wasn't sure from what. Clearly some large cat had been prowling around, but it had engaged with something else. The display, even knowing I had access to magic, really put into perspective the fact that humans weren't at the top of the food chain anymore.

I motioned my friends back inside and shut the door. "Okay, thoughts. Obviously something huge is living nearby and it likes coming by at night."

My two friends frowned at my words. Without prompting, Sam went to rummage in one of our supply bags and handed out breakfast rations. Grits, jerky, and disintegrating crackers. Munching loudly, Daniela brought up some points. "We need to get the crystal back here. As soon as possible. I imagine that whatever it was doing to keep murderous critters away when we passed out will help us *not* have a repeat of this; talking to it will be invaluable in settling up here. Not only that, we should try to find more things to hunt."

"How are we sure that the stuff we hunt isn't going to kick

our ass?" Sam asked, swiping at some of the inevitable crumbs from the crackers.

"I don't think we can know for sure. But if the attributes are right, it should be plausible for us to fight directly against stuff. The 0.1 growth is insane. I feel much faster already," Danny said, twirling her spork in the air.

"I agree with both of those points. Before we head out, I think we should fortify the Bunker exit. I might have been a bit ambitious with where I started to build our wall," I said, scratching the back of my head.

"Considering most of the garden I was setting up is mulch, perhaps I should move it closer to the pond. Maybe I can figure out how to make a small canal system to do some serious farming," Sam said, pointing to the four foot tall tomato plant inside the lobby. I felt relieved that he'd had the foresight to leave the original plant inside and used the cuttings to seed his magical garden. As I considered that, the fact that none of the plants had dissolved into particles struck me as strange, but I just added it to the pile of questions to ask the Entity when it was functional.

"I'll keep blasting a trench around us then and see if I can spot any more of those squirrels," Daniela said. "No sense dilly-dallying. If any of us are in trouble, two quick shots from the pistols. Preferably *at* the target of said trouble." The woman gave Samuel a look and the blond scratched his head sheepishly. She made sure to rib him about his accuracy at every opportunity.

"That's a plan then. If something seems to be out of hand, run. If we need to retreat to the Bunker or regroup, or *something*, then so be it. None of our lives are worth anything we build or make on the surface."

Finishing the rest of the meal in silence, we got to work. With some difficulty, I broke through the stone spike defenses I'd set up outside of our door. The base of the spikes remained, but we all stepped over them. They were a minor inconvenience to walk over, but they would allow me to have set spots for future ones.

Danny joined Sam on the walk to the pond, hoping to help him set up the garden and keep an eye on his back. Once the two were past the original outer perimeter I'd hoped to mark, I eyed a twenty-ish foot radius around the lobby. Cracking my knuckles, I braced myself for the gut wrench of magic and started casting.

Over the rest of the day, I made an inner perimeter. With only a brief break for lunch, I pushed through my discomfort from using <Stone Spike>. While I felt like a used rag that had been scrubbed on basalt rock, I'd made a discovery.

Between each casting of my skill, I'd kept the spell just at the edge of my mind. While keeping magic at the surface, but untriggered, Sam could enhance the growth of the plants under his care. With that inspiration, I kept the passive effect of my magic active during one of my breaks. The result wasn't obvious from looking at it, but it made itself noticeable quickly. Markedly in the discomfort my rear end experienced when I tried to plop on the once-soft earth. My passive ability allowed me to consolidate and compress the ground around me.

As the day was drawing to a close, and I worked on using my consolidating abilities within the semicircle of spikes I'd created, a whistle drew my attention. While it hadn't been the agreed upon call, I brought up my gun on my right and my skill on the left. With quick steps, I peeked between a gap in my spike wall.

Making their way slowly up the slope were Sam and Danny. After watching them carefully for a few seconds, I holstered my gun. They'd just been signaling their return. Walking to one of the two wide openings I'd made in the perimeter, the one facing northwest, I smiled at my friends.

"How was the planting?" I asked, motioning to their mud-encrusted pants.

"It went great. I didn't realize we were going to come back

to some primal stalagmite fort," Sam said. The two of them were gaping at what I'd accomplished within the day.

"It wouldn't have been so surprising if you two had come back for lunch. I didn't see you grab anything when you left, other than the shovels."

"I stuffed myself full of roasted tomatoes. Oh! I found out what my ambient magic does, Ron!" Danny said excitedly. She pulled out a trio of cherry tomatoes and I saw the ring for her magic blink into existence. A second later, the sweet and sour tang of tomato drifted in the air and she tossed me one of them. It was grilled on the outside.

"That's amazing!" I moaned through the gush of flavor. The prospect of surface-grown food had me immensely excited. There was only so much hydroponic grown vegetables and fish you could stand.

"And that's not all!" The woman held up a fist-sized skull and another gray cotton blob. "Snagged another squirrel. Sam didn't even hit it when I blasted it out of the sky, so I finished it off. I'm almost to my third Quotient!"

I gave my friends a hug in excitement. Pulling back on the instincts my uncle had ingrained in me, I coughed a bit awkwardly and disengaged. Thankfully, my friends were used to it enough to simply accept the gesture. I hoped it made my feelings about working together clear.

As terrible as the previous night had gone, the day showed we were determined to survive and thrive.

Showing off my own discovered passive ability, I compressed the mud on their pants. The clinging clay and sand crumbled away and drifted in the wind after some hardy pats from my friends. We spent some time relaxing and catching up on the fun mishaps of the day.

As the sky splashed orange and blue, our moods went somber. We shared a look and slowly made our way back within the lobby. While the two openings the perimeter had would allow most things inside in its current state, I hoped it would discourage any violent engagements right outside our makeshift home.

Giving the setting sun one last look, I slammed two spikes in an X again to bar the door. Sleeping behind the Bunker doors would probably be safer, but we were liable to suffocate, since I'd seen no ventilation. After a quiet dinner, I suggested making a guard rotation. Just in case. My heightened perception had allowed me to stir when our nighttime visitors arrived, but I didn't feel comfortable leaving our security to just my tired body.

My friends wholeheartedly agreed. While they slept, I mulled on how we could transport the Entity Cluster back to our growing abode. Engrossed in possible solutions, Danny startled me with a tap and a nod to my bedroll when my watch was over. The rest was lost to the darkness and blissfully dreamless sleep.

CHAPTER TEN

Neighbors

Sam shook me awake gently. I swatted his arm away and curled deeper into my sleeping bag. When he shook me harder, I jerked up as the last few days flashed through my groggy mind. "What, where!?"

"Calm down, Ron. Danny is putting breakfast together, but there is something strange outside that I think you should look at," my friend said. When I looked at him, I saw him scratch at the blond stubble just starting to grow in. Accepting his offered hand, I rose to my feet and waved at Daniela. The woman was hunched over our pre-packed breakfasts, adding in what looked like dried tomato slices.

Chagrined, I walked over to the open doorway of the lobby. With dramatic flair, Samuel pointed at a small herd of cows that were grazing peacefully in the space I'd barred off. I drank in the sight for several seconds before looking at my friend. "What are they doing?" I asked. It was a dumb question, since I could see they were eating, but Sam got my meaning.

"No clue. I tried to spook them with my magic and a few pebbles, but they just looked my way before going back to their business."

"Have they shown any… magic stuff? Attunements or anything?" I asked, gesturing to the larger-than-expected, but normal-looking cows. Normal, at least, based on the information we had from the world pre-Landfall.

"None that I could tell. There is that guy, though." Sam pointed out a darker-colored cow with a large set of horns spread wide from its head. As my eyes landed on the creature, its information populated on the implant.

<Bull>

<Attunement: Life>

<Refinement: Fertility>

<Perceived Metier Quotient: 2>

"Oh man," I said, scratching my head awkwardly.

"What? Did you see something?" Sam said, looking back at the creature he'd pointed out.

"I think the other cows may be normal cows, or something, but that's a mana creature. Attunement for Life and Refinement for… Fertility."

"Oh. I… see." Sam looked around at the gathered herd, and then back to the Life Bull. "Can we take it?"

"I… think so. But…" As soon as I realized that we could probably kill the bull, a better idea popped into my head. "How long have they been out here?"

"Eh, a few hours. They poked their heads against the door but just drifted over to eat the scraps from my first tomato planting. They are almost done." Looking over, I saw that the half-dozen animals had munched through the grass in the space with a vengeance. A few dark mounds in the space also told me where the tomatoes had gone after being eaten. Grimacing at the addition to our budding foothold, I turned to Sam.

Under my squint-eyed scrutiny, Sam tilted his head in confusion. When I wasn't able to hold back my smile, Sam backed away slowly. "Oh, look. Breakfast!" He bolted the short distance back to Danny who gave us a curious look.

My face remained split in a grin and Danny's morning person cheeriness flagged slightly. "Oh no."

"Oh yes. Best eat up, friends. We are gonna be honest to goodness cowboys today."

— + —

"This is a terrible idea," Danny complained as she hid behind a double barrier of my stone spikes.

"What's the worst that can happen?" I said from the other side of the four foot barrier.

"That cow goring Sam! What do you mean what's the worst that can happen!?" Danny said, glaring over at me.

I didn't meet her eyes, since my concentration was already zeroed in on my other friend and his approach to the bull. The seemingly normal cows parted as the human approached. Sam handed each of them a small bundle of fresh-grown magic grass before heading for the bull. With the herd milling around him and a wide smile on his face, the blond turned to the attuned creature. His smile slipped completely as he focused on the first step of his plan.

Sam had been vehemently opposed to my plan at the start, until I pointed out the fact that the bull was both fully grown already and just as likely to murder us all if we didn't deal with it. Instead of opting for the death option, we'd decided to try to tame it. Sam's arm lit up with a soft green light and I saw the ground around the bull rise and reach for the sky. As if it had sensed that something was amiss, a similar green glow encased the creature. Confirmation enough of its Attunement.

Unlike the mesh of vines I'd expected from Sam, a deluge of grass surged out of the ground to bind the bull. It lowed and its eyes widened as its attempt to charge was halted. My friend had preemptively rolled out of the way, but seeing the magnified effect of his skill, doubled down. Another surge of vines exploded out of the ground to grasp the Bull's head. This second casting looked like the ones he'd used before and seeing the weakened binding, the bull started to thrash. Sharp snaps marked the breaking of the bindings keeping the creature down. Another two casts from Sam thickened the vines again, but the snapping continued as the bull fought for its freedom.

Seeing that the attempt to bind it was failing, I moved in. Danny was a step behind me, but not for long. The woman shot by, giving Sam a hand as he struggled to stay on his feet. Clinging to the hope that my plan could still work, I summoned one, then another stone spike to form a cross *over* the bull. Its thrashing snapped the earthen pillars, and it sagged under their weight. My stomach heaved at my quick casting, but the bull redoubled its efforts for freedom. Loud lowing echoed out behind me as the herd responded to the bull's frothing frenzy.

Gritting my teeth, I summoned another cross to lock the bull's flailing horns. The pain was immense as I triggered <Stone Spike> two times simultaneously and dropped to my hands and knees. My eyes watered and I blinked the tears away to watch as the bull continued to thrash. Thankfully, with its thick neck caught right against the ground by two foot thick pillars of rock, its thrashing weakened. One final casting from Sam snapped into place around the bull, sealing its movements completely.

Taking a wary look behind me, I saw the herd calm with the quieting of the bull. The cows still shuffled around anxiously, pushed against the far side of my spike wall, but they went back to grazing. With some effort, I made it to my friends. The two of them were looking at the bull, having the strangest staring contest I'd ever seen.

"Quick thinking there, Ron. I don't think I could have nabbed him," Sam said weakly. The blond was nearly as pale as his locks, and rested heavily on Daniela. The woman gave their friend a look of concern, before looking me over.

"Are you alright?"

"Good as new." I gave her a tired smile before looking at the bull. The creature had calmed down completely and its eyes were flashing between us. "So, any ideas for the next step?"

Both of my friends glared at me, but eventually Sam sighed. When he was able to stand on his own, he brought his magic to the fore and revitalized one of the few surviving tomato plants. Before my eyes, the plant righted itself and bloomed. Several small red cherry tomatoes dropped onto Samuel's waiting hand and he walked slowly to the bull. The creature strained against its bindings once again, but stopped when Sam did too. The two stared at each other for several minutes before he took a few steps closer. When the bull tensed, he repeated the process of waiting and advancing. When he was a few feet from the creature, he dropped half of the tomatoes within reach of its mouth. My friend took a step back and smiled gently at the bull.

The creature snorted loudly, sniffing the curious red fruit before nibbling on one. The snorts increased as it dove back into the small pile, chomping through it and some of the surrounding grass in its desire to snag every bit that he could. Wary of its enormous horns, Sam set another three tomatoes and stepped closer.

When the creature finished eating, and then looked at Sam expectantly, Sam held his left hand out with the tomatoes for it to eat. The bull hesitated for several moments. I caught it looking between my friend's hand and his face and a chill ran down my spine. The creature had a noticeable intelligence beyond its reactive nature. When it ate out of Sam's hand and allowed the man to run his hands along its head, I could only hope we'd succeeded.

"Come say hello, guys," Sam said in a barely audible whisper. I hesitated, but followed my friend's lead and ran my hands along the creature's head. Its fur was thick and silky in a way I couldn't have expected. Up close, its horns were even more impressive as they shot out and up to the sky. Even with a Quotient of 2, I had no illusion that I matched up with the bull. This beast was many times physically stronger than me. It made me consider the effects Quotients had on us physically. If the rate of growth was proportional to the species… Another shiver ran down my spine as I thought of a *number* of creatures that did not need to be magically enhanced to be terrifying.

I'm not sure how long we stood there loving on the first

'friendly' creature we'd ever interacted with, but when the other cows started eating the vines binding the bull in their monotonous hunger, we stepped back hesitantly. At some point during our petting session, Sam had fashioned a halter from his vines and placed it on the bull's head. It had protested, but after some additional tomatoes and petting, it had calmed.

One final, surprising, development that happened was that when the bull worked to free itself, the soft glow of life-attuned mana radiated from its body. In response, Sam's body also glowed the same shade until the beast shrugged off my binding spikes. I stepped back, ready to throw out my magic if the bull charged. Instead, our bovine neighbor lowered its head and rubbed it into Sam's side. The man let out a nervous giggle as he petted the now-free bull and we all let out sighs of relief.

"Time for that final part of the plan then. I think we are going to need many, many more tomatoes, Sam." Mischievous smile in place, my two friends groaned. Having successfully appeased the bull, the real mission could begin. Retrieving the Entity Cluster.

Over the next hour, Sam wrung himself dry of mana to produce a rucksack's worth of tomatoes. He also used the growing plants and vines from his passive skill to craft several feet of cordage with Danny's help. While they tinkered with the finer bits of weaving, I chopped down a tree.

A wide-blade hatchet had been included in the set of tools Ben had supplied us. Taking hold of the rubber-handled, steel implement, I swung from the hip into the base of a roughly ten foot tree. My eyes widened at how far the blade sunk into the oak, but I shook my head. *Can't expect the same results after the increase in strength I've had.* Yanking my hatchet out of the tree took considerably more effort, but once it was free, I swung a bit slower. Before long, I was calling out 'timber' as the wedge I'd made forced the tree to topple. A few more strikes freed it from its stump, and I began to strip it of limbs. Chucking the larger branches towards the Bunker and then shoving the rest out of the way took a good half hour.

As I paused to assess the foot and a half cylinder of wood, I scratched my head as to how I would be able to split the thing lengthwise. Deciding there wasn't anything immediately clever I could do, I began to mark out the midpoint of the trunk. The process of raising my arm and dropping it onto the wood was even more monotonous than casting and waiting for my stomach to settle before casting again. Mid-swing, however, inspiration struck.

With a plan formed, I finished marking a one inch groove down the length of the log. I called Danny over and she helped me twist and flip the log so that the groove faced towards the ground. Instead of watching my ingenious idea, she patted my shoulder and returned to Samuel. Huffing in indignation, but excited to see if my plan would work, I bound each end of the log with an X of stone spikes. No shoving or kicking or pushing caused the log to shift, pinned under the compacted earth. I hopped onto the uneven wooden surface and glared a hole onto the top. I visualized the groove hidden underneath and where it would exit on the other side. Then triggered <Stone Spike>.

The result was a bit more than I'd expected, but worked splendidly. The condensed earth shot out of the ground straight into the groove before pushing deep into the wood. The stone of the two bind points at either end groaned in protest, but held.The spike pierced through the wood, splitting one end in the process. It wasn't perfectly centered, but it would work. Waiting for my mana to regenerate, I marked the other side of the log with a shallow groove in the hopes of guiding the split as much as possible. Two more spikes and the log was snapped mostly in half. Breaking and rolling the stone spike bindings released the tree and it *twanged* mostly apart. A few hatchet strikes later and I had two halves.

Excitement built in me as I worked on the biggest thing anyone in the Wildwood had for decades. The wood shaping was harder than I expected, but the work had me gleefully attacking each half of the log. Before long, I'd carved two holes on one end of both logs, as well as two indents perpendicular to the length of the wood. Taking one of the thickest branches, I set it onto the indent across both halves and hammered it into place. Repeating the process with the other indent, the Bull Sled 1.0 was complete.

While Sam and Danny finished the bindings that would hopefully attach the bull to the sled, I did my best to smooth out the bottom and top surfaces. I'd deliberately picked the closest, modestly-sized, and least-knotted tree around us, but it wasn't perfect. After some deliberation, and a delay on my friends' side due to an overeager cow that ate some of their tomato supply, I added another two perpendicular supports for the sled.

I was all smiles as Danny arrived and tied up some cord to reinforce my work, before doing a complex knot to the front of the sled.

"Man, I guess I am glad you and Sam spent that summer learning how to tie knots. Who would have thought it would serve us well here," I said as I watched her work.

"Sam did. He'd used them several times with his dad to fix up stuff in the greenhouse. Figured it would fill in gaps in our knowledge, should we need to move or secure stuff on the surface," Danny said, tugging on the single woven vine that secured the front of the sled. "This is a bale sling hitch, and hopefully will work as well horizontally as it's supposed to work vertically."

She continued to explain some of the other knots and weaves that they'd used to create the several foot long rope at her feet, but the terms and concepts flew over my head. She sighed in defeat and laid down on my rough handiwork. We watched the woods, listening to the occasional bird call and the wind shifting the leaves. The sweat covering us and the twinge of oppressive heat didn't bother us in the least. The space and freedom to *do* was reward enough to keep struggling for our little spot of land on the surface.

"You two gonna space out, or are we going to get us an alien rock?" Sam called out from behind us. He had the bull close in tow, a series of ropes tied to its head, horns and shoulders. My perception focused on the small red liquid dripping from its mouth, but that very perception allowed me to recognize it as tomato paste. With a jump in his step, Sam alternated between hitching the bull to the sled and feeding it a handful of tomatoes.

When the whole mess of wooden bars, metal clips and vine rope was complete, my friend nudged the bull in the rear. The cart took off after the bull and we all resisted the urge to cheer loudly. Sam had warned us it could spook the bull.

"Perfect! That's an amazing job, you two!" I said, half-whispering, half-shouting at my friends. Sam tried to glare for a second, but couldn't help the smile that worked its way to his face. Danny was the same. She adjusted herself on the sled, braced against one of the indents I'd carved, while Sam was at the head keeping the bull calm and guiding it. "Let's go get us a crystal!"

CHAPTER ELEVEN

Special Delivery

The trip back to the crystal was blissfully quiet. I worried the entire time that we would attract the attention of some deadly creature around us, but nothing happened. There was a small twinge of disappointment since an attack would have meant growing stronger too, but I pushed that thought back. Retrieving the crystal was more important.

"You know, we should give him a name," Sam said from the other side of the bull. Daniela and I were surf riding the cart to pass the time while keeping an eye on the surrounding woods.

"How do you know it's going to stick around?" Danny asked, turning towards the blond.

Samuel looked affronted, as if she'd gone up and slapped him. "Of course he's going to stay!"

"Sam, he's a wild animal. I don't think domestication has been a thing over the last two decades," I said, patting the creature's side gently. Its wrist-thick tail swatted at me and the bull snorted but kept moving forward without pause.

"I'll name him Raymond then. And you two have no say in the matter." Without another word, he turned back to the forest. After some time, he leaned down and started to talk to our bovine companion. He was whispering into its ear, but it wasn't incredibly difficult for me to hear with my increased perception.

"Don't listen to them. You are a big strong bull, and you are going to help us build a big strong settlement, while you get to have a big strong herd all to yourself."

I shook my head at my friend's antics, but a smile remained plastered on my face. There was no point in blaming Sam for getting attached, and hopefully the bull *did* stick around.

While musing on the potential of farming and animal husbandry with magically mutated animals, we arrived at the embankment I'd built up. One point of the crystal reached out from behind the mound and I saw some of the iridescent light it had originally.

Excited about the possibility that the Entity would be awake once again, I leapt off the side of the sled and rushed closer. Sadly, as I neared, no voice greeted me. When I was standing over the crystal, I could see that it had brightened considerably but was still only a shadow of its previous glow.

A few minutes later, my friends and Ray the bull pulled up beside me.

"No dice, eh?" Sam said as he fed Raymond another handful of tomatoes.

"No, but it definitely seems to have gotten brighter. Can you get Raymond turned around and we'll try to lever it onto the sled?" Putting action to words, I asked Danny to grab one of my broken spikes to use as fulcrum while I sought out a decent fallen branch.

After testing nearly a dozen, I found one that didn't crumble into rot. Propping the branch against the head-sized chunk Danny fetched gave us enough leverage to lift the tip of the Entity Cluster onto the sled. With that done, Sam had Raymond back up while I used the branch to keep the crystal from sliding. This whole process took nearly two other handfuls of tomatoes and over half an hour. For the first time since encountering the beast, Sam's inexperience at maneuvering the animal showed its annoying head. Nonetheless, with a final assisting push from me and Danny, the crystal was on board.

Sam had Raymond take a few steps forward and our ramshackle contraption held together well enough. A few hammering strikes with the back of my hatchet pushed one of the supporting slats back into place and we were off.

The return trip was much, much slower as our bull friend strained against the weight of the Entity Cluster. Other than a pair of squirrels, one of which Danny shot out of the sky before I even got my gun up, the return trip was quiet. When the already regrowing patches of land the fire had ravaged came into view, we knew we were home.

When my spike wall became visible through the trees, we heard the lowing of the herd. It wasn't the ambient, peaceful tones of the grazing animals, but one of panic and concern. My friends and I shared a look, and sped towards the Bunker.

Sam didn't even need to urge Raymond. Since the bull had heard the call of his herd, it had acted as if the large Entity Cluster was but a minor burden. At the base of the clearing, we could hear the herd's lowing increase in fervor. Far beyond, I saw something that raised my hackles.

A corpse, whose throat had been shredded. Ray must have seen the body at the same time, because he thrashed and managed to snap several of the ropes binding him.

"Cut him loose!" Sam shouted over the bulls wild snorts.

Without hesitation, I chopped down on the knot holding the bull to the drag sled. Without needing further prompting, Raymond was off. With only a few feet to build his charge, the bull closed the distance in seconds and disappeared behind my spike wall.

"We need to find out what's going on!" Putting action to words, I leapt over the crystal and headed for the wall. Daniela moved to rush past me, but I grabbed hold of her arm. "We don't know what's over there. We stick together."

The woman gave me a grim nod and we all matched pace to get to our small base. The scene was one of chaos.

Literal Fire Ants scurried all over the cows. Small gouts of fire rose from the ground wherever the creatures moved. Most were the size of rats, while three were equal in size to the cows. Raymond had locked horns to mandibles with one of the giant ants while the other two were moving to flank the bull. As I took in the mayhem, I saw that our bovine companion had already plowed clear through another of the giant ones and had stomped several of the smaller ones.

When I focused on one, their information blinked into view.

<Fire Ant>

<Attunement: Fire>

<Refinement: N/A>

<Perceived Metier Quotient: 0>

I fought back the urge to panic at the overwhelming number of enemies, seeing that if we didn't intervene, not only would the cows be decimated by the ants, we would follow soon after. With that cold realization, a plan snapped into place.

"Danny, try to save as many of the cows as you can, keep them moving. Sam and I are going to try to deal with the giant ones." I brandished my gun and flicked the safety off.

With huffs in response, the two of us parted around the dead cow's body. With a running start, I punted ant after ant, crushing their heads in a flash. It didn't do much to abate the tide.

A flare of fire followed by a muted boom marked Danny's first skill, followed by a half-dozen cracks of gunfire. The ants didn't like that.

A veritable surge of the smaller ones headed straight for her while one of the larger ones veered off from Raymond.

"Sam, help Raymond!" Gritting my teeth, I focused on the ant heading toward Danny. Keeping in mind how many I had available, I triggered <Stone Spike>.

The condensed earth rose up and caught one of the creature's limbs. With the sudden obstruction, it stumbled but only briefly. Thankfully, that was all I needed. With three shots, I managed to blow out one of its eyes, directing its ire toward me.

My own eyes widened when the ant spat a fireball in my direction. Reflexively, I cast <Stone Spike> at point blank range in front of me. Not a moment later, the heat and flames of the attack forced me to cover my face. Then the ant was on top of me.

The impact with the ant was like getting hit by a rogue storage container when I helped Ben on the storage floor. Except this one was alive, angry, and lightly coated in fire. My gun went flying as I grabbed hold of the insect's mandibles. A hiss escaped my lips as the chitin burned my hands, but I held on regardless.

It might have had something to do with the burning furnace breath and the prodding angry feelers reaching for my face.

Focusing through the madness a few inches from my face, I cast another <Stone Spike> toward the ant's head. Grimacing at how close the stone brushed passed me, I was glad when it entered right in its damaged eye. The insect struggled for several more seconds until it realized that it was dead. Several hundred pounds of crispy ant fell on top of me, and I was forced to summon another spike to keep it from crushing me. Ignoring the gut wrenching sensation of my magic, I crawled out from under the insect to rejoin the fight.

In the time it had taken for me to extract myself from the ant, my friends and the herd had done a number on the others. While the entire area was once again scorched bald, with most of the cows suffering from burns all along their fur, Danny was working through the ants with ease. As they surged to attack her once more, she lobbed a ball of fire right into their midst. It didn't seem to do as much damage as I expected, but the sound threw the herd into motion. The wild stomp of the cows flattened the smaller ants, leaving Danny to snipe the few remaining ones.

Raymond and Sam had also fully addressed their pair of giant ants. A torn ant head hung limply from Ray's horns while he charged the other ant. Sam was standing just behind Ray, reaching out towards the ant as vines rose up and bound it.

They didn't last long as they dried out quickly, but it was enough to keep the ant in place and distracted. Just before the bull could charge right through the creature's thorax, my perception populated the ant's information.

<Fire Ant>

<Attunement: Fire>

<Refinement: Smolder>

<Perceived Metier Quotient: 2>

A moment later, the information winked out as Raymond cleaved the ant in half, tearing right through the strings of Sam's <Vine Whip>. I held my gun up and scanned for any other threats. Just when I was about to blast one of the smaller ants to pieces, a thick vine rose up out of the ground and locked it in place. The creature chittered and struggled to bite at its restraints. Even if the vines looked like they were already drying out due to the insect's Attunement, they held. For good measure, I knocked it on the head and that seemed to daze the creature and stop its struggling.

Giving Sam a nod, I eyed the rest of our clearing. Only the one cow had been taken down, and the wound had already been cauterized by what I assumed was one of the bigger ants' attacks. Looking over the rest of the herd, I spotted burn marks on every single one. They were still quite agitated, but with the immediate threat gone, they huddled together and seemed to be nursing each other's wounds. Raymond limped over from the two corpses he'd generated and set his massive flank against the side of the herd. A moment later, the green glow we'd seen earlier when restraining him pushed out in a small bubble. The grass reached for the sky and, to my amazement, the burns on the nearest cow smoothed out slowly.

From what I could see, the bull wasn't privy to his own healing as he remained slumped on the ground. The rest of the herd slowly shifted to encase the bull, blocking him from sight. My friends walked up to me, Danny holding on to the rat-sized ant by the head and thorax. A small wave of heat reached me when she drew near with it, but her hold seemed to fully placate the creature. I didn't know which to focus on, the apparently docile ant or the healing herd of cows not two dozen feet away. *Leave it up to the surface to make each day interesting...*

Deciding to address the bull in the room, I pointed at Raymond. "So, big boy over there can heal things."

"Seems like it. He's still injured, so I don't know how that really works," Sam said, wiping soot from his head. I gave myself a look and noticed that I had a thin layer of ash coating my body, just like the rest of the clearing.

"Hopefully the Entity will have more answers when it wakes up," Danny added, using her ant as a pointing stick. When we gave her an awkward look, she shrugged. "Sam's got his little cow friend, figured I might be able to keep one of these."

"Danny, that isn't why I—"

"Shhh, you. Now, I'm going to figure out where I can keep him without too much trouble." The woman wandered off, ignoring the wisps of smoke coming off her outfit. I made note of the fact that the heat seemed to wash right over her without the same effect it seemed to have on me and Sam.

When I turned to my blond friend, he was working on cleaning off his clothes as much as he could. "I'll let you deal with that. Do you think Ray will be down to help us move the crystal closer?"

"That's probably a negative, I would think. At least not until he's recovered. That big ant left some pretty hefty cuts on his flank."

Resisting the urge to make a joke about eating a real fresh cow, I pointed over my shoulder at the dead cow. "What do you think about that, can we eat it or use it for something?"

My friend frowned as he looked at the half-charred remains, but nodded. "I think Danny and I may be able to get some usable meat from it. The rest... well, I can bury it near the crops and it will work as good fertilizer. If it doesn't disintegrate."

With that note, I remembered the ants scattered around the camp. Most of the smaller ants were blasted to bits or stomped flat, but the giant ones were big eyesores. "Think you can help me collect the Pith from these? I don't even know what I killed other than that one," I said, motioning to the ant still propped up by my spikes. Sam gave me a pair of thumbs up and went around the clearing nudging any bit of ant he saw, charting a slow course to the herd. *Probably wants to check in on Raymond.* A few seconds after he touched them, the creatures converted to the strange mulch his Attunement caused. I contemplated whether it would be more beneficial to have him convert it all, for the sake of fertilizing the area. However, when I saw the sheer amount of ant corpses, I opted to help.

The first creature was the one I'd killed. When I placed my hand on its carapace, the arm material immediately hardened into crystal then shattered like broken glass. The telltale particles of what we knew was Pith drifted up from the crumbled pile and split in two. The larger of the two clouds slammed into me while the other drifted towards the herd. *Probably headed for Ray.* With a smile on my face, I went about the whole clearing, touching the ones Sam hadn't bothered with.

As the final hair-thin wisp of Pith flew into my body, I pulled up my status.

Subject: Ronan Terrigan
Health: 100% (Unafflicted)
Mana: 100%
Metier Quotient: 2 (51%)
Dreg Accumulation: 16%
LPS: Wildwood, FL
Communications
Skills - *(1) Selection Available*
Traits - *(6% Banked)*
Attributes:

I nodded appreciatively at the growth of my Quotient and frowned worrisomely at the Dreg accumulation. It made sense, considering the amount of creatures we'd fought, but the Entity's warning about built up Dreg still rang in my thoughts. With the space around the Bunker entrance littered with small piles of rock and mulch, I went to fetch one of the empty duffles inside. Nearly an hour later, I collected the final bits of ant that had remained after they lost their Pith and the strange coal blobs.

I'd managed to keep count while collecting the pieces, and nodded in appreciation. There were ninety-three small coal blobs from the rat-sized ants and four slightly larger ones from the Smoldering Fire Ants. The larger creatures had dropped huge sections of their carapace, except in the case of the one Sam had nudged. That one dropped what looked like a soggy rubber pouch. After collecting all the Dreg I figured I was going to get, I headed for the sled with the crystal to bank it. Just in case.

While still a ways away from the Bunker, the walk to the crystal was brief. I'd seen both Danny and Sam stop by and purge their own Dreg before returning to whatever else they were doing. The oddest thing about it had been the woven leash tied around the small fire ant that Danny had fashioned, but I didn't comment on it as she headed back to the Bunker. I knew better than to question one of Danny's decisions on something.

I cast a look at the sky and saw that we wouldn't have much more daylight, so I set out to catalogue just what ant pieces we had available.

"Good to see you three have kept busy," a voice said behind me, causing me to spin and send a stone spike right into the side of the Metier Crystal. The crystal was unblemished, but it rocked slightly before my spike cracked against the tougher surface. "Ow. I didn't exactly give you access to spell chains just so you could use them against my body." There was a hint of mock pain in his tone, but it didn't last long. I blinked as I noticed that the light within the Entity Cluster had returned to the intensity of our first meeting. When I didn't reply immediately, the crystal continued talking. "Care to update me?"

CHAPTER TWELVE

Antsitting

"What the hell happened to you?" I exclaimed as I turned to the crystal.

"You didn't think all that tinkering I did to your brains came free of charge, did you?" the crystal retorted. I groaned in frustration at the piece of rock's cryptic tone. Thankfully, it seemed that was enough to get it talking again. "While I would like to talk for longer, I do not have as much energy restored as I need for full functionality. Please, update me on my sudden location change and what has happened so I can optimize my information delivery."

I did a double take, but started retelling what had happened since we'd last spoken with the Entity Cluster. From the fight with the Haze Wolf, to the trip back, snips of information about the Bunker and the potential for getting more implants, as well as the trip to retrieve the crystal. The light within continued to thrum at the same rate, without further comment through the whole development. At some point, Sam and Danny came to check in on me as the sky darkened. When I explained that the crystal was awake, but didn't have much time, they urged me to finish the tale.

"That is sufficient. I do not need many more details. As it would appear, you three have gathered enough Pith to draw the attention of larger predators in the area. I will be able to assist moderately with that, but it will keep me in stasis a while longer. Keeping up the costs of your spell chains has put a significant strain on my energy stores."

"Don't you need to be closer?" Sam asked, looking over his shoulder at the hill the Bunker entrance crested.

"No matter, I got it!" the crystal replied in a chipper voice. Then to the jaw-dropping horror of all of us, produced crystalline spider legs out of its body. The protrusions looked similar to the ones it had used to bind us before, but much more solid. One of those appendages waved at us before sinking into the ground and dragging itself forward, sled and all.

We stared in awe as it climbed right up to the edge of my spike wall and slowly oriented itself to the north face. "Would you be so kind as to remove these two spikes, Ronan? Being centered on your region will be the most optimal use of my deterrent."

Shaking myself of my stupor, I pulled the hatchet from my belt. Using the backside of the tool, I hammered away at it. I could hear the cows on the other side lowing in confusion, but I worked quickly. The sky had started to lose its orange and I didn't want to be outside during nighttime, even with the crystal here.

The spider-shaped crystal rose up and half dragged itself into the gap before dropping heavily. "That should do it. I should be able to speak and maintain the field within a few days. It will be faster if you three acquire more Dregs to bank. As I noticed you all realized, it helps restore my energy when I purge them. Now, I bid you three—"

"Wait, one question before you go. What are these spell chains you keep referring to?" I blurted out. I could see the light inside the crystal flicker, as if it was thinking over what I'd said.

"That would be your skills. However, I do not have the energy to really delve into that at the moment. Purge more

Dreg, get more answers. You three *are* supposed to be Warriors, after all."

With that, the crystal winked out except for a tiny flare of light in the center. In exchange for the glow, the strange static that I'd felt while excavating the crystal permeated the air around us. I let out a breath I'd been holding as I relaxed. *If the deterrent field didn't work, then we would have died that first night. I just hope it can keep away whatever that cat was from a few days ago.* I smiled as the thought crossed my mind. A few days ago. We'd been on the surface for quite a while now, and it had almost slipped my mind. With the crystal as secured as it was going to get, we retreated to the lobby area.

I'd completely forgotten about the fire ant, and when the creature hissed in our direction, I nearly turned it into a kabob. Daniela cried in alarm at my response, jumping between us and the creature. "Don't hurt Anthony!"

"You *named* it? Not only that, but you named an ant *Ant*hony?" I asked incredulously. "How do you know that thing isn't going to attack us in the middle of the night? I thought you'd finished it off out back when you joined us earlier."

"He will do no such thing!" Danny said, holding a hand to her chest as if I'd wounded her. "He's behaving. All I need to do is pull on my mana every so often and he mellows out!"

I cocked an eyebrow at her words and turned to Sam. The man looked dead on his feet, but shook his head when I focused on him. "Did you do something like that with Raymond? Use your mana to mellow the bull out?"

"Sorta? It was more like when I used my mana, Ray didn't see me as a threat. I think the tomatoes really helped though." The man scratched his chin in contemplation. "Maybe it's because we share Attunements with the creatures. Another thing we will need to ask the crystal."

"Yeah! And I have a bone to pick with that big rock. I'm Quotient 3, he's got two skills to answer for," Danny complained while gently stroking Anthony's carapace. I shivered as the insect seemed to snuggle into her side. Giant bugs were *not* my thing.

"We'll have to try to figure out some stuff on our own. I have a sneaking suspicion that the crystal isn't going to be as active as we would like."

"Because of the mana chain stuff you were asking it about?" Sam asked. I didn't realize when he had gotten our meals set out before us, even going so far as to pluck some tomatoes for Anthony, but he had a plate ready for me.

Nodding and taking the offered food, I chewed and contemplated. Based on the time we'd spent on the surface, those in the Bunker would be expecting us to return the following day. I didn't want to miss out on even a little bit of time working on our defenses, so I delegated some of my plans to Daniela. The brunette didn't look happy about it, and made sure to extract a promise that I would not attack Anthony, but she agreed in the end.

Thanks to Sam's ability to grow food, we hadn't depleted our rations nearly as much as we'd expected. However, getting more variety would be key and the only place we could get it was the Bunker. When I asked about the dead cow, Sam shook his head, explaining that he didn't feel comfortable with the way the meat smelled. While disappointing, I trusted my friend's judgement. Even if Sam was the most overly cautious out of us three, it was never without reason.

As the last of the daylight vanished along with our meals, I noted a good and bad thing that Anthony brought to the table.

"He glows..." I said, looking at the warm light coming off of the insect. Apparently, it not only generated heat but a bit of light. It allowed us to save on the battery-powered lantern we had, but would probably annoy me at some point in the night. When I voiced as much, Danny told me where I could shove it and turned to face the wall. She did keep a tight leash on her new pet though. *At least I know she isn't totally carried away.*

Before heading to bed, I replaced the two crossed spikes before our entrance. The presence of the crystal and the herd made me feel much safer, but it didn't hurt to be cautious. We did, however, forgo the night watch. I ran over the last few days in my mind, processing how the surface had been. It was an exhausting place, drawing everything we'd learned in the Bunker during our survival training to the logical extreme and then past it. However, even as I considered the mortal danger we'd encountered, I couldn't wait to get back outside. The world was a blank canvas, and we were the hungry artists.

— + —

A blink brought me back to the present. Breakfast had started off the same as the last few days. The biggest difference was Danny making a list of all the things we would need here on the surface. At the top of it was more plants for Sam to grow, followed by ammunition and a replenishment of our rations, just in case. As a side thought, I asked her to check if Ben had a mattock somewhere. The woman lifted an eyebrow in my direction, but I waved her off. When I asked her what she wanted to do with... Anthony... she glared at me.

"I want you to make him a stone pen. I would take him down to the Bunker with me, but I don't think they would appreciate it." She looked over to the ant who was eating some tomatoes Sam had handed it, and smiled. When she tried to pet it, its mandibles snapped on her hand. I jumped forward, expecting her to be injured but she just cooed at the insect. Small bleeding cuts opened on her hand, instead of the violent burns I'd seen on the herd outside. Still stunned by the ease with which she was enduring the injuries just for the sake of petting the creature, I turned to Sam.

The man coughed into his hand and shrugged. "Don't look at me," his eyes practically screamed. He didn't say anything, otherwise he would have gotten an earful from Danny.

I mulled in my head how I was going to make a pen for a rat-sized ant while guzzling my breakfast. You didn't need to breathe when you were busy. Plus, the bland taste didn't even register as my mind whirred with possible designs. Before Danny even left to head down to the Bunker, I had already broken the barring spikes at the doorway. The three foot tall pieces of rock made a muted thud on the ground before rolling over to where the other broken spikes were piling up. Over the course of our time on the surface I'd accumulated an astounding amount. Fifteen of the ones with a foot wide base and several of the smaller ones.

I heard my friends talking while inside, but I was focused on getting the pen complete so I could resume building our defenses. Possibly even start on an external building. Considering the method I'd used to bind creatures so far, I formed a triangular structure of thick spikes. There were wide gaps between the large spikes, but I hammered in the smaller, broken chunks to fill in the gaps. I looked at the two foot by four foot triangular prism and smiled. It looked ugly as all heck, but there wasn't a single gap large enough for the ant to squeeze through. When I called Danny out to see my masterpiece, she gave me a scalding look.

"I expected something better from you, Ronan," she said, rubbing at her temples. She looked sadly at the ant that was trying to burn a hole through her pants, and completely ignored me. "Sorry that Mommy has to go on an errand. Your Uncle Ron and Sam are going to look after you okay, Anthony?" *Chomp.* The fire ant ignored Danny's attempts to be cute, instead trying to once again wiggle out of her grasp.

Sighing wistfully, she placed the ant in the stone pen and I wedged one of the larger broken spikes to block it in. The ant wasn't thrilled about being stuck once again, and the moment Danny got a few steps away, small licks of flame escaped through the gaps in the stone. Sam and I shared a wide-eyed look, but Daniela just looked thrilled. The madwoman. With that, she wished us good luck and sauntered back into the lobby before we heard the thud of the closing Bunker entrance.

"She's crazy," I finally said.

"She just wants a friend, Ron. I may not be on the best

terms with Raymond, but I think it may work out. Who knows, maybe it's like one of those 'pets' from video games. Or 'familiars,' whatever the difference was." He made air quotes with his fingers and gestured to the mostly healed herd. "I think if I spend more time with the cows, we'll be able to get them more domesticated. Which will, in turn, require pens and fenced-in areas, but food has to come first. I'm going to work on prepping the farm for more crops, if you want to help."

Looking at the mess the cows had already made of his first garden, I had a sneaking suspicion what he was going to do with what he grew. A gout of flame drew my attention, making the decision for me. "I'll help build you something to deter them from eating your plants. Just get me away from this thing."

Sam chuckled the whole time we walked to his farm. And farm it was. I did a double take as I saw a veritable network of growing tomatoes shooting off from the edge of the pond. A trio of furrows had been dug in the earth and even from where we stood, I could see the dark brown of moist earth.

"How did you get all this set up?" I exclaimed. Suddenly, my efforts building the defensive wall felt minimal as I stared at what would almost match the grow area of the greenhouse floor in the Bunker. Not all of it was planted, but there was easily three hundred by four hundred feet worth of rows. Having worked for a few years with the growers after our daily lessons, I knew that soil-grown plants would require less maintenance and balancing than hydroponics. This farm would change everything about our survival on the surface.

Sam explained that Danny's ability to heat stuff up let her dry out the area around the pond. After that, it was easy enough for him to manipulate his vines to tear up the earth. The explanation didn't make me feel any better. Regardless of my feelings, Sam outlined some of his more immediate plans and I was completely onboard. Particularly setting up an area for the herd to graze.

"It will serve two purposes. One, it will draw the cows away from our main set of crops. Two, it should keep them interested in sticking around. The more familiar they are with us, the more likely we will be able to domesticate this herd for real." There was a gleam in his eye that I hadn't expected. I knew he was passionate about growing plants just like his father, but apparently the potential of the surface wasn't only pushing *me* to new heights.

For the next few hours, we worked together to make a makeshift fence around the farm crops and started another to hem in the herd with plenty of space. The exercise pushed our magic so that we could properly reinforce what we produced. We discovered that the farthest Sam could extend a single vine was ten feet, but the further it stretched, the weaker it got. Setting up five foot intervals of stone spikes, the blond weaved his magic through mine. As an extra measure, while I recovered my mana, he made notches on my spikes to improve the grip of his vines.

More than once, I growled in frustration at how the pain of my casting affected me. Not only that, but Sam's regeneration speed was faster than mine, making me the bottleneck of each section we worked on. My friend was supportive, as always, but it only served to bother me more. I wanted to be able to contribute more, but my body refused to cooperate.

Regardless of all my complaining, we finished the entire perimeter by lunch time. After the mental strain of forming the fence, we were wiped. The two of us rested, listening to the hum of wildlife that had returned to the area without Danny blasting stuff throughout the day. I kept an eye out and a hand on my holster the entire time, but nothing bothered us for a good while. Just when I was about to droop into a lazy noon nap, the lowing of the herd snapped us out of our mellow mood. Sam and I shared a look, then took off toward the bunker.

My jaw dropped as I saw the herd stampeding out of my spike wall, knocking two of the stone constructs over in the process. The culprit paused before the leader of our bovine neighbors. Raymond stared at the tiny fire ant with disinterest as it chased away the rest of his herd. The bull glanced our way, snorted once, then went back to sleep. The fire ant, on the other hand, noticed our approach and turned to stare us down. A few small gouts of flame turned some poor grass into cinders and then it was *off*.

The creature dragged its makeshift leash behind it and headed northeast into the forest. Without waiting for Sam, I took off on the insect's tiny heels. If I lost Danny's strange pet project, she would take my head off. When I passed by the entrance to the Bunker, I saw that the sneaky bastard had cooked my spikes into ceramic and then cracked a hole for itself.

"Anthony, you fiery pain in my rear, get back here!" I shouted as I crossed the tree line, my perception already straining to follow the small red blur in the forest.

CHAPTER THIRTEEN

Dreg Poisoning

The light dimmed the moment I entered the forest. Shifting rays of sun illuminated Anthony in spurts, and I gave chase each time I spotted its telltale red color. I was surprised by how fast the little critter was, not to mention its maneuverability. It got much further ahead of me with each log it swiftly climbed or each sharp bend it took around a copse of trees. With each minute that passed as I followed it, the prickling sensation grew stronger. I wasn't sure where the feeling was coming from, but I found myself holding <Stone Spike> at the ready on my left and my pistol on my right hand.

When I saw Anthony halt abruptly, then begin to thrash wildly, I knew something had gone terribly wrong. Not only that, when I finally pulled my eyes away from the little ant, I realized that Sam *wasn't* right on my tail. Instead, the sun had been muted further by a thick webbing that I was realizing covered absolutely every inch of the canopy above, yet only a few select strands reached down to the ground like invisible nets. What sent a further chill up my spine was that there was not a single spider in sight. My hand trembled as I thought about the tiny spiders we sometimes saw within the Bunker. Whatever kept the Dreg out of our systems down below had kept them the way they were meant to be. On the surface, and considering what I'd seen of the ants, I had no doubt that it wasn't a tiny harmless bug friend that had ensnared Anthony from the canopy above.

A slight hum echoed, and I spun with my hands splayed out on either side. There wasn't anything visible around me. Yet. My heart threatened to beat out of my chest, but I rushed over to Anthony. The little Fire Ant was thoroughly ensnared. I gave the world around me a glance, then holstered my gun.

"Anthony. I don't know if Sam and Danny are off their rockers, but I *really* hope you can understand me. I need you to burn your bindings off and climb on my back," I said, brandishing my work hatchet and chopping down on the largest section of web holding the ant.

The first strike barely did anything, as the string twanged like a musical instrument, so I hacked through as hard as I could. Anthony stopped thrashing wildly, and I really hoped it wasn't because something horrifying was looming over my shoulder ready to eat me. Instead of focusing on that bone-chilling and highly distracting thought, I set the blade down on the other length of webbing holding the insect and sawed like my life depended on it. As if waiting for that very moment, Anthony turned into a miniature bonfire. While the fire lasted only a second, it forced me to cover my face and look away. Right into the eyes of a man-sized version of a banana spider.

The arachnid's information populated through my implant. However, it wasn't the only one that did as my peripheral vision caught the other forms amidst the web.

<Female Banana Spider>
<Attunement: Air>
<Refinement: Gossamer>
<Perceived Metier Quotient: 3>

<Male Banana Spider>

<Attunement: Air>
<Refinement: N/A>
<Perceived Metier Quotient: 1>

Two smaller child-sized males flanked the female. The large spider clicked its mandibles and shifted slowly along their web. Her vivid yellow thorax sparkled with a silver shine, and the black spots formed what my terrified brain assumed was a skull shape. The spider stopped less than two hundred feet away, testing the bundle of strings that had just been binding Anthony with her long slender legs. The motion looked gentle, but I knew the webbing was surprisingly strong from how much resistance it had when I chopped down on it.

The males looked like smaller, gray-brown versions of the female. They'd moved in concert with the female, each of them having their little beady eyes trained on me. I flinched when warmth traveled up my pant leg and onto my back, but managed not to jump. *Apparently they can listen...* I didn't have much time to contemplate the tamed behavior Anthony exhibited, because the female leapt from the canopy, the whispered hiss of deflating air trailing her. Literally.

A glittering trail of air followed in her wake, and the spider closed the distance in a blink. Thankfully, my reflexes saved me once again. A stone spike rose out of the ground less than three feet away right as the spider crashed into it. My hastily erected shield, however, didn't last long as cracks sprouted from the single impact, and I could hear the hiss of two more spider butts heading my way.

Not bothering to double check if the warmth on my back was Anthony, I let loose with another stone spike as I turned to run. There was a loud screech as my spike impaled one of the males, but I didn't stay to look at the creature. However, just as I was about to dive behind a tree for cover, a thick strand of webbing struck me in the shoulder. I was sure that I would have stumbled forward from the hit had the spider not hauled me back with a surprising amount of strength.I could already feel my back bruising as I fought against the web reeling me in.

"Anthony! A little help!" I said as I dug in with my heels, locking eyes with the giant female banana spider. Rippling spurts of glitter shot out of its body, threatening to yank me back into its clutches. Even with the lingering fear of getting eaten by a spider, I managed to realize that the spider must have been wary about my stone spikes, which was why it hadn't charged me again. With my thoughts organized enough, I sent another stone spike right at the creature's head.

Moving impossibly fast, the spider crawled backward. The motion jerked me closer than I wanted to the arachnid. A small clacking, and the disappearance of the warmth on my back told me the motion had dislodged Anthony. *Focus on yourself, Ronan!* Even while still attached to the spider, I rolled to the side to avoid another thread of webbing which splattered against a tree somewhere behind me. I could feel the pressure of casting back to back building up in my gut without even risking a look at my mana pool. The male spiders weren't even anywhere in sight, so I was wary of getting attacked from behind.

In my panicked thoughts, I missed the silhouettes creeping beside me. A heavy weight crashed and brought me to the ground. A second later, I felt a lancing pain as one of the males bit my unprotected shoulder while the other tried to web me. Growling in pain, I unleashed a duo of stone spikes aimed at the space behind my back. The motion ripped the spiders, and a chunk of my shoulder, along with it.

The world grew increasingly hotter as the pain throbbed further from the bite to encompass the majority of my body. A pulsing warning flashed through my implant.

<Afflicted: Banana Spider Inflammatory Venom>

The warning winked out as the female yanked on the thread still attached to my vest. Like a beached whale, the giant spider pulled me closer and the pain grew. A gout of fire severed the thread, leaving the spider hissing its agitation. When I tried to stand, but failed to even get up onto my elbows, it charged forward like before. The world was a hazy blur, but the incoming flash of yellow managed to send some subconscious signals to my brain.

Almost mechanically, I aimed spike after spike at the spider's thorax. The pressure in my gut was so strong I caught myself dry heaving. A mass collided against my side and then the gentle tinkling of glass before a surge of energy pumped through my veins. I blinked some of the haze away before yet another sensation overpowered my body. Bone deep exhaustion. Not the sleep kind of exhaustion, nor the muscle exhaustion you get after some vigorous exercise, but an overwhelming pressure from everywhere that made even blinking my eyes a struggle.

While my body refused to respond, my mind whirled a thousand miles a minute. *Where's the spider? Did I get hit with a different venom? Why isn't my implant responding? What if Sam gets here and is ambushed by more spiders?* The inquisitive clicks of a Fire Ant drew me out of my spiral. I latched on to the little insect with my eyes like a drowning man to flotsam. If Anthony was still here, and as unconcerned as he was, then the spiders really were dead. Remembering that the ant had been able to understand me before I forced my mouth to cooperate.

"Sss...m. Ssa... mm," I managed, even if my tongue felt like it had weights attached to it.

The ant perked up at my response. I could almost see the warring thoughts in its compound eyes. However, after a few seconds of hesitation and shuffling on its little limbs, it headed away. The fight had left me so disoriented that the only way I would have been able to find my way back to the Bunker was with the help of the implant. *I really hope he didn't just head back towards his hive...*

I wasn't sure how long I laid on my side, but the shadows cast by the trees crept slowly across the ground. A few inquisitive squirrels, ones that looked unattuned, if a bit larger, sniffed around me before scurrying into the woods. With how exhausted I felt, it wasn't difficult to resign myself to wait for rescue. *Thankfully it doesn't hurt anymore...*Closing my eyes, I proceeded to go over the numerous mistakes I'd committed in the fight.

The first was losing sight of my surroundings. I could somewhat attribute that one to my freshness on the surface. Having space to run around as opposed to being stuck on a treadmill or circular track was still a new experience for a Bunker-born. With how much deadlier the wilderness was, and having found not even a sign of the world from before Landfall, mapping our surroundings would be imperative. *Better bring that up with the others, especially Danny since she is the fastest and most likely to wander off.*

The other major mistake was leaving Sam behind. We hadn't gone over each other's specific attributes, but if the growth of my friends mirrored my own, then I imagined strength was up there for Samuel. I'd always been faster than him, but not by much, and he'd always been stronger than me, but not by much. Still, getting 20% faster than the pre-Landfall humans was one way of stretching out that difference.

Getting caught by the spider's webbing was the last major mistake. I wasn't sure of where the line between attuned creatures and regular species was drawn. *Yet another thing to ask the Entity. I really need to write a list of these.* Putting down roots on the surface was going impossibly quickly, and too slow at the same time, thanks to the crystal's help.

As far as the engagement, I had to forgive myself for the blunders in expending my mana and understanding just how Anthony could have helped. It was hard to gauge just how much my perception had helped me in the fight, but I had a sneaking suspicion my reflexes on triggering Stone Spike had something to do with that particular attribute. *Now that I think about it, how did I manage all those extra skill triggers....?*

"Ronan!" a voice gently echoed through the forest.

A thrill of anxiety forced my eyes to look around wildly. My body was still locked in its strange catatonic state, but I managed to eke out something between a groan and a hiss. I was worried if my friend called out too loudly in the woods, more spiders or possibly something worse would come. A fireball sailed through the air above me, very nearly landing on me.

"I see him! Sam, he's under that spider leg." Danny's voice reached me, and the anxiety calmed. Both of them stood a much better chance of killing anything that attacked.

A hand lifted something off my body I hadn't realized was even on top of me, then turned me over. A frowning Sam looked me dead in the eye. "Ronan? Can you hear me?" he asked, shaking me when I didn't respond.

I blinked twice in quick succession. *I hope he gets it.*

"Yes? Blink twice again for yes, one for no."*Blink blink.*"Can you move? What happened?"*Blink…Wild blinking.* I didn't really have a yes-no way of answering his second question, but he seemed to realize it. "Right, it's not a yes or no question. Sorry. I'm gonna haul you back to the Bunker. Hopefully Alan and Alexis can figure out what happened. Danny, watch our backs!"

"Me and Anthony have it," my friend said somewhere behind Samuel as he lugged me over his shoulder. The woman and her Fire Ant came into view, the human with a concerned expression and the ant jumping for joy. Well, that was what it looked like.

My friends argued back and forth on what was the best path to take, but opted to let Anthony lead when the Fire Ant rushed off in the direction of the Bunker.

"Are you sure your ant knows what it's doing?" Sam asked.

"No, but he came back to tell us about Ronan. I think he's earned a bit of trust for it."

Sam huffed, but picked up speed to keep up with the wiry insect. Several minutes later, punctuated only by the hard breathing of both of my friends, I heard the lowing responses of the herd of cows. A few flashes of light in what I now realized was the afternoon light indicated Anthony's presence.

"Raymond, please, Anthony was just leading us back. We aren't here to threaten the herd," Sam said as we got closer and I noticed some of my spike wall constructions. The bull was out of view, but the deep, rumbling low that answered Sam made me think he'd heard. Once more, I wondered just how intelligent Raymond and Anthony were, at least as opposed to the other creatures we'd encountered so far. After the alpha had calmed the rest of the herd, Sam moved towards the entrance to the Bunker. The moment the group entered the inner perimeter, a flash of light came from the center section of the spike wall.

"Didn't think you three would get the energy quite so—" the crystal started to say, before cutting itself off. "Stop, bring him here!"

Sam halted in his tracks, pivoting to walk to the crystal's side. "What do you need with him?"

"Just set him down, I can deal with the rest. Be quick about it!" When Sam laid me down on the ground, I caught a glimpse of the crystal shining brighter than I'd ever remembered it being before that same brightness encompassed my entire vision.

When I blinked again, I found myself floating in an empty white space. It was similar to being submerged and floating in the bathtub down in the Bunker, except I was vertical. While looking around, I realized I was also buck naked.

"No sense covering that up. No one but me can see, and I have no interest in your anatomy, Ronan." I whirled at the sound of the voice to see a bobbing sparkler drifting a foot from my face. "To make it short, yes, this is me. The Entity Cluster. In the metaphysical flesh. Now, care to tell me what the heck happened to you?"

"Ehh… I fought some giant air-attuned spiders and nearly lost?"

"Of course you did. That explains some of this. Go ahead and open your status."

Unlike outside of the strange floating space, my connection

to the implant seemed to work. Immediately, my eyes widened in confusion.

Subject: Ronan Terrigan
Health: 43% (Envenomed)
Mana: -47%
Metier Quotient: 3 (2%)
Dreg Accumulation: 98%
LPS: Wildwood, FL
Communications
Skills - *(2) Selections Available*
Traits - *(22% Banked)*
Attributes - *Growth Quantified*

"Why am I envenomed? How is it possible I have negative mana and how did my Dreg accumulation get so high!?" I asked in alarm. I distinctly remembered the Entity saying high Dreg was bad, and if it matched up with anything the other Bunker survivors had told me about my real father, then possibly deadly.

"Before all that, tell your friends you are okay," the Entity said.

"What…? How am I supposed to tell them that I am okay? Am I not okay?" I asked, alarm causing my words to quiver.

The Entity didn't answer, and it almost felt like its attention was somewhere else, even if the blob of light didn't have a face or any other feature apart from its bobbing to tell me anything. When it didn't answer after I asked again, I resigned myself to wait, numerous possibilities churning in my head. Many not at all positive.

"Well, they aren't convinced, but at least they went to bed. Seems they aren't entirely without their rational minds," the Entity finally said, and I noticed that it was bobbing slightly faster.

"I think that's a bit rude, considering we were the ones that dug you out of that ridge," I said, my worries pushed back for a moment in defense of my friends.

"So, your envenoming is a result of getting bit by a venomous spider. Surprise. As for the rest, well, you have Dreg poisoning. You were one step shy of a Dreg affliction, the ones that turn into permanent traits." I could have noticed the deflection a mile away since the Entity didn't even acknowledge my previous statement. *I wonder which of us he pulled that trait from...* Regardless, I wanted the information too badly to derail its current explanation.

"That doesn't answer my other questions though. How did my counter get so high, and why is my mana negative? That doesn't make sense, you can't spend what you don't have."

"Just wait until banks become a thing. The folks in your Bunker probably know a lot more about that than you." When I glared at the bobbing light, it started talking again. "Right, well, the two aren't mutually exclusive, per se. The mana bar I provided for you three is made to gauge the internal reserves your body has available. It is entirely possible to pull from ambient mana, that pesky 'radiation' you all are so worried about. However, it is highly rich in Dreg, since it hasn't been filtered by an organism or an Entity Cluster. When the process is done *actively* by an organic life form, it is exquisitely painful and brings the side effects you experienced.

"Additionally, Pith acquired from air-attuned creatures provides the most Dreg for earth-attuned ones, such as yourself. You are lucky that ant nabbed the other spiders and pushed you to Quotient 3. Without the extra containment, your poisoning would have been an affliction."

"What does the trait situation mean? We haven't had much chance to talk since you updated our implants and gave us the skills."

The Entity bobbed to either side. "The implant will let you know once you are back outside."

"Why can't you give straight answers?" I asked, folding my

arms across my bare chest. I'd forgotten my modesty in my frustration.

"Because I have to keep you all alive and your implant interfaces functioning. If I run out of juice, then you three are also out of skills and out of my field of influence. I'll talk to you all when you get more energy, and please try not to be near dead next time?"

A breath later, the Entity winked out. Cracks appeared all throughout the white space around me and I blinked my eyes open to see refracted daylight through a crystalline pane. When I tried to take a breath, it caught in my throat instead of providing valuable oxygen. Just as I was about to squirm and panic, the crystal pressed in around me and ejected me onto the dirt. The whole process felt and sounded like being a chewed up piece of food getting spat out. Thankfully, after my discomfort, I was able to take a deep breath and come face to face with a larger-than-I-remembered version of Anthony.

CHAPTER FOURTEEN

First Old Man

"Anthony?" I asked as I tried to gather my wits. The now dog-sized ant clacked its mandible happily and nuzzled into my face. I was so taken aback that I just stroked its warm chitin as if it was completely normal. My mind spun with the memories of the previous day, but at least I recalled what the Fire Ant had done for me. "Thanks for getting my friends. Maybe next time don't run away, yes?"

As if he'd completely understood my words, the ant lowered its head before nuzzling me again. It was wild that I was interacting with an ant capable of spitting fire, and I couldn't help but laugh. It was possibly the fact that I'd survived by the skin of my teeth, that I was allowed more time on the surface, or the absurdity of my time on said surface. Any of those were crazy enough in their own right. So, it was laughing like a madman, rolling on the ground next to a confused Anthony, that my friends found me.

"Yup, he's back. Danny, did your ant fry his brains?" Sam said, a hoe propped over his shoulder.

"I thought we both knew he was cracked wider than one of his geodes. At least it seems the crystal didn't lie. Look, he's even got the weird skin thing it mentioned." Daniela poked me in the side, eliciting one final giggle before I settled my back on the ground.

"Hey, guys. Talked to the crystal some. Thanks for pulling me out of that mess."

"Maybe next time you don't run off into the woods faster than I can keep up, Ron?" Sam said. The blond set his hoe down to lean on it while inspecting me closely. "We are just glad you are okay...Well, *are* you okay?"

"I feel fine. The crystal said I should have gained a trait, but it didn't—"My words died in my throat as I ran my hand through my hair. While the *hair* was still smooth, my scalp had a sand-papery surface. It wasn't a particularly coarse one, maybe a very fine grain, but it didn't feel quite like human skin. When I ran my hands along arms and face, they too had the same feel. What Daniela had said about my skin finally registered. "Why do I feel like I have sandpaper skin?"

"You tell us, Ronan. You were the one who was just talking about traits. Does your implant say anything?" Danny asked, plopping on the ground.

"Right, the crystal said to check it. One sec."

With a thought, the lines of information for my status populated. Having seen most of that information while talking to the crystal, I instead concentrated on opening traits.

Traits:
Limestone Skin
The surface of your body has taken on some of the strength properties of compacted sediment.
Trait overbanked. Impact forces are minutely dissipated when making contact with soil interfaces.

"Well... Looks like I have Limestone Skin now," I said, rereading the description of how my body had changed. When I explained to my friends what it was supposed to do, their eyes widened in surprise. It sounded like only positives.

Probably wouldn't have been so positive if it had been due to a Dreg affliction…

"That's pretty crazy. So…" Danny shot a lightning fast jab into my arm. I winced in anticipation of the pain and probable bruise, but instead it was Danny who hissed. A fine scrape along her knuckles marked where she'd hit my arm. "Ouch!"

"Amazing! So you *do* have sandpaper for skin. Did that even hurt?" Samuel was leaning ever closer, inspecting where a thin strip of Danny-skin had stuck to my arm.

"It didn't, but I don't think Daniela was trying to hurt me. It just felt like a pressure more than anything." I paused for a second as I shook the realization that I wasn't quite human anymore. The three of us had stopped being completely human the moment we'd returned to the surface. "No sense lying about. What did I miss?"

"Ben is supposed to arrive today. We aren't sure, but judging by what I was able to get from the others, he should be here before lunch." Danny looked at the sky, gauging the time of day. "Which I'd say is any moment."

That was enough to get my blood pumping. Not only because another set of hands would help kick our modest foothold into gear, but because Ben was a veritable logistical machine. Out of all of our makeshift teachers, he had been the most prompt with assignments and with help when a particular subject eluded us. His meticulous nature had saved us once already, and having him on the surface would be extremely reassuring.

"We better get to cleaning up around here. We don't want the ol' teach to think we've been laying about while on the surface," I said, jumping to my feet.

"*We've* been busy. We didn't just get to take a crystal nap for a day," Danny said with a frown before her eyes softened. "Just take it easy. Thanks for looking after Anthony, Ronan."

I shot the woman a dazzling smile before a loud lowing broke the moment. Somehow Raymond had snuck in behind our group and was nudging at Samuel's pocket. The life mage chuckled and fed the overgrown bull a handful of tomatoes he'd stashed in his cargo pants. The whole scene caused a round of laughter from us, and confusion for Anthony. Without really discussing what we were going to do exactly in preparation for Ben, Danny walked off with Anthony, while Sam led Ray back to his herd.

"Man, I need to find me a pet..." I mumbled to myself. Nonetheless, I knew what would be the first step. Solidifying the exit out of the Bunker.

Whatever restorative powers the crystal had, I felt like a new man. A gentle mental prod at my <Stone Spike>skill told me it had remained the same cost, but my mana pool had expanded. I couldn't help a grin from spreading on my face. I took a moment to reevaluate the perimeter I'd enclosed. With the pen for the herd mostly complete, we could push our home out. Focusing on the thick spike I had used to mark the 'entrances' through our spike wall, I triggered my skill.

As I'd thought, when I focused on the middle of the compressed earth, the spike rose up higher. What I hadn't expected was the additional girth of the spike. Instead of the foot wide base, nearly two feet of stone quickly used up the original spike's earth to compress it into a stubby version of my others. It looked like a proper cone instead of a thick spear.

I scratched at my stubble as I considered what had caused the change. The skill had still taken roughly twenty percent of my mana... I slapped a hand on my face. *Twenty percent of a mana pool that had increased!* My eyes looked for a spot close to the tree line and I unleashed my skill again. Even with the expected decrease in size and width thanks to the distance, the stone spike was still a foot thick at the base. The other aspect that I noticed was that the gut wrenching pain that came from casting was near negligible.

Picking a point closer to the Bunker entrance, some twenty five feet further from the current spike wall, I triggered my skill again at close range. A divot carved itself out of the ground where I'd targeted the spell. Then the earth in the center *leapt* out of the ground to double the size of any of my original spikes. The two foot base let the tip of the spike reach just over six feet. I could barely contain a cackling laughter from escaping me as I reassessed what I could do with my skill.

Remembering my request to Danny, I rushed into the lobby to the Bunker. Arrayed on the desk were a variety of duffels and a metal-reinforced plastic crate. Making the obvious assumption, I flipped the locks open on the container. There were a number of smaller tools, a gardening set, and a series of saws, but the one taking up the bulk of the crate was what I was after. It wasn't exactly what I had requested, but then again, I doubted the people who stocked the Wildwood Bunker would have differentiated between a pickaxe and a mattock.

Nonetheless, I lifted the length of wood and pointy steel out of the crate and made my way outside. Sam could feed us. Danny could defend us. The spot left for me was something I had always wanted to do: build.

After some rough measurements of the divot my new maximum-sized Stone Spike created, I demolished every other Spike I had constructed around the Bunker entrance. Every time my mana was topped off, I filled the section I'd broken through with a six-foot spike. Then I lopped the top foot with my pick. I repeated this for the entire space minus the two openings I'd created originally. The space now occupied by the Entity also threw a slight wrench into my plans. Instead of coming up with some elaborate way of dealing with it, I opted to just cast two large spikes on either side of it. The two pushed against the crystal without so much as scratching it, pinning it in space.

Just as I was starting the second part of my wall construction, a gasp caused me to pivot instantly. A slack-jawed Ben stared at what I'd built before his eyes landed on me. I hadn't even heard him arrive, but a smile crept up on my face.

"My God... Ronan...You all weren't lying..."The man barely managed to get the words past his lips, but all I could do was laugh. He had barely seen anything.

"Welcome back to the surface, old man," I said, bowing as I

gestured out one of the openings in my wall. As I'd expected, Ben walked right by the wall he'd seen me magically working on. Tears rolled down his stoic face, but I didn't pay attention to those. When I arrived at the surface, if we hadn't been attacked, I was sure I would have reacted much the same.

Instead, I reveled in the joy of his expression. While coming to the surface meant freedom for all of us in the Bunker, it meant a return to their home for everyone outside me and my friends. He was touching everything and staring at the sky, his eyes glazed over. It was honestly more direct emotion than I could remember seeing from Teach. It didn't take long for the surface to subvert that.

"How did you—Ahh!" I didn't see what caused Ben to leap back within the wall, but I had a good guess. The Labrador-sized shape of Anthony flicked its antenna about to get a read on the new human. "What the hell is that!?"

Apparently a trained response, he moved to draw his sidearm. Before he had a chance to accidentally shoot the insect I'd already gone through hell to save, I cast Stone Spike between the two of them. Not a second later, the round punched into the compressed earth. Thankfully, it was only enough to crack the spike and not penetrate to the now-spooked Fire Ant.

"That's Anthony, Ben! He's... Daniela's pet," I said, as I put myself between the man and the ant. "He's not gonna hurt you. Right, Anthony?" The insect nodded its head vigorously, feelers twitching in alarm. Before I had to spend too much of my energy dealing with Ben, my friends crested the western dip... followed by Raymond.

"Oh, Samuel, there is a bull behind you!" Ben said as he aimed his weapon. Thankfully, I was able to stop him before he shot the bull and wasted yet another bullet. As much as I didn't think Ray was going to attack us, if he got hurt, I would not want to deal with the enraged creature. A slight shiver ran down my spine as I thought about the large ant he'd plowed through.

"He's Sam's pet…erh… domesticated bull… thing. Just don't make it angry. Like by shooting it."

"What kind of nightmare menagerie are you kids building up here?" Ben asked, turning wild eyes on me just as my friends arrived.

"The kind that lets us deal with the other nightmares roaming the surface, Teach," Danny said, waving at Ben while running a hand on Anthony's carapace.

"It might take a bit, but they aren't bad. Raymond even has a small herd we might be able to milk once he's a bit more settled in," Sam said in way of greeting. The man had produced tomatoes and was shoving them into the bull's mouth. Said bull was staring intently at Ben. "He's a friend, Ray. Just another human, you know, one of us." The life mage channeled his mana while feeding the bull and I noticed the creature's flexed muscles relax visibly.

Instead of responding, Ben stood unsteady on his feet until he plopped against my spike wall. The man's gaze traveled through the humans arranged around him and the two clearly changed creatures from his life on Earth. He took a deep breath, then let it out slowly.

"Okay. Right, magic and such. That's normal now. Where is the… talking rock?" The three of us turned slightly and pointed out the glowing iridescent light set directly into my wall. "Right. Glowing crystal right there. Dummy me." Ben reached back around to touch where the implant would be and I saw him blink something out of his vision.

"Take your time, Ben. As much as we want to get things set up, you should take your time to get situated," Samuel said, already leading the Fertility Bull away. "Sorry to run, but I think Raymond isn't totally settled with Ben. I'll check in later!"

"Ron, think you can watch the newbie? I saw some traces of Fire Ants in the forest, and I want to make sure we are prepared if they are scouting us out," Danny said. I noticed her leg turn slightly towards the northwest as she spoke.

"Sure, Danny. Just stay close and make sure you take

Anthony, at least." The ant perked up at the mention of its name.

"Sorry, Ben. We can talk tonight at dinner!" The man in question waved weakly before turning to me.

"Come on, let's make sure you are purged then you can get situated while I work." The man took my hand when I offered it and we both made the short walk to the Entity. Ben placed his hand on the crystal at my beckoning and the hum of mana in the air picked up.

"Another one, eh?" The crystal spoke up. Unlike its usual boisterous volume, it was more a whisper. However, I was thankful it had opted to interact with Ben. Before my old teacher got a chance to pull his arm away, the crystal grew out to encompass it up to the elbow. "Hmmmm. A member of the pre-Landfall generation. I'll give him the status sans mana and purge him of that nasty cancer-turned-Dreg, but you'll have to get him more Pith. From my readings, he should be earth-attuned. Best of luck, Ronan."

The light in the crystal dimmed significantly just as Ben's arm was freed. He looked around wildly, coughing out a phlegm with dark blood, before taking a much deeper breath. "Did that thing just give me souped up chemo for a cancer I didn't even know I had?"

"Something like that. I can talk about the details during nighttime, but you should probably take a seat and process the changes he just made to your implant." The man looked me in the eye for a second before nodding.

As he walked back towards the Bunker entrance, I heard him mumble to himself. "I knew I should never have started smoking. Damn apocalypse…"

I shot the man a soft smile before I noticed my incomplete work. Rubbing my hands together, I got back to work on the wall.

CHAPTER FIFTEEN

Magic Infusion

For the next part of my plan, I concentrated on my casting of Stone Spike. Picking the spot perpendicular to the tall spikes, I began to create makeshift beams that ran the entire top length. With the broken top section, the pointed end was able to rest on the next cut off spikes, essentially forming columns. I repeated this for the entire wall then took a step back to marvel at what I'd managed. It wasn't anywhere close to smooth, but the gaps were now much more reduced and there were horizontal lengths of stone bracing the top of the wall as opposed to jagged tips.

"I hope Sam can coat this until we can find some clay…" I mumbled to myself as I paced out the space inside the half circle. While I was debating how close together to place the support columns, two gunshots pulled my attention. I checked in the direction of the Bunker entrance, but all I saw was Ben rushing out, gun in hand.

"What happened?" he asked, eyes scanning around.

"One of the others must have engaged a creature. Let's go!" I said, snatching the pickaxe as I went. With my increased attributes, Ben struggled to keep up. Seeing himself lagging behind, the man urged me on so I put on the speed. Making full use of my new mobility, I reached the tree line where a blaze was picking up. *Danny!*

A moment later, I was at the edge of the flames. Sure enough, the fire mage was lobbing fist-sized projectiles at some of the giant ants we'd encountered before. While they looked to knock back the three giant ants trying to surround my friend, they weren't doing a whole lot of damage. Not only that, from the coloration on Daniela's face, I knew her magic was extracting its toll on her body.

Bracing for the pain, I aimed a Stone Spike at each of the ants. When the three casts released back to back, the gut wrench brought me down to a knee, but the spikes found their mark. One pierced one of the ants right at the thorax joint, cleaving it in half. The other two were impaled. My friend didn't miss the opportunity to let loose with another fireball that hammered one of the ants down onto my spike hard enough to punch through the other side of the chitin.

A double tap of gunfire told me Ben had arrived, and the man quickly dispatched the last giant ant, the newbie's itchy trigger finger finally getting some use. A sweating Danny rushed around the space where the fires were starting to crank out and held her hand out to the flames. They flared for a second before leaving a smoldering, blackened bark on the trees. The branches and grass along the ground burned up into ash.

The woman took a breath, walking over to Ben and me. A red blur practically screamed at my senses and I erected another Stone Spike next to my friend. Without waiting to see what had lunged at Daniela, I brought my pickaxe down in a vicious blow. The pointed end of the pick punched clear through the ant's head and its information appeared in my implant a second before it died.

\<Fire Ant\>

\<Attunement: Fire\>

\<Refinement: Lance\>

\<Perceived Metier Quotient: 2\>

The ant in question was about half the height of the giant ones, but much longer. The mandibles clacked one last time around my stone spike, showing their jagged chitin points, before the creature slumped. My pick came away with a wet squelch before the ant started to crystalize. Ben panted beside me, and Daniela gave me a grateful shoulder pat as she plopped to the ground.

"This can't be good," I said, shaking off the rush of absorbed Pith.

"No, I don't think so either. I'd eat my boot if the ants weren't scouting us out, maybe even weighing our strength." Daniela checked her pistol before holstering it. With the numbers advantage, Daniela had been forced on the defensive. The weakened effects of her flame attack against the Fire Ants was a concern. The smaller, rat-sized ones at Quotient 0 seemed to die from the concussive force, but the bigger ones were more able to shrug off the effects.

"You guys have a nest nearby?" Ben finally asked.

"That would be my guess. Or at the very least, one of their food lines runs close this way," Danny answered. "You two got any water?"

When the two of us shook our heads, she wobbled to her feet. "I'm gonna go grab some before I get heat stroke. Just in case Ben goes boneless on you, Ron, try to brace him. He pegged that one real good and it's gonna be a doozy for a Quotient 0 to absorb." The woman pointed over her shoulder as she stumbled back towards the Bunker camp.

"What does she mean 'boneless' and 'absorb'?" our teacher asked, his usual confident air wavering under the onslaught of new things.

"Just try to relax, Ben. Touch the last ant and you will gain its Pith. That would be essentially its power. That will attune you to mana, which is what the Entity mentioned before. The process can be… a bit rough. It will pass and you will be stronger for it, don't worry."

"When people say not to worry about something, the only logical thing to do is to worry, Ronan," the man said flatly.

"Fair enough." I chuckled. "But you aren't getting away from it. As soon as I touch it, the Pith will leave it and split into all who had a hand in the creature's death. Proportionally, as far as I can tell."

"Ahh, crap... What the hell!" Ben slapped the top of the giant ant whose brains he'd splattered. We watched as the creature turned to crystal then shattered into floating particles. The fragments split almost evenly in three, the one that pushed into Ben's chest a tad thicker. I remembered how my body had reacted, and held on to my old teacher as his body snapped straight, then went slack. Setting him down gently, even with my improved strength, was a task. Once I made sure the bulky man was still breathing, I looted the rest of the bodies.

Further influxes of Pith made their way into me and towards the camp where I assumed Danny was hanging out. In place of the large ant corpses were more chitinous plates and blobs of smoldering coals. The Lance Ant, however, had dropped both of its mandibles. Without anywhere to really put the carapace, I dropped it next to Ben and kept watch. While the man did whatever happened while his body became attuned, I practiced swinging my pickaxe smoothly.

It was an unwieldy weapon, but I knew that if push came to shove, it could work as a club. It was basically just a club with one pointy and one flatter end. On my third successful strike against a tree, I noticed how my increased perception was helping me keep the tool directed at my target. I wouldn't call it precognition, but my eyes were *just* able to track where the pick head would hit if I concentrated hard enough. Such insight allowed me to twist my grip and get the head to hit exactly where I wanted it to strike.

At some point during my impromptu training, Ben started to stir. I wiped the sweat off my head and leaned against a nearby tree. Since I was taking a break, I made sure to take in the sights and smells of the forest around me. As dangerous as the surface was proving, it was worthwhile to be grateful for the opportunity to even be here.

Sure enough, a few minutes later, the older man woke up screaming bloody murder. When he realized it was just me and him, plus he wasn't actually feeling like a sack of abused potato chips anymore, he calmed. "That's not something I *ever* want to repeat. Please tell me that isn't common, Ronan."

"Not as far as I know. It's only ever happened to us while we attuned. Every other time we absorb Pith, it's painless. How's the old body?"

"I feel… great. Even better than when the crystal took that stuff out of me."

"Check over your status, is there anything different?" I asked, gesturing to the loot and starting to make our way back to the camp.

Ben was quiet while he mechanically hoisted some of the chitin plates and I grabbed the rest with the mandibles. I let the man take his time with coming to terms with his new body. He finally snapped out of it when I went to check on Danny and he saw what she was up to.

The brunette was inside the Bunker's lobby arranging some of the goods she'd brought up with her. Something of what she was doing positively appalled the man in charge of the Bunker's storage, because he immediately started correcting her. Something about ease of access and proper categorization in anticipation, he said.

"Before you get too caught up, I think we should purge the Dreg we all got. Maybe I can have a little chat with the Entity."

"Sounds good. Apparently Sam had to get rid of another of those air squirrels that was attacking his crops. He and I already got rid of ours, so hopefully you two can pitch that sparkly rock to answer more questions," Danny said, setting down what she was arranging so as to not agitate our old teacher more.

Ben and I walked to the crystal's immediate vicinity and the static in the air returned. A moment later, the light within the crystal flared and stabilized. "Dreg? And no one is dying? I am shocked, Ronan. It also appears you got dear Benjamin here his Attunement. Congratulations on your new allegiance to the Dreg Warriors, Mr. Burks."

"He's really talkative for someone that doesn't talk much," Ben said while crossing his arms.

"As I've explained to Ronan, it takes energy to speak with you all. Energy I do not always have the capacity to spend. However, thanks to this latest influx, my lattice mass is sufficient that we can hold this conversation. I will keep it brief, since I am sure you will want to unlock new skills before I have to return to being dormant."

At the mention of new skills, my mind sputtered. *More magic?* I obviously knew that all of us had skills available to unlock, however I hadn't pieced together that it was the Entity who was granting them. Was it finally time? Before I had the chance to ask that, Ben brought up his own question.

"Why don't I have these 'skills' and 'mana' that you gave to the kids?"

"That is simple enough to answer. You were born before mana permeated every inch of this planet. As a result, you do not have your own internal mana to draw from and replenish. This is what allows me to impart the spell chains onto Ronan, Daniela, and Samuel, the 'skills' you are referring to."

"So what, I'm going to be a regular human here while they go off blasting magic left and right?" Ben asked, and I could see the furrows on his bald head. I could understand that frustration. While I hadn't had access to magic for long, if it was taken away and I saw someone utilizing it, I would feel inferior to them. Even if I knew Ben would be imperative to returning to the surface, magic or not, the man didn't seem to see it that way. "I didn't come to the surface to be relegated to some safe corner somewhere."

"While you will not be 'blasting magic,'" I could practically hear the air quotes in the Entity's tone, "your rise in Quotient will also net you a longer life and better physical abilities. Not only that, but your refinement and containment attributes don't deal with your mana pool, but instead with empowering your body and whatever traits you form. Spell chains are only one way in which mana takes form, Benjamin."

It was obvious Ben had something more to ask, but he didn't say anything else. Taking that opening, I prepared to ask two of my most pertinent questions. "Why do some of the things we fight disintegrate but trees and the like don't? Also, what are these things?" I asked, holding up one of the smoldering blobs we'd acquired from the ant attack.

"That one is a tad more… complicated. I will answer the second and hopefully the first as a result." I saw the light in the crystal dim slightly. "Look at it again. A shortcoming in my system programming, I will admit."

When I focused on the blob in my hand, information flitted in my vision from the implant.

\<Quotient 2 Infusion>

\<Fire - Smoldering>

\<Integrity: 99%>

"Okay, so these things are infusions?" I asked. Ben had moved around to look at the smoldering blob in my hand.

"That is what it would translate to, roughly. This is because you are able to infuse the remaining Pith into objects." The Entity paused for a moment as if deliberating on what to say. The flickering brightness of the light inside it was a clear indicator of when it was thinking. *As much as artificial intelligences think anyway…* "Enough of them should also allow you to fuse objects together, so long as you have the mana to manipulate the process."

"Before I dissect that bit of news, I thought that what we didn't absorb from the creatures got turned to Dreg within us," I asked, recalling our previous discussions. "That cloud that comes out of the creatures holds the Pith and the Dregs are what our bodies can't process, no?"

I did my best to keep my frustration out of my voice. The sporadic access to the Entity was aggravating at best and dangerous at the worst. We could only hope his field would keep us protected from the stronger creatures, so I couldn't get too angry at it.

"In general, that is correct. However, there is Pith within the creature's body. The energy and essence of the creature is *also* stored in its matter, after all. When it dissociates, you receive it all in four parts. An item, your Pith and Dreg, and finally the infusion. The stronger the creature, the more of each you will receive as the energy is more densely stored. If you want to draw comparisons, the material is the Dreg portion of the body, while the infusion is the Pith."

"Okay, not many details there, but I can live with that. What about the dissociation?"

"You will need to shield your mana when interacting with the creature in question. And,"the Entity raised its voice as it anticipated my question, "I will provide you a memory package for that. It will also include how to *use* infusions, at least in the simplest of ways. There are many ways that not even I am aware of, not to mention the combinations of infusions beyond that.

"As for the dissociation. When you interact with Pith, it seeks to be drawn. Just like your concept of energy, it isn't created or destroyed, but merely transformed. By shielding it before it can dissociate, you essentially lock the Pith in place. This will make it so that you do not receive any of the four manifestations, lest you consume its matter."

"While I don't have any context, I think I get it," Ben inter-jected. "We either get the concentrated drops and energy, or the whole body. Right?"

"You are correct, Benjamin. The term 'concentrated drops' is also a good way of describing the item and infusion. The entire composition of the creature is condensed into those two, which makes the item much stronger than if it was simply harvested from the body. Not to mention there is no other way for you to acquire infusions."

"Good to know those Fire Ant chitin bits will have a use. However, why don't we absorb some things? We don't know how to shield things yet," I said, bringing it back to my original question.

"This is where it gets complicated. Things live their lives saturated by mana. This you know and have experienced personally when you drew from the atmospheric mana actively." I winced at the memory. "Organisms may or may not attune. This can be as a result of a list of factors as long as the catalysts for complex life in the universe. One line of reasoning is that the more complex and ancient an organism is, the more likely it will attune to a type of mana. This is further complicated because organisms that are both complex and ancient, such as trees, do not directly contribute to the death of creatures. Which is a catalyst for Attunement, as Benjamin can attest."

As clear as the Entity had made the explanation, it had too many open ends. The main thing I could pull from the whole thing was that bigger things were more likely to attune. This would in turn make them creatures of mana and then leave them to have their Pith absorbed upon death. *About as imperfect as all the other information we've been operating with here on the surface.* With that thought, I decided to contact Sam and Danny.

I opened the connection between us using the implant. A beep of white noise rang in my ears for a moment before I heard Danny's voice.

"What do you want, Ronan? I am trying to hydrate and deal with twenty thousand tiny pieces of ant shells, while you and Ben stand around talking to rocks."

"Those would be carapaces, Danny. Ants don't have shells," Sam interrupted.

"Don't get smart with me, Samuel, I know where you live."

"We live in the same place, Danny."

"Why, I'll—"

"Hey, guys. Just… come to the crystal. It said we might be able to get another skill," I said, cutting off the tirade that I knew would be coming from Daniela. When she wasn't being extremely cooperative, she was usually busting everyone's chops for no real reason. I don't think I was done with my message when Daniela burst out of the lobby.

"Shiny dude, you owe me two skills," she said, pointing accusingly at the Entity.

"I'll be right up, Ron. Keep her from burning down the camp, yes?"

While I had been listening to Sam, my other friend had proceeded to talk up a storm. Ben had even taken a few steps back just to whisper in my ear. "Has she always been this... jumpy?"

"I think not having her mom here to keep her in line has let her blow up more often. Plus, she has the space to be loud out here. You scream in the Bunker, and half of it knows about it."

"I can hear you two perfectly fine. What, just because I am demanding what I was told was mine, I am causing a scene?" The woman crossed her arms and huffed in indignation. I could have sworn I saw a puff of flame extinguish itself under her armpits.

"There are only the four of us here, Danny. You don't need to get so up in arms about it," I said. Ben made the smart decision of staying silent through the engagement. As much as he was our elder and we respected his opinion, Danny barely cared about that outside of her parents.

"I would like to pose that I, too, be counted as present." We all turned to the forgotten Entity. "Thanks to you all, emotions are a thing I am having to contend with. If I were to warrant a guess, I am feeling somewhat offended by this whole exchange."

"Maybe you should join the conversations more often, buddy," Daniela shot back.

"As I have already explained to Ronan and you, if you wish for your skills and status to function properly, I need to conserve energy." There was a hint of anger in the Entity's tone. *That bit is definitely from Danny. Oh boy...*"Would you like me to drop the protective field keeping the creatures of the forest away? Or maybe take your <Flame Blast> away?"

Thankfully, before Daniela could escalate the situation further, Sam arrived. "What did I miss?"

"Let's not talk about that now. The Entity said it should have sufficient energy to allow us to pick another skill. That won't put you in a precarious position, right?" I said, quickly changing the topic.

"That is correct. For your understanding, and so that we are *crystal clear* on what I am doing here, purging Dreg allows me to build mass. The more mass, the larger my mana pool and regeneration. Once I reach the next categorical size, my ability to process information and tasks will increase exponentially. Due to the way our minds are structured, I don't even know what I will be capable of doing until I reach that point."

"Do you have any recommendations for us?" Sam asked.

"Well, based on the information I have about combat engagements in your 'video games,' I would say that you three are filling very specific roles," the Entity answered. "Your Attunements are also linked to why you play those roles so well, but the science behind Attunements is complicated. Ronan and Benjamin can tell you two more about that."

"Wait, you three have been basing all of this implant stuff and your abilities on *video games?*" our old teacher said, flabbergasted.

"Has been working pretty well so far. Plus, how else would you explain all of this madness but with magic?" I said, meeting the man's eyes.

"That...Damn. That's a good point. Carry on, I'll just stay an old man in the back." His frown and the actual step back he took elicited a chuckle from all of us. The lingering tension lifted instantly. I noticed a smile twitch at the corner of his mouth, but he kept a frown on his face. *Crafty Teach, you did that on purpose.*

"Right, so, roles. I can take a guess. I'm some kind of support, while Danny and Ronan are damage dealers," Sam said.

"Close. As damaging as Ronan's skill is, I believe he is acting as the group's tank. From what I have observed, he has used his direct offensive skill for defensive and utilitarian purposes more than to actually deal damage."

"Hmm, I guess you are right," I said, suddenly looking back on our fights in a new light. "What are you suggesting?"

"I believe that Samuel would benefit from a direct defensive skill, Ronan would benefit from a materialize defensive skill, and Daniela would benefit from a materialize offensive skill."

"Don't you pick what skill we get under the different categories?" Daniela asked.

"Not exactly. While I have the knowledge of the links in your spell chains, the magic manifests differently for each of you. Your body picks which of the ones I give you knowledge of fits you best, so to speak."

"Well, might as well get it over with. We gonna be out the whole night again? If that's the case, I'd like to grab some dinner before going through this whole song and dance."

"The process should only last a few minutes. That last time, I was configuring the reprogrammed interface for your implants and compiling information to transfer to your brains. I think the time investment was warranted."

Danny lifted her arms up in a sign of surrender.

"Wait. Could you expand your field of influence?" I asked. Considering the main threat we'd encountered were the Fire Ants, I wondered if it was possible to keep them from even running into the camp at all with the help of the Entity.

"That will require more mana regeneration than I have at my disposal. Most of it is currently spread out around your camp already." The light within the crystal bobbed in response. I wanted to ask more questions, but I knew unlocking skills would be more valuable than spending time speculating about the Entity's behavior and limits. We'd gotten so far on trust, there was no sense doubting its capabilities.

"You guys go ahead, I'll give Ben a more detailed run down of the status and our skills." I put my arms on my friend's shoulders and nudged them forward gently.

"I'd like to know why you look paler than when you lived in the Bunker. There shouldn't be any lack of sun in Florida. At least *that* hasn't been changed by the apocalypse," Ben said, pointing to the most obvious feature of my Limestone Skin.

"That's a bit of a long story." I pulled Ben a little ways from the crystal. "You see, Anthony wasn't really being cooperative…"

CHAPTER SIXTEEN

Two Birds, One Wall

"So, then I came out of the crystal already changed."

"Is that what is going to happen to me?" Ben asked, more than a bit alarmed as he looked at his own arms.

"No idea, Teach. I will say it is pretty minor, and I'll take any advantage when things all around us are trying to kill us," I said, crossing my arms while watching over my friends. I absently ran my hands down my arms. As much as I was getting used to the Limestone Skin, talking about it brought it to mind. Without a clock, I had no idea how much time had passed, but I gauged it at roughly thirty minutes. The sun was already beginning to set when the Entity released them and they blinked their eyes while looking off into space. *Probably looking at their status.* "Is it my turn yet?"

"One sec, Ron…" Danny said. The woman held up her hand and fire concentrated in her grasp. The circular pattern for her skill spun around her arm before sliding off it like a fallen bracelet. The fire stayed attached to the spell chain. Unlike her <Flame Blast>skill, the fire condensed further. Then a pair of fiery wings sprouted from the center sphere and the whole thing took to the air above us.

"What the hell?" I said, following the speedy ball of fire as it circled lazily around us.

"It's called an <Ember Wisp>. It's a little elemental ball of fire that I can direct with my mind!" Danny said, clapping her hands in excitement. She squinted her eyes and the ember wisp spat out a thin gout of flame into the sky before dissipating. "Man, that takes a ton of mana."

"My skill is called <Health Bump>. It should let me restore the health of those I touch, which will come in handy. I don't know about you guys, but I am tired of leaving everything to the increased healing our Quotient gives us," Sam said.

"Wait, what do you mean increased healing?" I asked.

"You didn't notice the burns in your hands disappear, or the scrapes we got while putting together the herd fence? Or Danny when she got cuts from the air squirrels?" *I hadn't.* I could vaguely recall the Entity mentioned something about that when we first spoke, but those had been stressful times. "It isn't super fast, but we are healing much faster than we ever did while living in the Bunker."

"Samuel is correct. Your internal mana will seek to reach homeostasis and assist in healing you. This is likely why you did not experience the enhanced regeneration while living underground. Life-attuned organisms often gain ways of more directly affecting this process. Not only to heal, but also to enhance for short periods of time," the Entity provided helpfully, but I could hear the exhaustion in its tone.

While I didn't know how something without an organic body could get tired, I wasn't going to pretend I really knew the minutiae of being an artificial intelligence.

"Just don't give Sam an excuse to use his new skill while you play around with yours, eh Danny?" I said before pressing my hands against the crystal. Immediately, my consciousness was pulled into the crystal, like when I was envenomed. "Woah."

"Welcome back, Ronan. It is good to have you here on better terms than the last time. This space is what I developed to properly impart skills. The last situation required a more...

rushed transfer of information. I am optimistic this process will be much smoother," the floating ball of light that represented the Entity said.

Without more prompting, the skill selection appeared before me. Knowing that I was going to follow the Entity's recommendation, I selected the defensive materialize skill. A surge of information flowed through me, however it wasn't an immediate dump. Controlled rivers of details and concepts that I couldn't entirely grasp joined the mass of information that made up my <Stone Spike>skill. Slowly, that information concentrated enough that I felt the mental 'button' for the skill take shape in my mind.

<Earthen Barrier>

<Compress surrounding earth to provide a protective barrier>

Those descriptions are positively unhelpful...

"You may test the skill in this space. It will still drain your mana, so be aware of that, but it will be in a controlled environment, and you will still see the effect."

Doing as asked, I pushed the button for my newfound skill. A simulacrum of the camp, sans the walls and everything I'd developed, manifested around me. The swirl of brown patterns I'd associated with my <Stone Spike> formed. Instead of around my wrist, it took shape on the ground where I'd been looking. The earth bulged, thinned, then formed a small embankment. As far as barriers were concerned, it was more of a bump. Rising roughly a foot up and four wide, I doubted it would even cover me if I laid prone behind it. The drain on my mana was close to <Stone Spike>, just shy of twenty percent, but so was the 'barrier.'

"Is this all the skill can do?"

"Not remotely. However, I do not know how the specifics would transfer to humans. Attempting to use the skill back to back or with other types of earth should yield different results. I am confident in your abilities, Ronan."

"That's a big vote of confidence."

"Not only do I have no one else *to* put my confidence in, but you three have already managed to provide me enough Dreg to grow more than I had in years. Perhaps I will find out why there haven't been Dreg Warrior analogues where Entity Clusters have interacted with humans once I achieve a sufficient category…"

The light of the Entity flickered briefly before continuing. "I understand my limitations are frustrating for you and your people, Ronan. However, I want you to understand that I am just trying to give you all the best chance to achieve your goals. I do not fear death, because I have never really been alive. This is not the case for you."

My jaw worked itself open and closed, but I had no words. I hadn't been expecting that level of candidness from the Entity. It made my previous frustrations with it petty and misplaced.

"I will work to continue spreading my influence. Though I will be out of contact until the next time I have sufficient mana to bestow your new skills, I can implement some triage options should you be in urgent need of my assistance. Let the mana strengthen you against the Dreg."

With that, I found myself back at the camp. The real one. A surge of information flowed through my mind. It wasn't nearly as intense as when the Entity provided us the spell chains for skills, but it was significant. A line of text manifested before my eyes before fading away. Thankfully, there was only a lingering headache this time.

<Pith Mana Lock>

<Miscellaneous skill for managing dissociating matter>

<Infusion>

<Miscellaneous skill for transferring Pith into objects>

<Place your hand on the forehead of anyone you'll want to pass these skills along to. It will drain almost all of your mana pool, but you are the only one with a big enough one to complete the transfer. Best of luck, kids.>

When the line faded from view, I watched the Entity Cluster dim to a mere shadow of its usual brightness. Standing as close as I was to it, I could still sense the static in the air that indicated its field of influence. *Now that I think about it, we never did thank you for the skills.* "Thanks. We'll keep churning the Dregs your way. This is just the beginning."

There was the slightest pulse of light within the crystal. It was so small, in fact, that I thought it might have been a trick of the light. Regardless, I took it as the Entity's positive response and I smiled. As much as I wanted to test out my skills more, the darkening sky and the grumbled conversation of my friends told me it must be dinner time.

"Finally! I could barely wait to eat these roasted tomato-enhanced dry flakes of mock food…" Danny said when she saw me finally walking over to the entrance. "You've been standing there for almost an hour, Ronan."

"I got a set of skills from the Entity," I said. Without waiting for my friend's response, I pushed into the lobby space. The telltale signs of Ben's organization were already spreading into it. Primarily, the fact that all our bedding had been moved behind the counters in the room, the food items to the right hand side and the rest to the left.

"Hold the comms. You got more skills?" Daniela said. The woman was in front of me in a second. She was much faster than she had been before, which was already faster than either me or Sam.

"If you'd been paying attention to my conversation with the crystal, you'd realize we discussed how we might be able to keep the corpses from turning into Pith and items."

"What does that have to do with getting new skills?" she asked, crossing her arms and pouting.

She really can't keep herself out of trouble, huh? Instead of answering her, I placed my palm on her forehead. With my practice triggering my skills, orienting my mind to the <Pith Mana Lock> and <Infusion> was easy. Instead of actually casting them, I tried to *will* the information into my friend. The world turned into a blurry mess of pain. A blinking indicator highlighted my mana pool, which sat at just six percent. The crystal was right, the transfer had taken nearly the entirety of my mana pool in one go.

"Holy crap! Ronan, what was that?" Sam said as he helped me to my feet. I hadn't even realized I was down on one knee. Ben had caught Danny before she'd fallen back. *Maybe that's why the crystal grabs us when it transfers the spell chains. Didn't know it packed quite that much of a punch.*

"He gave me two skills..." Danny said, staring off into space, obviously looking at her implant.

"Once I recover, you and Ben are next," I said, looking at my blond friend. "But before any of that, I could use some food!"

We spent the next several hours enjoying the prepackaged meals and the fruits of Sam's magical labor. Ben was thrilled to have some surface food after so long. The four of us reminisced about the Bunker and discussed our dreams for the future. Me and Ben were particularly ambitious, but Sam's dream of acres and acres of farmland wasn't far behind. It was with these thoughts in mind that we all fell asleep.

Before calling it a night, I transferred the skills to both Sam and Ben. The pre-Landfall survivor was hesitant after the conversation telling him he couldn't have skills. Oddly enough, the skill appeared as a trait for Ben. I hoped the man would still be able to use it, but the minutiae of the Entity's system was certainly out of my reach. It could also just be an error due to the generational difference it mentioned, and the transference had failed somehow. Either way, the moment I'd recovered enough mana, I crossed two stone spikes to seal the entrance and fell asleep the moment my head touched the sleeping bag.

— + —

Gentle lowing served as our morning alarm clock. Once my brain had enough time to boot up, it ran into hyperdrive. There was much I had to do and test with my new skill. I didn't bother rousing my friends. Instead, I chowed down the dried eggs in the insta-meal before nabbing my pickaxe and clearing the entrance. The sound of crunching rock was enough of a wake up call, and I smirked at the protesting calls from behind me.

My vigorous exit spooked some of the cows, but over the last few days, they'd mostly become used to our presence. Instead of charging off, they merely trudged a small distance before resuming to clear the hillside of grass. I took a deep breath of the surface air. *There is no way I will ever get tired of this.* With that out of the way, I walked up to my spike wall and grimaced. In the dawning light, it looked completely terrible. I wasn't one for aesthetics, but I couldn't believe I'd built something so hodgepodge. Just to check, I kicked it and it all held together even with my enhanced strength. The design itself wasn't faulty, but I didn't think even if Sam covered the entire wall in vines I'd be able to live with myself knowing what was underneath.

"Suppose it's time to try out the Entity's suggestions..." I mumbled to myself. I focused on the space right at the base of the wall and cast <Earthen Barrier>. Instead of the simple mound I'd seen take shape, I saw the material surge between the spaces left by my stone spikes. The barrier rose a good four feet before stopping, having covered the disastrous ugliness of the updated wall. When I looked at my mana pool, the casting had still taken roughly twenty percent, as I'd seen in the Entity's simulacrum, but the overall volume ended up greater.

Upon closer inspection, I could see striations of stone amidst the compacted earth of the wall. *Maybe it creates the barrier from the surrounding materials...* I gave the concrete building where the Bunker entrance was a look. It only took a moment for me to realize how dumb of a decision that would be. With how little I knew about the skill, and my magic in general, the whole wall could collapse due to a flaw I created. *Or it will be magnificently strong... No!*

After turning back to the wall I'd created, I decided to cast the skill again. Instead of trying to build up the wall further, I would concentrate on the section I'd already raised. The circular pattern took shape on the ground, spinning partially through the earth as if it wasn't really there. When I pressed the mental trigger for the skill, my breath caught in my throat. The gut wrenching pain that came from casting returned and I looked at my mana pool to see it had dipped by nearly forty percent.

The barrier that had been just a compacted mound of earth, however, became the same consistency as one of my stone spikes. I received a solid thunk when I rapped my knuckles on it. The pain of the magic was quickly forgotten as I realized what I needed to do to achieve step one of our little fortified camp.

Over the course of several hours, I worked to raise double height, stone spike reinforced barriers. This process was much more mana intensive than casting the stone spikes had been originally and by the time I was done, I laid back on the ground gasping at the sky. I'd been so caught up in constructing the wall, the comings and goings of my friends had gone completely unnoticed. The occasional echoing blast of fire from the forest and grumble from the lobby area told me Daniela and Ben were working on something. A peek around the openings of my wall showed me Sam was equally engaged with Raymond in what appeared to be his attempt at cow herding.

With lunch quickly approaching, I decided to head into the lobby after pinging my friends through our implants. As effective as gunshots were for getting their attention, I realized we'd been underusing the comm system now built into us. Getting an affirmative from both of them, I pulled the door open.

The inside of the lobby was completely transformed. While before there had been a general sense of organization, the space was now meticulously arranged. Something akin to an actual kitchen had been set up on the right counter. A small burner and gas tank was set up at the edge, while a few containers held the insta-meals like a makeshift pantry. A half-open box had been repurposed for the sake of leaving a few handfuls of tomatoes accessible.

The opposite counter was loaded with the weapons Ben had provided us, the ones he'd brought with him, as well as a few of the larger tools he'd lugged up from storage. *He must have gone down to the Bunker again...* I realized as my eyes continued to take in the room. Behind the counters were the four spots that marked our bedding. However, instead of laying on the ground, they were settled atop long, flat crates. I wasn't sure what was stored there, but considering they seemed to be acting as bed frames, I couldn't imagine anything important.

The organization spree didn't end there. On the left hand side of the room were several vertically stacked crates. To my surprise, I saw small displays showcasing an inventory of what was held within. The entire left-most stack was just chitin plates from the ant's raid, as well as various other supplies, a trio of empty water barrels, and two crates that said they contained the sum total of our infusions. The breakdown of 106 infusions surprised me, but I wasn't going to complain about having our resources clearly noted.

When I spotted Ben, he was waist deep inside a vertical tent-like construction, cursing up a storm. There were a number of wrenches and grease streaks on the ground around him.

"Hey, Teach. You need a hand?" I said.

"God—"A painful metal thud came from the flap-covered man. Grumbling all the while, Ben extracted himself from his work. He was rubbing his temple where a bruise was already forming. "A little warning would have been nice, Ronan. I very nearly met my maker just then; I thought that snippy ant was back to mess with my organization."

The man's shirt was covered in various stains, and I could see an oil slick pattern on his head where the sweat and oil warred for dominance of his wrinkled baldness.

"Just took a break for lunch. What in the world did you do here? How did you get all of this done so fast?" I said, gesturing around at the significant improvements the one man had wrought in the lobby. My hand lingered pointedly on the contraption he was working on.

"Right, well, I've had a long time to get good at organizing things and counting them." He chuckled while he grabbed a rag to wipe his hands and head. "Knowing what you have, and where it is, is often underrated. When I used to run the lab at my university, they would dock our pay if things weren't prop-erly documented. It's just a logical extension that our excursions to the surface should follow. As for what this thing is... it's a shower."

He explained that while it wouldn't be optimal, he could set it up outside of the lobby once he had it assembled. It had a filtration and pump system that he was working to bypass so that we could use simple gravity until we figured out how to get electricity working on the surface. "I suppose with magic that might become obsolete at some point, but in the meantime, hygiene is essential. Just because you like to go around looking like the mud you play in doesn't mean it's healthy for you or your friends."

"Hey, I clean up after myself just fine," I said, crossing my arms defensively. "Anything else you care to criticize?"

"Actually, Ron, since I have you here, I was wondering if we could talk about something," Ben said. Sweat immediately broke out along my back. Teach wrung the rag in his hands as he waited for my response.

"S-sure, Mr. Burks," I said, dreading what was to come. If I was honest with myself, I was surprised it had taken Ben as long as it had to broach the topic.

"Your dad... uncle... Well, Dale. I think you shouldn't be too hard on him."

"Ben, I'm trying not to be. Really, it's just... it's been a lot to take in," I replied after a few seconds of awkward silence between us.

"Ronan, the secret...It always took its toll on him. I don't know how many times he came to talk to me when you accom-plished something just to break down in tears.Now that it's out, you'd think things would be better, but everything came to a head in the worst way possible." Ben shook his head as he leaned back against his half-built contraption. "We know better than most you three aren't kids anymore, but you need to remember you *were* our kids. I may not have been related to you three in any way, but I saw you as my own rugrats."

The admission physically ached. It was something I hadn't really thought about, even if I already considered the people of the Bunker our family. What did the specific title a person held matter if you cared for them?

"I'll talk to him. Not sure when I'll muster it, but you are right that things moved terribly. He didn't deserve that." I sighed.

"Good!" Ben said, slapping me hard on the shoulder, wincing as he scraped along my Limestone Skin. "I've never been the best with the touchy feely stuff. I'm more of the background listener kind."

"Same boat, Teach," I grumbled.

The bald man roared with laughter, pulling me into a half-hug as the tension between us dissipated.

He once again attempted to explain to me some of the mechanical aspects of the filtration and pump, but the material went over my head. Instead, I focused on how many aspects there were to life in the Bunker I had never considered. Obviously, food and water were the main ones, but hygiene was also a big part of it. What use was it returning to the surface and being protected from its beasts, if we died of an infection or something? *We have healing magic now, dummy.* Even while mulling over that caveat, I wasn't willing to bank on magic being the solution to everything. Being envenomed had had immediate effects on me, and I could only imagine what illnesses an Attuned Earth had to offer.

"How long has he been spaced out like that?" Danny asked.

"I think it was right around the time I started describing the head pressure value for the pump. So, five minutes or so?" Ben replied. The man was using a small knife to slice tomatoes, sprinkling them over top of our insta-meals.

"It's rude to talk about a person, especially when said person is right there," I said, approaching the snickering pair and grabbing one of the offered meals.

"No need to feel bad, Ron. We know you were probably off somewhere in your head planning some crazy shenanigans for us to have to deal with," Sam said, placing his arm on my shoulder. The blond's dazzling smile nearly dissolved my frustration, but I managed to throw out a good-natured grumble.

The four of us shared the meal, laughing and detailing what we'd managed to accomplish in the day. After the sobering step back Ben had forced me to take, I realized just how much we'd managed to accomplish and how much of the groundwork for the future we had available. Samuel told us he had finally gotten the herd to stay in the area near the fence we'd created. Daniela had been working to clear out the game trail to the east, all while acquiring wood for when we needed to use it. Both of my childhood friends commented on the impressiveness of my wall, excited by the prospect of more *space* to really settle into the surface.

Step by step, the foothold grew deeper.

CHAPTER SEVENTEEN

Infusing

The rest of the afternoon I spent laying the groundwork for the first room of our fort camp. Calling forth my mana with ease, the circular pattern formed around my hand. As I held it, the ground consolidated once again. After a few minutes of the slow process, I stopped.

"What if…?"

While I was much more comfortable with calling forth <Stone Spike> without actually casting it, I tried to imitate the result with <Earthen Barrier>. Sure enough, a brown colored circle formed around the area I would have cast the skill. Keeping the skill from triggering was a bit more slippery than my spikes had been, but I managed to hold back the effect.

The diameter of the magic circle was roughly the same as the width of the basic barrier. My mana dipped much faster than if I was just holding my other skill, but the entire area under the magic circle compressed as if I'd set a large weight overtop. After a few seconds, the ash and grass roots had been pushed out of the ground, leaving a relatively smooth circle in place. The effect was much more uniform, and intense, than when I'd waved my hand around. It could have been because of my initial work in flattening the area, but I had a sneaking suspicion it had to do with the nature of the skills.

By the time I'd finished inspecting the compacted circle, my mana had completely regenerated. Remembering how draining stacking two <Earthen Barriers> on top of each other had been, I opted to just spend mana to get the space within the first wall flat and even. While in the process of pacing out columns and marking them with my pickaxe on the new hardened ground, a veritable cascade of water fell from the sky.

I blinked. It was as if someone had turned on the shower while I was fully clothed. Looking up gave me the simple answer, which was punctuated by a sharp crack of thunder. A lancing line of lightning manifested itself in the distant sky and I realized that at some point during the afternoon, clouds had blanketed the sky. Dirt and sweat rolled down my body and all I could do was stare up at the storm. The first bit of rain I'd experienced. It was a surreal feeling. I stuck my tongue out, tasting the dirt-heavy droplets of fresh rain and marveling at the taste. Not even the boiled surface water tasted as fresh and *natural*.

At some point during my commune with nature, I heard chittering. An unhappy Anthony appeared from the area of the woods where Daniela had been and scurried into the lobby. The Fire Ant used one of its forelimbs to open the door and when it was inside, it shook its thorax while flames coated its body. The visual of a dog drying itself was a weird thing to attribute to an ant.

"Suppose that's it for today. Glad I got the herd fed again before this storm." Sam sauntered into the space I'd cleared and paused when he stepped on the fruits of my labor. When I turned to my friend, I could see his boots were already coated in mud. "Did you turn the ground into stone, Ron?"

When I explained what I'd done, he looked pensive. Before I had a chance to ask what he was thinking about, Daniela grumbled her way into camp. The woman gave us each a look before walking straight into the bunker. Sam shrugged and headed in after her. I gave the slowly intensifying rain a longing look before stepping inside.

Our friend's grumbling and, from what I could see, her ant's, had continued unimpeded inside. Daniela was chattering away at Anthony the whole while, complaining about 'sky water' and how it had no business coming down from above. I'd never considered that one of my best friends would be both a fire mage and a cat. When I said as much, she glared in my direction while I removed my soggy clothes down to my trousers. At that point, she had the decency to blush and look away, putting an end to her tirade while Sam and I hung our clothes from the mostly modified shower.

"You know, once upon a time that would have been considered awkward," Ben said while tinkering with the arrangement of tools and another series of crates. By my mental count, the man had either hidden boxes within other boxes, or he'd taken yet another trip down to the Bunker.

"We aren't living in the past, Mr. Burks. Plus, I don't see a dryer anywhere here," Sam said, going through one of the crates for a fresh change of clothes. He pulled out two vacuum-sealed bags with a t-shirt and a pair of jeans. I copied my friend after wringing some of the water out of my clothes. It was hard to remember a time when I'd ever had my clothes so thoroughly soaked. Our teacher huffed and resumed taking stock of what we had available.

Suddenly without anything to do but listen to the rain, I twitched with pent up energy. *Guess I know why kids invented that 'rain rain go away' song...* There was still some light filtering through the clouds, mocking me with the potential of the rest of the day. When I turned to see if my friends would commiserate, they were all thoroughly engaged in other tasks. Samuel was tending to the original tomato plant, an intense look of concentration on his face as he channeled mana into *two* circular formations. Daniela was talking to Anthony nonstop, and from what I knew about the Fire Ant, it was listening. Probably learning too. Ben was still stacking and counting away with a clipboard.

That left me. Wallowing on a rainy day. It was certainly a novel situation compared to wallowing in the Bunker with nothing to do but browse the archives, play games, or assist one of the floors. I almost resigned myself to zoning out for the rest of the day, maybe a little daydreaming about plans for the fort camp, when Ben pulled out some of the infusions to count.

A glance at my status showed the two skills burning a hole in my metaphorical pocket. I walked up to the crates where Ben had separated the infusions we'd acquired. There was an over-whelming amount of the ones that belonged to the smaller, unrefined Fire Ants. I plucked one of the cool, smoldering blobs and let the information populate before me.

<Quotient 0 Infusion>

<Fire>

<Integrity: 96%>

*Hmmm. They must lose integrity over time also...*It was something to keep in mind. Considering how many of those we had, I grabbed a handful and set up shop near the door. After some consideration, I grabbed one of the little plastic containers that our insta-meals came in. Ben gave me a questioning look, but turned back to his work while I focused on mine.

Unsure of how exactly the process would work, I gently pressed on the information associated with the Infusion skill. The blob in my hand brightened slightly in response. When I concentrated on both it *and* the skill, a hovering thread of crimson red unspooled itself from the infusion. The thread snaked in the air without a care for gravity. I could feel my mana reacting to the process, draining. It was a slow trickle, but it didn't stop while the thread remained.

Testing what would happen, I released the skill. The thread winked out and the infusion was left darker. A look at its infor-mation revealed that it had lost a significant amount of integrity, nearly twenty percent in that short period. *Gotta do it in one sitting, or probably make sure it's properly attached to whatever item.* Not wanting to waste any more of the infusion, I willed the thread to unspool. Picturing my mana pinching the end of the thread seemed to do the trick as I directed the crimson line in the air.

With a mental flick, the Pith made contact with the little plastic tray. Two things happened immediately. First, the plastic melted as if I'd put it to the torch. Black acrid smoke suffocated me for a second. The other was that the rate of mana draw spiked hard enough that I felt it twisting my gut. The entire infusion had transferred into the tray the moment I willed it. I coughed and spat out the acidic flavor of the smoke. The black goop that remained of the tray sizzled once before hardening again.

"Ronan, what did you do?" Ben asked, waving a rag in the air to push away the last bits of smoke.

"Testing," I said between coughs. The taste of plastic really lingered. "Trying out using our infusions."

"Was that what you intended to happen?" he asked, poking the charred tray.

"I am going to say that infusing plastic with fire is a bad idea. I wonder how the Pith from the other Attunements will react…" I said. My mind was already running a mile a minute. What the little exchange had made me realize was that certain things needed to withstand the *type* of energy of the Attunement. Without waiting for Ben to say anything else, I grabbed one of the small gardening shovels we had available and another empty plastic tray. I contemplated saving the air infusions we'd gotten from the squirrels, but I figured learning about the process was worth using them. What use was it if we kept them, only for them to destroy whatever we tried to infuse later because we didn't understand their behavior? I grabbed the cotton-looking blob and let its information appear in my view.

<Quotient 1 Infusion>
<Air - Flight>
<Integrity: 98%>

With the air infusion in hand, I crouched next to the black

goop and set the new tray next to it. After giving Ben a meaningful look, he backed up. Just to be careful. The air infusion unspooled the same way as the fire one, leaving a gray thread for me to control. Taking my *own* step back, I flicked it at the plastic tray.

The thread made contact with the tray and I felt the dip in my mana pool. While the Quotient 0 Infusion had made me feel the draw, the Quotient 1 Infusion made me pay attention. It was through gritted teeth that I watched as the Pith wrapped around the plastic tray, vibrating it.

Small bits of the plastic chipped as it vibrated against the floor before the shaking stabilized. My mana kept flowing into the connection and I watched in amazement as the tray lifted up into the air with a gentle gust of wind. The tray floated gently in the wind like a falling leaf. Then violently exploded into shards of plastic.

"Gah!" Ben and I screamed in unison. Thankfully, we were standing over the tray and far enough away that we didn't get any plastic in our eyes. The rest of our bodies, however, got pelted by the fingernail-sized bits. Ben, who was still wearing his combat vest, only got a few stuck in his arms. In my case, I took most of the blast straight to the chest.

My health only dipped ten percent, but the pain radiating from all the small wounds certainly felt like it should have taken a larger portion of it. Samuel was at our side instantly. The blond looked at all the little pinpricks of blood with worry, but when I explained the actual damage, he took a breath in relief. Ben had only taken four percent damage, so he waved off Sam in my direction and went to fetch some tweezers. *I didn't even know we had tweezers up here.* After handing Sam a pair and grabbing some for himself, my old teacher started to pluck plastic from his arms.

"Sorry, Teach," I said, wincing as Sam helped me out of my shirt. Some of the plastic bits plinked off my skin as we tugged off the fabric, while others just cut through the fabric. Without much preamble, he started to pluck them from my body.

The old man waved it off. "Most pain I've felt in years was getting attuned. This is a walk in the park, really. And what can I say? Experimentation comes with a price. I could have just as well left you to tinker with magic nonsense alone, but where is the fun in that?

"Plus, I've been trying to get these skills-turned-traits to work with no success. I feel like I am just missing something to get the effect to... well, work," Ben said, sighing. "Who doesn't want to use magic to build crazy stuff, you know?"

All I had to do to respond to that statement was look at the work I'd been doing already. As for his experimentation, I really didn't have a better response than 'because magic,' so I remained silent; I knew I was throwing things at the wall to see what stuck. Mostly because 'feeling' the magic was the root of my own experimentation, but I would need to keep the possibility of failure in mind while infusing.

It only took Sam ten minutes to get me all patched up. And by that I mean that he finally got to try out his skill on a live human for the first time. "Stay still. Not sure exactly how this is going to pan out. The Entity only had me cast it but he didn't have the mana to give me a target."

The life-attuned in question called forth the magic circle that correlated with his direct skill and then placed his hands on my shoulder. A surge of soothing warmth traveled down my body, numbing the areas around the plastic shards and leaving me painless. It wasn't total numbness and it was quickly followed by the feelings I expected from being bare-chested, minus a dozen cuts. The little cuts oozing blood stitched themselves back together before my very eyes.

"Impressive," I said, as I looked my healed body over. There were paper thin scars where the wounds had been, but other than that, there wasn't any evidence that I'd been hurt. One of the pieces of plastic had actually pushed itself out of my skin to plink on the floor, the original wound not even leaving a trickle of blood to mark its passage.

"Mr. Burks, get over here please. I need to test some stuff..."

Sam said, thoroughly lost in thought while walking back to his tomato plant. It took me a second to realize that it didn't quite look like a regular tomato plant anymore. The fruit was a darker red and the vertical stem was thicker than the trellis supporting it.

"Wish me luck. I survived your infusion explosion to be killed by the one with healing powers!" the man joked as he walked after my friend.

Daniela hadn't even moved from her spot through the whole ordeal. She gave me an amused wave, then returned to talking with Anthony like nothing had happened. I shook my head at her while I gave my body a look. Instead of trying to clean myself, I stepped outside and rinsed off in the rain. After some consideration, I decided to conduct the next part of my infusion experiments outside.

There was no sense in stopping now—*I already took the plastic shards to the chest!*—but nothing said I couldn't take my precautions even further.

Ignoring the pouring water and occasional thunder, I stepped out of the area I'd compressed. I dug a hole on the soil and went back inside to get the fire infusions and the little shovel. By the time I returned, the hole was filled with runoff water and mud.

Now familiar with the process, I triggered the Infusion skill. Making sure I aimed the thread at the metallic portion of the shovel, my mana started to drain like I expected. The metal of the shovel quickly jumped to a dull red and the rain falling on it instantly hissed into steam. With a nudge from my boot, the shovel went into the hole. The water that had accumulated instantly boiled over, but it only lasted a few seconds until I felt the draw on my mana ease.

I left the shovel in there for several seconds more, just to be sure it got a proper chance to cool, before I fished it out of the muddy water. The rubbery handle was completely gone, likely melted like the plastic tray had been. The metal, on the other hand, had a slight red tinge to it. It was cool to the touch, and when I scratched at the surface with my finger, nothing came off to indicate it was some kind of residue. However, when I brought it up to my eyes, information started to scroll before my eyes and the shovel was outlined in gold.

<Insufficient Pith Enhanced Shovel>

<Attribute: Undetermined>

<Trait: Undetermined>

Did the Entity anticipate this? I didn't realize we would be able to analyze items. While it wasn't clear what exactly I could do to reach a 'sufficient' amount of Pith in the shovel, trying to infuse it again was the simplest thing I could think of. I placed the enhanced shovel next to the muddy hole in preparation to kick it in again. Before I started infusing it again, I noticed that some of the mud that touched it flaked before turning back into mud when the rain hit it. The slight change was so mesmerizing that I didn't start the infusion until a crack of thunder shook me out of my thoughts.

"Focus, Ronan. Possibly dangerous magical process here." I pulled another infusion and began the transfer of Pith. The tug on my mana was more intense this time, and I watched nearly twenty percent of it vanish before the whole thread had unspooled and the infusion vanished. I didn't even wait for the metal to heat before I nudged it into the hole. The reaction this time was much more violent. Steaming bubbles of mud splattered my boots and I took a step back. The cooling process also took longer, but I watched intently as the muddy surface stilled other than from the falling rain. Making sure to wait a full sixty count, I reached into the hole and pulled the shovel out.

The first thing that caught my attention was the fact that the edge of the tool had acquired a wavy pattern to it and the tang beneath where the rubber had been thinned and lengthened. Instead of the original six-ish inches, it was nearly a foot in length. The red tinge hadn't changed. A trill of excitement rushed through me as I brought it closer and it was highlighted in gold once again. The information remained the same. I frowned down at the changed shovel then looked back at the Entity Crystal.

"You can't answer, but maybe when you get a chance, give a more thorough indication of how close to sufficient it is? I'm kind of scared of infusing this again," I said to the air, hopefully not talking to myself. A cow lowed in the distance, and I chose to take that as affirmation that at least *someone* was listening.

Just for my peace of mind, I dug the makeshift quenching hole deeper, up to my elbow, and set the shovel just short of tipping into it. With now-practiced ease, I focused on the third fire infusion and flicked it at the shovel. My mana was still transferring into the process when I shoved the metal in the hole. Sure enough, a small geyser of muddy water and steam rose up from the hole. I was thankful I'd dug it deeper.

The water churned as if something alive was moving in it but quickly stilled. Before my eyes, the mud in the hole hardened. The surface started alternating between solid and liquid until the shovel cooled. I stayed a full five minutes just to make sure it was okay to handle and I *dug* the metal out. The handle end had been sticking out, but the rest was embedded in the mud after the water evaporated and geysered out.

The shovel was nearly unrecognizable. The metal was now thoroughly red with only a tinge of the original silver black. The handle had lengthened by another inch or so, but the actual digging portion was what had morphed the most. The wavy pattern that had taken hold after my second infusion was much more pronounced, and several small spokes that resembled flames reached up towards the handle. It looked as if the actual shovel was a flame frozen in time, then cast in red-colored steel.

When the no-longer-mundane tool was in scan range, the golden outline encompassed it and new information appeared before me.

<Quotient 1 Enhanced Shovel>
<Attribute: Strength>
<Trait: Baking Aura>

I had no idea what the lines meant other than the obvious. It wasn't clear how the shovel had a Quotient of 1 when I had used only Quotient 0 infusions, but I wasn't going to complain. It was yet another thing to ask the Entity. *I really need to write these down for the next time it can talk.* Shaking that distracting thought, I swung the tool in the air experimentally.Nothing interesting happened other than the fact that I was sure I looked ridiculous out in the rain. Then I remembered I could now show off my success to my friends. Instead of hoarding the shovel like a greedy crafting dragon, I rushed back into the Bunker's lobby.

CHAPTER EIGHTEEN

A Room in the Wild

Understandably, my friends were all ecstatic about my success. When they got close enough to the item, much closer than I had needed to receive the prompt, they told me the information they saw was the same. We speculated a few possibilities and when I described how the metal had changed, they agreed that it was probably curing the mud somehow.

"It's not hot to the touch right now, but I wouldn't put it past this weird metal to do *something* we just don't know how to activate," Ben said. The more I watched my old teacher interact with the magic around us, the more I could see him adapting. I'd been concerned the older members of the Bunker would struggle with that. I also had to consider that he was among the 'younger' group of those below and must have been at least familiar with fantasy games and some of the things the Entity had used as inspiration from our brains.

"Can I see it? I want to try something," Daniela said, holding out her hand. The older man passed the tool over and Daniela held it tightly in both hands as she summoned her magic circle. Immediately, the circle vanished as it was sucked into the tool. The heat coming off the tool quickly filled the small huddle we'd made to discuss the infused equipment. We all took a step back, as Daniela chuckled in surprise. "It's still drawing mana from me."

"You think that's how you make use of its trait?" I asked, ignoring the heat and watching the tool for any additional change. It almost looked like the red coloration had lightened, but I couldn't be sure.

"Yeah. I am also pretty sure that it's how you access the attribute. I instantly felt much stronger."

"Danny, check your status. See if it says anything about it," Sam said, a frown reaching his face as he looked between the tool and his overgrown tomato plant.

We all remained quiet while she stared off into space. The heat continued to reach us, even if it didn't seem to get any hotter. It might also have been a result of my still partly wet clothes, but I ignored it regardless. A few seconds later, she huffed in surprise.

"Yeah, there is a pair of brackets next to my strength attribute with a [+0.1]," she said.

"Can you deactivate the item?" Ben said, wiping some of the sweat that had started making its way down his considerable forehead. Daniela nodded and the heat was gone as if it hadn't been there. *The metal definitely lost some of the red when deactivated.*

"Strength boost is gone. That didn't take a whole lot of mana actually, but I don't know how it would be affected if I use my other skills," Danny said. She placed her other hand on the shovel head and I winced. She didn't so much as flinch. I should have expected that considering she'd been holding the metal handle all along, but I'd been more focused on the effects of the tool. "Anyone wanna give it a try?"

"You think it will work with mana from other attuned?" I asked as Sam took hold of the shovel.

"Nothing to do but try?" he shrugged as he called forth his direct skill spell chain. Just like with Danny, it sucked itself into the metal and the heat bathed us. "Checks out. This is an interesting way of giving other attuned access to the other elements. A sort of neutral ground for our attuned mana."

"It was hard to make just that one tool. I also feel like something unusual happened. I only used Quotient 0 Infusions but it's a Quotient 1 Item. We'll need to look more into it," I said.

"You better get working then! Maybe on something more useful than a garden shovel?" Danny said.

"I think I am about done with experimenting for today, but I'll let you know if I have any more success. Considering the fact we can make tools that might improve our attributes, even if it costs mana, infusion crafting just climbed up in my list of priorities." I made a mental note to myself to talk to Ben about getting at least one set of each metal tool we had infused with fire. "For now, I am starving!"

The rest of the evening was a whirlwind of conversation. We all spoke about the exciting possibilities of crafted items and how they would give us advantages in the wilderness. Ben was curious enough to actually try to activate the shovel, but he wasn't successful despite a few hours of trying. Sam and Danny were the most excited, listing things they thought I needed to infuse first for them. When I told them no, they looked thoroughly shocked until I reminded them that they were able to do it themselves. If they wanted something specific from *me*, then they would have to wait for when I got around to it.

Of course, I didn't tell them that I already intended to work on an infusing area within the room I was building outside, because they didn't need to know that. It was funny to see how quickly they were okay with waiting when it involved them risking explosions or magical geysers in the process. I didn't know what that said about me. I couldn't blame them, however. Sam wanted to keep working with his herd and farm. Danny I wasn't too sure, but she seemed to be content blowing stuff up in the woods. Considering the unknown dangers of our surroundings, I was glad she'd taken the initiative. Not only did she have Anthony to accompany her on her fiery escapades, she had the most damage potential, aim, and speed. She was *built* to be a scout. Even as worried as she made me with her going off alone, I knew she wasn't reckless. Her response to the Fire Ants was proof of that.

As I placed the defensive X of stone spikes on the door, my thoughts drifted to the threat of the Fire Ants. Building up our fort would be a good first step, and getting the Entity to expand its influence was another. However, even the crystal hadn't been able to keep the Fire Wolf away forever. It was possible that it was simply depleted after giving us our skills, but I had a hunch it had to do with its Quotient as much as it did with it running out of energy.

The highest Quotient we'd encountered was level 3. It wasn't hard to draw the connection between predators having higher Quotients since they could potentially take Pith from their kills. The Gossamer Spider and the Haze Wolf were threats we'd been lucky to manage. Venturing out into the woods and learning how best to use our skills was at the top of the list after I finished the first fortified room.

"Rocks-for-brain, it's morning time and people want to go about their jobs!" Danny said, nudging me in the side and eliciting me to roll over.

"You don't need me to leave," I said from under my arm. The light from the room's lantern was like a lance into my retinas.

"True, but they are *your* stone spikes. Now move it, daylight is a burnin' and I have trees to clear."

With a groan, I rose to my feet. Focusing my eyes briefly on the space right through the crack at the bottom of the door, a stone spike materialized and knocked my defensive X to the ground. The cast was so effortless I actually gave myself pause. It shouldn't have surprised me, considering the week of work I'd been doing, but it did regardless. Danny thanked me before heading out the door. Sam and Ben weren't far behind as they went off to work on our budding farm. The trio waved to me even as I was trying to fully wake up.

"I wish we had more of those coffee snacks..." I mumbled to myself. The little chocolate-encased beans had run out about five years ago. I wasn't a particular fan of their taste. Bitter had never been something I sought out in food. However, the shot of alertness they provided was invaluable when I was going through school. Mornings had never been my friend.

Regardless, I munched on some fresh-roasted potatoes and tomatoes that Danny had graced me with. With Sam dedicating himself to growing the farm, and with the help of Ben to manage it, we'd been able to add russet potatoes, peas, and rainbow chard to our dietary combinations. We'd even sent a load down with Ben. He'd been acting as our de facto point of contact with the Bunker. Once I'd gobbled the meal down, I tied up my boots and stepped out into the shade.

I couldn't help but smile at the success of my work. Several stone spike columns rose up around me, holding a hardened stone roof over our first surface-built room. The light in the space came from the Entity cluster directly in front of me and the two openings diagonally from the Bunker lobby. Throughout the last week, I'd used <Stone Spike> to create makeshift beams that I filled in using <Earthen Barrier>. The result was a vaguely geodesic dome pattern of stone spikes that was filled in by earth. I'd wanted to experiment with windows, but without glass or something similar, I opted for the defensive effect of plain walls.

My other major success had been in testing the extent of my compressive abilities. If the first cast of <Earthen Barrier> cost about the same as a <Stone Spike>, the second cost double, and the third triple. However, by the third casting, the compressed earth turned into a semblance of actual stone. When I'd been testing the compression limits of my skills, up to the fourth cast, it had given me trouble to break through even with my pickaxe. Doing that level of compression on the entire building would take many more days, since it drained my entire mana pool in one go and left me wheezing on the ground any time I tried it.

With that completed, I was ready to put the finishing touches on the building and work on some more infusing. For the first part of the morning, I worked to dig out little trenches at the base of each entryway; each gap was about a foot wide. Once those were completed, I made sure to gently compress the ground to create a smooth surface with a roughly trapezoidal cross section. With those done, it was time for me to get the rest of our group.

I'd discussed the general idea with them the night before, and they'd thought it would be a good solution in the meantime. Between the four of us, we lugged several of the logs Daniela had been working to clear away and debranch. When I got near her work area, I was surprised to see how much she'd managed to clear. A good ten foot wide path headed northwest away from the Bunker, before hooking north out of sight. The logs in question were strewn about the edges of the path, so we collected those nearest to the Bunker's clearing.

We brought ten logs and then worked to cut them down to about seven feet. With my increased strength and targeted use of my <Stone Spike> to pin and split the still green wood, we had what we needed just after lunch. Using a hatchet, we got the half logs as trimmed as we could and set them in the groove I'd made. Sam then used his skill to wrap them tightly together. My friend used some knot wizardry on par with *actual* magic to weave his vines, tying off the rest of the makeshift door.

"Ta-da!" I said, presenting the door to my friends as if they hadn't just helped me make it.

"This is the ugliest door I have ever seen." I opened my mouth to protest, but Danny cut me off. "Yes, this includes the ones we saw in simulations and movies."

With how much work we'd been doing on the surface, I'd forgotten my friends were quite resistant to my antics.

"This is pretty heavy," Ben noted. Our old teacher struggled to make the log door slide properly in the wedge I'd made. "Suppose that is part of the point of the design."

"It should give us some more space to store things while leaving the lobby for housing. I would like to add a few more buildings to the space, but I think this is enough for now. We should split one of the logs to make a little walkway across the groove I made and that should let us walk across without worrying about falling in the hole."Matching word to action, I was already picking through the sections we'd cut. We laid two halves of a log inside the groove and finished the other door into the space in record time.

"Congratulations on building the first vestibule of post-apocalyptic Earth," Ben said.

The man patted me on the shoulder as we all admired the sealed space I'd created. Sam and Danny were already trying to stake their claims over certain sections of the new room. The vestibule was far from perfect, and much larger than any pre-Landfall one actually was, but it was a starting point. The structure was a testament that returning to the surface was not a pipe dream, but a real possibility. It would require all of us to work together, Metier Crystal included, but we were on the right path. Our hands were already paving the way.

CHAPTER NINETEEN

Traces

With the vestibule area complete, I took an hour just to clear out the space within. My 'friends' quickly scattered back to their tasks when the prospect of more physical labor was brought up.

There had been an inordinate amount of stone spikes broken and set to the side from all the times I'd locked us in. Moving those out the western door and away from the more trafficked area took a fair bit of muscle. I hummed to myself as I planned the first project for the space, daydreaming of it while lugging the stone. I wasn't sure what use we could have for them, but at the very least, I'd be able to use them as reinforcements for buildings if push came to shove.

Once those were out of the way, I used a flat head shovel to clear up the last remaining bits of grass inside the vestibule. What was left was an unnaturally smooth floor ripe with possibilities.

"Step one: punch a hole in the wall," I said to myself. It was a funny thought that it was the first thing I planned to do with building, but it served a purpose.

I hefted my pickaxe and used the pointed end to mark off the eastern third or so of the vestibule. Then I picked a spot roughly at hip level and dug a wrist-wide hole to the outside. With the hole in place, and smoothed out with the help of a smaller shovel and gentle taps of my pick, I raised the ground right in front of the hole.

The draw of my mana barely bothered me as I cast <Earthen Barrier> four times over a few minutes. The first two raised the floor to make a rough table that I smoothed out using the chisel head on the back of my pick. When I'd regenerated enough mana to cast the skill again without discomfort, I consolidated the table. It wasn't at the degree of hardness that the walls or the floor had, but it was sturdier than the plastic counters inside the lobby room.

Once the shell of my workstation was complete, I carved out a deep cylindrical bowl with the top leveled just above the hole I'd made. With that complete, I repeated the process on the opposite side of the wall. Instead of carving just a deep bowl, however, I hollowed out the entire section. A half-dozen trips with a bucket to the pond, and very confused looks from Ben, Sam, and the cows, I had a trough of water filled. With the last two buckets, the water crested the hole and filled the basin inside.

It wasn't revolutionary, but it would make it easier to fill and have access to water within the vestibule for whatever I needed to work on. And the first thing I was going to work on would almost certainly require quenching.

I brought out a few chitin plates and laid them out on my work space. Unlike when I had first picked them up, the creature drop now gained a golden outline in my eyes.

<Chitin Plate>

<Attunement: Fire>

<Quotient 0 Density>

It didn't surprise me that the hand-sized pieces I'd selected all showed as Quotient 0. The bulk of what we had had come from the rat-sized insects. I'd been tempted to experiment with the larger pieces we'd gotten from the stronger ants, but getting the hang of infusing was more important than a piece that *might* be immediately helpful.

I pulled a handful of fire blobs from my pocket. The moment I set them on the workspace, they nearly rolled into my basin. Grumbling all the while, I dug five divots into the stone. With the infusions safely stored, I focused on the chitin plate.

The material was perfectly smooth everywhere but the edges, which were ridged. It had a fair bit of give to it. I opted for a worthwhile experiment, so I sent a message out to my friends not to be alarmed.

I took the piece of any chitin outside and set it against the stone wall. Taking several steps back, I fired a shot from my pistol into the center of the plate. To my utter amazement, the piece of ant carapace stopped the bullet. There were several spidering cracks all along the body of it, but it still held together when I bent it between my fingers.

Since I was already shooting for testing purposes, I put three bullets into the side of my magic-constructed vestibule. The stone took the blows fantastically well and only chipped a little bit.

After informing my friends through the comm that I was done wasting bullets, I patched up the wall and set the cracked chitin plate aside. No one said I couldn't start a new collection of stuff on the surface, and technically the infusion area would sort of be my office. With positive thoughts of building an actual office for myself at some point, I cast <Infusion> and flicked the unspooled thread into a fresh chitin plate.

The plate thankfully didn't melt, but I used another gardening tool to push it into the basin. There was a hiss as it plopped into the water, but nothing quite as explosive or violent as the shovel's experimental infusion. With the rake I'd used to push it into the basin, I fished out the plate and scanned it over. Other than a seemingly random pattern of darker red veins along the outer surface, it was unchanged. The information on the plate also hadn't changed other than the name, which left me scratching my chin. It hadn't turned into an 'item' like the shovel had, but it also wasn't prompting for more infusions.

<Quotient 0 Infused Chitin Plate>

<Attunement: Fire>

<Quotient 0 Density>

"Curious…" I sent my friends another message while I took the infused piece outside.

"Ronan, I just want you to be aware that the Bunker has a limited amount of ammunition. I'm aware I told you all not to be so restrictive with using the weapons at our disposal, but I didn't exactly mean this," Ben said.

"What are you even doing?" Danny asked. I heard her grunt, coinciding with the explosive sound of her <Flame Blast>skill somewhere to the north.

"Infusing," I responded cryptically, opting to fire into the infused chitin plate. My focus zeroed in on the piece of ant carapace as it *flexed*, then the bullet pinged to the ground. Just for good measure I fired two more shots back to back into the material, but it just wobbled with the force. My enhanced perception pointed out something surprising. There was a slight haze around the plate, somewhat similar but less intense than the one the Haze Wolf had generated when it attacked.

Somewhere in the back of my mind, I heard Danny and Ben asking more questions. Instead of paying any mind to Ben's 'lecturing voice' and Danny's 'you are ignoring me again, rock brain' speech, I picked up the chitin only to drop it again. It was scalding hot. I was no firearms expert, but I was fairly sure things that got shot didn't suddenly get hot like that. At the very least, not with a low caliber weapon. On a hunch, I went back inside the lobby and found the biggest hammer I could find. As it happened, it was a sledgehammer.

Like a proper scientist playing around with magic, I quenched the plate in my outside basin. After double checking that it was cool to the touch again, I laid it on the ground and whacked it as hard as I could. A gust of hot air blew past me as the sledge's head impacted the plate. When I touched it, the chitin was warm. I repeated the quenching-hit process a few times until I was fairly sure of my assessment.

"It's turning some of the force of the blow into heat..." I said to myself. Obviously there were a number of specifics I could test. What portion of the force would turn to heat, what the max threshold for force transference was, as well as how much abuse it could take overall. The sheer number of possibilities made my head spin. However, I needed to be realistic. The researchers downstairs got lost for *weeks* every time they encountered something while working on the implants. That was not a luxury I had. *Yet.*

With the main effect of the infused material at the very least identified, I decided to try one more thing. I left the plate on the ground and retrieved the pickaxe. Sam and Danny had teased me over the previous week about how I carried it everywhere, but I didn't mind. It was an odd thing to use as a weapon, that was for sure, but with my enhanced strength and perception, I liked the flexibility it offered. One such offensive benefit made itself known when I hit the infused chitin plate.

Instead of flexing like it had managed with the bullet and the sledgehammer, the pick side of my tool punched clear through the chitin. *Oops.*

My breath caught in my throat for a second when the heat released by the plate spiked, flash drying my mouth. The veins that had appeared on the chitin dulled before my very eyes and the heat blew away with the gentle breeze outside. I coughed and licked my lips in an attempt to get some moisture flowing. When that failed, I dunked my head into the outside trough of water.

"Note to self: keep mouth closed when testing infusions, material or item alike," I croaked. I'd only taken a little swig of the water in the trough, but it had done wonders for my throat. I tried not to think about the sheer amount of dirt and nastiness that was in the stagnant pond water.

I put the second broken plate next to my first and proceeded to infuse several more of them. The process was exhausting, as it drew my mana each time, but with each infusion, I could feel the strain lessen. I'd also felt something similar while using <Stone Spike> and <Earthen Barrier>. The only thing that seemed to remain somewhat equally exhausting was summoning the passive form of either of my skills. *Yet another thing to ask the Entity. If it knows.*

I was so lost in my thoughts, Sam's arrival went mostly unnoticed. When I dropped one of the plates in the basin and it hissed, he exclaimed in surprise and my focus finally landed on him. There was now a full stack of twelve plates on the right side of my workspace, plus the one cooling in the water.

"What the hell, Ron?" he asked, as he looked at the stack of enhanced chitin plates. "Are these all infused?"

It would have been easy to point out how quickly my friend distracted himself from his outrage, but I was excited to share the results of my afternoon of crafting and experimenting. When I explained that the plate hadn't turned into an 'item' like the shovel had for some reason, but had instead remained a component, he'd been disappointed. At the mention that it somehow converted kinetic energy into heat to lessen blows, his excitement matched my own.

"We need to get more infusions!" he said, motioning to my entire setup. "If there are even more magic effects like this, we've got to find them all. You think it will be consistent based on what you infuse?"

"Not sure. The heat the plate puts out is similar to the shovel, but I haven't tried to channel mana into it. I've only been hitting the plates and making more."

"Let me try. Shouldn't take long to check…" Sam drifted off as he grabbed hold of a chitin plate and summoned his direct skill magic circle. The veins on the plate brightened in response to the magic, but it didn't suck up the formation like the shovel had on activation.

We discussed possible causes for this. The simplest would be that the plate didn't respond to magic, only force, but we agreed that it was likely because it hadn't formed an item. There was no linked attribute. Of course, we couldn't be sure why it hadn't turned into an item, or if items could present themselves in some other way, but we felt it was a reasonable assumption.

It was during this debate that Daniela practically manifested into the room. If my perception hadn't increased, I wouldn't have noticed her approach at all before she ran into us. As it was, I barely had enough time to pull Sam out of the way. Danny stumbled into a roll and laid face up, panting. Sam and I were immediately on alert. I grabbed my pickaxe and he pulled the infused shovel from his belt.

"It's… all good… guys…" Daniela managed through ragged breaths. I didn't relax immediately since I spotted a red blur moving towards the entrance. When the shape stopped before the door, I realized it was Anthony. The ant didn't look winded, but its legs were shaking.

"Daniela, what the hell?" I asked, setting down my pick and turning a glare at my friend.

"I… found something!" She didn't elaborate. Sam's frown turned into a glare. "Okay, okay. Geez, you two are so serious all the time. I found a road. An old asphalt road, as far as I can tell."

A thrill of excitement flowed through me. There were traces of humanity left on the surface. Suddenly, the urge to explore I'd been suppressing jumped to the surface. I would never want to do that alone like Danny, not with the dangers of the wild, but with my friends?

"Did you find anything else?" I asked. She flinched slightly and I made sure to tone down my intensity a bit.

"I saw some kind of building in the distance, but I didn't go much further out. I've been moving up and down fairly quickly along the game trails in the hopes of avoiding anything outside of the Entity's range. I've been shifting east since I hit a wall with the ants. Their resilience to my fire makes them a pain to fight solo, but with my limited skills…" Daniela paused to glare at the Entity. I was sure I spotted it flaring its light when the woman turned around. "I opted to look for something else to fight. Based on what I saw, the game trail had to have been an old dirt road."

"You think that's what they used to get stuff over here to the Bunker?" Sam asked, taking a step back and helping her to her feet. Daniela absently pet Anthony when he nuzzled his mandibles against her leg. It looked like it should hurt, but she didn't seem bothered while talking to us.

"It's possible. I haven't seen anything else that could have been a road and even *I* know it takes a whole bunch of resources to build something like this place." She gestured vaguely behind us and down, where the Bunker entrance was.

"You're not wrong. I saw them working on this place when I was still in school. The speed with which they built it made me a bit hesitant to actually join it, but it was a better option than being annihilated on the surface." The three of us turned to see a downcast Ben leaning on a full-sized shovel. The shadow on his face could have been a result of the setting sun, but I doubted it. "I'll tell you all about it someday. I don't know if anyone other than your family, Elias, and myself ever spent time at this site."

As if trying to change the topic, he pointed an accusatory finger at Sam. "You forgot to bring water. Just because we can use the pond water on the plants doesn't mean I can drink it!"

"Oh, sorry," he said sheepishly. The blond scratched the back of his head awkwardly and immediately used me to explain his distraction.

"All I did was share my wonderful results of testing magically enhanced materials. How could you *not* be enthralled?" I gestured with a grandiose sweep of my arm to the pile of chitin plates. In the process, I also turned enough to see a woman in her late forties glaring at us. *I really need to install a doorbell or maybe some jingling bells on that Bunker door.*

"You four didn't even deem it relevant to welcome me? Have you lot lost track of time or your specifically emphasized request to the mayor, Ronan?" Ava narrowed her eyes when she spotted her daughter and her pet ant. "I hope you've been feeding that thing properly."

I honestly couldn't be surprised by Ms. Holmes' response. Out of the people living in the Bunker, those I could imagine being the least impacted by returning to the surface included both of Danny's parents. Ava would just brush the whole deal off as another problem to deal with, while Juan would go with the flow to a frustrating degree. I couldn't wait to see the pair help us take the surface.

"Ah, Mama. We… weren't expecting you," Daniela said, straightening up more than Ben's shovel. Anthony swiveled his head left and right as he tried to reconcile the strong family resemblance of the two Latinas. It was quite comical, since the poor ant looked thoroughly confused.

"Of course you weren't. And what is all this? I don't remember all this dark and gloomy cave nonsense last time I was aboveground." Ava gestured at my stone vestibule. "Would it kill you to have some light in here?"

Straight for the jugular is it? I winced at her words.

"Give the kids a break, Ava. You should be damned pleased with the work they've done here. Now, how about we get you up to speed, eh?" Ben said. I was surprised how quickly Teach had jumped in to defend us, but it emboldened me to respond as well. Only slightly, though. I was still terrified of Ava.

"We needed more room, and there are dangerous creatures all around on the surface. Putting in windows at this time would have compromised that."

She huffed but said nothing else. Instead, she cracked a smile and gave Danny a huge hug, kissing the top of her head. We were all a bit caught off guard, but Daniela responded as any of us would have. She immediately complained and tried to extract herself from her mother's embrace.

I suppose it's not how I would have reacted. No. Shake it off, Ron. No self-deprecation now. There are things to prioritize. I proceeded to gesture everyone inside. Our little gathering had taken longer than I realized and the light of day was already fading. Sam,

Ben, and I sealed the wooden doors while Danny led her mom into the lobby space.

Somehow, there was already a fifth bunk space set up that hadn't been there before. When I looked at Ben, he gave me a cheeky smile. He'd known Ava was coming and didn't tell us.

"Ms. Holmes, are there any updates you can give us about the Bunker?" I finally asked as Danny roasted potatoes and tomatoes in a bowl. Her mother plucked one of the probably scalding vegetables and chomped on it. She didn't give any outward indications that she'd been burned.

"Nothing other than a community meeting today. People voted on whether they would want to come topside or not," she said casually. She also gave Danny an appraising look that I didn't know the meaning of. Her daughter couldn't have seen it as she was focused on using her magic to cook, but I hadn't missed it.

"What was the verdict?" Ben asked, leaning forward on his crate-bed. We'd opted to start using the crates as chairs, and simply rolling up our bedding for the day. It was a nice way of having everyone gathering together for meals, and served as an impromptu 'round table' for important discussions.

"We only have five surface volunteers as of right now, myself included."

"People don't want to return to the surface?" Sam asked in confusion. Ben sighed loudly. I could feel my eyebrow twitch that the question even had to be asked.

"It isn't that they don't want to come back to the surface. If I had to guess, it's more along the lines of them being scared. I pride myself on being fairly flexible." Ava snorted at Ben's comment and he pointedly ignored her. "But you need to remember that everyone in the Bunker is older than forty, other than you three. Life in the Bunker was incredibly boring, but it's incredibly *safe*. Up here? Not even remotely. The information we've made everyone aware of regarding your first trip up, as well as my own, sent many people running. Figuratively speaking."

My old teacher had a point. It was a point I hated, because it made sense and would inadvertently limit us. There was only so much we could expand, or would *need* to expand, if there were only a few of us. "It's not as much of a problem now. Mayor Barnes told me he thought they might not be able to make more than six implants at the moment, so getting more people on the surface wouldn't be possible."

Ava visibly winced. That couldn't have been good.

"Please tell me there isn't more bad news," I said.

"It's not the worst, but we may have gotten a bit ambitious with our implant making. Elias and I felt confident enough to make one on our own while Alan worked on another. Suffice it to say, we are not nearly as good as Alan. I would expect two more at most."

I sighed. Loudly. The weight of responsibility I'd put on my shoulders grew slightly. We wouldn't have nearly as much help as I hoped for on the surface.

"It's alright, Ronan. We'll figure it out. We waited almost thirty years for this, it doesn't have to happen immediately," Ben said, rising and placing a supporting hand on my shoulder. Sam and Danny smiled at me. Daniela even gave me a thumbs up, like that was what I wanted to see.

"Did I miss something? I thought you would be the one making decisions, Ben?" Ava asked. She looked downright puzzled about the exchange.

"Mama, Ron has always been our leader. Sure, he's kind of lazy, and stubborn, and honestly a little borked, considering how he plays with magic," I sent a glare in her direction, "but he's not led us astray. Plus, I'd rather him be at the front when we get attacked. He's the one with stone skin."

"Stone... skin?" Ava seemed to do a double-take and looked intently at me.

I gave her a smirk and a shrug. "That's a long story. I never intended to be a leader, but I can't shake these two off my tail." Sam punched me in the arm at that. "I never said I *wanted* to!"

We all laughed, and Ben added his own two cents. "This is

not our world anymore, Ava. It is theirs. Ours is long gone, but we can hopefully help them build."

The mood sobered at that, and I was once again reminded that coming to the surface wasn't only a big change for me and my friends. The other Bunker members were survivors of Landfall. Their entire lives and families were gone. In a bid to change topics back to our original conversation, I asked the next most relevant question.

"Who agreed to come up?"

"That would be me and Juan—but he has to remain because they still need a cook—Dale, Alan and Emilio." Ava counted off on her fingers. "Elias wanted to come, but basically the entire population opposed that. So much for free will."

It didn't surprise me that my fa—uncle was among the volunteers. Not that his job wasn't essential, but with Sam subsidizing the food of the Bunker and Sam's father managing the waste treatment floor, he should have been more than free to spend time on the surface. Being closer to me, regardless of what it took, was probably at the top of his list. That was a whole can of emotional worms I didn't want to open, but I knew my uncle would be invaluable on the surface. "Alan? And which Emilio, C or D?"

"Cantero. He didn't even say anything, he just raised his hand when we asked who was willing to get the implants to go topside." Ava shuddered. "He's like a ghost sometimes."

"He really is silent. One time, he came to request two water filters from me and he just stood there for thirty minutes, without calling out. I know, I checked the security cameras," Ben said.

"Right. As for Alan, he thinks being on the surface will let him push his research further. We agreed that he would get the last implant he could make. So we will probably get *two* people or just him next time. Just in case there is a complication while making the implants," Ava explained.

We ate in silence for several minutes. The only sound was the wet crunch of potato wedges and roasted tomatoes. Daniela had really outdone herself, even without any real seasonings. The meal managed to distract me enough from my emotions to formulate a plan moving forward. *If people don't think the surface is safe, then all I have to do is* make it *safe. How hard could that be?* I would have laughed out loud at that thought had my mouth not been full of starchy goodness.

The rest of the evening was spent running my plans by all of our growing surface members. There had been a major addition—a delay, if I wanted to be honest to my own perception of the situation—but it had to be done. An old saying drifted through my mind, something about it 'taking a village' to raise a child. While a budding camp on the surface wasn't necessarily an infant, what was a camp without people?

CHAPTER TWENTY

Elder Talkin' To

"Is this really necessary?" Samuel asked, adjusting the straps on his armored vest for the fifth time.

"Do we need air to live?" I shot back.

"I don't know, do we?" Sam asked, tapping his chin in contemplation.

I rolled my eyes so hard I thought they might fall right out of the sockets. "Rhetorical question, Sam."

"Really don't see why you need to head down to talk to everyone, much less bring me with you!"

"If they want to quiver in their recycled plastic boots, then they are going to get an earful from me. I'm not going to force anyone to come to the surface, but the only candidates are our immediate family and a handful of others! Out of three dozen people, there needs to be more courage piled up even if it takes some peer pressure."

"Truly inspiring the masses here," Sam said, taking his own turn to roll his eyes. "Let's just get this over with. The farm still needs a few more touches before we can go ahead with your plans."

There was no point arguing, so the two of us made our way

towards the Bunker doors. A much less strenuous process thanks to our improved attributes, the two of us found ourselves back on the engineering floor a few minutes later.

My feet froze for a moment as emotions I'd been keen to ignore swirled through me. The revelations of the last time I'd gone down to the Bunker pulled at my focus, fraying it before I'd even started 'preaching,' as I was sure Daniela would call it. A comforting hand pat me on the shoulder, bringing my derailed thoughts back in order. "Thanks, Sam."

"Just be glad it was me and not Danny, otherwise that hand would have gone right for your temple," the blond said, chuckling.

The two of us made our way down familiar stairs that now seemed claustrophobic in comparison. The floors passed us one after the other before we arrived at the laboratory floor. We were the only ones with implants so communicating, even when through the blast doors, required good ol' fashioned walking. Not surprising either of us, we found our targets working away behind the glass walls.

Elias turned to scan through a monitor when he noticed the two of us standing cross-armed. The old man nearly leapt straight to his death, but managed to compose himself after a few minutes. Alan did nothing more than wave casually over his shoulder as the implant he was working on took his whole focus.

"Ronan! Samuel! I wasn't expecting you two to come down so soon after Ava left," the old mayor said, dabbing at some of the sweat on his face.

"I'll get right to the point, sir. We want to talk to the Bunker. All of the Bunker," I said, not mincing words.

"You... Does this have something to do with the implants?" Elias asked, clearly unsure about how to deal with my aggressive approach.

"In a way. Can you gather them for us? We'll be waiting on the engineering floor." I waited long enough for Elias to give me an uncertain nod before returning to the stairwell. Sam followed a step behind.

"That really the best way to go about this?" Sam asked. "Elias has never really worked against us."

I paused, mulling over my words and using my newfound discomfort with the Bunker to harden my resolve. "You're right, but he also still sees us as people that need to be managed. Meek balance isn't going to cut it when things are trying to kill you."

"And that's how you want to appeal to the other Bunkerites? Maybe we would have been better off sending Danny for this."

"What would you have me do? Just the fact that people we've known our whole lives want to fold like a bad hand hurts. I'm not going to take it laying down."

Samuel didn't argue any more, and the two of us made our way to the engineering floor unimpeded. Unsure of how things were going to play out, we pulled chairs and a handful of benches from the storage rooms and laid them out facing the Bunker exit. Then, we stood patiently.

Surprising no one, my uncle was the first to arrive to our impromptu meeting. After waving at us, Dale hovered uncertainly at the edge of the rows of chairs. My chest tightened as he picked a seat close, but on the far side of me. I'd been the one to push him away, but the 'space' he was giving me held a physical weight I hadn't expected. Thankfully, sources of frustration quickly made themselves manifest and my thoughts turned from my dad.

Most of the members of the Bunker were well into their fifties with a handful of exceptions. As each of them arrived to the engineering floor, they got the distinct displeasure of being glared at by one of the youngest three members of the Bunker. The response to that was mixed, and I quickly realized that the choice of returning to the surface wasn't as clear cut as I expected. Hesitance, fear, and a healthy dose of actual anger was intermingled in the faces of the Bunkerites.

Despite the cues that my improved perception was handing out like candy, I knew that I needed to present the facts and challenge their expectations. If that didn't work, then the surface wouldn't be a place for them anyhow; their contributions would be negligible or detrimental.

As I took a mental attendance of everyone present, I realized that Elias had somehow managed to actually get the entire Bunker, sans those above ground, to show up. With them all arrayed before me, my confidence flagged a bit. Gritting my teeth through the surging fears, I started to speak.

"Ava brought to my attention that only a small number of you wish to return to the surface. While I understand there is probably some hesitation due to fear of the world outside, or even the implant procedure itself, I want to reassure you that it will not harm you."

I started pacing, working my way through my thoughts and disappointment in their initial responses. "The surface is as safe as it is going to get without more help. Danny, Sam, and I can only do so much, and your help would change everything. Something we've discovered the more time we spend on the surface is the immediate benefits. Health, unparalleled. Space, unbound.

"By returning to the surface, you aren't only helping us but you are helping yourselves! I'm sure you've all been made aware of Sam's cultivation efforts," I said, gesturing to Samuel even as he blushed. I made a point to look at those who spent the bulk of their time on the greenhouse floor. "We aren't a closed system anymore, and it would be foolish to ignore it."

"You would have us turn into monsters, then," said Smith. Disdain dripped with every word. He'd been one of the angry faces I'd seen enter the floor. "We saw what your father did. What's to say you aren't the same?"

"Our powers are safe. I understand that my… father struck fear into you; I ask that you recognize that he didn't hurt any of you. I'm not trying to be callous, but would the Bunker have survived as long without returning to the surface had he not done what he did?"

The Bunkerites murmured amidst themselves and I felt the pang in my chest again. People I'd trusted to have my back and who'd supported our efforts with the implants to our face were faltering under uncertainty.

"Punch me in the face," I told Sam through the implant.

The blond blinked, taking a moment to turn to me as he responded through the implant. "Come again?"

"Punch me. In the face, if you would."

Samuel wavered for a moment, but then shrugged and clocked me right in the jaw. Stars flashed in my vision for a moment, but I'd been bracing for it. The force was also dispersed gently through my skin, reducing the actual damage that punched through to my brain. The sound of flesh on flesh silenced the discontent discussions in the background. I had regained their undivided attention even if some looked more frightened than before.

Samuel shook his hand out, blood already dripping from where he'd scraped his knuckles on my Limestone Skin. I rubbed my jaw as I gestured to Samuel. "Could you use your magic, Sam?"

Giving me a knowing look, the blond flourished his formation of the <Health Bump> spell chain before healing himself. The skin scabbed over before the scabs themselves shrunk visibly, leaving mostly unblemished skin behind. Also making a show of the gesture, he placed his spell chain against my cheek and healing energies cleared away the last bits of my discomfort.

"We don't know what we are truly capable of, but living in fear and remaining in the Bunker does not provide the solution.With the help of the Metier Crystal assisting us, you don't even need an implant to simply live on the surface."

"You would have us risk our lives when nothing remains?" My hearing picked out Alexia's words from the crowd. Some of those near her turned to her and June placed a comforting hand on her shoulder.

"I don't want you to risk your lives!" I said, some of my frustrations leaking through. "I want you to *live* your lives! Alan is working on the last of the titanium we have so that more of us can forge our way. We plan to reach further and look deeper, so that our powers become your strength. We don't want the people we think of as family to be discarded, or forgotten, or to simply waste away in a hole in the ground!

"You need to be willing, if not actively working to return to the surface. Now that the door has been thrown open, on your pasts *and* on your futures, you can't expect things to remain the same!"

"The more things change, the more they stay the same," someone mumbled from within the crowd.

It took all I had not to growl at the people arrayed before me. There was a certain safety in numbers that they had against me and Samuel. Their united front against returning topside helped them remain detached from the responsibility they held to the future of mankind. I was almost sure that some even justified their hand in our education as that contribution I was asking of them now.

I huffed, crossing my arms and doubling down on my glare. Many of the people gathered couldn't even meet my eyes.

"I thought we all wanted to return to the surface, but I suppose I was wrong. Regardless of what you all contribute, I am going to build a future up there. I may have been born here, but I belong up there. You all not realizing that, *especially* when you *were* born on the surface, is… sad. Life in the Bunker might be cozy, but if your life doesn't leave a mark, did you really live?"

Most of the fear had been reduced to wariness and the uncertainty had been changed to curiosity. Samuel stepped forward, prompting everyone to ask their questions in the hopes of us addressing their concerns. People scattered almost imme-diately, but most remained in the area even as some fled further below.

I barely heard Sam as he reassured people to the best of his ability, leaning on his new healing powers to make the interac-tion doubly effective. It was one thing to see healing and another to be rejuvenated by it yourself. The fact that most of the residents had one ache or another also worked in his favor.

I wasn't sure if it was my demeanor, or my very verbal response to their response to the surface, but no one approached me. I panned my eyes across the gathered crowd, burning their expressions of hesitation into my mind. It hadn't turned out how I wanted, but I would take uncertainty over outright denial. Sprinkled amidst them were our immediate family, beacons of the hope to live free again. My eyes lingered on Dale, and I hesitated to approach him. With a knowing shake of his head, my uncle stepped away and started to engage people in conversation. It was so natural, so smooth, that my speech could be considered garbled gibberish.

Almost an hour passed in that fashion. No further questions reached us as I pulled Samuel along behind me. Elias had expressed interest in discussing things further, but I'd cited other priorities. As much as I worried for the people of the Bunker, they could take care of themselves. The surface needed trail-blazers, and the job title was practically stamped into our implants.

CHAPTER TWENTY-ONE

Away from Home

"Are you sure you all have everything you need?" Ava asked for the seven hundred and ninety third time.

"I believe we do, Ms. Holmes. Much better packed than my last saunter through the woods," I said, pointing over my shoulder at the hiking pack stuffed with supplies.

"From what I hear, that shouldn't be reassuring at all, Ronan. And please, just call me Ava. You were right. You are no longer children, and I should also reciprocate the respect you all have always given me." She crouched lower in an attempt to whisper to me alone. It wasn't at a level that our enhanced senses wouldn't have picked up, but I was sure that was deliberate. "But you keep them safe, or you'll make me go out there."

She'd said that like she had access to magic or firearms much more powerful than what we had, but I had no doubt she *would* come after us if it came to it. We'd planned to be out overnight, two at most, so the bar for returning was set.

"You kids have fun!" Ben said, casually holding a rifle up on his shoulder. Daniela's mother was similarly armed.

"Benjamin! They aren't going to go watch a movie or out to a restaurant!" Ava said, outraged.

"True, but what would you rather they do? Be miserable?" he asked, smirking in the dawn light. Ava mumbled a number of expletives in his direction. Daniela and I laughed as we walked closer to where she'd been clearcutting trees.

"Come on, veg head. We are burning daylight!" Danny said, patting Anthony's head as the ant walked towards the pair of Landfall survivors. She assured me the Fire Ant wanted to accompany us, but she'd instructed him to protect Ben and her mom. For the first time, I noticed how much larger he'd grown as he stood next to Ben. Still dog-sized, but possibly a bigger breed like a Labrador or German Shepard. As I frowned in its direction, strings of information populated in my vision.

<Anthony (Fire Ant)>

<Attunement: Fire>

<Refinement: N/A>

<Perceived Metier Quotient: 1>

Why didn't I think to try to inspect him before?His Quotient is higher. It also shows his name, curious. Good to know that we can somehow get domesticated creatures to grow in lev—

"*Samuel!*" Daniela shouted right by my ear. I turned to see our blond-headed friend speaking feverishly fast to Ben, all the while walking in reverse.

"And make sure Ray gets at least two handfuls a day. If he looks ornery, just give him an extra one. Oh, and make sure to mend the fence on the south. One of the—"

"I got it, Sam. Shouldn't be a problem to deal with the herd while you are away," Ben said. I could hear the exasperation in his tone. Knowing how neurotic Sam could be, I pitied the amount of tasks he'd left our old teacher. Sam eventually turned around, and both Ben and Ava waved in our direction. Anthony flicked his antenna from side to side.

"Did my mom tell you about the medical titanium stuff?" Danny asked as she took the lead. It looked like a straight shot for most of the way, so I just made sure to keep an eye on either side of the cut path.

"Something about medical grade kits and Ti-6Al-4VELI?" I said.

"Wow, you really do know how to pay attention," Danny said.

"I think that's more a selective memory type issue than an attention issue, Danny. If you recall, Ronan is very good at many things and very bad at others." Sam took the opportunity to throw out a barb.

"Oy! I would say I am mediocre to decent at least. We just have different interests," I said, crossing my arms.

"Right. I don't know if I could even call your cooking skills mediocre, though. Doubt that you'd be able to muster something even if the Entity put the knowledge straight into your head as a skill." Danny laughed along with Sam.

I kept my mouth shut. This was one of those exchanges where the more I talked, the more flustered I would get and they would just end up winning. None of that so early into the trip. We all walked in silence for several minutes before Sam threw out the most impatient sentence known to road trip movies. "Are we there yet?"

"Samuel, we've been walking for less than fifteen minutes. Sure it's only about a mile to the road, but we aren't in a rush to get anywhere. We don't even know if there is *anywhere* to get to," Danny said, glaring in his direction.

"But, Raymond and the farm—"

"Will be fine. Ben and my mom are adults, they can handle some responsibility."

"Unlike someone I know," I mumbled under my breath to Sam.

"Hey, I heard—" When she turned around, a <Flame Blast>manifested immediately in her hand. Instinctively, Sam and I threw ourselves to the side in clumsy rolls. The ball of fire traveled in a slight arc to splash against the side of a tree not far behind us.

As much as I knew she might have wanted to splash *us* with the fire attack, I knew she would never actually hurt us. Instead of questioning why she lobbed magic behind us, we turned and poised at the ready. A <Stone Spike> spell chain appeared in my left hand while I unslung the pickaxe from my back. It was clumsy and slow, but I still kept my eyes trained on where the attack had landed. When the flames cleared, I saw the telltale yellow of a banana spider as it scurried into the woods. Then it was gone.

"I must have cut through their territory. This is the third or fourth I've seen, but they run every time I hit them with magic." Daniela had pulled out one of the Haze Wolf fangs and was gripping it as a dagger. Sam had pulled out the infused shovel. I wasn't sure what he planned to do with that, but at least he also had a skill at the ready in hand.

"That would have been nice to know, Danny!" I said, frowning as I turned back to look at the flames. She didn't reply right away, instead she put away the fang and used her passive magic to snuff the flames. They'd been starting to spread. I resisted the urge to ask her how her heating ability worked like that. Instead, I stared at her expectantly.

"They never did anything but run away! Plus, with us three, I didn't think it would even be an issue. There've never been more than two that I've seen," she said. She crossed her arms and huffed.

"I agree with Ron on this. That would have been good information to have," Sam said, crossing his own arms. "I think we need to be on the same page moving forward with combat. As much as I am sure he dreads thinking about it, he's got the most experience with the spiders."

My body shivered involuntarily as I remembered how close I got to being a meal. However, I agreed with Daniela's assessment. "I don't think you are wrong, Danny. Avoiding a direct encounter with the spiders is also really high up on my list, and if they avoid your fire, then we should take advantage of that. As for telling us... that is part of why you were scouting. To tell us the good *and* the bad."

Daniela looked properly mollified, so I took the lead as she hung back. It was rare that I was the strict one in our group, but I knew Daniela could be a bit flippant about such things. The rest of the walk went on in silence and without any new encounters. When I spotted the broken fragments of roadway, a skip entered my step and I was the first to arrive on the asphalt.

It was indeed a road, but the earth had moved fiercely to reclaim it. Of what I knew was probably a near thirty foot wide road, possibly ten feet remained in the middle. It ended abruptly and stretched into the distance to the north, where I could see an overgrown structure. I scanned the area around the road. Black rocks littered all around the trees where the shoulders of the road would have been. Even the portion at the center was cracked by tree roots and tough grasses that couldn't care less that humans had once trod there.

When my friends reached me, I was running the rocks through my finger and poking the sections of road that had held together through the quarter century after Landfall.

"That's the building I told you about. Should only take a few minutes to get there," Danny said, pointing to the overgrown mess of vines and moss. She'd definitely lost some of her enthusiasm after our encounter with the spider, but I only felt a bit guilty. It was important information.

The three of us still discussed what the building could be from a distance. It didn't look like a warehouse, or a house-house for that matter. When we were less than a hundred feet away, it became obvious what we were looking at.

"It's a gas station," Sam said. I agreed. Six overgrown fuel pumps rose out of the ground. Most of the metal was rusted and the sections not covered in plant matter had chunks missing. The front windows of the building were missing, but we could see a long counter inside as well as several tipped shelves and displays.

The soft crunch of the asphalt changed as I walked onto the concrete slabs of the gas station's foundation. There wasn't a single one that had escaped untouched, but the concrete had held up much better to the test of time than the asphalt. The three of us kept our weapons at the ready as we walked closer to the building. It was unlikely that anything would make their home inside something so covered in rust and, from what I could tell, spilled oils and chemicals.

I wasn't sure how mana reacted with chemicals, but my hunch was explosively or poisonously. Neither appealed to me, so I stayed outside of the building proper. The gas station looked like one big room with another far in the back corner. I eyed some of the metal scattered around the place and made a note to possibly try to collect it in the future. Most of it would probably not be usable, but I didn't think there were still metal mines left on the surface anywhere. Especially not in post-apocalypse Florida.

When I explained my reasoning, my friends agreed that it would be a good place to try to grab materials in the future. Daniela took some time to clear the plant matter away with her passive skill, exposing the remains of a red and yellow paint pattern before it flaked off under the heat. Once that was done, there wasn't much more to the area, so we continued to follow the road east.

"How far is the town of Wildwood?" I asked, trying to gauge the distance using my implant while also paying attention to the road. I wasn't very successful.

"Give me a sec, I'll look it up. Keep an eye out for me." Sam placed his arm on my shoulder and spaced out. Concentrating on looking at the LPS, he used me to guide his steps.

"This road doesn't show up on the pre-Landfall map. Based on where the map shows us, we are about a mile and a half from the main road, 301, which runs north-south. The city seems pretty evenly split with The Villages to the north and the actual city of Wildwood more to the south along the main road."

"Okay, we should get to the main road and then we'll decide what to do from there," I said, tapping Sam on the shoulder to signal him to leave the map for now. With a semblance of a direction, we headed east on the road.

As we walked, I could hear creatures off in the woods to either side, but nothing jumped out to attack us. The whole time, I focused on trying to identify some of the creatures. Several didn't appear to be attuned, but three I spotted were. One was an air squirrel like we'd seen. In fact, that was what I saw the most. Mostly blurs of gray that I was fairly sure were the critters traversing the woods. The other two were completely new.

An earth-attuned deer plowed right through a tree with ease, froze on the spot when it saw us, then bolted back the way it'd come. The creature had barely been within view long enough for me to notice it was Quotient Level 3. The last, a Quotient 1 death-attuned skunk strolled across the road with not a care in the world. Even without being born on the surface, we'd been raised with media from before Landfall. Skunks were at the very top of the list of animals *not* to mess with on a primal level.

Both of the creatures, and the way we'd encountered them, once again reminded us that we were just another group of animals moving through the forest to them. Potential prey for another predator. Daniela's movements lost some of the comfort she'd been moving with, even after being rebuked about the spider's presence. She now kept her hand on her pistol and her head swiveled to the side more often. While it wasn't exactly the reaction I'd hoped to incite in her, I wouldn't complain about it.

Not long after encountering the skunk, the road widened. Even with the strength of the forest reclaiming most of the road, a much wider swath of asphalt remained in the center. Some ways north, I could see the crumbled ruins of several buildings. Many looked like they'd been hit by more than age, erosion, and overgrown trees. That was certainly a concern, but they could prove to be good sources of materials for our growing fort.

To the south, maybe a thousand feet away, I could see a road median split the asphalt. While the north remained a consistent width, more or less, the median provided yet another avenue for the trees to tear up the road. What immediately made me decide that I wanted *nothing* to do with going south was the information that populated in my eyesight.

<Coconut Palm>

<Attunement: Earth>

<Refinement: Geodes>

<Perceived Metier Quotient: 6>

A tree taller than the others swayed gently in the wind. I could see several clusters of coconuts at the top of the palm, each glimmering like hidden pearls. My friends were deep into discussing which direction we should try to go by the time I was able to gather enough of my wits to join them.

"North. Yep. North."

"What? Why?" Sam asked, confused. All I did was point to the tree in the distance. He started walking in the tree's direction. I was surprised we'd not seen any attuned plants, but if this was going to be how we found them, then I wasn't sure I *wanted* to find any.

"Fair. North's got my vote," Samuel said, stiffening then walking deliberately slow back towards me.

"What are you two hemming and hawing about?" Daniela had to walk a full fifty feet closer to the tree before she stopped, turned around, and dashed back to our group. "Never mind. Let's go."

A frown crossed my face as I realized that Daniela's perception was so much lower. It was possible there were other factors in getting the implant to trigger an information reading, but it was something to keep in mind. Just because she was the fastest member of our group didn't mean she needed to *always* be the scout. I shook off that train of thought as I realized my friends were already on the move.

With the frightening prospect that a tree could kill us, and had probably killed more things than the three of us, we made terrible progress along the road. With the appearance of our first attuned tree, I grew suspicious of every other tree we encountered. We were in a forest, after all, surely there had to be more attuned plants.

I tried to keep a mental tally of all the structures we encountered. However, few, if any, looked accessible. Most of them looked like they would be more trouble than they were worth at the moment, so I just filed them away in the back of my mind.

When the sun reached its zenith, we made camp in the shade of a standard tree. Still paranoid, I checked all the nearby trees by stabbing them with a thrown rock and a scan before I set up an outward-facing ring of spikes to surround our camp. It wouldn't do much against some of the bigger creatures we'd encountered, but I hoped it would deter or at least give us a chance to respond to any threat.

While we were eating lunch, we discussed what we hoped to find.

"I think updating the map should be a priority," Danny said. "Like that tree, we need to know what we need to watch out for. Maybe I can get my mom to help update the map whenever she goes down below ground."

"That's a good idea. I also think gathering materials should be a focus for us. I know this is just getting a look at what's around us, but getting more titanium and other metals to use back at the Bunker will be important," I said, washing down the insta-meal with a swig of water. It was important *not* to get a proper taste of it.

"Didn't know you were an aspiring blacksmith, Ron?" Sam said, repeating a similar procedure with his food. I was glad he was able to magically boost those tomatoes more and more each time I ate one of the insta-meals.

"I'm not, but I think we'll need the metal for equipment and tools. Maybe even a proper cart for Raymond. The titanium is for the implants, obviously."

"Should we be focused on finding some of that? None of the people in the Bunker really want to come to the surface," Danny said. "All your little sermon did was stir the pot."

I frowned as I thought about how our meeting with the

other Bunkerites had gone. "True, but I still want them to have the option. Plus, it is only a matter of time before we go looking for the other Bunkers. Having implants ready for *those* people to come topside will be the key in having multiple camps."

"You really are being ambitious. Are you sure we shouldn't temper our expectations a bit, Ron? What's to say the other Bunkers survived? What's to say there even *are* other people our age? You heard them down in the Bunker, Ava only survived with the help of a crystal. What are we—"

"We can't think like that. We'll figure something out. Plus, there is always the possibility that—" I cut myself off as a wave of nausea rippled through me. My friends didn't notice it. I jumped to my feet, abandoning the last of my meal. A moment later, the sensation traveled up my legs and into my gut. It was very similar to the discomfort I'd felt when I overdrew my mana, and I was not soon to forget that feeling. "Something's coming."

My friends set down their meals and moved to flank me on either side. Already my pickaxe had found its way to my hands. I pressed tightly against my stone spike wall, watching the trees around us and the road to our left. A quartet of shadowy shapes walked purposefully down the road, barely paying attention to their surroundings. My blood pumped loudly in my ears as I considered the possibility that one of my biggest hopes would be a reality.

When the twisted features of two humanoids, a wolfhound, and a rolling gelatinous mass became clearly visible, my heart sank. When the wolfhound turned pitch black eyes in my direction, it jumped back into my throat.

CHAPTER TWENTY-TWO

Insidious Tendrils

"That's not good," I said. The wolfhound snarled and a fire flared along its spine. "That's much worse."

While the creature wasn't anywhere near the size of the Haze Wolf, the heat didn't look any less potent. Having spotted us, the humanoids turned in our direction and promptly unleashed blasts of ice and fire respectively.

"<Earthen Barrier>!" I said, using my voice to focus on the skill faster. The rising earth used my stone spikes to climb higher and a proper barrier blocked the blows from the humanoids. "Return fire, please!" I shouted over the tinkle of shattering glass.

My friends finally snapped out of their shock. Daniela let out two gunshots, one striking the wolfhound and the other one of the humanoids. Instead of the spray of blood as I'd expected, a gout of fire flared from the wound. The gelatinous mass started to roll in our direction while the humanoids took cover on the opposing side of the roadway. There wasn't much to their expressions but an eerie, smooth head, yet they seemed somewhat agitated.

The wolfhound shook off the shot and bolted in our direction. A trail of flame appeared on the ground as it approached, and I concentrated on its path. My eyes tracked its movement and I cast a half strength <Stone Spike> where I anticipated the wolfhound would be. The tip of my spike was off, but I still managed to get the creature to crash into the body of it.

"Sam, try to snag it!" Without needing much more prompting, the magic circle for his vine skill transformed the grass around the stunned wolfhound. With the hound dealt with for the moment, I had enough time to see Danny hammer the slime with <Flame Blast>. The blob ignored the attack almost completely, and I only heard the slight hiss of something boiling for a second before the creature's rolling put out the fire. Then it *oozed* through the gaps in my spikes and directly onto me.

"Ronan!" Sam shouted a second before all I could see was green and brown sludge.

Without thinking, and suffering the price for drawing on my mana too soon, I impaled the blob with two half-cost <Stone Spikes>. It only marginally slowed the creature, or whatever it was, before it started to part its body around them. "Don't worry about me, focus on those things. Danny, make sure you kill the hound!"

"What do you think I've been working on!" she shouted, letting loose with her gun again. I didn't get to pay much more attention to their engagement as the slime rolled through my spikes and headed straight for me. Thick, slimy residue remained on my spikes and the creature was a tad smaller than when it had oozed through our defenses.

"Oh no you don't," I hissed, calling forth my mana, but just in its passive form. The creature was subject to damage, all I needed was to deliver solid blows. I two-handed my pickaxe and swung wide across its body. The majority of it ignored the blow, but a wet splat off to my left told me I'd removed some of the creature's mass.

There was no way for me to know if the compressing effect of my magic worked on the slime, but it certainly *felt* like it was adding more force to my blows. Regardless, the creature didn't seem fazed by my attack and instead continued to roll forward unimpeded. That was when I started hammering it with blow after blow using the chisel side of my pick. It wasn't as effective as a shovel, but slowly I could see the gelatinous creature shrink.

When the creature was about to my waist, it stopped moving. My next blow had been anticipating its continued motion and I swung without any resistance. The top-heavy weapon carried me to the side and down to a knee. Surprisingly, instead of capitalizing on my blunder, the creature *reshaped* itself into a wall and *ate* a fireball that had been aimed at me. My eyes traced the origin of the attack, and I could see that the fire humanoid had crossed the street and was bolstering the wolfhound somehow. Its flames were brighter and more intense than before.

I heard a growl of frustration from Daniela, but quickly concentrated back on the gel. It still hadn't advanced, but the top portion of its body thinned into some kind of amorphous appendage and waved. Waved. Like a friendly child might have to a stranger. I was so stunned, I actually waved back in response, forgetting where I was until a splash of frost hit my barrier not far from Sam's side of the fight.

"If you aren't going to attack right now… Sam, Danny! Switch sides. Samuel, try to buy time for an <Ember Wisp>."

"What about the slime!?" Sam ducked out of the way of another blast of ice before spotting the waving slime. The size to which his eyes opened would have been perfect for a cartoon character. "What the hell are you doing, Ron?"

"I think he's friendly!" I said, keeping an eye on the slime, but moving to Danny's side of the barricade. A nudge from me sent her back over to where the icy humanoid was attacking.

"He came with the things shooting magic bolts at us, rock brains. How is he friendly!?" Danny asked in outrage. Her eyes were focused on the skill in her hand just as her wisp took to the air. "Get the ice dude!"

With those simple instructions, the mana construct flew ten feet up into the air and zoomed across to the left.

I eyed my mana and winced. The initial attack had taken most of it, and I had only regenerated enough for a few half-powered spikes. I didn't get to deliberate much because the wolfhound had managed to free itself. The fire humanoid was standing still behind a tree that was charring just from its presence, but the incoming lupine threat removed any chance of striking it.

The hound leapt over my barrier easily, aiming for where Danny was recovering. There was a deep blush along her body and I knew she had to be close to her mana limits. I pulled my pistol out and fired into the hound at close range. The sound left my ears ringing a bit and the creature managed to shrug off the damage somehow, but it focused its attention on me. *Good enough.*

I roared a primal scream as I charged it with my pickaxe held out in front of me. Clearly, the creature hadn't been expecting that because it tried to backpedal out of the way.My skin hissed under the blaze, and for once I felt the effect of my Limestone Skin protect me from the worst of the fire.

With the metal head of my pick between us, I concentrated on the hound's torso. A <Stone Spike> ripped clear into the hound's ribcage and through its sternum. Unfortunately, the skill had been aimed toward me. *Worth it,* I thought with a grimace. My own spike tore a gash in my left shoulder, but thankfully my skin and adrenaline mitigated most of the pain of the engagement.

The hound twitched, still alive, but incapacitated thanks to its impalement. Despite its near-dead state, thermodynamics still snuck into the situation. The once-on-fire creature still threatened to give me a severe burn just from exposure. My legs failed to hold me up and I pitched forward.

"Woah there. <Health Bump>!" Sam slapped my injured shoulder and sat me down before peeking over the top of the wall and letting loose with his own gun. A howl marked that he'd hit at least once. Daniela was on the ground, reloading her gun with shaky hands, and I slid closer.

"I'm… almost out. Is that ice… dead?" Thick drops of sweat rolled down her forehead and I fumbled with one of our packs for water. Instead of just giving it to her, I dumped half on her head *then* handed it over. A thin mist rose off her body, and I could only hope she hadn't pushed herself past her mana pool.

At some point, the blob rolled closer. When it nudged me with its appendage, I very nearly sent a spike through it. It used its limb to point to the right, and I saw the fire humanoid was moving to flank us. Sam and the <Ember Wisp> were focused on dealing with the ice one while we'd hunkered down to try to recover a bit. The small, lobbed flames of the wisp crashed against the freezing projectiles, seemingly neutralizing the energy of the attacks.

A string of expletives ripped themselves out of my mouth at the oversight. As the one with the highest perception and the leader of our group, I should have been aware of where all of our enemies were regardless of who I was directly fighting. Saving that internal beratement for another time, I sent two half-powered <Stone Spikes> at the fire humanoid. The first it blasted with a concentrated explosion of fire as the spike formed. The second, it *let* hit. Instead of punching right through like I expected, the creature caught it with its arms. A moment later, the fiery aura that clung tightly to its skin flared just like the hound's had done, and it was charging towards me.

A stone spike appeared in its path, but it only managed to clip the creature. Its fiery cloak diminished slightly, but then there was even *more* speed to its charge. I glanced over my shoulder to Danny, who was struggling to rise to her feet, as I set my own in a wide stance. It would not get past me. My pick was held tightly in my right and I held a skill ready on my left arm. I swore the advancing creature smiled, its information flickering through my eyes now that I concentrated on it long enough.

<Dreg Tendril (Human)>
<Attunement: Fire>
<Refinement: Spread>

<Perceived Metier Quotient: 2>

Processing that information wasn't immediately relevant, but at least I knew what it was called. When the tendril was ten feet away, I released my spell. Thankfully, the creature had been both intelligent and dumb enough to try to anticipate my attempts to impale it, because that wasn't what I did. The earth at its feet heaved as <Earthen Barrier> formed and turned the tendril's charge into a flaming tumble. I swiped my pick horizontally, catching the humanoid with the pointed end somewhere near center mass. Its momentum ripped the pick from my hands as it continued to tumble past me to my left and straight into the gelatinous creature. Its body sizzled like fresh onions on Juan's skillet while the fire cloak around the tendril winked out.

Mouth agape, I watched the creature slide the tendril's body *through* itself. The corpse, unmoving, flopped wetly to the ground, pickaxe and all. I shuddered involuntarily before I focused back on my friends. Danny had reached Sam and was firing into the ice humanoid. I watched one bullet chip the tree the creature was using as cover. The one that followed sprayed its ice-filled brain out into the woods.

My friend pumped her arm. "Try to ignore that, snowman!"

"Did we get them?" Sam panted, wavering on his feet and leaning heavily on my makeshift wall. My eyes landed on the hound. The creature was still struggling weakly and now that I calmly looked at it, its information appeared before me.

<Dreg Tendril (Wolfhound)>

<Attunement: Fire>

<Refinement: N/A>

<Perceived Metier Quotient: 1>

With that information acquired, I kicked it deeper onto my <Stone Spike> and it stilled. "Now we did."

"What about that thing?" Danny gestured at our unexpected blobular ally. The creature formed another appendage and waved at my two friends. "Are we supposed to kill it?"

"It helped us fight! Why would we kill it?" Sam asked, gasping in surprise. "Sure, it was with the others, but why would it attack us now?"

"It's one of those tendril things too. I don't know about you, but considering Dreg-related stuff has only caused us heartache, I say we get rid of it."

My eyes focused on the gelatinous creature and I concentrated. Through the end of the fight, it had shrunk considerably more and wasn't taller than my knee. Other than that, it still looked like someone had taken lime Jell-O, thrown it into a mud pile, rolled it into a ball, and left it out in the sun. I wasn't sure why, but it took a significantly larger amount of concentration than any other creature we'd encountered for its information to be populated through the implant. It was also particularly unhelpful.

<Dreg Tendril (???)>

<Attunement: Earth, ???>

<Refinement: ????>

<Perceived Metier Quotient: ????>

"That's really all we know about it. It wouldn't be fair to judge it just because it was with an aggressive group, now would it?" Sam said, having taken a moment to look the gelatinous Dreg tendril over.

"I suppose you are right, Sam. What do we do with it, though? As a matter of fact, what do we do about this whole excursion?" Daniela asked, waving at what I now realized were the charred remains of one of our bags and most of the surroundings.

"We keep an eye on the tendril and attack it if it does anything funny. As for our little trip, I think for now we should gather up whatever we can and move camp. My mana is tapped and my health could use a few bumps."

"Ha! Hilarious, Ron. Don't you know the joke? Don't bother the healer. I think you are patched up enough for your own regeneration to top you off," Sam responded, deadpan. The life mage was already separating out the parts of our supplies that hadn't been affected by the fight. He made it a point *not* to look at me.

Daniela nodded, reloaded her pistol, and walked slowly to the growing inferno on our side of the road. The humanoid fire tendril had lit the tree it used as cover and Daniela struggled against the flames somehow. *Another thing to put on the mental tally of questions.* With my friends engaged, I did the only thing left to do: loot.

The first target was the wolfhound. Rough black fur with red accents was matted with orange ichor of some kind. The creature was still thoroughly impaled, and I felt a twinge of guilt about the way I'd killed it. Until I remembered it'd been trying to roast me. With a nudge of my boot, its body crystalized into a deep shade of red cinnabar. I barely had a moment to admire the mineral before it crumbled into particles, floating into me and Sam. A trail of Pith flew through my wall, presumably to where Danny was firefighting.

As the Pith settled within me, the nauseous feeling returned but disappeared much more quickly than previous times. I hadn't even realized that my nausea had disappeared when I'd killed the tendrils. A look over my shoulder told me the slime creature was still right behind me, which was another strange development. Why did the other tendrils' presence induce the sensation of absorbing Dregs, but not the blob?

I ignored the question for the moment, instead collecting the two drops from the wolfhound. The item was a perfectly skinned section of its pelt, and there was the expected Quotient 1 Infusion. I almost added 'how does the Pith know to separate certain parts' and 'how does it pick a pattern to remove them' to my list of questions for the Entity. *You already have enough things to ask. Just accept that it's magic and move on.*

The loot went to a grumbling blond when I passed him to get to the fire humanoid. A whole *new* string of questions flowed through my mind. The one that stood out the most was: were there humans that survived on the surface? While the tendril only looked humanoid, there were a few things that appeared distinctly human. Its lower body had some kind of cloth rags and the proportion of its limbs were pretty similar to what I knew of human anatomy. While it was entirely possible that the faceless, red-skinned creature was some strange mutation of another animal, I couldn't bring myself to believe it.

What I also noticed was that it didn't look to be an *old* human either. The Dreg might have been able to halt a human's aging somehow, but if that wasn't the case, then that meant they had to have survived Landfall as children or been born *after* the crystals struck the surface. Both of those possibilities made me swell with hope. It also made me shudder at what had happened to them. *Are these the side effects the Entity was talking about?* That went to the top of the list of things to ask.

I contemplated using the <Pith Mana Lock> to bring the body back to the Bunker, but I wasn't confident we would be able to keep nature from interfering with a dead body. Attuned vultures and ravens, or more wolves, were things I did not want to lead back to the base just to look over the corpse. Before I lost my nerve, I nudged the corpse with my hand and it crystallized into a now-familiar cinnabar-esque mineral before the Pith spread to us.

The feeling of power from the Pith and the nausea from the Dreg did a number on my stomach. I hadn't opened my status to look over the gains, but the other creatures whose Pith we'd absorbed hadn't produced quite as violent of a reaction. Regardless, their drops were what I was most excited about.

One way of getting used to killing things was that we got tangible benefits out of it. Surprise tangible rewards added something extra to the situation.

The drops were a length of bone and the tendril's fire infusion. Comparing the piece of bone to my own body, it was probably a forearm bone. Ava would be able to tell us more. The information on the implant merely called it 'human bone.' I *did* add that as a question to the Entity. Where exactly were our implants drawing the information they displayed from? It wasn't a priority, but getting more detailed information or anything of that sort could be invaluable when we encountered threats.

When I handed Sam the loot, he grimaced. "Human… What—"

"No sense speculating or feeling guilt, Samuel. We knew the surface would be different and we always hoped there would be survivors. As for what this means for that, and my…father… We shouldn't dwell on it. This is not a good sign, but it is *a* sign." He took the bone from me, the depth of his frown uncharacteristically deep, but he nodded.

The walk across the road was tense. Considering how much noise we'd made, attracting creatures was a possibility. I almost didn't want to entertain the fact that the human tendrils acted intelligently. Few animals I knew of would think to seek cover or bolster their allies like they'd done to the wolfhound. Having to deal with souped up animals was enough of a concern.

Regardless, I arrived at the body of the other tendril. Unlike the fire one, who'd been neutralized by the slime, this one was still positively frosty. The ground around it and the blood spray that had exited him were all turned to ice. Instead of giving it the decency of a hand tap like I'd done to the other human, I nudged it with my boot. Sure enough, some of the frost transferred to the tip of it. *Yet another thing to keep in mind.*

With that unpleasant thought in mind, I collected a human heart and a water-ice infusion with Quotient 2 density. The infusion looked just like the bead of water I expected, and the heart looked like any of the numerous anatomical representations I'd seen in my classes, sans blood and the rest of the circulatory system. While the heart didn't beat or anything strange like that, I felt it trying to pull on my mana. The sensation was disconcerting. I let the spell chain for <Stone Spike> form in my hand and it was immediately sucked into it.

Then the heart beat. I yelped and dropped the organ on the grass where it beat for a few more seconds. Each pulse spat out a small wave of frost across the blades of grass before it quickly melted. Less intimidated by the development, I grabbed it again and sent mana into the heart. Sure enough, it beat with ice but I didn't feel the cold.

"You are going straight into the infusion workshop!" I exclaimed. It was hard to not be excited about having an instant refrigerator on hand.

When I moved to cross the street again, my eyes focused on a group of silhouettes walking in the distance. It was hard to discern what they were outside of some kind of quadruped, but I didn't spend any further time looking them over. I activated the comm in our implants. "We're going to have to cut the trip short. There are some more *somethings* incoming. Danny, help Sam load up. I'll keep an eye out. Stay on the other side of the road and we'll join up when we get to the intersection for the side road."

"Got it," Danny replied. "I've got one more tree to put out." Sam echoed her response and I saw him move around the makeshift wall I'd made. When Danny rushed over, she grabbed hold of the pack he handed her and they pushed south. The figures hadn't moved much further down the road, but I didn't want to risk watching them any longer. I turned and mirrored my friends' progress on the other side of the road.

CHAPTER TWENTY-THREE

Gathering Thoughts

I was so caught up in retreating that I completely missed the rolling blob of slime following me. The only reason I did notice was because Daniela had a fireball at the ready. We'd met up at the smaller road branch not long ago, but the moment she'd crossed the road, her <Flame Blast> splashed against the asphalt beside me. The sound of surprise I made couldn't really be put into words.

"What the hell, Danny!?"

"That's close enough, blobby. Why did you follow us?" she asked, the skill held threateningly in her hand.

When I looked over my shoulder, I spotted the green-brown gelatinous tendril poking a shaking appendage around a tree. It waved the appendage in the air like a flag before flattening itself on the ground. Even with its decreased size, it still covered a significant space. As the gel substance it was made of flattened, I noticed two things. One was the fist-sized Metier crystal at the center of its body. The other was the fact that said crystal was emitting a distinct brown light intermingled by flashes of the iridescence we'd come to associate with the Entity.

"What the…" Danny said, lowering her hand and letting the skill drop.

"It has a Metier Crystal. That's the only thing in its body. Maybe that's why it didn't attack us like the other tendrils," Sam speculated. Almost as if to confirm his thoughts, the slime reformed and nodded its appendage vigorously. "Wow, and it *can* understand us, not just communicate."

Its appendage pointed in my direction, before the slime rolled around on the ground quickly. For a gelatinous mass, it sure was expressive.

"Are you saying that's because of me, somehow?" I asked. An appendage nodded in response. "Okay, well, I don't think you should follow us. You could lead more of the tendrils to us, even if you directly won't."

The appendage rose up in the air, then shook itself side to side. The slime vibrated with agitation. When it rolled in our direction, we all took a step back. The slime's appendage formed again, and it seemed to point at each of us briefly before the whole creature deflated. Its gelatinous mass sagged to the ground enough that I could see the glow of the crystal inside it.

"It's not worth the risk, Ron. Let's get going," Danny said, tugging on my torn shirt in the direction of the Bunker path. I nodded and walked after her, but not without giving the friendly tendril another look. Its appendage rose up for a moment before it slunk back to the ground. Its bulk was out of sight as we moved around the trees and onto broken asphalt.

— + —

No creatures stumbled on our path. With the now-familiar surroundings, getting to the Bunker took just under an hour. I still held some trepidation about the lack of attuned trees and plants, but I tried to relax when I remembered my discussion with the Entity. When we passed the overgrown gas station, I finally felt comfortable enough to zone out a little bit to look my status over. Instead of opening up the summarized bit of information, I populated my skills, traits and attributes. The results were surprising.

Subject: Ronan Terrigan
Health: 94% (Unafflicted)
Mana: 98%
Metier Quotient: 3 (22%)
Dreg Accumulation: 15%
LPS: Wildwood, FL
Communications
Skills - *(2) Selections Available*
Traits - *(6% Banked)*
Attributes - *Growth Quantified*
Skills:
Offensive - <Stone Spike>/ Imbue/ Materialize
Defensive - Direct/ Imbue/ <Earthen Barrier>
Misc - <Pith Mana Lock>
- <Infusion>
Traits:
Limestone Skin
Unformed (0%)
Attributes:
Strength: 1.40 > 1.41
Mobility: 1.31
Perception: 1.52 > 1.53
Refinement: 1.13
Containment: 1.93

The information scrolled slowly before my right eye while I kept my left on my friends and surroundings. There were two things that stood out to me the most. The first was the fact that I'd gained much more Dreg from the tendrils than almost any other creature. I hadn't bothered to open it and look at how much I got from each body, but fifteen percent was almost the amount I received from the whole *swarm* of ants. We'd only fought three things, and all of them had been of a lower Quotient than us. That was reflected in the Pith gains, but the Dreg... *That's probably why the feeling of nausea was so strong when we absorbed their energy.*

The second thing was that I'd actually increased my attributes outside of a rise in Quotient. Considering how much stronger I was compared to when I first arrived on the surface, I had doubted it was possible for me to get past that value.

Before I could spend too many mental resources, an excited Anthony surged our way. The creature had a deep blue line painted across the top of its body which initially gave us pause. Thankfully, Ben and Ava weren't far behind.

"You are all back! What happened? Ronan, why are you shirtless? Daniela, is that smoke coming off your hair!?" Ava immediately went full mother hen on all of us. The only one who had remained mostly untouched through the encounter was Samuel, but I'd done my best to keep it that way. Other than dirt and grime from travel, our healer was pristine.

"We're okay, Mama. Can we get inside and we'll explain everything?" Danny said. I heard the lowered tone of her voice and finally noted the sag of her shoulders. She hadn't exhibited anything close to what happened to me while taxing my mana, but I hoped hers wasn't more subtle. She'd been mostly quiet the entire trip back other than engaging the slime. It was entirely possible she'd been dealing with something in silence.

I have to talk to her. She probably still thinks we are unhappy about the spider situation. I had to admit, I handled that situation poorly *and* in the wrong place. If I intended to be the leader, I needed to be understanding as well as direct. The loud monotone voice of the Entity shook me out of my self-reflection.

"Ah! Wonderful! It seems you all are really kicking it into high gear on the Dreg front. And no life or death injuries, I see. Though it appears someone manhandled some fire." We stepped over the gap of my sliding doors to see that the Entity was illuminating the inside of the vestibule perfectly. "Hold on. One, two... Why are there seven of you now?"

"What do you mean?" Sam said, turning to count all of us. "There are only six of us?"

"What about that thing in the ground behind you?" While we knew it was technically possible for the crystal to point out what he was talking about, it wasn't necessary. All six of us, ant included, turned to see a mound of dirt we hadn't noticed there before. Under our scrutiny, the wobbly mass of the slime appendage rose out of the ground, pointed itself in our direction, quivered, then sunk back out of view. The mound didn't move.

"I think it's pretending we didn't just see it," Sam said with a chuckle.

"I think I need to blast this thing so it stops following us," Daniela said with much less enthusiasm. She didn't move to cast her skill, but I suspected that had to do with exhaustion rather than lack of desire.

"You three care to tell us what the hell that thing is?" Ben huffed. Ava and Ben had, admittedly, reacted fairly well. They both had their semi-automatic rifles pointed at the poorly hidden gelatinous blob.

"That," I said, gesturing to the slime, "is part of the story. Entity, are you okay to talk for a while?" A brief look at my status showed that it had already banked my Dreg and presumably that of my friends.

"I have sufficient energy for an extended conversational period. However, based on the encounter your elders had here at the base, I will say it would be prudent of me to expand my field of influence further. Sooner, rather than later, that is."

When I gave Ben and Ava a look, they both shrugged. "We got attacked by another swarm of ants. Thankfully your mom is a crack shot just like you, Danny. She even went through her whole 'combustion phase.' Nearly gave me a heart attack," Ben said.

"Should have stayed in the Bunker if you can't handle the heat, baldy," Ava shot back, rolling her eyes in his direction. *Don't need to look far to see where Danny gets her snark.* "Ben and

Anthony did a fantastic job keeping the critters occupied while I hit them. After I came to from the less-than-relaxing exfoliation of attuning, we gathered up all the stuff they dropped into a crate next to your work space, Ronan. Ben's been moving some stuff to your work area."

"Yeah, I also put the scrap metal that my rifle became in there. Let's say that you don't want to get caught between those ants and a hard place with only a gun in between," Ben said, grimacing as he looked northwest.

"Sounds like we aren't the only ones with a tale to tell. Anyone up for an early dinner? I'll make us some chairs," I said, eyeing the slime mound one more time. "I'll tell the slime to join us."

"I don't want it anywhere near my stuff!" Danny said as she made her way inside.

Good to know she isn't tired or dejected enough to stop being the physical manifestation of a pain in my butt. Before I went to talk to our stealthy friend, I raised two mounds of earth facing the crystal. Then I made rough backs to them with half-powered <Stone Spikes>. A quick strike from my pickaxe sent the tips crumbling to the ground.

"Thanks for turning my bedroom into a dining room," the Entity quipped. It had remained silent through the constructive endeavor.

"I aim to please. Plus, I figured having dinner under the magical light of a possibly interdimensional being would be a nice touch."

"It *will* be nice to actually interact with organisms beyond just existing."

I didn't pause what I was doing, but the depth of loneliness in the Entity's voice was something distinctly human. On the short walk to the slime, I thought about how I would have felt living for decades without really being able to communicate. Probably not well.

The slime slunk further into the ground when I approached, as if it would be able to hide better.

"Hey, we all know you are there. Come on out." The appendage poked itself out of the ground and pointed itself in my direction. The lime green creature quivered and I realized it was probably scared. Danny hadn't exactly been welcoming. "It's alright. You are already here, and considering you helped us in the fight against the other tendrils, I don't plan on driving you off. I can't promise you won't have to deal with the occasional fireball from my friend though. She has a bit of a… fiery personality."

While it didn't look like the slime appreciated my puns, it did extract itself from the ground. It was as if the very earth took its shape. It was a bit frightening to think we might not have noticed the tendril stalking us, so I gave our surroundings a hard look. The slime rolled along behind me, jiggling in what I interpreted as joy, while I stared out over our clearing. I could see some of the burn marks on the ground and even a toppled tree to the north. The herd looked to be intact, but considering their previous experience when they angered Raymond, I wasn't surprised.

"Ronan! Food is getting cold and it's story time," Sam said, poking his head out of the vestibule to call out to me.

The slime and I made our way back to the bench-chair-things I'd made. I took one of the ones furthest from the crystal and the slime sunk down to a flattened circle. *Maybe it's more comfortable like that?* Anthony and Daniela took the opposite spot from us. The ant prodded at the slime with its antenna, but the gelatinous creature only jiggled in response as if it was giggling from tickles. Before I got much of a chance to consider how weird the current situation was, Daniela passed me a used insta-meal tray with a heap of tomatoes and potatoes.

"Bon Appetit. Eh… does that thing eat?" she asked after passing food to everyone.

"Not sure. Let's see." I flicked one of my potatoes onto the slime's bulk. It stayed on the surface of the creature for a sec before it sucked it in with a slurp. The potato faded from view a moment later. "I'd say yes?"

Daniela didn't say anything, but she went back and returned with a tray for the slime.

"Right, so you two had a fun party without—" A loud slurping sound interrupted me. We all turned to see the slime's appendage reaching over the food tray and sucking up the potatoes and tomatoes like a vacuum. The sound was sloppy and reminded me of the wet flop the fire tendril humanoid had made when it passed through the slime's body. It did not stop until the last bit of food had disappeared into the slime's body.

"I would very much like to hear your side of the story first, Ronan. Particularly, how you acquired this creature whom I am struggling to identify even within the inner layer of my influence," the Entity said.

Ben and Ava weren't in a rush. Both were already stuffing their faces with food, as were Sam and Danny, so I gave the recounting of our day. It'd been barely twelve hours, but the sheer amount of things that happened took almost an hour to retell.

Samuel described the damage to our gear we'd sustained, and Daniela retold her experience summoning the wisp offensively for the first time, as well as fighting the budding forest fire. I'd been right in assuming it had taxed her. She mentioned that she'd never dipped quite that low in her mana pool before.

Both of the adults seemed shaken by our descriptions of the tendrils. Being entirely honest, I'd been ignoring the whole 'possibly human' avenue in my own mind for the sake of sanity. The casters had been put solidly in the 'enemy' category. The logical part of my mind, however, refused to leave the nagging possibility that I'd killed a human. Considering what their reception of us had been, I didn't necessarily feel *bad* about it. *I wonder what that says about me...* The whole situation, however, left me wondering about what we would be forced to do in the future.

Our group, even the Entity, speculated on the nature of the tendrils. Unfortunately, without much more information, it was conjecture. It wasn't like their drops could elaborate on how they'd gotten the way they were, if they had been humans, or how they'd come about if they weren't. Not many things on Earth had humanoid forms.

Eventually, with our story out of the way and heavier concerns set aside for later, our two older companions talked about the attack from the Fire Ants. Ten of the smaller ants, as well as two of the larger Smolder Ants had made an appearance. They had initially attempted to attack the herd, but Raymond wouldn't have any of that. He single-handedly crushed one of the larger ants while the rest tried to swarm over the relatively un-magically enhanced pair. Ben had beaten the larger ant while Anthony wrestled it and Ava had blasted neat holes in all the smaller ants.

"Okay, exciting day on all fronts then! Speaking of, Ms. Ava, if you would please walk over here, I will augment your implant." The Entity connected with Ava for less than a minute before releasing her. It looked like it was getting better at giving us access to statuses; she barely staggered. "As for your gelatinous friend, I have an inkling of what he is. The short answer? Nothing good."

"Are they nothing good for us or just in general?" Danny asked. I could have sworn I saw the glyphs for her spell chain forming in her hand even as the Entity explained.

"I do not believe this creature means any of you harm. It… has bonded to Ronan? Comparing it to what you and Anthony have, as well as what Samuel has with Raymond, would not be far from the truth." The light inside the crystal fluctuated for a moment as if it was considering its words. "What it is, is something new. Something new to the information I have available at my present category, anyhow."

"Well, out with it, man…ehrm… crystal… Entity?" Ben said with excitement before fumbling with the terms with which to address the alien rock.

"Calling me Entity as you have been doing is fine, Benjamin. What this slime is, to use the term most adjacent to your knowledge, is a Dreg-Infused Entity Crystal."

While I suspected something along those lines, I didn't really know where it *or* the tendril creatures overall stood in the growing mountain of things we needed to be concerned about. Thankfully, the Entity had anticipated our question.

"Like the tendrils you encountered, it is something that has been nearly overwhelmed physically by the presence of Dreg. As you know, mana can cause mutations in organisms. The rampant versions of these mutations are the result of Dreg afflictions. While these provide immensely more power to the creature involved, they come at a cost that cannot always be paid by the organism. The cost is something I cannot ascertain, as the structure of Dreg is foreign to me. However, it appears that some portion of the Category 1 Entity has been able to take control of the mutations and corruption."

As if seeking to affirm that deduction, the appendage of the slime moved up and down rapidly. The creature had remained both still and perfectly silent the whole time after eating, I'd nearly forgotten about it.

"Ah, it appears to be fairly intelligent also. I cannot begin to guess or compute the nature of such an... unholy union. Your language choices are certainly strange. Anyhow, I believe I may be able to remove and purify most of the Dreg within. As for the change that led it to become... wobbly in nature and attuned at that, I do not believe that is currently in my power."

"As long as you don't think it will be a threat, I don't have a problem with it," I said. Ben and Ava shrugged, while Sam nodded and smiled at the gelatinous addition to our group.

Daniela stared intently at the slime for several seconds before she blurted out, "Fine! But you have to name it Blobby!"

That was apparently agreeable, because the slime wobbled up and down, jiggling all the while. It was a strange sight to behold, but actually an impressive display of its control over its body.

"I suppose you are Blobby, if that is fine with you?" I said, addressing the slime directly. It nodded with its appendage, then rolled closer to my side. *While I said I wanted a pet just like the others, I hadn't realized it would be... this.* I actually quite liked Blobby, and the more I thought about its abilities, the more I thought they would synergize well with my defensive role as a tank.

I *had* been surprised that Daniela had already been holding one of her patented terrible creature names at hand.

"Weren't you extremely concerned about the slime since the moment we met it?" I asked.

"Yes, but then it helped us. And then its little arm just waves around, and its body is so expressive and cute!" Blobby rolled closer to Daniela and reached out with its appendage. The woman hesitated for a moment, but shook the firm gel a moment later.

Blobby didn't look particularly cute to me, and what I'd seen it do with the fire tendril sent chills down my spine, but I did find the idea of having an amorphous blob of matter as a pet pretty cool. It wasn't much of a stretch to say I had a pet rock.

"While I am glad to have access to a status and a new… friend, I would like to discuss the piece of news the Entity revealed to us," Ava said. Her tone immediately sobered the mood, even with Blobby's silly jiggling body directly in front of us. "And what you three have brought to our attention. The tendrils and *human* tendrils, at that. How does this change our plans?"

CHAPTER TWENTY-FOUR

Making Preparations

"I don't think it should," Daniela said. We'd all remained silent after Ava's question. I'd already been brewing on what the existence of humans on the surface meant, but I wanted to hear the thoughts of the others.

"From what you described they sounded like a much, much stronger threat than just the regular animals," Ava said. Her tone wasn't dismissive of Daniela's comment, more testing.

"True, but it also means that there could be others out there. Others that could benefit from our technology and, at the very least, our help."

"What do you think we can provide, Daniela? We don't even have enough titanium or manpower to produce more implants. As much as I believe in you kids, I don't know if you are ready to go on a wild goose chase for people that might not be there. Or worse, people that may be corrupted by Dreg. Is there any way to tell?" Ben directed his last question at the Entity.

"I may be able to provide an index of comparison for tendrils, but it is not something I routinely dedicate power to.

Considering how unorthodox our arrangement already is, however, it may be an appropriate use of resources."

"No."

"Ronan?" Ben asked.

"There are more important things than being able to tell how far gone a tendril is from another. They are a threat like everything else on the surface. Are we ready to face them if there are more of them? Probably not. But if there are other humans out there, we can only be stronger together."

"What would you do about... err... creatures like Blobby?" Ava asked, grimacing at using the name in a serious context.

"We judge on a case by case basis," Sam interjected. "If they attack us, like the two humans we met, then obviously they aren't friendly. If they assist us like Blobby did, then they might be allies. The reactions in between will have to be at our discretion. Just like they were back before the world went to crap."

"So no investing in a tendril meter, for now at least. What is the next step moving forward, then?" Ben said, crossing his arms and leaning his bulk on the earth spike I'd made as a back rest.

"More of the same, I think. Our main objective is to return humanity to the surface somehow. Getting to the other Bunkers is going to be key, but we are going to need more than the three of us and a mismatched crowd of creatures." I gestured around at my friends and at Anthony and Blobby.

"You don't think us old timers will be able to pull our weight?" Ben countered with a frown.

"Mr. Burks, I think I get what Ron is getting at. We've already seen it, in fact. Most people aren't going to want to risk going out for the sake of a maybe. Maybe they have the surface secure. Maybe they have enough food and comforts. Maybe there will be other humans out there. It is going to be up to us to turn those maybes into yes or no," Sam said.

"As far as I recall, there was still a fair bit of opposition to the implants and trips to the surface. If it wasn't for our parents, you, and Alan, the others would have squashed it," Danny added. Ben's frown deepened, but he conceded the point.

"No sense arguing in circles, and based on your tones, you all sound in agreement to head back out into the wilds," Ava said. She continued once we all gave her a nod. "Then before you go out again, we need to solidify our foothold on the surface more."

"Mama, we are already—" Daniela started before her mother interrupted.

"I am aware of how much you've done. Sam's farm is nearly able to produce double what the greenhouse floor can, Ronan has built this whole space basically by himself, and you were the one who discovered the path into our old world. However, I think we can all agree that you might need some more preparations.

"There are steps and infrastructure we can put in place to help you should something go terribly wrong. Least of which is getting the farm to a size that doesn't depend on Samuel to sustain itself. Further defenses in the perimeter and a Quotient or two on top of the ones you all currently have would do wonders for your safety. Not only would that give you more skills, the Dreg will strengthen the Entity." Ava counted things off with her hand, giving our group a knowing look.

"Those… are very fair points." My mind flashed back to our engagement with the human tendrils. While their individual power hadn't been much stronger than our own, their coordination compounded their abilities and the extent of their magic control seemed broader. The Entity had reminded us that our skills were a shortcut to what creatures, and people, that had grown up with mana would be able to do. The outcome had Blobby not joined us in the fight and instead attacked us would *not* have been pleasant. There were matching looks of contemplation on my friends' faces.

"Well, what do you propose Ms…ehm… Ava?" Sam tried to address Danny's mom formally before she gave him one of her patented stares. The one mothers gave their children when they were about to do something they had told them not to do again. While I didn't have personal experience on the mother front, I'd seen it enough from Ava to Daniela and the occasional time from my uncle.

"You all need to train more. Ben got me up to speed on everything you have been working with, and I think it's about time I give you all the once-over to optimize your development. Other than that, you will keep doing what you have been doing."

"There is one more thing you can also do," the Entity said. "As I know Ronan has already been considering, using the ant hive as a location to gather Dreg and materials is a good step. I will focus energy in expanding my field of influence to keep you safer in the meantime, but culling them will also provide valuable experience. The ants are the threat you are most familiar with, and thus the least likely to surprise you."

"That is a good point. We can discuss that after I get a good metric for your abilities. I'm not underestimating you," Ava added, halting Daniela's argument, "but is it going to hurt to plan for the future and have markers for development? I did this for you kids growing up, no reason I can't do this now."

"But with magic," Ben added, throwing a smirk at us.

"Yes, yes, magic and all that stuff we don't really understand. All it will take is time." Ava sounded extremely confident, and I had to admit it felt good to have someone as interested as me in quantifying the development of our abilities.

"With that being the case, I will make a slight modification to my plans. I will spend part of the growth I acquired to expand my influence but only maintain it during the night. This should allow me to have an hour or two of interaction during the day where I can discuss any questions you might have. If the creatures I've warded away are any indication of the biomes around this area, then the ants really are your easiest targets for growth," the Entity said.

The Entity mentioned that we would know when it was awake for questioning the following day and promptly dimmed.

It was a clear indicator that the discussion had been drawn to a close. We spent a few more minutes planning under lantern light before calling it a night.

Blobby was a bit hesitant to enter the lobby, unlike Anthony, so I formed a raised earth cubby next to my infusion workspace for it. The slime jiggled in excitement, then rolled into the space and melted. The change was instantaneous. The lime green gel camouflaged to the exact shade of brown as the consolidated earth and Blobby was almost invisible. It alarmed me for a moment before the little appendage waved as if bidding me good night.

"This is gonna be interesting…"

— + —

"Alright. Step one will be to see how you all work together."

Ava stood before us, exactly like what I would have expected from a drill sergeant from one of those old military movies. She'd woken us all up at the crack of dawn, and had us line up along the eastern portion of the clearing. This was the area with the most trees other than the path that Daniela had carved. It was the secondary reason Sam had opted to create his farm along the west and southwest portions of the hill that hid the Bunker.

"What are we supposed to do, Mama?" Daniela asked.

Anthony was standing beside her. The ant's gaze shifted from her to her mother as if it still had trouble picking which was his master just based on the facial expressions and mannerisms. Blobby had waved at us as we exited, but made no motion to join us. If Raymond was on this side of the Bunker, then we would have the strangest trifecta of observers.

"You'll be clearing your *own* training space. As of now, you have chopped through trees using an axe and your explosive skill. However, that leaves stumps that make it hard to really use the space for anything." Ava gestured to the mess of stumps to the northeast. "For this training space, you will want clean dirt, a reinforced stone wall on the south side which abuts the Bunker, and another section of Ronan and Samuel's trademark fencing as a barrier to the east. You have until lunch, otherwise we will be adding additional days of training to whatever time-frame we decide to mark for you three to attack the ants."

When none of us moved, she clapped her hands loudly. We scattered before realizing that talking about our plan of action would be useful.

"So, alternatives to choppy chop?" Daniela asked.

"Well, maybe we can cut the trees like we've been doing and then deal with the stumps afterwards," I suggested.

"I have an idea," Sam said. "But I don't know how well it's going to work."

"Hey, you are the resident plant expert, so if you know how we can get rid of these trees, I am all for it!" I said, patting the blond on the shoulder.

"Most of these trees are live oaks, which means their roots tend to reach *out* before they go deep. If you can consolidate the ground right around the base of the tree, Ronan, then we can dig and cut a trench through the roots. Once we have that, I can use my <Vine Whip> and maybe a blast or two from Daniela to knock it down. Moving it after that might take a long while, though."

"It's better than just doing what we've been doing. We'll give it a try and see how it works."

Without delay, we picked a medium-sized tree in the space we were looking to clear. Hoping to expedite the process, I concentrated and summoned two of the spell chains for <Earthen Barrier> at the foot of the tree. Immediately, the ground sank a good inch before dropping slowly as it consolidated. An extensive system of roots became exposed the more the ground lowered, sending cracks spidering through the radius of my passive skills. The strain was notable, but it was something I was getting used to dealing with.

"That should be good!" Sam shouted, moving in once my spell chains faded away.

Both him and Danny had hatchets in hand, while Anthony used his forelegs to dig out the earth for the trench. I joined the group with the chisel side of my pick and lopped roots with each strike. Before long, we had a good foot excavated around the tree and the largest roots chopped clean through.

"Time for you to shine, veggie head," Danny said.

"Really thought we were past those poor insults, Daniela. We are in our twenties." Sam sighed, concentrating himself on a spot far from the tree.

"Don't act high and mighty, you languished in the quip trenches same as me. We fought on the frontlines of the pun war that tortured Ronan through his teens. How could you abandon our—"

"Danny, please let me focus."

Sam's tone was serious, which prompted our verbose friend to be quiet for a moment out of sheer surprise, I reckoned. A moment later, a thigh-thick vine exploded out of the ground before wrapping itself around the tree right below where the branches started to grow. Sam's face scrunched up in concentration, and we heard the creak of wood as his skill pulled on the tree. The massive specimen tipped, but refused to fall over completely.

"Hit it, Danny," I said, casting two half-powered <Stone Spikes> aimed up into the bending trunk. The spikes pushed the tree further but it still refused to give. A flare of fire splashed against the top of the tree, causing it to pitch further. Sam let out a loud groan before the root ball of the oak sprayed all of us with loose dirt. We'd managed the uprooting.

"Yeeessss!" Sam shouted, before wobbling and taking a knee. Danny tended to Sam while he recovered his mana and I considered how effective the method had been. While there were still roots to deal with, as well as the extensive branches all along the crown, it was faster than chopping, if more mana intensive. When I noticed that Sam's vine was still attached and perfectly green, I approached my friend.

"Sam, are you able to reconnect with that thick vine you grew?"

"I've… never tried," he said. He still looked a bit dazed, but there were thoughts connecting in his mind. "Everything I've grown before either got destroyed really quickly or was thin enough I forgot about it."

The man rose up to his feet and focused on his magic. I wasn't sure how much mana he'd managed to recuperate, but I wasn't going to stop him if he was coming to some kind of realization about his abilities. The light of his spell chain formed around the base of the inanimate vine before it jerked and uncoiled from the tree. Sam moved his hand around in the air while the vine swung around, imitating his motions. After a few seconds, he lowered the vine to the ground and the light of his mana winked out.

"It works! And it saves me an insane amount of mana. All I have to do is spend mana to manipulate the vine, but nothing to grow it. Give me a few minutes, and I'll be ready to try another tree. Maybe I can use this for the tomato plant…" He drifted off in thought, so I motioned Danny over to another tree that was in range of Sam's whippy assistant.

Daniela instructed Anthony to start delimbing the tree we'd cut down while she and I worked on the trench around the next tree. It was a great division of labor, since I saw the ant spit out small gouts of fire to help it saw the branches with its mandibles.

The two of us worked in silence while Sam continued to mumble to himself. I debated continuing to work in silence, but opted to bring up what I thought might be a source of tension between us.

"I'm sorry about the way we attacked you over the spider issue," I said. "It was important that you knew, but I think we may have come off a little strong."

"There's no need to apologize, Ron. I can be… impulsive, you know."

"Like turning a wild insect into your pet, or naming *someone else's* pet?" I said, quirking an eyebrow in her direction in between pickaxe swings.

"It seemed like a good idea at the time!" Danny blushed and continued to chop through roots. "I didn't want to distrust Blobby, but the fact that those *things* are out there has me worried."

"You aren't alone, Daniela. Not only are Ben and your mom here with us, but you've got Sam and I. We haven't failed you…yet."

"Very funny. Ha. Ha." There was a slight smile on her face before it flattened. "I just want to push forward. You always have your nose to the grindstone whether it's for good or bad. Sam's head is always in the clouds if he isn't planting something. I just don't know what I bring to the group. The mishap with the spiders is just the latest of my blunders."

For what must have been one of the first times in my life, I felt my own frustrations echoed back at me. It made me realize that maybe feeling worthless or disheartened wasn't something unique to me, but something people around me also experienced. Logically, it made sense. All three of us had been born in a Bunker after the world ended, with no good prospects for the future, and so we had to deal with that reality. Whichever way was needed.

Daniela opened up about her desire to move and go and run around whenever possible. While I understood the feeling, it resonated much more deeply with her. She wanted to explore, to learn about the *world,* as opposed to its systems like Samuel, or its intricacies like myself. She spoke the whole time while we worked, and I felt the tension between us flow away with the gentle breeze around us.

I also conceded that her points had much merit and that I would try to be more open about my feelings and concerns. Making sure we took the time to check on each other would be key to handling the significant stresses the surface had already put on our shoulders and I had a suspicion they were just starting. Even if we all pushed forward in different ways, doing so *together* was the most important thing.

By the time we'd finished the trench, it was much deeper than the previous one. My mood was at an all-time high, happy to know where each of our heads were.

"What are you two smiling about?" The blond's head was tilted to the side in confusion, but we just chuckled and told him to get a move on with the tree.

CHAPTER TWENTY-FIVE

Consolidating

Despite our best efforts and the removal of all the trees, Ava strode over to our group, frowning. We were all soaked in sweat, the sun at its zenith. In Danny's case, some of that sweat was evaporating into the air at a visible rate, but the woman didn't seem bothered so I didn't comment on it.

"You have done wonderfully, but still did not finish up the details I'd assigned. Can you concede that we will have an additional day of training?" Ava asked, keeping her hands at her sides while looking us up and down.

"A bit unfair, but I agree we could have done better," I said, wiping off sweat and crossing my arms. My friends nodded since we'd already discussed what we would tell Ava when we weren't able to finish her task. Danny was already mostly dry and Sam was still trying to catch his breath. *Maybe I pushed a bit too hard to try to finish and get out of the extra day.*

"Understandable, and that is because it *was* unfair. I'll admit I didn't think you three alone could clear that many trees before lunch. Much less add the features I'd recommended. Recalculating your capabilities as they are boosted by magic will be imperative for me to assess your development. Now, lunch.

Then I want you all to finish the training area before dealing with your usual responsibilities."

We all groaned, but trudged past the smirking woman. I couldn't help but recall all the times she'd run us through our biannual physicals and then essentially grounded us with physical training. The outcome of that had now saved our lives for the entire duration of our stay on the surface. If Samuel, Daniela, and I weren't as fit as we were, I doubt we would have survived the first day.

With food in our bellies, we got to work on the training space. This part was almost too easy. Twelve casts of my <Earthen Barrier> formed a six foot tall, doubly reinforced wall that sprouted right out of the side of the hill hiding the Bunker. My pickaxe opened up a few holes on the unsupported side of the wall for Sam to thread his vine fence. After raking an astounding amount of charred grass courtesy of Daniela and Anthony, while waiting for my mana to recuperate, I raised a dozen <Stone Spikes> for him to make the fence.

Ava scrutinized the training area for a full ten minutes, but eventually nodded. The three of us let out sighs of relief and took a well-deserved bit of rest. There was still plenty of light left, but we sat with our backs to each other and recounted how the day had panned out so far. The consensus was that it had been extremely productive. With the realization that we *wanted* to make even better use of the day, we groaned to our feet and split off across the Bunker clearing.

Sam rushed over to grow another batch of fresh food and tend to the herd. Danny, with help from Anthony, started to work on clearing out the stumps that led to the old road. She even snagged the pickaxe from me.

As for me, I started to work on the infrastructure of the camp overall. Using the passive form of my defensive materialize skill, I consolidated paths from the vestibule to the edge of the farm as well as towards the old road. My mana consumption was obscenely high. While I'd gotten used to the mild discomfort of using and regenerating it almost constantly, I was exhausted when I plopped into the benches before the Metier Crystal. Since the makeshift meeting spot sat all of us, we'd opted to use it for our meals moving forward.

The heat of the day lingered inside the vestibule, but the thorough coat of sweat I wore helped to stave off the majority of my discomfort. It did mean that I needed a shower of some kind as soon as possible. When the others made their way over to join me, Danny's arms laden with food, I asked Ben about the shower.

"Well, I got it rigged to take from a container above it. Had to splice in a two way valve, but the heating element takes more power than any of these batteries we've got up here can handle. None of the ones your grandmother was able to adapt to function while subjected to mana were ever very portable."

"With how dirty and smelly I am right now, I'll take a cold shower any day. Plus, it's like a billion degrees out. Who would want a hot shower?" Daniela and her mother both raised their hands. "Never mind. I don't know why I asked."

"You two do know I have magical fire powers, yes?" Daniela asked.

Ben and I exchanged a look. I had to resist the urge to facepalm. Even with everything we'd experienced and how much we'd been using our skills, our basic thinking was still a bit… Bunker-locked.

"I'll get it set up after dinner then. Just need a hand getting it through the door now that it's fully assembled. I can set it just outside of the vestibule so it will give everyone a tad more privacy," Ben said.

"Put it around the east wall. I'll make a little open top shower room and tomorrow I'll make a basin to store water for back to back showers," I said, already picturing the space in my head.

"*Early* tomorrow or *after* your training, Ronan." My groaned response just made Ava's smirk widen.

While we continued to eat our food, a bright flare of light from the Entity pulsed over us and I felt something being sucked from the air. It wasn't something I perceived with my skin or saw with my eyes, but somehow I knew that it had pulled its influence back.

"Greetings. It appears my plan to interact with you has been put on a much more restricted course than I'd hoped," the Entity said. The light pulsing with its words was weaker than before it had expanded its influence yesterday.

"What's going on?" I asked, tensing at the serious tone of the sapient rock.

"Nothing for you to be concerned about. There is, however, a substantial amount of wildlife moving through this area. Most of it is unattuned, and that has cost a pittance to divert, but there are still *many* attuned. My reserves have been taxed just keeping them away, but I believe I can manage a brief conversation."

With us now more settled, we discussed what would be the most beneficial question to ask. Ben had technical questions about *what* the crystal was made of, Ava wanted to ask about the effects of mana on the body, and both my friends wanted to know when it would be possible to acquire more skills. When I remained quiet, the whole group turned to me expectantly.

"What? This is a group discussion, we can all decide what to ask. We should be quick, Entity has a knack for winking out mid-conversation."

"That is not entirely representative of what has happened. I thought we'd come to an unders—" the Entity said before I raised my hands in a placating gesture.

"I'm just kidding. Don't let Danny's temper get a hold of you again," I said pointedly. The brunette across from me blushed furiously and looked away while the crystal pulsed inquisitively. "We appreciate all the help you've given us so far."

"To get back on point," Ava started. "Considering you were the one who thought about enlisting the Entity in our attempts to return to the surface, why don't you act as our liaison? We can give you our questions and you can optimize when we ask them."

"Are you all really okay with me picking what we ask?" Everyone nodded as if they'd agreed on this before.

"It would be terribly inefficient to discuss what we should ask every time someone gets a question; it is even more inefficient if the Entity has limited time," Sam pointed out.

With that out of the way, I considered the questions everyone had, as well as the ones I'd been stacking up in my own mental list. Knowing the plan for the next few days of training, I focused on a question somewhere between Ava's and one of my own. "My attributes grew without getting a Quotient increase. How exactly does that work now? I can't imagine that I'd be able to grow stronger than I've already become thanks to the levels."

"That would be correct, were you solely human," the Entity responded enigmatically. Thankfully, none of us had a penchant for dramatized conversations or the crystal probably would have continued being vague. "That is to say, your Attunement changed you fundamentally. As I am sure you all know, using mana extracts... a cost, let's say, from your body. Yes?"

"I believe so, yes. I get this pain-soreness-gut-wrenching feeling thing. Danny spikes crazy fevers, and Sam gets woozy. All of these have debilitated us at one point or another."

"Indeed. This feeling should *also* be minimized as you grow more accustomed to your mana."

"What does that have to do with attributes?" Danny asked. "My strength and mobility have gone up, but the change is a tenth of what we would get from a Quotient."

"Ah yes. Well, as I mentioned before, your attributes are computed values of an extensive list of factors. The reason why I opted to show your attributes to the mathematical hundredths place was because anything beyond that is constantly changing. Up, down, steady. Unless your body makes a concerted shift so your average is higher or lower, that number will remain steady.

"As for what your mana has to do with attributes, well, the longer you remain within a Quotient, the more likely it is for your body to stabilize. This, in turn, lets you achieve higher averages. That level of... comfort, shall we call it, is a good indicator that the power you wield can be used more efficiently and effectively."

"So we should opt to stay at each level for as long as possible?" Sam asked, tilting his head. I was sure he was running all kinds of scenarios where we wouldn't be able to *ignore* a level up.

"Yes and no. Growing your Metier Quotient will increase your survivability, and it will also let you passively grow your attributes *at a higher level.* And no, because the creatures around you will certainly try to take your Pith, and there is only so far comfort will train your body before your attributes plateau in your Quotient."

"Okay, there are like three questions wrapped up in that one, but I'll keep it on topic. Why would growing your attributes at a higher level be more important than doing so at a lower level? If I understand the way the math has worked so far, we've all become ten percent better than the human average with each Quotient. A little growth at each Quotient would add up greatly," I said, frowning at the Entity. *There is so much we don't know.*

"That is correct, however your gains would be mirrored at higher Quotients. Beyond the first threshold of levels you will also gain *more* power with each Quotient and be forced to stay in them longer *regardless,* due to the jumps in Pith cost. Training as you have been doing will be key to improving your attributes and skills. Quotients and traits, however, will be just as important for you to close the gap on the other beasts on the planet." The light inside the Entity flickered for a moment. "The nighttime neighbors are waking up. I will attempt to join you in the future, but if the volume of creatures does not decrease, it will be difficult."

Without another word, the light in the Entity Cluster shrank to a pinprick. The sensation from earlier returned, this time spreading out from the crystal as if blanketing everything around us.

"See? I told you you'd be the man to ask the right questions!" Sam said, smiling and scraping his leftovers onto Blobby's bulk. The slime jiggled in elation as the food sunk out of view. After exchanging looks, everyone else also disposed of their food onto my pet before heading into the lobby.

I held my head in my hands as I tried to piece together the information the Entity had given us. It was true I tended to overthink things, and there wasn't much I could do with the information other than file it away as something good to know. It did mean that we could push ourselves to eke out some attribute gains, however we could, while focusing on getting more Quotients. Getting some confirmation that we hadn't been wasting too much of our time was definitely a comforting thought.

My train of thought derailed as Danny shouted, "Dibs on the first shower!"

Ben and Sam hauled the unwieldy rectangle through the door and the need to shower jumped up in my list of priorities. Theorizing on the maximizing of our future could wait for some cleanliness. One usually does their best thinking in the shower anyhow.

— + —

Surprising no one, that night's sleep was the best we'd had since arriving at the surface. I hadn't realized how much the small commodities of the Bunker had shaped my life until they were gone.

Making the best use of my time the previous day, I'd actually created the little roofless space for the shower *while* showering. This left us to eat breakfast in a hurry and meet Ava in the training space we'd cleared away. The woman had her hair pulled up in a tight bun just like her daughter, and her eyes combed over us with vivid intensity.

"In order to optimize the time you spend training, which will be until noon, you three will create the exercises for each other. From what I have gathered, you have all developed different ways of using your skills just from practicing. I would like to get the basics of those to be as natural as your movements. The week I have allotted, plus the extra day, will not be enough to accomplish this. Why might you ask? Because there is always something to improve." At this point she began to pace up and down, while gesturing to the ground around us.

"For your first round of training, I want you all to focus on *precision*. All of you attack with a certain... wildness. Daniela, you throw big flashy sprays of fire. Samuel, you *always* try to tangle without considering where your vines could be used more effectively. Ronan, while your ability is extremely utilitarian, it is costly and you need to really think about how you use it."

Those are some on the spot comments. How did she break down our weaknesses so easily? That was a skill I wished I had. Before I could get too far into my leadership train of thought, she laid out the exercise we would be doing.

The idea was that I would practice forcing <Stone Spike> to form a size based on my will. This would therefore reduce, or increase, the cost of the skill. So far I'd been able to control a full-power versus a half-powered <Stone Spike>, but I'd never tried to regulate it based on size.

With that in mind, I would be creating the strongest and largest single spike that I could for Sam to attack with his vines. He was supposed to break down the entire structure from top to bottom, using only his skill. For Danny, I would focus on making a person-shaped earth dummy. Ava expected me to create a larger middle spike, then form four smaller prongs to represent its limbs. Daniela's goal was to accurately hit and damage *just* the ends of each then finally hit the body with a bigger attack.

It was an extensive, roundabout, but ingenious way of getting us all to train each other. It also benefited from wasting no resources other than our mana and the discomfort that brought. With the plan explained, and a brief moment that Ava took to measure *something* around our bodies, she left us to our own devices.

"I suppose I am up first," I said. My training relied on my friends destroying my targets, but considering how much time I would be spending regenerating mana, I also decided it would be as good a time as any to practice swinging my pickaxe.

After I set my tool-turned-weapon down on the ground, I focused on the space in front of Sam. The spell chain for <Stone Spike> appeared in my hand, but I held it tight. The ground below me was unconsolidated, so when the mana congregated around my arm, it responded in kind with its passive compressive effect. I pictured the top of the Spike reaching higher than the six foot maximum I'd discovered at Quotient 3. Not only taller, but also wider. The gut-wrenching feeling of drawing on my mana pool hit me like a physical blow, but I didn't drop the skill. Instead, I buckled down and flicked my hand at the ground like I'd done with the infusion threads.

The ground before Sam dipped considerably, then heaved, then exploded up. A four foot wide, eight foot tall spike of compressed earth pulled itself out of the ground at my command. It was beautiful. The sand and organic matter inter-mingled on the ground around me had been separated perfectly, leaving a smooth sedimentary rock version of topsoil just a few feet away.

Then I *let* myself fall to the ground. My two friends hovered over me as I curled into the fetal position, hoping to help ease the pain stretching my muscles like some medieval torture device. The world was agony for several seconds, but it slowly faded away.

"Ronan? Are you okay, man?" Sam asked. His hand was glowing green where I presumed he'd been trying to use <Health Bump> on me. If it'd made a difference, it was lost on me.

"Yeah, I think so. I didn't exceed my mana pool, but it was a close deal. It also wasn't as intense as when I transferred those skills to you guys and Ben, but... I definitely felt it. How long was I out?"

"Probably a minute?" Danny answered. "You dropped like

a rock and I barely had time to catch you. I didn't think you weighed as much as you did."

"Are you calling me fat?" I asked, taking Sam's offered hand to rise to my feet. My muscles twitched from the effort, but I pushed past it enough to give my friend a mock gasp.

"Rock brain," she said, punching me in the arm and causing my muscles to tense again.

Sam squared up against a giant piece of stone after he was sure I wasn't about to seize up again. His vine whip barely left chips in the stone after he broke off the tip. Once I'd recuperated enough mana, I cast <Stone Spike> a ways from the horticultural fanatic.

Unsure of how to manipulate my mana *down* without causing the spell chain to dissipate, I cast it quickly instead. The desired result was there, if completely inconsistent in both size and direction. The stone spike dummy had an upraised arm, while the other pointed directly down. One of its legs was thick and short while the other was a lanky little thing pointed forward.

"Didn't know you were into disco, Ronan," Danny said with a smirk, giving herself twenty paces to the dummy.

"This is going to be a long week," I sighed.

CHAPTER TWENTY-SIX

Passing the Torch

My focus was razor sharp as I summoned a spell chain on my left hand and another on the right. Groaning as the mana flowed out of me, I cast a thick stone spike vertically out of the ground. With my other hand, I tugged on the hardened sand to form four smaller spikes sprouting from the larger one. The pronged dummy was complete. Without missing a beat, I dismissed and resummoned spell chains to both of my hands and joined them together to raise a triple-empowered <Stone Spike>. The earthen structure towered out of the ground, then compressed down to its impressive eight foot height.

Then I took a knee to let the wave of discomfort wrack its way through my body. It wasn't entirely bearable, but at the very least it didn't incapacitate me like before. Once I managed to shuffle out of the way, my friends engaged the stone constructs. Danny let out a volley of three <Flame Blasts>. Unlike her usual flashy attacks, these were much more muted. The red and orange glows of the fireball in her hand were much more compressed. The brief second she held the attack in hand, my eyes were swimming in the flames.

A wave of heated air passed me over as she cracked the top

three tips of the dummy. Her accuracy had always been amazing, and now it was starting to incorporate the lobbed magical projectiles.

While I watched her charge up another attack, a spray of rock fell over me as Samuel attacked my empowered spike. A vine twice the size of my skill cracked like a whip. The tip of the plant disintegrated in a spray of green matter, but so did the section of stone that Sam attacked. Samuel gestured with his arms, the vine responding to each of his subtle movements. I'd never been to an orchestra, but if he didn't embody a conductor, I didn't know what did. The massive organic limb reduced itself chunk by chunk, but soon the <Stone Spike> was all but rubble. Dramatic as he was, Sam plopped straight to the ground.

A conflagration of fire and bits of stone pelted against my Limestone Skin. The heat was mostly abated, but bruises formed along my back. Thankfully, my regeneration was already replacing the five percent health Danny's collateral damage had done to me. Considering the discomfort of dumping out my entire mana pool, the fiery rock barely hurt, but I still gave Daniela a glare.

"You still splash too much with the empowered version," I complained.

"It's a fireball! What do you expect? We can't all *think* about where your attack is going and make it happen," she said. She had to pause to dab at the sweat off her body as it steamed.

"She does have a point. The accuracy of your attacks is a whole other kind of scary, Ronan," Sam said from the ground.

"Hey, I'm not the one with the crazy leaf tentacle taking up half the training area," I complained. When none of us said anything for several seconds, we started laughing. It was a relieved laugh and an excited cackling.

The first half of the week had been an utter mess of experimenting and wasted mana. However, once we'd figured ways of circumventing the limitations and side effects of our skills, our flexibility had jumped to an astounding degree. For all of us, the main factor we were able to tune was the scale of our skills. Daniela and I focused on regulating the intensity of our attacks, as well as precision. In Samuel's case, he had to figure out how to effectively use his vines offensively.

The results of our near-ceaseless efforts over the past week and a half were sprayed around us in rock form.

"Impressive! That was a magnificent display of something that should have been physically impossible!" an energetic voice called down to our group. All of us spun in surprise to see Alan smiling at us. His eyes were wide and there was a twitch in his step. Almost literally. The man had trouble standing still.

Ava and Ben flanked the brains of the Bunker as he trudged forward excitedly. They revealed a *second* person as they moved down the hill. My uncle. The greeting I was about to call out froze in my throat as all the conflicting emotions I'd kept bottled up these past weeks bubbled to the surface again. While I managed to wave at their approach, it wasn't much of a greeting. Sam and Danny, on the other hand, shook hands vigorously with the new surface arrivals and motioned for my uncle to join us. After a moment of hesitation, I saw him start to walk.

"Children, please, tell me what you've discovered. These two," he pointed over both shoulders, "have been keeping me apprised, but they also told me that us old timers can't quite perform the same as you. I would love to know how that works, exactly."

Alan leaned forward on the balls of his feet. As he stood, he nearly hovered over Daniela and was close to bumping heads with me and Sam. His deep blue eyes bore holes into ours. We all took a step back, letting the man realize he'd been overexcited. When he didn't react, Ben stepped forward and placed a hand on Alan's shoulder.

"Let them catch their breath, Alan. They just finished training, and I think everyone will benefit from a talk over a meal. Yes?"

"Why, of course! My apologies. I will catch you all once the food is ready. I *must* look at that plant over there. And that rock.

Oh! And look, some of the fire is still smoldering." With that as his excuse, Alan proceeded to comb through the remains of the training area.

"Did we ever find out why he talks like that?" Daniela asked.

"Danny, it is rude to pry into people's past like that!" Ava gasped, scandalized.

"He was only sixteen when you all entered the Bunker though, wasn't he?" Sam asked, looking between our group and the man poking his <Vine Whip>.

"Alan was very close with our family," my uncle said. He stepped up beside Ben, wringing his hands all the while. "Your grandmother spent a lot of time looking for people from all over the world to work with, and Alan was her protégé. This was only made all the more intense after we were locked away in the Bunker. I fear that losing his family made him latch on to Ingrid and her work. When *she* passed, well, it became much worse."

I had to resist the urge to look at Alan again. He'd always been one of the unpredictable elements of the Bunker, and honestly a great source of excitement if we had some strange question another of our teachers couldn't answer. The only thing we'd never been able to get him to talk about was the past of the Bunker or the time right before Landfall.

More than once, he'd been scolded by Elias for 'misuse of limited recreational resources.' We'd always benefited from it, but we'd never pried into why he had so many quirks. The presence of yet another link to my family added to the weighted chain of responsibility over me.

"It isn't your prerogative to deal with the past, Ronan," Dale said, placing his hand on my shoulder. I almost flinched, but I nodded my head in silence instead. Emotional perception had always been my uncle's uncanny ability.

When awkward silence followed the engagement between us, Danny clapped her hands to draw our attention. "I'm making the food! Ronan, you are going to have to make some more chairs since we are up to a population of seven on the surface."

"Danny, I don't know if I would call seven people a 'population,'" Sam argued. He added the air quotes to emphasize what he thought about the brunette's word use. My two friends' mock argument alleviated the mood and everyone quickly dispersed into the vestibule and the lobby.

"Blobby, Anthony. Can you guys keep an eye on Alan for us?" I said, poking my slime partner in its gelatinous mass. All three older people jumped in surprise when I poked a nondescript mound that had blended in with the dirt. Blobby raised its signature lime green gelatinous periscope to look around, then my words finally seemed to register. The slime moved its bulk out of the little dip it'd created for itself next to my workspace and rolled down towards the edge of the woods. The dog-sized silhouette of Anthony met up with my slime and they headed towards the training area. I couldn't deny that I wanted to see how our eccentric researcher would react to the two, somewhat tamed entities.

"There have certainly been some developments since *one* of you two took a trip down below," my uncle said.

When I averted my eyes, Ben chose to respond in his place. "What can I say? There's been more excitement and things to do on the surface than there has been since the Bunker's early days."

I tuned them out for a moment as I focused on the space around the Entity Cluster. It wasn't cramped, but it would be if I just added two more spots. A smirk found its way across my face as a sneaky way of using my skill came to mind.

With a crack of my knuckles, I hardened the raised earthen sections of ground. The makeshift benches shrunk slightly as soil particles materialized in the gaps and were pushed closer together. With a twist of my hand, the section at the base of them received a boost of mana. Then I mule-kicked the rock bench.

A loud scrape of stone on stone drew the attention of Ben

and Dale as they saw me break off the seats. My uncle gave me a confused look while Ben just looked at me curiously when I repeated the process with the other three-person bench. I didn't answer as I focused on <Stone Spike> and splayed my fingers out while focusing on the corners of the bench. My control wasn't perfect, so the bench tipped back in my direction. Four small prongs sprouted from the bottom corners of the stone bench.When I straightened the stone bench and tested my weight on it, the thing barely budged. Just as a precaution, I added another pair of prongs midway and checked it again.

"Tada!" I said, gesturing to the now mobile bench. Both men gave me an appreciative nod. I could tell my uncle wanted to say more, but he settled on a 'good job.' With my prototype complete, I finished converting the other legless bench and created a whole new one from scratch. *Or mana. Wherever the soil was coming from. It worked.*

Ava, Sam, and Danny came out not long after that, surprised to see that I'd made the equivalent of a Flintstone's sectional couch while they prepared the food. Considering all the other things we'd seen since coming to the surface, a piece of stone furniture was low on the list of surprising things.

"You just can't beat dirt grown!" My uncle immediately complemented Daniela on her cooking efforts and gushed about the freshness of the food. He was in charge of much of the miscellaneous task of tending to the fish in the hydroponics system and dealing with the waste water processing of the Bunker. If anyone was to judge the quality of food based on its origin, it would be my uncle.

"Sam has been working on something over on his farm for a while, but he hasn't let any of us approach. He barely lets Ben help him or keep an eye on him," Danny said between bites.

"And it will stay that way until I am ready," the blond huffed.

Sometime during our meal, a ravenous Alan joined us. Daniela had even prepared food for the man's two non-human bodyguards, so when Alan plopped his butt on the bench,

Anthony and Blobby took positions next to him. Everyone but my uncle gave the exchange a strange look since Anthony had propped its abdomen on the bench and Blobby was settled in next to Alan. Instead of sucking in its food like the vacuum it usually mimicked, its appendage touched the food and it flowed into its body.

"Since when were those two ever polite eaters?" Sam finally asked.

"Oh? These two gentlemen? Why, they are wonderful conversationalists! You see, Blobby quite enjoyed when I fed him some of Ronan's mana-infused aggregate and Anthony *loved* munching on Samuel's <Vine Whip>. From my observations, I believe it is a key part of their development. It will require some further study once you three return from your next excursion," Alan stated matter-of-factly. The amount of words he was able to get out between mouthfuls was impressive.

"Wait, how do you know about the excursion?" I asked.

"Those two like to talk a lot, and I tend to like to listen. Plus, what else do you think the people down in the Bunker have been talking about? It's like someone gave them social media again. You'd think they would have learned some self-control after a quarter century underground," he replied flatly.

"Well, I guess that's one way of bringing up the next topic of conversation." Ben set down his food and looked at me and my friends. "Are you three still going to head towards the ants?"

"Yes."

"Yep."

"Mmmhmm," I added since Ben had waited to ask his question while I was chewing on a baked potato.

"Ronan, what have I told you about your manners!?" my uncle cried. When all he got in response was a shrug and a round of laughter, he crossed his arms and made it a point to look away.

"With that decision out of the way, is there anything we can do to help you three before you go?" Ben asked.

"Well, we are going to be leaving the camp in your hands

and everything that comes with that. I can't think of anything else," Sam said.

"You could force Mama to cook," Danny said, eliciting a groan from everyone. Even Alan.

"Torture aside, I think I speak for everyone here that we want you to succeed." Ben had a serious expression on his face.

"Ben, we aren't going to push ourselves too much. Our goal is to hit the next Quotient before we try to travel the old paved road again. If things get too spicy, we'll run away or figure something else out. The surface has been nothing but wake-up calls, and for once, I am not going to be sleeping in," I said, trying to convey my determination.

"Bad choice of words. He's definitely going to sleep in," Danny argued.

"Yes. He's never been much of a morning person," Sam added.

"*Anyways*," I said, ignoring the snickering from the people that were *supposed* to be the adults, "we are hoping it will be a short trip. While Ava's training hasn't raised our Quotient, the flexibility with which we can use our skills has gone through the roof."

"What about your work with the infusions?" Ava asked, gesturing to the series of crates now stacked in the corner of the vestibule.

"The Entity has helped me make a bit more progress on understanding infusions, but I would like to increase my Quotient more. I think I am just shy of having enough mana to do some of what he's been teaching me."

"That's what you've done with the three times it's been around?" Danny asked.

I nodded. As it'd warned us, the Entity hadn't been present for *most* of the days we'd remained at the camp. "I'm trying to figure out how to make full items instead of infused materials. Considering how many ant plates we have, I want to improve our armor so that we can take bigger hits."

"Why not just infuse our guns?" Ava asked.

Thankfully, Teach answered that for me. "He welded the whole thing together." The man retrieved a hunk of metal from inside the lobby. While the gun *looked* mostly intact, the slide refused to move and the grip had warped enough that you couldn't put a magazine into it. Ben passed it around, head hanging low. "It was one of my favorites..." he mumbled.

"Okay, well, if that's all you got, I think you three should take it easy today. We can handle the chores and tending to all the stuff. Only do what you *want* to do. Considering how hard you all have been working, some rest is well deserved," Ava said.

I already knew what I wanted to do with my day, but Sam and Danny looked a bit surprised with Ava's proposition of an off day. Had she said we needed to train more, I would have done more, but I was part of the school of thought that you should work hard and play even harder. Since coming to the surface, those two tasks just happened to be the same so far.

After that, we all quickly dispersed throughout the camp. Only Alan and the two pets remained in the vestibule. The harebrained researcher didn't say anything, but just observed everything I did as I prepared to infuse. It wasn't the first time I'd seen him do that, but it was the first time he'd directed his analytical stare at *me*. It took all I had to concentrate and not shudder under his intense gaze.

Before actually starting on a new piece, I checked over what I'd accumulated over the week and a half of work. Two dozen small chitin plates, five of the torso-sized chitin plates and the wolfhound pelt we'd received. The small plates I worked with the Quotient 0 Infusions as I'd been doing. The larger ones, those we got from the Smoldering Ants, I infused with their own Quotient 2 infusions. I didn't want to start testing how a Quotient 0 infusion translated into materials acquired from creatures with Quotient 2. The fact the metal shovel had taken *three* would have put my stock of infusions behind if I hadn't wrecked a few chitin plates while testing. With my lack of skill, I wanted as much training as possible to be able to make better things in the long run.

Handling the threads of the higher Quotient infusions had been an identical, if more taxing, process to using the Quotient 0 infusions. I'd worried that the wolfhound pelt would have caught fire. When it *did,* but didn't actually burn, I called that a success. I didn't risk testing them under gunfire either, since I had plans for the larger plates.

Every piece I'd worked had turned out to be an infused material, and not an item. During my brief lessons with the Entity, it explained that infusing worked the same way that the spell chains of our skills did. There had to be a link between the target, intent, and potency. Materials had potency, but no target or intent. Target was what shaped the item, while intent was what bound it to an attribute in the material. When those conditions were met, it would be recognized as an item.

The shovel, I realized, already had a target and an intent built into its form. While that might have also been true of the pistol Ben and I tested, it might not have been the right combination; the simpler explanation being that I just wasn't skilled enough at infusing. Nevertheless, there were two things I wanted to do before we left the camp.

It was risky to experiment with infusing using an Attunement I hadn't handled before. However, having better equipment would be vital to surviving longer in the wild. Pushing all those doubts and speculative thoughts from my mind, I fished out one of the infusions we only had a single copy of.

<Quotient 1 Infusion>

<Earth - Crystal>

<Integrity: 97%>

It was among the first we'd acquired, but it had been the only one of its kind we'd acquired. As far as we knew there were life, death, air, water, fire, and earth Attunements. We hadn't asked the Entity if there were more, but it wasn't important. The death Attunement we'd only seen in the skunk. If the trend for that Attunement continued, I wasn't sure if I *wanted* to meet any more. I shook my head, focusing on the task at hand.

I set my pickaxe on my workstation. Even with the brief

amount of use against my magical projects and enemies, there were a number of chips on it. The pointed end even had a slight bend to it. It was a fairly standard tool. The five pound carbon steel head with a three foot fiberglass shaft had performed admirably outside of its intended uses. I aimed to improve that.

With a press of the mental button for my <Infusion>skill, the little blob of mud and rock unspooled out of my hand. The dirt brown thread hovered in the air as I manipulated it with my mana. I watched the bar that represented my mana slowly trickle out as I contemplated how to infuse the pick. I doubted that anything would catch on fire like when I used the ant's infusions, or vibrate like the air infusions, but it was still equally likely to hurt me.

Before I could hesitate much more, I flicked the thread at the steel head. Instead of letting go as I'd been doing previously, I retained a firm hold on the thread as it wound through the head. The draw hiked up significantly, almost to the same amount as infusing one of the Quotient 2 chitin plates. I grit my teeth against the discomfort inside me, but I wrapped the thread around and around the pointed end. When I got to the point of contact with the shaft, I tied a hasty knot in an X before continuing to wind it around the chisel end of the pick.

The steel groaned as if I'd placed it under the lab's hydraulic press. When I ran out of thread to manipulate, a surge of mana transferred from me into the tool, taking me to my knees. Or it would have, had Alan not been right over my shoulder to catch me. Neither of us said anything as the pickaxe transformed via the infusion.

A ripple of crystal, similar to when I absorbed the Pith out of a creature, ran through the whole pickaxe. A brown light concentrated in the joint between the metal head and the shaft before crystalline growths sprouted from the material. I heard the fiberglass snap, but a pulse of mana surged within the weapon, filling in the hollow space inside the shaft. I stared dumbfounded as the metal point elongated and the chisel short-ened but widened like a fin.

The magic finally dissipated away, leaving a much deadlier version of a simple tool. I hefted the now much heavier weapon in both hands. The whole thing had to have gotten twice as heavy and the shaft didn't have a single bit of the hollow flexi-bility it once had.

"Marvelous. Molecular manipulation and force application all wrapped into one…" Alan whispered from behind me. "May I?"

My eyes remained locked on the newly enhanced weapon as Alan tested the short crystals sprouting from the top with a flick of his finger. A perfect bell chime answered the strike. As if it had been waiting for that response, the item's description flashed in my vision.

<Quotient 1 Enhanced Pickaxe>
<Attribute: Strength>
<Trait: Crystal Growth>

"I will need a detailed explanation on this process as soon as you are able, Ronan. This…This changes everything!" Alan said. His eyes had a fire within that made me flinch back, but he didn't attack me like I'd expected. He handed the enhanced pickaxe back to me without explaining what exactly changed before he vanished into the lobby.

Ava poked her head out and raised an eyebrow. I explained what had happened, getting an appreciative whistle from her when I showed her the pickaxe, and a nod of understanding when it came to Alan. "He went straight back into the Bunker. I wouldn't worry too much about it. He is probably getting ready to come up with some other crazy plan that puts yours to shame."

The woman returned to the lobby and I found myself a bit lost. After the intensity of the infusion, and the rollercoaster of emotions interacting with Alan always was, I sat at one of my stone benches for the rest of the afternoon. I had one more thing I wanted to put together for our trip the next day; it wouldn't take too long to set it up if I got up early the next day.Instead, I worked on getting familiar with the trait and feeling of increased strength my improved pickaxe gave me.

The light shining in from the doorways dimmed and my friends quickly returned for dinner. It was a muted affair compared to lunch. Alan was still down in the Bunker. Everyone appeared excited about my success with the pick, but Daniela cornered me after we all finished dumping our leftovers into Blobby.

"I've got dibs on the next weapon. And I want it before we go back out there." She pointed her thumb over her shoulder in the direction of the old road.

When I lifted my hands up, accepting defeat, she huffed and stormed away to help Samuel clean up for the night. The rest of the evening went by in a blur and my internal clock was screaming at me to get up. It was time to give our fiery neighbors a warm welcome.

CHAPTER TWENTY-SEVEN

Raid

Before anyone was awake, I'd already made my way out to my workstation. I didn't have a particular plan for how I wanted to armor us, but I knew it couldn't hurt to add some actual protection that the surface creatures couldn't penetrate as easily. The three armored vests we'd been using while traveling lay before me. Mine and Daniela's had already been replaced after all the damage we'd taken while fighting, but we didn't have an unlimited number of them.

Instead of trying to figure out a way of attaching the infused chitin, I removed the Kevlar padding on the front and back of the vest. I marveled at whoever designed the things since it was a fairly simple, but effective, piece of equipment. It was all attached with Velcro. After those were removed, I used a bit of tape to attach the chitin to the front of the plates before strapping it back into the Velcro. It was a tight fit, but I didn't think it would fall out. I repeated the process with both mine and Sam's vests. Then I replaced Danny's. Her torso was small and lithe enough that the large Smolder Ant chitin plates would have hampered her movement. Instead, I taped two of the smaller plates on the front section and one to the back.

With that done, and one last large plate left, I used a healthy amount of duct tape to fashion myself a shield. *More of a buckler if I'm honest...* If Alan saw my construction job, he probably would have had a heart attack. When *Ben* saw it, he was going to have one based on the amount of tape I'd just used up. I tested putting my hand in and out of the makeshift enarmes. It was quite snug, but with the tendency with which things tended to attack us, I didn't really plan to take it off while traveling. Comfort be damned over safety.

"Cutting quite the figure this morning, Ronny," my uncle said from the doorway. I spun to see the door pull closed behind me and the man holding out two trays of breakfast food. A look through the cracks of the vestibule's wooden doors told me that dawn was well on its way.

"Thank you. I have every intention to not get eaten by an ant today," I said, unequipping the chitin shield and setting down my enhanced pickaxe with all due haste. As serious as I was about all the defenses I'd just made, I couldn't shake the feeling that my uncle had walked in on me or something. It was ridiculous, but the flash of guilt made me reflect on how much I had been avoiding him.

"Nothing to be ashamed of. I have every confidence that you three will return victorious, only to head out and return victorious again," my uncle said. He hesitated slightly before placing one of the plates on my workstation. He didn't say anything else, just let his gaze drift over the scattered pieces of chitin and the dips where I kept the fire infusions for easy access. He gave me a weak smile before taking his food to one of my stone benches.

To my surprise, Blobby stirred and wobbled his way over to my uncle. The slime jiggled its appendage in protest until my uncle conceded and tossed it a potato wedge. The lime gel shivered as the food sunk out of sight and my uncle giggled in response. I hadn't even touched my food yet.

"Ronan. I... know that things are awkward between us. I didn't come to the surface *only* to try to work on mending our relationship. What… Well, what I am trying to say is that you don't need to worry about me being here. I did come to the surface with my own tasks, but should you need me, I will be there. Hopefully not out there," Dale gestured through the wooden door, "but if that is where you need me, then I will be there too."

"Why?" That was all I managed to say.

"You are my nephew, Ronan. You might not be my son by birth, but I raised you as if you were. I'm not trying to hold that over you like some kind of obligation that you have to love me. That would be unfair to you and uncharacteristically selfish of me. At least, I hope it would be uncharacteristic," he added with a slight smile. I couldn't help a snort-laugh from escaping me. He pinned me with his deep brown eyes. My increased perception noted the tension in his shoulders and the gray in his five o'clock shadow.

"You have given me everything without anything in return," I said. Unable to keep the words from spilling out. "But why did you keep that from me? I would have loved you regardless. Knowing more about you… about Mother and Father. That was all I wanted for a long time and you had those answers all along."

"That's right. I should have told you the truth a long time ago. Elias wasn't really enough of a reason to keep my mouth shut."

My uncle went quiet for a moment, and I could practically see the gears turning in his head. "I… I was angry at Marcus for many years. I didn't resent him leaving or what he did to avenge your mother and free us, but he could have stayed. He could have stayed until he had to leave. It took me a long time to realize he didn't want to taint your future, or Sam and Danny's, with the horrors he'd committed. His presence was a reminder of what humans were capable of when something got in their way."

"I'm going to try to find him," I sobbed. There were tears streaming down my face that I hadn't even realized I needed to shed. As much as I wanted to be mad with my uncle, I believed every word he said. He'd always been nothing but sincere with me. When my mother had come up, he'd always deflected like everyone in the Bunker, but he'd cared. He cared about my rock collection, he worried about my hopelessness, and he tended to our futures. Not just mine, but everyone's in the Bunker. Alexia and June may have been the doctors of our physical bodies, but Dale Terrigan was the heart of the Wildwood Bunker.

And I realized that I wanted him to be the heart of Wildwood Camp. The warm fire and comfortable bed that we returned to after facing the horrors and enemies of the surface. My uncle pulled me into a hug and I continued to sob into his shoulder for a long minute. As I cried, I felt many of the chains I'd put on myself spread out. I didn't have to carry burdens alone while surrounded by people who cared about me.

"Then I hope with all my heart you find the brother I lost," my uncle whispered. The moment ended abruptly as my uncle and I were tackled to the ground by a lanky blond's fierce hug.

"Yay! Finally," Sam shouted as he wrapped his arms around us.

"Samuel!" my uncle cried in surprise before breaking out in laughter.

"Hey! I didn't approve of this dog pile!" Daniela jumped on top of Sam, knocking us apart like a bowling ball to human pins.

An excited Blobby and a confused Anthony hovered at the edge of our group, unsure of how to deal with the mound of humans. Ben smirked from the doorway while Ava held her head in her hand.

"Was it too much to ask everyone to be professional right before our kids head out into giant ant territory?" Ava asked, head still in her hand.

"Would you rather they leave tense, or relaxed? Come, Ava, you don't want me to tell Juan you've been nitpicking again?" Ben joked. Ava immediately straightened and coughed into her hand.

"Right, I suppose a little lightheartedness is beneficial at times. Are you children ready to go? I hope you all return by sundown if at all possible."

"Let's go kill some ants!" Danny said excitedly. Anthony chittered at her. "I mean, some bad bugs!"

— + —

"These are pretty sweet, Ron," Sam said, knocking on the chitin under his vest.

"How come you two got the big plates and I got the small ones?" Danny complained as she adjusted her vest. Even with the smaller plates, it was bulkier than before and she struggled a bit to get it on. When I pointed to her twisting and turning to try to get into the vest, she sighed in defeat. "Fair enough."

"Here is an empty duffle for any sweet loot you guys might find on the way," Ben said. "Are you sure you want to leave Anthony behind, Danny?"

The ant was hovering next to Ben, using its antenna to check out the fire mage still struggling with her armor.

"I don't want to risk him getting mixed hormones or pheromones or something and attacking us. I haven't scouted out this way, so it may be entirely possible that we need to run away, and I don't want to worry about leaving Anthony behind," she answered once she was finally able to adjust her armor. "Plus, I think having him give you a hand while we are away will be good. Don't want something to come knocking without you all having something to protect you."

"You do see this rifle in my hands, yes?" Ben said, hoisting the gun onto his shoulder.

"Sure, but things out here have shrugged off bullets more times than I want to think about. Anthony brings a little bite to your group."

As if the Fire Ant had been waiting for the word, he snapped his mandibles loudly, causing Ben to jump. He glared at the giant ant but his gaze softened when he looked at us.

Blobby had been waving at the gathered adults since we'd started standing at the edge of the woods. *I need to spend some more time explaining human norms to it,* I thought to myself.

Regardless, we packed up our supplies and water and made our way into the woods. Less than ten feet into the trees, we walked through a near imperceptible bubble of energy. Neither Sam nor Danny reacted to the change, but I had my suspicion that we'd just crossed the Entity's area of influence. While the implications of that weren't clear to me, I was content to know that the Entity had been keeping the camp safe through its efforts.

The rest of the trip was an exercise in patience and attention. Unlike our first few ganders through the woods, particularly when we went to retrieve the Entity Cluster, we paid rapt attention to our surroundings. I walked at the head of the group, keeping an eye on everything at ground level, while Danny and Sam alternated in keeping an eye on the foliage overhead and our surroundings. Blobby just did as Blobby did. The slime rolled a ways forward past us, waved its appendage and settled to wait until we met up with it. The gelatinous blob repeated the process for the whole hour free of encounters.

Throughout the whole week, I'd been so concentrated on training that I hadn't even bothered to check my status. I knew we hadn't absorbed any Pith or Dreg, so I went straight to what I was most interested in.

Attributes:
Strength: 1.41
Mobility: 1.31
Perception: 1.53
Refinement: 1.13 > 1.16
Containment: 1.93 > 1.98

The gains to my refinement and containment were small, meager really, but it was a trackable improvement. My mana still regenerated a percent every few seconds, and I didn't feel like I could cast more <Stone Spikes> or <Earthen Barriers>, but the constant drain of using my magic's passive ability or activating my pickaxe would be just a bit easier.

While I had my status opened, I focused on the LPS. A brief glance at my map told me we'd traveled almost a mile north-west. The only signs of life we'd encountered were trees and more trees. The further we went from camp, however, the more scorch marks we saw marring the bark of the oaks and pines around us. Another thirty minutes, and we ran into the markers of Fire Ant presence we were looking for. Cleared trees.

A clearing composed of translucent off-white sand and scattered debris sprawled for miles before us. The transition from woods into sandy ground was nonexistent. There was a tree line even sharper than the one at the Bunker. Scattered amidst the sands, we saw hundreds upon hundreds of the Quotient 0 ants milling about. They dragged chunks of plant matter and non-descript piles of rot out of sight. We skirted the tree line to finally spot flattened ant piles. Holes big enough to fit the Smolder Ants led underground and out of sight.

"This is not just sand, this is ash," Danny whispered. The woman was rubbing the white substance between her fingers. I shuddered as I looked back at the field all around us and the sheer amount of destruction the ants represented.

"Let's stay out of the way and observe. This is... more than I expected. We might have to retreat and entrench ourselves even deeper in the camp before heading out again," I said.

We moved to a small grove a ways from the tree line and observed the ants in the distance. Every so often, a scouting group similar to the one that had attacked Danny would come from the edge of the trees to the east carrying a spider corpse. There was a military efficiency to the scouting groups that contrasted sharply from what the smaller workers were doing. From what I could tell, it almost looked like the weaker workers didn't have much of a will until one of the larger ants approached them. Wondering if that was potentially something we could exploit, we continued to watch the creatures go about their business.

One group of scouts scurried empty handed out of the woods not far to our left and we all tensed as they passed us by. As they crossed paths with another group that had been coming from the spider's territory, both paused briefly and exchanged antenna waves before heading north further into the cleared space. As I tracked their movements, I could have sworn I saw a gout of fire rise out of the ground in the distance.

When no other scouting groups appeared for over thirty minutes, I got an insane idea. As if they'd read my mind, my two friends immediately had counter arguments. My hands went up to halt the initial deluge of protests.

"How else are we supposed to get stronger? I don't want to take the risk, but doing nothing means this is a wasted trip. As much as I feel the benefit of training our skills, the Entity is right. Quotients are going to be our best bet at survival. Plus, more Dreg means more energy for it and traits for us," I said, meeting my friend's eyes.

"There is no guarantee they won't retaliate," Sam said.

"They've already attacked us. In mass, if you need me to point to the stockpile of materials and infusions we got from it. If more than we think we can handle come at us, then we'll retreat. Twiddling our thumbs isn't going to get us anywhere."

"Ah, bork. Ronan, if I get bit because of you, we are going to have some words when we get back to the camp," Danny said as she climbed one of the nearby trees.

Sam just shook his head, but used his <Vine Whip>skill to bring two person-high, thigh-thick stalks of death to our side. Raising berms of spiked earth to either side of us, I created a funnel to limit how many ants could come directly at us without climbing or being impaled. Once we were set up and our mana restored, I turned to Blobby.

"I need you to watch Sam's back, okay? I'm still not entirely sure what you can do, but defend him like you would me. Got it?" The slime gave a little headless nod and rolled to be right behind Samuel. His vines hung limp over the crown of spikes I'd made for defense, but I knew they would respond to his commands.

With a deep breath, I walked out onto the sand-ash. Only a few feet into the ants' territory, a dozen Quotient 0 ants spotted me. Like the horde of senseless insects they were, they charged. Bracing my left leg, I called forth a spell chain on my shield arm. Just before the ants reached me, I heaved the ground beneath them with <Earthen Barrier>. Three of the rat-sized ants actually took to the air while the others weren't able to stop their charge and crashed right into the mound of hardened sand-ash.

My pickaxe whipped through the air as I pushed the pick through one, two, and three of the crashed insects. I didn't bother to shake the small creatures off my weapon before I swung it wide. The ants caught on the other side of my swing flew through the air like small, smoldering projectiles.

One of the ants that had flown up with my initial cast managed to wiggle its way into my personal space to clasp onto my left leg. A hiss escaped me, but all I did was punch down with my shield and the creature was crushed. The burning pain lingered in my leg, but it had reminded me that while fragile to my current powers, they could still swarm me. And swarm me they did.

My initial engagement had only drawn a dozen, but I could already see two more groups of ants surging in my direction. A <Stone Spike> spell chain formed in my shield hand again and I splayed my hand out while focusing on the surviving ants of the first group. All but one of them got a sand-ash rock right in the gob. I stomped on the last remaining one before hightailing it back to my friends.

It was a good proof of concept for how I could deal with creatures, but I wasn't dumb enough to think I could keep a whole swarm off alone.

"Aggro!" I yelled as loudly as I could without risking my voice echoing through the Fire Ant territory.

"We can see that, rock brain. Get a bump and get ready to tank," Danny called from above. I could barely see the woman as she hung, legs clasped around a branch, spell chains poised on both hands. Her fists were closed, which was unusual for how she cast her skill, but I didn't pay it much mind.

Sam wordlessly tapped my leg with his healing skill and sweet relief flowed through me. The attack had done a mere five percent damage, just a shade more than getting peppered with exploding plastic while infusing, but every percent counted. Just when I took my spot at the head of the funnel, fiery death rained down on the approaching ants.

As if Daniela had fired a shotgun, stone pellets shredded several of the incoming ants with a single cast. The closed fist suddenly made sense as I watched the brunette release a handful of tiny gravel that was instantly hit with her skill's kinetic and thermal force. From experience, we knew that fire against fire wasn't as effective, but Daniela had come up with a counter to that weakness without even letting us know.

Atta girl. DPS for the win! That was all the time I had to focus on my friend before the survivors of her attack reached me. A vine came in and slapped away any Fire Ant trying to flank me, while I kept a steady core workout. That is to say, I swung my pickaxe left and right while keeping my legs firmly planted on the ground. Each time I was on the backswing with the widened chisel head of my weapon, I lashed out at any ant that got overeager.

This went on for less than two minutes, but my muscles burned from the effort of keeping the tidal surge of ants from reaching us. Thankfully, only a few ants remained scattered around us. Danny dropped down from above, crushing one underfoot before she ran two of them through with the wolf fangs we'd acquired on our second day on the surface. I hadn't even noticed she'd had those on her.

"You guys better rest up, I saw another wave of them heading our way," she said, finishing off the last straggler.

I plopped to the ground, groaning and flexing my hands.

The start of some serious calluses were making their presence known. *I didn't even know limestone could get calloused…*"Should we retreat?"

"If you think you can handle another round of that, I think we'll be good. Blobby didn't even get involved in the fight." Daniela pointed to the slime which appeared to be shaking its appendage like a cantankerous old man shaking a cane. Not getting to fight had apparently bothered the gelatinous tendril.

"Here, take a bump, Ron. I've got to rest up but then I'll be good to go," Sam said as he passed a flow of refreshing energy through me. I hadn't realized his skill could restore exhaustion and muscle aches as well as it did, but that would be something to experiment with in the future.

"Based on that response, I am going to say you are all down to hit this next group." My friends gave me sweaty but fierce smiles. Daniela's smile faltered when she looked back at the ants. A surge of fear-borne adrenaline jolted me to my feet. "What's wro—"

The words died in my throat as I watched the horde of ants pause at the edge of the tree line. One of the ants in the swarm stood out from the others. My perception let me glean its information even from our distant spot.

\<Fire Ant\>

\<Attunement: Fire\>

\<Refinement: N/A\>

\<Perceived Metier Quotient: 1\>

The information itself wouldn't have inspired the chill down my spine. It was what the ant did next. As if it had decided its compatriots were part of a buffet bar, the large creature snapped the heads of several Quotient 0 ants with its powerful mandible. Before our very eyes, Pith ejected itself out of each corpse, and the dog-sized ant swelled inch by inch. As if having sent a command along its pheromone lines, another of the ants snacked on the buddy adjacent to it. Soon the twenty-ish horde had turned into four mean insectile drones.

The lead ant who'd taken control morphed one last time before its information updated before me.

<Fire Ant>

<Attunement: Fire>

<Refinement: Blaze>

<Perceived Metier Quotient: 3>

"Form up!" I shouted just as the cannibalistic elites surged in our direction.

CHAPTER TWENTY-EIGHT

Pinched

The Blaze Ant had grown to be nearly the size of Raymond. Its buddies were now the size of dogs, meaning they were at least Quotient 1. My eyes were locked on the enormous creature as it shouldered a tree out of its path. It didn't rip out of the ground, thankfully, but a significant chunk of bark instantly flamed, charbroiled, and disappeared in the wind.

"Sam, can you slow it!?" I asked, setting my pickaxe down on the ground. There was no sense trying to meet the creature's charge. I would've ended up the same or worse than that tree. Instead, I focused my mana on both of my hands.

"Getting ready to deal with the smaller ones!" he responded, just as vines sprouted out of the ground to pin the three smaller ants. Small gouts of flames erupted from the creatures' mouths, pivoting left and right to try to burn or bite their unexpected bindings.

To answer my call for assistance, two claps of fire splashed against the Blaze Ant's head. The strike was enough to slow it just a tad. The missed step after the strike gave me the opening I needed.

"<Earthen Barrier>, <Stone Spike>, <Stone Spike>!"

The words ripped out of me like commands to the very earth, which heaved up a mixture of sand-ash and topsoil to meet the behemoth's charge. The outside edges of my barrier stretched higher, pointed inward to increase the catch area of my attack. The ant still forced its way through my barricade. One of the spikes impaled its abdomen before snapping off at the base. With impressive dexterity, the creature tipped its wounded body out of the way as I released another stone spike right in its trajectory. Liquid fire spilled out of it in response, eliciting a trilling chitter from the creature before it lost most of its momentum.

A net of vines tried to wrap around it, but they instantly shriveled thanks to its boiling blood. I chanced a look behind the creature to see Danny flicking her wolf fangs into one of the ants before the other two managed to get free. Then the largest ant turned back to me with hate-filled compound eyes, drawing me back into the fight.

"Sam, help Danny! Then come save me!" I shouted as my war cry. Not particularly inspiring, but I wanted to kick my life mage friend into overdrive.

After all the constant casting, my mana pool was at less than twenty percent, so I figured it was time to finally use the trait and attribute boost of my weapon. Brown light flickered in my hands before it was sucked up into the crystal center of my pickaxe's handle. A surge of strength filtered through me and I jumped towards the ant.

Its front leg moved impossibly fast for an injured bug. My perception and boosted strength gave me just enough reaction speed to put my chitin shield between me and the blow. A pulse of heat spread out from the impact, but I was still thrown off course. Worried that I would impale myself on my own weapon, I hugged the pick head before tumbling on the ground.

My health flashed an angry warning as it dipped to sixty percent from the single blow. Something in my chest groaned as I stood, warning me that something in there was close to breaking.

"That the best you got!?" I coughed out. The ant turned back my way instead of heading for my friends. A hazy line of red light formed around the Blaze Ant's antenna. A light that I distinctly recognized from Daniela's skills, even if it lacked the crisp, yet unknown, patterns. The primal skill unleashed a flamethrower, plain and simple.

Thankfully, I was still channeling mana into my pickaxe. When I hunkered down on the ground with my chitin shield covering my head, a thin dome of crystal sprouted from the head of it like a glass umbrella. Both of my defenses were… inadequate, to say the least. Tongues of fire licked at the rest of my body and my Limestone Skin only muted the heat slightly. I screamed in pain as my clothes smoldered.

The retort of two pistols brought a merciful end to the flames. As soon as the pain hit full on, I lost concentration and the pickaxe fell from my hand. The crystal umbrella, glowing a faint red even during the day, shattered when it lost the mana feeding it. My shield didn't last much longer either. The heat melted the adhesive on the tape which left the tape enarmes around my arm; the chitin plate fell to the ground next to where I shivered from the pain.

A pair of fingers snapped an inch in front of my eyes. I blinked and focused on Sam, who was hovering over me with another of his deep frowns. "Ronan, can you hear me?"

"Y-yes," I chattered through gritted teeth. There was so much pain. My thoughts jerked from one thing to the next as I shook. Then a blanket of relief flowed through my head and down my neck before it was stifled on my shoulders.Another surge of cooling energy flowed from my forearm up to my shoulder and down to my fingers on both hands. A last bump hit me in the navel, and my shivering eased significantly.

I blinked again as the world snapped into sharpened focus. It was the standard amount of focus I had, but everything had had a hazy outline while the pain overwhelmed my brain. I had enough wherewithal to catch Sam's head before it hit the ground.

My body still had enough pain receptors kicking to be distracting, but not enough for me to miss the fight not thirty feet from me.

Daniela weaved around the leg strikes of the Blaze Ant, dodging them with her high mobility. It was a close thing as I watched claw after claw barely miss my friend. I scrambled on the ground for my pickaxe and checked my mana pool. Back to twenty percent. Even the few seconds between getting scorched and healed hadn't afforded me much of my magic back. That, however, wasn't going to stop me.

I plastered a grimace on my face to try to distract me from the pain as much as I could. It wasn't super useful, but it got me walking. Daniela spotted me hobbling closer and darted behind one of the nearby trees, getting the ant to turn away from me as it chased after my friend. My legs churned faster as I grit my teeth. At my mental beckoning, crystalline growths crawled along the head of my pick.

When the creature was turned almost all the way around, I dropped the widened chisel end right onto the stone spike I'd lodged in its body. The Crystal Growth trait had let me add mass to the weapon, and the strike pushed the sand-ash rock clean through the chitin. Surely some of my attributes had something to do with that, but I didn't trust my body enough to have done more than lift and drop the tool.

The ant let out a strange insectile wail I didn't ever want to hear again before it pivoted its body away from Danny. A gout of its boiling blood sprayed the air and I resigned myself to my burning fate. Before any of the stuff could land, a gelatinous half-dome of lime green materialized around me. I heard Blobby's slime bubble under the onslaught before evaporating away into nothing.

The much-reduced tendril plopped to the ground and coalesced around its crystal center. I didn't think, grabbing the corrupted crystal in my free hand before the ant finished turning. A half-jump stumble took me behind a tree as the ant bit down where I'd been standing. Loose tree mulch and dirt showered around me, and I really wished I had enough mana to throw out a <Stone Spike>. Then I remembered it didn't need to be a super strong one or even do much damage. The damage would come from my pick.

A spell chain formed in my left arm. The mana moved as if it was threading through mud, but I still got the spell out quick enough to pin the creature's body. Two thin spikes formed a triangle over the ant's thorax. I had no doubt it would break through them if given a single chance, so I rushed in. A gout of flame similar to what the smaller ants had blazed out of its mouth, but thanks to its compromised position, I ignored the attack with a jump.

My senses screamed at me. One of the ant's legs had managed to free itself enough to protect the head and work to swat me out of the way. My body wasn't in a position where I could dodge, so I tried to brace myself for the impact. It was going to be too slow. For me.

Blobby once again expanded. The slime had somehow used its senses to prepare a defense against the Blaze Ant's sudden attack. Gel flowed down my arm to brace my neck and Blobby's appendage reached out as if it was going to catch the claws careening towards me. The slime *did* catch them, eating through the momentum as if it was a custom made mattress of comfort. Unfortunately, as effective as the tendril's gel body was, the ant still slapped me away like a fly. *Insect irony, Ron?*

With that last useless thought, I once again tumbled through the air. Thankfully, the earth was my friend. Sorta. I felt what should have been a bone breaking skip through the woods turn into a body bruising one as my Limestone Skin transferred some of the impacts into the earthy medium. Without me to distract it, the Blaze Ant shook off my stone bindings with ease. My body stopped on its back and I got a good view of the ant heading towards me to finish me off.I couldn't really blame it, considering how many of its pals we'd killed.

Both Blobby and I struggled to shift out of the way, but we

were at our limit. The ant would get to us before we could get out of the way.

As the ant loomed over us, it practically licked lips it didn't have at the prospect of us as a meal. When it *didn't* clamp down on me, I opened my eyes to see what the wait was. My friends were the answer to that.

Two lashes of foot thick vines wrapped around the Ant's legs. With the oozing green ends, I recognized them as Sam's earlier stalks. Then a screaming Latina dropped out of the tree canopy, right onto the ant's head. Daniela planted her wolf fang daggers into the creature's eyes, releasing twin gouts of boiling blood. Before any of that could get on her, she let loose two <Flame Blasts> into the handle-ish roots of the fangs.

The flames portion of her attack did next to nothing against the ant's fire-attuned body. The two daggers, however, embraced the kinetic energy and punched into the creature's brain. The Blaze Ant dropped instantly.

"Danny!" I managed from the ground. The woman rode the creature down flawlessly and did a front flip worthy of a pre-Landfall gymnast. "Wha—"

"You didn't think I spent the whole time scouting without trying to pick up new skills, did you? And I mean skill skill, not the magical one," she added.

"Where is Sam?" I tried to get up, but failed utterly. A look at my left leg told me my knee was either dislocated or something there was broken. As the adrenaline of the fight lessened, the cumulative pain from all my injuries flared up again and I flopped to my back. Thankfully, Blobby shifted enough to catch my short fall and prevent me from aggravating my body more than it was already.

"Are you okay?" Danny reached out towards me, but when she saw the burn marks, she hesitated. *She probably sees my twisted leg too.*

"Answer to that is…no. However, I am okay, and my health is holding at twenty-ish percent. How's Sam?"

"Present, accounted for, and thoroughly enDregged.

InDregged? Whatever the term is for the atrocious agony of using external mana. If <Vine Whip> wasn't a constant drain skill, I would *not* be doing so hot." Our blond friend stumbled from around the giant ant's bulk. He looked a bit drunk, which was a new sight. The Bunker survivors had managed to make a poor man's version of vodka many years ago and Sam had always denied trying it. It tasted like burning toilet water, but it was more about the experience.

"That would be Dreg poisoning. What's your Dreg up to?" I asked, trying to focus on the conversation and not on my injuries.

"Oh, it's only up to twenty-one percent. Boy, was it a doozy, though!" Samuel proceeded to sway even while standing in place. That was a bit concerning, but not the biggest problem.

"How is your mana doing? Danny, are there any more ants coming this way?" I asked, my mind sputtering. Thoughts struggled to connect, but I at least had the presence of mind to ask about possible reinforcements.

"Holding at ten percent, captain!" The blond struck a poor salute.

"None that I can see, but I wouldn't trust hanging around after all the noise we made," she said. The brunette also moved to hold Sam up as he hiccupped and swayed dangerously close to falling.

"Okay, before all the adrenaline leaves my system, if you have enough mana to use <Health Bump> on my leg, please do it. If not, I want you to try to find something to make a splint, Sam. Danny, start triggering as many of the ants as you can. Start with big boy over there." I pointed to the Blaze Ant. "Then do a quick run through and check for other ants that might be coming. We'll gather what loot we can after that."

"I got one left in me, cap!" Sam said as he sauntered over to me and slapped my leg. "Oops. That looks like it would hurt."

The iron taste of blood filled my mouth. I'd bit my tongue to try to stop myself from screaming. It was partly successful. Thankfully, I heard a sick pop and my leg straightened. The healing would have probably hurt as much as the initial slap. Daniela was already making her way around the open space. The Blaze Ant was disintegrating into ash before our very eyes and I saw Blobby roll away from us and vacuum up two of the small Quotient 0 ants into its body. After how much the slime had shrunk, they sat snug against the Metier Crystal core.

Instead of moving to assist Danny, Sam plopped on the ground and hit the snooze button on the whole engagement.

"Great. Just what I—" My words cut off as a veritable wave of Pith surged from our dead attackers. Each trail split in three, but we'd slain so many ants I couldn't keep track of which went to who and from where. The trail from the Blaze Ant, however, was clear as day and hit me like a spark of power. Goosebumps ran down my skin as the smaller trails of energy also filtered into me. The ones that flowed into Samuel forced the man awake. I made note that none went to Blobby; yet another oddity of the tendril.

A rush of soft warmth flowed through me as I felt my Quotient rise. Most of my burns and pain winked away in an instant. Before I got a chance to give my status a peek, Daniela rushed into the clearing. The woman plowed right through the ash mound of the Blaze Ant and over to us.

"We've got about two dozen Q0's coming our way," she said, already holding our gear and provisions. I tested my legs, then wobbled to my feet. Thanks to the Quotient and Sam's healing, my legs were back in travel shape.

"Start grabbing what you can. Blobby, if you can grab stuff and not eat it, please help Daniela," I said as calmly as I could. "Sam, give me a status on how drunk you are."

"On a scale of one to ten? It was eleven and now eight," he droned. He was still on the ground, but I managed to help him to his feet.

"Start walking home. You see some loot on the way, grab it. We'll catch up."

With my friend shambling home, I looted the three Q1 ants before sifting through the ashes for the Blaze Ant's loot. The chitin plates clacked where I'd stuffed them in my armored vest. The echoes from the forest made me want to twitch as if the ants were right behind me, but I focused on my task. It was a truly astounding mound of ash. After a few tense seconds, my fingers brushed against a scalding hot object that forced me to draw my hand back. After another unfortunate second of hesitation, I snagged the burning thing and braced for the pain.

Surprisingly, the object was cool to the touch. It gave me a start as I realized it was the ant's stinger. Pushing that out of mind for the moment, I scrounged the infusion from the ash mound and started to head towards Sam. Neither Danny nor Blobby were anywhere in view. Just as I trudged through where the ant's head once was, I tripped.

Had I had the coordination and senses of my pre-attuned body, I would have fallen flat on my face. Instead, I managed to catch myself on my injured leg. The motion sent a shot of pain through me, but at least I didn't fall. What laid on the ground at my feet made the whole embarrassing near-tumble worth it. Daniela's two fangs and a Metier Crystal the size of my fist. Without thinking, I stuffed them in my waistband and tucked the crystal under my shoulder. My pickaxe was the last thing I needed, and I swung that over my shoulder as I hobbled away from the ashen territory of the Fire Ants.

It didn't take me long to catch up to a wobbly Samuel. The man held the chitin plate I'd made my shield from like a baby. He was doing a poor job of not stumbling into thick oaks that were nowhere near his intended destination.

"Hold these, Sam," I called from behind him. In a swift movement, I passed him the crystal and the stinger. Then I slipped my pickaxe into my belt and threw his arm over my shoulders. The two of us kicked it into high gear as much as we could. The forest chittered with angry sounds as the ants pursued.

My legs burned as I fought against exhaustion and the lingering pain of my injuries. Sam's and my breaths were ragged by the time Daniela came into view. She was holding a duffle that looked to be stuffed full, and had her gun trained behind us. It clapped twice before the empty click told us she was out. She huffed in frustration and tried to cast one of her skills, but it fizzled in her hands.

"For...get it! Get...to the clearing!" I shouted between gulped breaths.

The woman turned and sprinted. If I hadn't been watching her, I would have said she just vanished, but a brief second later, my perception highlighted her form traipsing through the trees. Trusting that she would be able to get help, I soldiered on. At some point during the endeavor, Sam got enough of his bearings to hit us both with a <Health Bump>. With the slightest bit of stamina restoring us, the sounds of the pursuing ants quieted. Not gone, but muted by the surrounding trees between us.

The minutes ticked and we managed to make it into the clearing. Daniela, with what looked to be a fresh weapon in hand, helped take Samuel from my shoulders. Dale and Ben grabbed ahold of us and dragged me back a ways. Our entire group retreated slowly towards the vestibule, where I spotted Ava holding a rifle. As professional as ever, the woman didn't even flinch as we collapsed on the ground. Alan rushed over to us with a series of bandages and water.

He gave Sam a look-over, noting his drunken demeanor, before focusing his efforts on me. He didn't comment on my injuries, or the lack thereof on my friends, as he cleaned the burns that remained and bandaged them. His eyes burned intensely as he hesitated slightly. He'd felt the slight change to my flesh thanks to Limestone Skin. Regardless, he finished patching me up, handed me a canteen with water, and trained a pistol on the woods.

"Incoming!" Ava called. "Focus on the backline, leave the closest ones to me."

The five members of our group still standing started to alternate shots into the woods. Ava and Danny took a life with each shot, while Ben, Alan and my uncle took a few to hit their speedy marks. One of the larger ants hesitated on the edge of the woods. It was just outside of my perception range, but judging by its size, it was one of the Q2 variants or possibly a Q3. If insects could glare, I was sure that one was doing it. It tried to take a step forward, but it touched something it very much didn't like. A ripple of energy passed through me and I turned just in time to see the Entity Crystal's dimming light. *It must've been trying to cross into its area of influence.*

Chittering angrily, the ant looked at the dead bodies in our clearing before retreating back into the woods. Everyone held their breath for several seconds until the Entity broke the silence.

"How kind of you to bring friends. Maybe next time, do not anger them quite as much?"

CHAPTER TWENTY-NINE

Recovery

"Comes with the Dreg Warrior territory," I said, finally laying on the ground and releasing a weary sigh. It had only been a few hours since we'd left, but I could have sworn it was a few days.

"It appears so. Look, your strange gel pet is coming." Sure enough, Blobby rolled *slowly* into the clearing. There were two Q0 ant corpses inside its body as well as several red-black blobs floating around inside him. As laborious as the tendril's movements looked, its jiggle spoke of unbridled excitement.

"You three care to catch us up? It's barely been six hours," Ava said, flicking the safety on her rifle and turning to regard us. Apparently, she'd been so focused on the ants, she'd missed our less-than-stellar state. "Oh my God! What happened to you two?"

Samuel was still utterly trashed and I looked like something left in the oven overnight.

"Fire Ants. Dreg poisoning. The usual," I said casually.

"Very funny, Ronan. Are you two okay?"

"Nothing our healer here can't fix." Of course, Sam picked

that moment to hurl on the ground beside him. "Once he's less drunk."

"What? How is he drunk?" my uncle asked. Dale patted Sam gently in the back, supporting him as he emptied the contents of his stomach. While I hadn't anticipated he would get intoxicated like he had by Dreg poisoning, I did warn the blond not to eat those snacks while we scouted the ant territory.

"That's a long story. Entity, are we safe?" I asked.

"Clear as far as I can see. I appreciate the Dreg, for the record. Not having to hold your breath while talking is appreciated." Everyone looked visibly confused at the crystal's antics. "It is a metaphor for what I have been doing with my mana and influence. I do not need oxygen. Yes, you are safe. Story time, if you would?"

— + —

Everyone was very eager to hear what happened. Before we did any of that, we collected the little present the ants had brought to our door. Ben and Ava nudged fourteen of the Q0 ants, pushing Ben into his second Level and putting Ava very close. In the case of my uncle and Alan, the Pith triggered their Attunements.

My uncle started sweating profusely before a sheen of frost covered his entire body. In the case of Alan, flakes of skin burned up and drifted away like ash off of coal. Neither of them were conscious while this happened, since their bodies locked up the moment the process started, but it was still distinctly fascinating. I somewhat regretted not seeing Daniela's mom taking on her air Attunement.

Once all the loot was secure inside the vestibule or the lobby, and both Dale and Alan had received the reprogrammed connection to the Entity via their implants, we sat down to talk. It took well over an hour for us to recount our brief raid on the Fire Ant hive. The part that surprised everyone the most was the degree to which I'd managed to concentrate the physical damage to myself. Considering I was supposed to be the tank of the group, I took that as a compliment. My uncle, of course, frowned the entire time as I talked about getting slapped around by a car-sized ant.

"Why didn't you shoot them from afar? That seemed to work pretty well with the ones here," he asked. He shook his head, small flakes of ice falling from his hair like snow, before pointing at the pile of Q0 chitin plates and infusions. Ben was hard at work separating all the loot by type. He really had an astounding dedication to organization.

"I can provide an answer, Dale," the Entity started. "That would be because of the exponential growth factor certain creatures gain from Quotients. From Ronan's experimentation with the materials these creatures provide, I can say that most of their growth is centered on survivability. Each Quotient makes the ants roughly three times more durable either in carapace strength or hardiness overall. The bullets of the current weapons at your disposal would have a tough time penetrating unless it was a direct hit. The chitinous armor of the ants also throws some ablative properties into the mix."

"As long-winded as that was, that about covers it," I said. "I hadn't considered that Quotients would affect creatures like that, but it makes sense. We aren't exactly the same as when we were at Quotient 1, either. There is a big difference between half an inch of chitin and a full inch of it."

The revelation deepened all of the older member's faces. Except for Alan, who was going through the loot, infusions, and his status like a child on Christmas Day. Or, at least how I pictured Christmas had been pre-Landfall.

"We'll deal with that problem as it comes. What's the plan now?" Ben asked, frown still etched on his face.

"I think it will be good if we take a day to gather ourselves and plan then."

"Can we make that three?" Sam asked from where he was propped against the vestibule wall. He hadn't made it all the way to the benches, and no one wanted to move him after he had passed out.

After some mumbled agreements, me and my friends were left alone in the vestibule while the others tended to the camp. My uncle basically told Daniela that if she didn't let him cook dinner, she would be barred from the lobby. He even had a small cook stove ready to go, so Daniela's passive magic wasn't necessary.

"I wanted to speak with you three. As you are aware, I have access to your status and to your Dregs. Thanks to your efforts, I should be able to impart another set of skills onto each of you while keeping my functionality as I have. A bit more, and I will be able to have more stable connection times. Alan has already expressed explicit interest in speaking with me. At length."

The three of us chuckled. It hadn't surprised me that Alan had already been trying to eke out as much from the Entity as he could.

"Do you have any recommendations for us this time?" Daniela asked. Her tone was much more level and less demanding than when we'd discussed our skill acquisitions with the Entity.

"Actually, I do. From your tale, it appears that you three should continue to focus as you have. Perhaps, spreading the damage taken with Ronan a tad. As such, I believe the offensive imbue skill for you, Daniela, the defensive imbue skill for Samuel, and the defensive imbue skill for Ronan."

"That sounds fairly reasonable. Actually, wait a sec." I looked over the loot, searching for the Metier Crystal I'd found. "Did you guys see the crystal that was with Danny's fangs?"

"You mean the thing Blobby is sucking up into its body?" Sam slurred.

If the Entity had been able to pivot with us, I was sure it would have. Daniela and I spun just in time to see the crystal disappear into Blobby's bulk. The slime even had the audacity to burp loudly. *I didn't even know he could burp...*

"That is unfortunate. I could have significantly increased my mana capabilities with a cluster of that size. If you did indeed acquire that from your insectile foe, then that would explain why you three struggled so hard."

"Wait, back up. Explain," I said. Blobby was jiggling erratically, but what the Entity said drew my attention.

"As creatures grow in Quotient, it is possible for them to form clusters of purified mana. That is, what we Entity Clusters are imprinted on. They give the creature enhanced capabilities and control over their Attunement mana. Should I gain access to one such crystal, my mass would increase proportionately to that crystal and so would my strength."

"Ah! They are rare mobs!" Sam chuckled. "They drop the best loot."

"From my understanding of your games, Samuel is correct. It is not often that creatures form pure clusters. It is also not clear if they form as a result of their abnormal strength or their abnormal strength is just a result of the formation early on in the organism's development."

"Ugh. This is making my head hurt. Can we just get our skills and take a nap?" Daniela complained.

"That is certainly okay. I do not believe it would be in your best interest to practice your skills over much. As far as your Dreg, I would suggest you give your statuses a look. You and Samuel have now accumulated enough Dreg to form a trait. I believe Samuel has enough to overbank his own. Daniela, you are at the borderline threshold. Considering Samuel's... odd state, I would recommend you let him acquire his trait before you."

The three of us took a moment to review our status. Except Samuel. I wasn't entirely sure what he did while we both stared at our implanted displays because he was *already* looking off into space. In my case, I went for the full breakdown. Thanks to the health and mana bars at the edges of my vision, I knew some of the overall information, but I wanted the numerical breakdown.

Subject: Ronan Terrigan

Health: 91% (Unafflicted)
Mana: 100%
Metier Quotient: 4 (3%)
Dreg Accumulation: 0%
LPS: Wildwood, FL
Communications
Skills - *(3) Selections Available*
Traits - *(69% Banked)*
Attributes - *Growth Quantified*
Skills:
Offensive - <Stone Spike> / Imbue / Materialize
Defensive - Direct / Imbue / <Earthen Barrier>
Misc - <Pith Mana Lock>
- <Infusion>
Traits:
Limestone Skin
Unformed (0%)
Attributes:
Strength: 1.41 > 1.52
Mobility: 1.31 > 1.41
Perception: 1.53 > 1.63
Refinement: 1.16 > 1.26
Containment: 1.98> 2.08

A grimace took over my face. I'd been expecting the growth from my risen Quotient, but my strength had gone up by 0.11. The fight hadn't been particularly physically exertive compared to what I'd been doing daily. That meant that the marginal gain to my strength had been a result of the thorough beating I'd received. My thoughts scattered when Daniela finished her own status check.

"All done. You can take him, but I want the skill."

"Very well. Samuel, if you would?" The Entity's crystal flowed open like a closet door of perfect glass. Sam tried to make his way over, but failed miserably. Daniela and I were forced to give him a hand. A muted thunk was all we heard before the Entity Cluster encased my friend. A trill of panic clenched my heart. He could suffocate within.

"Don't worry. You did the same thing, remember? Hopefully he won't be so wobbly when he comes out," Daniela said, patting me on the shoulder. "Now, Entity. Skill me up!"

Daniela placed her hand on the portion of the crystal where our friend *wasn't* and it sunk an inch in before her eyes rolled into the back of her head.

"You know, you do some freaky stuff to our bodies," I said.

"That may be true, but not as freaky as what your gelatinous companion is doing," the Entity retorted. When I turned, I watched Blobby mitose. Like Play-Doh being molded, the lime green creature stretched in the middle before a wet pop snapped both parts of Blobby. And then there were two.

"What the hell, Blobby!?" I wasn't sure if I should be impressed, alarmed, or scared that the creature had been able to do that.

As if trying to communicate a response, both Blobbys held up an appendage in the air. They were perfect mirrors. A moment later, the Metier Crystal cores rose to the surface like driftwood. One had the brown light surge within, while the other looked to be more or less pristine. At the edges of it, the same brown was starting to crawl along it with each passing second.

"Did you somehow use the new crystal to duplicate yourself?"

Both slimes nodded their appendages vigorously. Having tested the ability, Blobby surged and melded into itself and waved as if nothing had happened.

"Curious, and concerning. If it is this easy for this creature to corrupt and imprint onto other clusters, the tendrils may be a bigger threat than I could have anticipated," the Entity said gravely. I held the silence between us as I contemplated Blobby's new offensive capabilities and the unknown trouble the tendrils were presenting themselves as. And we'd only met them once! "On a positive note, I believe my hypothesis on your spell chain development was correct. Daniela will be much more potent moving forward."

"What are you talking about?"

"I will let her explain," it said cryptically.

On cue, the Entity released Daniela from its crystalline hold. She stumbled a step before shaking her head like someone had smacked her. Before I had a chance to ask what was going on, she lifted her hand and flames licked the length of her arms. She grabbed a hold of the fang tucked in her belt and the flames crawled down her arms and onto her makeshift weapon.

"Oh yes. I am a fan of this one…" Her voice drifted off and a chill ran down my spine. The fire flickering in her eyes didn't look entirely reflected. As suddenly as she'd utilized her skill, she cut off the mana. "I got something on top of my new skill. That was <Heat Touch>, by the way."

"Well, don't keep me waiting!" I tried to push past my somewhat irrational fear into the prospect of something exciting.

"With the three categories of offensive skills, I was able to use another of those skill points for something called <Freeform Offensive>. It's supposed to let me manipulate spell chains to do whatever I want!" she said excitedly.

"That would be *some* of what you want. You three haven't come anywhere close to understanding the manner in which we form spell chains. However, with the current catalogue of information at your disposal, I believe your minds will be able to start incorporating some of those benefits. A warning, if you would. Using the <Freeform Offensive> will be prohibitively expensive on the mana front, but it will give you much flexibility. Please, be cautious," the Entity said. It put a dampener on our prospects of more free magic use, but it was a fair warning.

Throwing magic around shouldn't be done willy-nilly. Especially not when your friend seemed to have a bit of a pyromaniac streak hidden inside.

"Got it. I'm gonna go mess around with this. Tell Dale I won't fight him about dinner this time." With that, Daniela was already speeding towards the training area. Had she not been walking on the path I'd solidified, she probably would have thrown up a dust cloud with her pace.

"Don't forget you still need to get your trait!" I shouted after her. All I got was a dismissive wave over the shoulder. "Great. Who would have thought I would be the adult in this situation?"

"It does appear you and Sam hold much of the calmness in bearing. Except when intoxicated. Samuel does appear unduly inhibited."

"What can I say? Friends help keep you grounded," I shrugged.

"Friends… of course. Would you like to acquire your skill?" the Entity said quickly. There was something suspicious about its change in tone, but I let it be for now. As much as I bugged Daniela about being aggressive with getting skills, I couldn't deny my own excitement. <Earthen Barrier> had changed the game for me; it had even given further functionality to <Stone Spike>.

With no hesitation, I sunk my hand into the crystal surface. The world winked and I was deposited once again in the white space hosted by the Entity. Its pulsing light hovered next to me.

"I believe you are now familiar with this process?" I nodded and mentally selected 'defensive imbue.' The familiar deluge of information pressed down on my mind. The surprising thing was that some aspects of the information felt familiar. So familiar, in fact, that my brain rejected it outright. The non-overlapping sections of information settled into the back of my mind, leaving the mental button for a new skill. The headache that followed was also less intense than with the previous bits of knowledge I'd acquired.

<Earth Shell>

<Soil will grow out of your body to reinforce it>

"That's not disturbing at all," I said flatly. "Are you the one who writes these?"

"In a sense, it is *you* who wrote these. I cannot describe the effects more than this without actually seeing the skill manifest through you. I also like to be brief."

"Now that is just a lie, but I'll take your word on the other part." Sighing, I pulled on the information and hovered my mental hand over the skill's trigger. "Here goes nothing."

The skill triggered instantly. Similarly to how Daniela's <Heat Touch> had worked, sand winked into existence around me. Instead of obeying the laws of gravity, they zipped back onto my body. Layer upon layer of sand sedimented along my arms as my mana drained. When said drain was at almost thirty percent of my total, I stopped channeling the skill. No new sand was added, but the compacted soil had formed solid chunks of stone around my arms up to my shoulders.

My arms were locked in place, however.

"Well, that doesn't seem very practical," I said, wiggling my arms ever so slightly.

"Perhaps a simulated enemy would be to your benefit?" the Entity asked.

"You can make those?"

"Certainly. At a cost, of course, and they won't provide you any Pith. This is all going on inside your mind." When I didn't object, the Entity drew half of my remaining mana away in a second. A Q1 ant chittered angrily at my feet before lunging.

"Gahh!" I screamed in surprise.

The creature's mandibles clamped around my immobile arms and only managed to scratch the surface. Its legs flailed and did manage to score some cuts along my body, but I shook my arms and the creature flew some distance away. Now that I focused on our surroundings, I could see that the Entity had also populated our training area from reality into its mental landscape.

Considering how effective the <Earth Shell> had been, I cranked my arm back and used my whole body to throw a haymaker into the ant's face. With my arms still locked in place, it *had* to be a whole body affair. Regardless, the attack proved super effective. My encased fist slammed the creature into the ground with earth shaking force. Its eyes bulged as its insides were unable to handle the blunt force trauma. The creature was dead.

A few seconds after the impact, chips started to form along my shell, like cracks on overly dry soil. This time, when I flexed my arms, most of the shell crumbled to dust. All that remained was my encased left arm, and the rock equivalent of a bracer.

"Good for cutting attacks, bad with blunt attacks," I mumbled to myself. As much as the Entity classified <Earth Shell> as a 'defensive' skill, I could already see the offensive uses for the new skill.

"On the surface, yes. With practice, you may be able to reshape <Earth Shell> to different uses. Ah, it appears that Sam is waking up and Daniela is returning. I look forward to speaking to you soon now that you are at Quotient 4. Your infusion goals are within reach." With yet another cryptic message, the Entity spat me out of its mental landscape.

"Good, we can eat dinner now. What were you doing in there, Ron?" Daniela asked.

My mind scrambled at the sudden change in perspective and all I managed was, "Huh?"

"You've been stuck there for most of the afternoon. You okay?"

Sure enough, the sun was already falling and my uncle was laying out salad bowls with some dehydrated-looking bits of potato on top. The whole scene was utterly strange, partly because I didn't know we had access to leafy greens or dehydration technologies. The other strange part was how nonchalant everyone was about interacting with a sapient crystal or the giant ant and gelatinous construct jiggling its way over to its own bowl of food.

"You're right, it is a tad strange."

I jumped high enough to hit my head on the vestibule ceiling. Samuel had casually exited the cocoon embrace of the Entity and laid a hand on my shoulder without me noticing. What I *did* notice were the hair-thin roots growing out of his hand. "Samuel, what the hell!?" I asked in alarm while rubbing my head.

"Oh, my bad. These are from my trait. I've got a Decentralized Nervous Root System now. I'm able to get impressions while touching living things," he said. He still looked a tad drunk, but nothing compared to before. He watched the small roots in his hands before they disappeared into his skin. *Freaky, but possibly useful.*

"Are you two done gawking at each other? I already ate dinner and I want to get this whole trait thing out of the way!" Daniela said in agitation.

If one could wait aggressively, then that was what Daniela did. She didn't rush her food, nor did she move around impatiently, but her eyes were set on the Entity Cluster throughout dinner. When that was done, she excused herself, gave her mother a hug, and then entered her crystalline cocoon. We all waited for a few hours, chatting and trying to dispel some of the stress our attack on the ant hive had caused, but she did not come out. A brief query of the Entity responded that she was alright, merely processing the changes.

Trusting in the Entity, we all went to bed except for Alan and Ava. The former, because he'd only gotten glimpses of Samuel receiving a trait. The latter, because even after all the assurances and the fact that both Samuel and I had acquired traits, she wanted to be there if her daughter needed her. It was a bittersweet display for me. Pushing past thoughts of my parents, I collapsed into my bed while my mind swam with infusion crafting. I was determined tomorrow would be the day I succeeded.

CHAPTER THIRTY

Reinforcing the Cracks

Turned out it took half a week for the Entity to resurface after giving Daniela her trait. When the woman finally exited the crystal, the Entity stated that its influence was being tested regularly by smaller ant groups. Other than that, it mentioned nothing else for three days.

As for the last person to really engage with the Entity, Daniela appeared shaken by the change she'd experienced. While Samuel's trait manifested at will and mine looked like a poor tan unless you ran your hand over me, hers was distinctly noticeable. A set of gill-like flaps outlined in red-tinged skin had formed on either side of her neck. The red extended down her neck and out of sight into her chest and back. 'Radiator Gills,' she said they were called. The trait *had* ended up overbanked according to her, which supposedly let her handle changes in internal temperature much more easily by expelling heated air.

When I complained about how much more diverse my friends' traits were compared to my own, they reminded me that I could possibly have died had my skin not been muting some of the damage from the Blaze Ant. They didn't hear much more from me on that topic.

Thanks to the Entity's comment about encroaching ants, we started a watch rotation just in case its influence was breached somehow. While Ben had insisted that we conduct a proper watch rotation, I insisted on simply flipping my sleep schedule. My uncle refused to leave the task to me alone, so we split the evenings so that the others could work throughout the day unimpeded. Considering *what* the others did, they benefited more from the daylight.

During my night shifts, I took some time to appreciate the sheer magnitude of the sky. Most of the other times we'd been outside past dark, something had been trying to kill us, we'd been unconscious, or we hid away before the stars and the moon came out. Thanks to the Entity, it was at least mostly safe for us to look outside through the half-open door of the vestibule.

My uncle and I spent a lot of time catching up. Our conversations were still a bit stilted, but he finally felt free enough to talk about the past. I soaked up each bit of information, feeling any lingering threads of resentment toward him unravel as he painted the picture of the early days in the Bunker.

He told me how my parents had gotten to know each other, and how much trouble he'd actually caused for Marcus Metier as he got situated in a job. Unlike most of the people in the Bunker, Marcus had been an unexpected addition. His reputation on my grandmother's team was 'brilliant, but volatile,' and not even my grandparents' reputation could shield him from government pressure. It was a bit of a wake up call that so much could happen to so many people, and I'd hardly been aware of it. It shouldn't have been a surprise, considering how many lessons on the pre-Fall history we'd been given, and how many documentaries we'd seen through the simulation terminals.

All of those thoughts swirled in my head, and it took quite a while for me to return to any productive state of mind. However, I let it happen. I knew that if I let things run in the background of my mind, they would just end up detracting from the tasks I needed to complete. So, I returned to gazing at the sky as my mind spun through knowledge old and new.

I watched the moon sparkle like a giant star, but after some consideration, I wondered if those were fragments of other Metier Crystals. They had, after all, been broken off course by humanity. *Was there Dreg on the moon?* That was both a pointless and daunting question, but it managed to wiggle itself into my mental list regardless. It was also enough of a nagging thought to break my reverie of celestial bodies; if I ever wanted to deal with the possibility of mages in space, I needed to get to work.

The first thing was to take stock of what we'd accumulated thanks to the raid. As a result of Ben's efforts, we'd gotten everything cataloged. A total of twenty-five Q0 plates, twenty-seven Q0 infusions, three Q1 plates and infusions from the slightly bigger ants, as well as the Q3 stinger and infusion of the Blaze Ant. It wasn't an inconsequential amount compared to what we'd amassed before. While everything was still of a low Quotient relative to my current level, my efforts had been rebutted with those 'poor' materials.

I was sure part of my issue was lack of practice. After less than a month, I couldn't expect to be an expert at an entirely new skill that required entirely new pathways I wasn't even aware humans could have. Regardless of the reason, while waiting for further assistance from the Entity, I churned through infusing plates and manipulating threads as much as I could. That particular aspect had been the only thing the Entity said I would probably manage without using my Quotient and reserves to brute force the process.

My control had improved so much, in conjunction with my increased mana pool, that I even managed to infuse two plates at a time. It was extremely uncomfortable and left me coiled up on the ground, but grew less intense the more I practiced. I took that as an improvement.

And so, on my thirty-fifth plate, the Entity chimed in. "It appears you are almost passable at manipulating those Pith threads."

Considering how concentrated I'd been on winding the threads as tightly around the chitin plate as I could, it was a wonder I didn't jump and hit the stone ceiling again. Instead I grit my teeth. The mana drain ramped up, but the infusion finished almost instantly.

"You could have waited a minute," I said, setting the chitin down on my workspace with a sigh.

"I apologize that I've not had as much time as we'd wagered. The stronger you have all become, the stronger the threats around you seem to dislike that. Countering them has taken a considerable effort."

I waved my hand dismissively in the air. If all I had to endure from the Entity was a fright here and there, it would be a bargain to have it protect us. "You are doing what you need to, to keep us safe. I'll work with what I've got."

"Indeed. I believe it is time that we increase that repertoire of things at your disposal."

"Do you have enough time?" I asked. My voice came out in more of a whisper than I wanted, revealing my unspoken optimism.

"Should do. I've surged my influence further and nothing tested against it. It is back to a passive state, you are present, and we have the rest of the evening. Unless the insects and other denizens of the night decide to give me a break, this will be all I'll be able to manage until you return with more Dreg. If I did not think infusion could strengthen you more than I could protect you, this would not be an expenditure I would make."

"Don't have to tell me twice. Give me a minute to recover my mana and we'll start." I cleared my station of everything except for Daniela's wolf fangs and several of the infusions I had available in the workstation cubbies. By the time I was done, being as meticulous as was reasonable, my mana was back at one hundred percent.

"Not hard to guess what you've chosen to work first," the Entity said matter-of-factly. "However, we will start with the pelt you acquired from the tendril. Manipulating infused materials will be the first step, and practice, for creating infused items."

Not questioning the direction of the lesson, I sifted through the loot crates to retrieve the pelt. I stretched out the maroon and hot rod red hide on my workspace. The fangs went on either end to keep the thing from coiling back into the roll in which it was stored. Its information manifested in my eyes as I looked it over.

<Quotient 1 Infused Wolfhound Pelt>

<Attunement: Fire>

<Quotient 1 Density>

A half-smile crossed my face as I recounted the battle and how we'd managed to make it out.

"Good. As this object has been infused, that means it is subject to being shaped by mana. The thing that was keeping you back from completing this was your control of the threads. That is to say, you need to control threads that are already part of the object. This process happens naturally to a certain extent, as the nature of the Attunements integrates with the object being infused. It is the same process that leads to the formation of traits or Dreg afflictions.

"What I will have you do is pour as much of your mana as you can manage into a specific section. Our goal is to split the pelt into strips which you can then use for further crafting. As your testing efforts have shown, damaging infused materials is exceedingly difficult. Along that same vein, forceful manipulation in what are... human techniques risks the irreparable destruction of the material. However, convincing the material that it should change form is possible with mana and more infusions.

"Take one of the Quotient 0 infusions, stretch its thread lengthwise down the pelt, and focus on the infusion acting like a cutting edge. Do not be frugal with your mana."

After that extensive explanation, I mechanically did as instructed. It failed immediately. Sure enough, the mana flowed out of me, pinched the infusion, and layered on top of the pelt.

The moment I tried to command the thread into the already infused material, it rebutted itself like a fiery whip. Literally. The thread took on the physical manifestation of a red hot line of fire as it snapped and struck the stone workspace. A black char mark was the only thing to indicate its passing.

"Do not try to meld them together, you are using the power of the infusion to *change*, not to empower."

Frown deeply set, I grabbed another infusion and held the thread with my mana. It was a bit like how I imagined tele-kinetic powers would work. Mental hands that were there, but not really, held the two ends of the Pith thread and pressed it against the pelt. Instead of flicking or manipulating the thread as I'd been doing, I pictured a garrote. I wasn't actually killing anyone or strangling anything, but the visualization worked. The thread made contact with the pelt and *parted* the material instead of trying to join it.

The result was lackluster. Some of the hairs on the pelt drifted off, turning into ash, but the hide itself was unperturbed.

"Very good, now you surge your mana through the thread and use it to splice the material," the Entity said from behind me.

My stomach clenched in anticipation of the gut-wrenching pain that would follow. Mana flowed through me and into the thread, causing the red glow to flare into pure white until it winked out. The infusion was spent. While I hadn't managed to cut all the way through, the pelt's two halves were hanging on by less than two inches. The discomfort of channeling large amounts of mana was overshadowed by progress in a new skill.

The Entity remained silent as I worked through six other infusions to get the pelt cut into eight, long, inch-wide strips. At the midpoint, the pelt had produced a roughly three foot strip with shorter sections for the rest. As I looked at the longest strip over, I was surprised by the slight change in description of its information.

<Quotient 1 Infused Wolfhound Bindings>
<Attunement: Fire>

<Quotient 1 Density>

I wasn't familiar with many leatherworking concepts. Bindings, as I understood it, were just a type of strap that was used for any number of things. That the Entity had picked up on that was impressive and showed just how engaged it was with its own system. Before my thoughts had time to wander, the Entity got my attention again.

"Wonderful. Once your mana recovers, you will be able to start working on getting an item made. The only instruction I might be able to provide for this next portion is that you need to try to visualize as strongly as you can what you'd like the infusion to change about the material. Bonding, cutting, shaping, shaving, molding. All of these things can be done. The infusion you select, as well as your personal mana, will affect how this process works. Earth-attuned infuse differently compared to fire-attuned, for instance."

"How do you know all of this?" I asked, trying to internalize the information the Entity gave freely. Considering it was a sapient rock, and didn't appear to have any particular Attunement, unlike Blobby, I didn't know how it could know all of this.

"Part of this is from the knowledge the Entity Clusters have acquired and made available to my category. Some of it has come from creating the system tied to your status. Being connected with you all has provided me significant insight into how mana is changing you and the world around you. My current efforts in that department are… poor. I hope that when maintaining my area of influence is negligible, or I achieve the next category, more information will become available for me to share."

"That would certainly be helpful. I'm not sure how we'd have made it on the surface without your help and skills."

"You would have found a way. Thanks to the amalgamation of your memories, I feel fairly confident when I say you three are the personification of the expression 'rub some dirt on it.' Encountering organisms as determined as your kind is somewhat unprecedented. As much as the Entity Clusters are determined to exterminate Dreg from existence, it is not actually something we believe can be achieved. It is merely part of what we are. Humans do not follow that mentality."

"Seems a bit sad, if I'm honest. Striving towards something, but believing it will always be out of your reach," I said.

The Entity's glow flickered for a moment, before stabilizing. "Yes, I suppose it might appear that way." The two of us lapsed into silence for the next several minutes as my mana regenerated from the ninety percent dip the crafting had left me at. "I wish you success, Ronan. Should I miss your departure, let your friends know I await your return."

With that, the crystal dimmed into a pinprick and the wave of pressure of its influence flowed through me and outwardly to cover the camp. I didn't comment on the Entity's bout of self-reflection, or the implied fact that all the Entities shared a common objective they thought impossible. However, the efforts and strides that we'd made on the surface did resonate with what I'd said to the Entity.

"We can only go so far without help. Surviving might have been possible on the surface, but your help is the key to thriving." There was no response from the Entity, but I was fairly sure it heard me. If it wanted to talk, it would find a time. But that was for later. Our equipment wasn't going to craft itself.

Looking closely at the fang, and trying to keep the image of a dagger in mind, I wrapped the bottom portion with one of the medium-length strips of pelt. The pseudo leather was soft on the fur side, but tough on the inner side, so I put that section on the outside. If I intended to bind it using infusions, then the grip would matter more where the weapon would be held. The two ends curled away from the fang since they were unsupported and I was fairly sure an actual leatherworker from before the apocalypse would have been appalled at my winding pattern.

Nonetheless, it was wrapped. Where I assumed was the root of the fang, I left about an inch to act as a sort of pommel. Getting the somewhat uniformly thick fang to turn into an actual blade would require some work. *How was she even using these things as weapons?* While I wondered about my friend's combat equipment decisions, I etched the rough shape I hoped to accomplish into the stone of my workspace. It would be a joke to fix the damage, so I tried to get creative.

The root of the fang was wide, but fairly straight, while the actual portion that would sink into prey had a slight bend to it. The whole thing was about two inches wide throughout and eight long. In an attempt to account for what I knew was my poor skill with modifying infused materials, I left the bend as it was and just thinned the top edge. I sketched in some shoulders by thinning the handle area of the weapon. This formed a pseudo guard and made the pommel stand out more. On a whim, I added a slight edge to the pommel as a tiny secondary blade. For maximum possible damage, of course.

The etched shape on my workstation was a total mess. Regardless, it did help me visualize the proportions I was trying to accomplish and the features I wanted to have in the weapon. I laid down the fang over my etch.

"Okay, before I try to shape it, let's bind everything together," I mumbled to myself. "How do I do that?"

The Entity had mentioned that each Attunement, and its corresponding infusion, would act like the element. And the only thing I could think fire helped bind together was metals with welds. *Nothing to lose, I suppose. Could explode in my face, but I don't think that will happen.*

Making sure that I had my mana fully restored, I held a Q0 infusion pinched between my fingers. I pretended that it was the electrode and the workstation was the welding table. My hands shook ever so slightly as I activated <Infusion> and the fiery thread of Pith zipped towards the fang.

My visualization had been right, at least. However, the thread only lasted long enough to 'weld' the pelt about half the length I'd wrapped it, so I repeated the process with yet another infusion. I was quickly losing track of how many materials we had at our disposal, but I was sure Ben would alert me if we were getting low. Possible future shortages aside, the second infusion disintegrated and the fang's description changed. A change that marked very good news.

<Insufficient Pith Enhanced Fang>

<Attribute: Undetermined>

<Trait: Undetermined>

The updated information mirrored what I'd gotten from the first real infusion I'd completed. Which meant the fang was already on its way to an item. Before I started pumping Pith into the actual fang, I needed to shape it. Somewhat. I could only hope that the changes the actual material underwent while being infused would help smooth out my mishaps. And mishaps followed.

I spent one infusion shaving off the blade using the method the Entity had helped me visualize. It worked poorly. The blazing thread shaved off the material just fine, but I wasn't dexterous enough to get smooth strokes along the bone. The slivers of bone immediately turned to cinder when they separated off the main fang.

Apart from that debacle, I managed to shrink the fang around the handle, but it pushed its mass into the 'blade' and some into the pommel as if someone had carelessly squeezed a Play-Doh version of it. It was nowhere near the smoother finish I'd aimed for. That whole process had taken another two infusions and the fang looked even worse by the end.

"What, on God's green Earth, is that thing?" my uncle called from the door. I'd been holding my head, wallowing as hard as I could about the horror I'd created. *There is no way Daniela will forgive me for messing up her fang weapon.*

"It's a… dagger?" I said in defeat.

"I do so hope you mean it is a poor attempt at one," he retorted.

"You know manual crafting stuff has never been my forte. That's always been Sam and Daniela's thing. Not even my first attempt at building this room looked as bad as this thing."

"True, but there is nothing that says you can't learn to be

better. Plus," my uncle picked up the botched weapon and turned it over, "it still looks salvageable. Can you do more of your infusion thing on it?"

"If you focus on it, it should show up as 'insufficient Pith.' If I pump infusions into the actual fang to complete the item, it will change with the infusion I add. I just... I don't know if it will be able to fix the mess I made."

"Well, it's not gonna fix itself, now is it?" he said, echoing my thoughts when I started crafting. He handed the fang dagger back, smiling all the while.

"Even *I* have trouble staying as positive as you. Got a tip for it?" I asked, retrieving a handful of infusions. Considering the fang was a Quotient 3 material, I suspected it would take a few.

"Survive the complete annihilation of your society and home world. Most other problems seem a tad small in comparison."

I did a double take and turned to my uncle. He was smirking knowingly, forcing a chuckle out of me. *Who would have thought he had a dark sense of humor too?*

Regardless, I set the dagger down on my etched outline. The initial sketch I'd managed had been bad, but somewhat close to the shape of the fang. In its new mangled state, it looked nothing like it, but I kept that image in mind as I triggered <Infusion>. "If it starts to smoke, or catch fire in general, help me shove it in the basin."

When my uncle nodded seriously, I flicked the Pith thread at the fang dagger. The effect was underwhelming, but notable. The fang absorbed the thread like a drowning man drawing air. The scratches I'd done to the fang recovered as its surface liquified for a split second. The item still showed as having insufficient Pith, so I dumped infusion after infusion. So many infusions, in fact, that I had to pause to recover my mana and let the discomfort in my gut pass.

By the ninth infusion, I was getting a bit nervous. Each additional one caused the dagger to put out a brow-roasting wave of heat. The actual dagger wasn't hot, but when we plunked it in the basin, it churned the water into a boil. *Some kind of heat aura?*

"Is this…common?" my uncle asked hesitantly.

"I've come to learn that there is no 'common' with infusing. I just hope for replicable and somewhat manageable. I really hope this takes."

Delaying was pointless. With nine infusions spent, the dagger was either going to blow up in my face or give me an item. And so, I chunked three more infusions into the dang thing.

The first set of infusions had softened and smoothed out many of my botched crafting mishaps. The last three gave the dagger the crisp edge a deadly weapon needed. The sheen of the repaired bone turned into a shine as the off-white tinged to maroon. The eleventh infusion sharpened a rose red double-bladed edge on the curved blade of the dagger as well as on one side of the pommel. The final infusion melded my poor leather grip with the bone, alternating rust-colored leather and white bone. Then the whole thing flattened and flared with one last slap of heat.

<Quotient 2 Fang Dagger>

<Attribute: Strength>

<Trait: Desiccating Haze>

I had no words. Even with my nearly botched attempt at modifying the materials, the weapon looked deadlier than ever. The blade was easily ten inches now, with a downward flare of bone to cover the top part of the smooth handle. The pommel had even turned out exactly as I pictured it, adding yet another pointy danger to the weapon. It was also the highest Quotient item I'd managed. Ideas for what needed to be made, how much time I was willing to invest, and just what the heck I could *actually* manage flowed through my mind.

A predatory grin split my face as I held the weapon out to my uncle to inspect. "Now we're cooking with gas."

CHAPTER THIRTY-ONE

Venturing Again

"Why all the secrecy, Ron?" Sam asked.

He was covered head to toe in less than stellar smelling goop. The life mage had spent the rest of the week I used to infuse dealing with a compost pile. Him, Ben, and Ava actually managed to deal with some Q0 worms that were eating our crops. Sam had somehow used his trait to influence the bundle of nerves and digestive tracts that were the creatures. According to him, they would help him mitigate the drain on soil nutrients that his magic-enhanced growth was having on the farm.

Nonetheless, he looked eager to return to the toil of his farm.

I'd asked everyone to stay around the crystal after lunch. Technically, I was supposed to be heading for bed, but my surprise couldn't wait until I'd managed to readjust my sleep schedule.

"I'm done. Well, done for *now*. With this, we'll be in the best position we can to venture further out," I said. While talking, I spun around and flicked open a crate that I'd done my very best to keep out of sight for the last week.

Gasps of surprise erupted from everyone present, except my

uncle. He'd been right beside me as I worked on the infusing projects' final stages.

Their other tasks forgotten, my friends reached slowly into the crate. Alan hovered as close as he possibly could to them while they turned over their new gear. Ben and Ava did their best to hover over their shoulders while my uncle and I stood back, arms crossed, smirks wide.

"How did you manage all of this? When did you manage all of this?" Daniela asked, eyes still glued to the harness and dagger with a little tag that read her name.

"The Entity gave me a crash course, and I've been working on these during my night shift. You all didn't think I just spent it staring out at the stars, did you?"

"Honestly? I kind of did," Daniela replied. She was suddenly very interested in one of her loose curls. Samuel was similarly looking away from me, half-turned, as he eyed his own breastplate. I could only describe their expressions as sheepish.

"Man, that hurts deep, guys. But I'm too excited, so I'll push past those wrongful schemas about my personage and tell you about my loot crate."

Just to remind myself, I focused on the five pieces I'd made. Their descriptions populated in my vision.

\<Quotient 1 Augmented Chitin Shield\>
\<Attribute: Strength\>
\<Trait: Force Dispersal\>

\<Quotient 1 Breastplate\>
\<Attribute: Strength\>
\<Trait: Force Dispersal\>

\<Quotient 1 Chitin Harness\>
\<Attribute: Strength\>
\<Trait: Force Dispersal\>

\<Quotient 2 Fang Dagger\>

\<Attribute: Strength\>
\<Trait: Desiccating Haze\>

I'd managed, with marginally more success, to replicate the dagger process with the other fang; near identical weapons in all but the overall shape of the blade. For whatever reason, the second dagger blade had come out a bit wavy.

Next, in order to get a better hang of infused material modification, I created a shield for myself. Taking the chitin plate that had mostly saved my behind during the Blaze Ant fight, I slapped on four of the smaller Q0 plates. Two on the top and two on the bottom made the whole thing look like a fat H. After using some infusions to actually weld wolfhound bindings to the back, I had enarmes that wouldn't be melting off right away. Hopefully.

Lastly, I combined everything I'd managed to practice into armor for Sam and Danny. For the more agile member of our little party, I crafted a harness with overlapping Q0 plates that gave her a fair bit of protection while minimizing movement restrictions. Her armor had used up most of the wolfhound pelt bindings, but it allowed her to have the harness on by itself or over her current body armor. I didn't have anything that could serve as an adjustable strap, so I made it tie at the waist.

For Samuel, I kept the design super simple. Two of the larger plates, one in the front and one in the back, bound together by shoulder straps and a tie belt at the waist. Two of the Q0 plates acted as small pauldrons over his shoulders. As for the infusions, I'd used higher Quotient ones to test out a theory of mine.

If my level to infusion ratios were correct, then each subsequent level was three times the previous one. It would also explain the requisite effort to get to higher Quotients. If creatures only provided you a fraction of their own Pith and *that* fraction was relative to their level, Metier Quotient 5 was a ways off. I was sure there were more specifics that I didn't know about, but the multiple of three had been consistent throughout my infusing.

Regardless of my own magical speculations, my friends were ecstatic with my success. Before I could even get another word in, both were already slotting the armor on and Daniela twirled her daggers. "Amazing! It's giving me +0.2 to my strength. I can *see* the change!"

The flash of red that came from her spell chains formed, then fizzled for a moment. "I can't gain the bonuses from both items?" she asked, confused.

"Right. Well, I am hypothesizing that is because it is a Q2 Item, hence it boosts its attribute as if you'd gained two levels. We'll revisit that if we can make some more higher level items. As for the multiple item use? Haven't been able to figure it out. From what I can tell, it feels like some kind of magical interference. Mana from one item doesn't play nice with the other, so they don't stack. Or something else entirely." I threw in a shrug. "Still working out the whole 'we have magic and magic items' bit of this whole thing. At the very least, it gives you some options. I haven't had much time to really figure out the minutiae of the item traits, but at the very least, they will offer us more protection than mundane armor."

"Ronan, this is astounding. We *must* discuss this. This exact outcome is what I believed would let us circumvent a major problem in creating the implants," Alan said when he was finally able to gather his thoughts. He'd been clutching my H shield like it was going to run away from him.

"I'm probably not the best person to talk to about that, but feel free to run any questions by me. The Entity is obviously your first choice, and you might be able to look over my first item. That garden shovel, as flamboyant as it is now, isn't what I would call optimal. Dale might be able to give you an outsider perspective too. He's watched the final infusion for most of these, and usually I am lost in the process while it happens."

Astute as always, my uncle picked up on my deflection. He immediately presented himself as a target for Alan, giving me a look as he led him out of the vestibule. It was hard to hide my snickering.

"Sneaky, Ron. I suppose the important question now is what is the plan?" Ben said, crossing his hefty arms. Ava had been talking in hushed tones with Daniela while Sam was still struggling with his armor.

"Two days before we head out again. Should be enough for me to switch my watch schedule with Teach and my uncle. Goal should be the same, try to get as close to the city as we can. Getting more people onto the surface will improve our chances all around and that requires more titanium. Plus, we might encounter more tendrils. If we come across any small groups we can handle, following them wouldn't be the worst idea."

"That works for me. I got the last of the worms handled yesterday, and I've got a decent chunk of grass grown for the herd. Raymond still is chunking through a huge amount of tomatoes, but I think we can handle that today," Sam said. He finally managed to adjust his armor. He cut an impressive figure now that the unrestricted food and constant physical exercise had let him fill his form some.

"How about you, Daniela? I don't have any objections, but how has your training been going?" Ben asked, taking a seat at one of my stone benches.

"Poorly. Better than before, but not great at all." The woman's mood dropped a bit, but not entirely. She was still twirling her daggers with a smirk on her face.

"Is that what you've been doing? Actually, I've been out of touch, focused on the crafting stuff. Samuel, did you even get your skill?" I asked, suddenly remembering I hadn't checked in with him.

"It's alright. I can forgive your astoundingly large oversight since it got us this sweet gear. My new skill is called <Adrenal Surge>. It lets me give a temporary boost to all attributes. About a Quotient level's worth, actually, even if it only lasts ten seconds per cast."

"That sounds amazing!" I said. Already, ways of exploiting the skill were flowing through my mind.

"Has its uses, yeah. But anyhow, I am okay with two days."

"Danny? Any objections?" I asked.

"Nothing much is going to change for me in two days, so not a problem really. I'll work with Anthony to start bringing more logs back to the camp. At this rate, we won't need you to make a wall, Ron. We'll have enough logs for our own palisade." She shrugged and played off her frustrations, but my perception highlighted the tightness around her eyes like a beacon.

"Well, better get to it then." I clapped my hands as I rose to my feet. "Now, anyone seen my gelatinous companion?"

Two days later, we were once again standing on the path towards the old road. This time, we were considerably more prepared, and stronger. My hubris hadn't reached Greek-hero levels to think nothing out in the wilds could deal with us, but staying stagnant in the camp would get us nowhere. We needed more resources to bring the others out of the Bunker. And we needed to know if there were *humans* that survived.

Parting with my uncle was much more touchy feely this time, as the two of us had mostly reconciled. When he let me out of his death-grip hug, his eyes had set in a firm stare. "You will find what you are looking for."

He then proceeded to crush Sam and Danny, as well as Anthony. If Blobby hadn't mitosed right out of the way, the slime would have also been a victim of my uncle's affection. The two smaller Blobbys rolled further down the path and waved at the group. If the thing could talk, it would have been hurrying us along.

"You all heard the slime. Stay safe, okay? Running away is always an option," Ben said, handing over the rucksacks he'd packed for our trip. We were determined to stay out at least one night, even if just to set up a forward base in one of the broken down buildings.

With the last of the goodbyes out of the way, we trudged on through the woods. Once again, the trip was uneventful. We did manage to spot the first true bird creatures far in the sky. It was only a series of vague silhouettes, but it brought a whole new set of terrors to mind. Getting plucked from the woods like worms for a meal was not a visual I wanted to live. Regardless, before long, we were back on 301, weighing whether we should head north or south.

Now that we were a higher Quotient, I was tempted to head closer to the Geode Palm. Fortunately for our health and well-being, a small bird decided to risk the tree instead of us.

"What's a swallow doing here?" Sam asked. He was squinting at the creature from the road intersection.

"Is it not supposed to?" Daniela asked, shifting a bit closer to inspect the blue-chested bird.

"Well, it's not impossible, but I wouldn't expect a bird from the Bahamas to be all the way—" Sam's explanation was cut off as a crack of thunder reached us. The swallow had reached for a coconut on the ground, possibly aiming to pick it up. It hadn't even made contact with the shell before the coconut ripped itself apart. Glimmering shards of crystal shredded the bird into red mist. We watched as the Pith rose out of the hardening corpse and suffused the tree.

"Well, that made the decision quite easy. Let's *never* mess with that tree," I said, already turning around and walking down the road. My friends weren't far behind.

We walked in tense silence for a few minutes, keeping a watchful eye on the increasing number of ruins around us. It didn't take long for us to reach the site of our encounter with the Dreg tendrils. Unsurprisingly, my reinforced wall was still there, and I finally saw the true extent of the blaze Daniela managed to contain. Several of the trees were scorched half way up, but that bark had fallen off to reveal still-healthy patches underneath.

"Should we just fortify this spot?" Daniela asked. "You already have half a wall up."

"We are still really close to the camp. Going further might mean we run into more things, but there's no sense setting up where there isn't anything for us to work with," I replied.

"Could always set up a secondary farm. Let it grow by itself, and just check it from time to time," Samuel suggested.

"Not a bad idea, but I would say that's something for the future. Once we aren't looking over our shoulder for bloodthirsty trees or faceless humanoids. We'll go another mile and see if we don't spot anything noteworthy. We shouldn't be too far from the town."

My friends agreed, and the three of us opted to slink on the edge of the road instead of walking out in the open. Even if it slowed our progress down, the trees prevented us from being clear targets. Less than five minutes of trekking and our layman's attempt at stealth proved beneficial.

Two humanoids, definitely tendrils, ambled slowly down the road. One looked like he'd been green at one point, but rolled around in some muddy earth, while the other had a similar red tinge as the one we'd encountered before. When my eyes spotted them in the distance, I immediately raised a bunker of <Earthen Barriers> around us. It took forty percent of my mana, but it helped block most of us from view. Anthony clambered up a tree, while Blobby camouflaged as a particularly squishy rock.

"What's the play?" Sam whispered.

"Danny, how fast do you think you can close the distance?" I asked, trying to use my increased perception to estimate how long we had before we were forced to act.

"Ten seconds, four if they get as close to your mound as they can."

"I don't think we'll get that lucky. I'll confirm their Attunements, then Sam will bind them both. You and I will try to take them out. As quietly as possible. If there are more, we don't want to draw them in."

Nods from both of my friends. My hand curled around my pickaxe in nervous tension. When the pair were less than a hundred feet away, their information flickered through the implant.

<Dreg Tendril (Human)>
<Attunement: Life>
<Refinement: Blossom>
<Perceived Metier Quotient: 2>

<Dreg Tendril (Human)>
<Attunement: Fire>
<Refinement: Spread>
<Perceived Metier Quotient: 2>

"Life on the left, fire on the right. Both Q2s. I'll focus on the fire one, in case it can burn through Sam's <Vine Whip>," I whispered. A spell chain formed around my shield hand, its light hidden by the earth and the chitin.

"On my mark," Sam said. Daniela had her hands on top of the mound, feet curled up, ready to spring. "Three, two, one... Go!"

A spell chain formed around the two tendrils' feet. Wrist-thick vines sprouted from the earth within seconds to trap their legs. The fire tendril managed to get its hand out of the tangle and I could see the uneven spell chain even from afar.

"Nope. <Stone Spike>!" The earth right behind it surged up and into the humanoid's shoulder. The hardened earth punched clean through the flesh, spraying orange ichor that smoldered on the ground. The spell chain fizzled in its hands. Tanking my mana again, I cast <Stone Spike> again. The four foot spike I'd first manifested thinned immediately, and another pushed out of its side and into the tendril's kidney. Or at least, where I thought the kidneys would be on a regular human.

A flash of red pulled my attention to Daniela. The life tendril had managed to slither out of the vine's grasp somehow.

Purple flowers had formed around its body, leaving a thin haze of pollen in the air. Instead of delving into that unknown mess, fire flowed down Danny's arms before encasing her right dagger. She then proceeded to toss it. The blade flipped once through the air, faster even than the dexterous brunette, and planted itself in the tendril's chest.

Scorch marks formed around the wound and the tendril's mouth opened wide in a silent scream. Whether or not it *could* scream I didn't find out, as Daniela closed the distance and nearly lopped the tendril's head off its body. The fire tendril tried to unleash another skill, but I triggered <Stone Spike> one more time. My third spike removed its other kidney from the equation. The attack gave Daniela more than enough time to repeat the semi-decapitation move she'd done to the other humanoid.

Both slumped as Sam's vines tightened around them. Daniela took a step back, ready to strike out if one of the two tendrils somehow managed to come back to life. When they both bloomed and disintegrated into mulch, she slid her daggers in her belt and retrieved the loot before hurrying over to us.

"That was—" Sam held up his hand to cut Daniela off.

"Don't even jinx it. We aren't much further from where we last fought some, so it is entirely possible there will be more. Ronan, think you could smooth out the aftermath?" My friend was right, of course, so I called forth the passive effect of my mana and smoothed out where his vines had cracked the asphalt. The black-tinged rock compacted very differently than anything I'd worked with up to that point, but I still managed to make it look somewhat natural. The mulch pile, I swept into the many cracks on the road.

"Anything noteworthy in the loot?" I asked Danny as I met up with them.

"Infusions, as usual. Bone from the fire one and a tooth from the life one. Are you sure we want to hold on to this?" she asked, pointing at Sam's bag. I was sure she'd gotten rid of the strange materials as soon as she got the chance.

"Materials are materials. Your daggers came from a wolf's teeth, if you recall. I'll figure out what to do with them."

"Let's get going. If we are going to set up a small camp further away, having as much time as possible will be important," Sam said.

"I'll scout ahead, then report back if I see anything. I can move faster and more silently than either of you. Plus, if I get caught in a tough fight, I'm sure you two will hear me." With that Daniela offloaded her pack onto Sam and took off down the edge of the woods. Her form, even with the dark red accents of her armor, was lost in the foliage within seconds.

"You know. If we are this strong at ambushes with Quotient Level 4, I don't want to know what actual ambush predators will be like," Sam said. His little comment sent goosebumps running down my body and I nudged him in the direction Daniela had taken.

"Come on. Better not stay out in the open then."

CHAPTER THIRTY-TWO

New Humans

"Guys, you are gonna wanna see this," Danny said through our implant comms. I'd almost forgotten about the feature again, but made a mental note to myself to send a message back to camp if we decided to rough it overnight. The flexibility and stealth they provided was something I couldn't help to keep ignoring.

"Care to elaborate *at all* on that?" Sam sent back in reply. There was tension in the blond's usually carefree demeanor for some reason. I even noticed the strange nerve connections from his trait curl and unfurl around his hands.

"You two just head directly north, then take a right at the next big road. I'm in the corner building about a block down." The connection clicked shut a moment after.

"She's gonna lead us into trouble, you know?" Sam said, sighing heavily.

"Usually I would say that I'm counting on it, but we aren't in the Bunker. I just hope it's not *another* problem to deal with," I said. I took Daniela's bag from Sam and we picked up the pace through the woods. My senses were just barely able to keep up with our increased speed. The effort of keeping my attention spread out, while also looking for potential threats, kickstarted a mild headache that I had to push through.

While moving through the woods, we noticed evidence of some recent clear-cutting. In the Attuned Earth, plants seemed to grow quicker by default even without being actually attuned or aided by magic, making the stumps all around us an intriguing surprise. The second surprise came in the form of sprawling fields of cultivated food.

It was one whole cleared space, but there were a variety of split sections. Rows upon rows of cabbage, watermelon, some kind of pepper, tomatoes, and a kind of bushy grass covered nearly every foot of the land. The line of trees ringing the space also looked too uniform to not have been purposefully planted. As I followed the edge of the field, there was yet another surprise on the far side. What looked like a grove of fruit trees cast a shadow over some of the crops. Bright orange orbs hung heavy from the trees.

"Oranges…" Sam said, breathlessly.

"There has to be humans close by. Why else would all of this remain so organized? There is no way this survived over two decades while keeping those cleared rows of plants," I said. My eyes roamed the fields off in the distance, but a grove of pines blocked my vision further to the east.

Originally, we'd planned to continue north into the town proper. If the fields were extending westward from a settlement, then that would be the best option to pursue instead. Sam and I shook off our wonder and slinked into the dilapidated building beside Daniela.

The structure was a one story building with raised ceilings, its cracked and crumbling concrete walls sporting numerous holes with a layer of ambitious grass attempting to claim the gaps. The woman waved us over and had us crouch down behind a series of rusted, overturned cabinets.

"I've seen some movement from both ends of the farmland, but nothing clear."

"What do you mean 'movement'?" I asked. I couldn't hold a

bit of the heat from entering my voice. *Did she already forget our conversation on cooperating with each other?*

She held her hands up in a placating gesture. "This just happened, Ronan. And I say movement because the wind isn't blowing, but the bushes on the west and the pines to the east are moving. Nothing I can pick up without going out into the open."

I bit back the retort I'd been crafting. *Seems Sam isn't the only one tense about being out here.* The presence of the farm also pushed adrenaline through me without an appropriate release. If there were humans, that would change our goals. Short term, that was. The other Bunkers could still use a hand in rejoining the surface.

My cheeks puffed as I let out a deep breath slowly. Instead of dwelling on my leap of reasoning, my eyes roved the tree lines. Sure enough, some of the pines were swaying in an erratic pattern. From our spot several hundred feet away, nothing but the shadows cast by the trees were visible.

On the opposite side of the trees, amidst the bushes, a figure stood surrounded by shivering bushes. I leaned forward as much as I could out of the building.

"There is someone in the bushes for sure. I can see them in the shadows, but they aren't moving. Something else must be all around them," I let my friends know.

Almost an hour of agonizing silence passed as the figure in the bushes waited for *something*. That something apparently was lunch time. Just when Daniela started to pull out a quick snack, the thing in the bushes emerged.

Out of the cover of the tree, my senses screamed at me. Some primal response, similar to what the Geode Palm had inflicted me with. The distance was much too great for me to identify the creature with my implant, but I was fairly certain it was Q6 or higher.

My friends tensed right beside me, staring down at the humanoid making its way across the field in front of us. Enormous palm fronds sprouted from its back like wings, but otherwise it was a green copy of the other tendrils we'd encountered. Samuel twitched next to me, but didn't say anything as a strange group exited the pines to the east. If I hadn't been so focused on the approaching group, I would have paid more attention to the peculiar manner in which the trees swayed out of the way.

My eyes failed to really process what I saw.

For lack of better words to describe them, an orc, two dwarves, and an elf sauntered out from amidst the trees. However, they weren't completely those things. It was as if a human canvas had received a severe splash of those mythical creatures.

The orc had more of a green-gray hue to her skin, while two prominent tusks yawned out of her mouth. Otherwise, she might have been any teen from my simulation lessons or pre-Landfall media. The dwarves were short and hairy. In excess. The elf was reedy thin with what looked like hot pink matte skin. He had sharp, pointed ears and earlobes. That last feature was not common in elven lore as far as I knew, and the skin really depended on what fantasy story you were reading. Considering there were fantasy races swaggering up to a plant man corrupted by a magic poison, I made a mental note that I probably didn't really know anything. Not anymore, anyhow.

My ears strained to hear, but I was only able to pick up a word here and there. "Fail," "pay," and "unfortunate" from the tendril. "Attack," "wildlife," and "damages" from the orc woman. The tendril's demeanor didn't shift at all, but I noted the bushes behind the Dreg creature stirring once again. That didn't bode well for the other humanoids.

"They are gonna get attacked," I said. Some kind of agreement had been broken and the tendril wasn't on the breaking side.

"What can we do?" Sam asked, a slight quake in his voice. I knew that if we had to jump into action, he wouldn't hesitate, but his feelings were written on his sleeve and clear in his voice.

"We wait," Daniela said flatly.

She was gritting her teeth and I knew she was ready to jump in the mix. However, she was more than smart enough to know that something more was going on here and exposing ourselves wouldn't be a good outcome.

With my focus split on my friends, I missed when the tendril had turned around and walked away. The humanoids hesitated, as if wanting to go after it but fearing a response to that behavior. When the elf placed a hand on the orc to hold her back, the entire group sighed in resignation and started to walk back towards the trees.

As soon as they did, the tendril flicked his fingers without turning around, and three boars the size of small cars charged out into the field. Their stomps left chopped salads in their wake and trails of steam drifted from their snouts. The glimmer of crystal on their tusks told me all I needed to know about their Attunement even if I was out of range for the implant.

The elf immediately turned and heaved the ground right in front of the boars. It wasn't in the same fashion as I used <Earthen Barrier>. Massive trunks of wood pried themselves from the ground to slow the porcine threat.

The move gave the other humanoids time to gather their wits. Fiery hair sprouted from the orc woman, and the dwarves held hands. It was an odd display, but when I watched a bright red, patternless spell chain form like a crown above the gray-green woman's head, and a tan colored one around the dwarves' waist, I knew it wasn't just for show.

Sure enough, the orc woman's fiery hair swelled and took on the shape of a hand. With it, and the help of another well-timed surge of wood from the pink man, they held off the three boars from reaching the dwarves.

The elf pulled a machete from its belt and started to wail on the closest boar. With impressive speed, the elf managed to stay out of range of the boar's tusks while giving it the thousand cut death. The orc lady was hair-wrestling one of the other boars into a smoldering submission, but the third was moving to flank the whole group and the scattered logs the elf had raised.

The dwarves were still locked together even if their spell chain looked thicker than any I'd seen from my friends.

"They aren't going to make it," Sam whispered.

A string of expletives found their way out of my mouth before I focused on the third boar's trajectory. A mental slam later, and the ground right next to the orc lady swelled. Two <Stone Spikes> pierced the boar in the chest, halting its advance and eliciting a squeal audible from our building.

The stones gave the two dwarves enough time to finish the longest skill I'd seen. A chunk of the earth right behind them rose up into the air. The tilled and organic rich soil immediately halved in size, creating small clumps of hardened stone. Said stone then accurately propelled itself like a hailstorm into the boars.

Having anticipated, or at least planned for, some aspect of their companions' attack, the elf and orc had disengaged from their foes just before impact.

The boars were sturdy enough not to get shredded by the stone hail like the swallow, but I doubted they would be more than pudding after they were buried under the attack. A dust cloud rose up out of the ground, but the orc and elf were quick to dart in and deal finishing blows to the entombed creatures.

With a start, I realized that the tendril was nowhere to be seen, and the opposite tree line was as still as could be.

"Ron, we need to move," Daniela said, urgently.

"What, what happened?" I asked, turning on a dime, expecting something had snuck up on us.

"No, I saw what you did. When they go collect the Pith, some of it will give us away!"

The pieces clicked and I was getting ready to head off into the woods alone when Sam grabbed my wrist. "The bodies aren't disintegrating."

"Wha—"

"They are extracting them from the rubble, and they aren't breaking down," he clarified.

I shifted back to the broken wall. Sure enough, the dwarves

were reaching into the mound and hoisting the boars out. The orc and the odd-colored elf worked together to extract the last body. Their discussion didn't last very long, but it was heated. The orc pointed to my stone spikes, their tips cracked inside the closest boar. The only word I was able to hear even with my senses tuned in was the word 'alone.' The others in the group looked around as if even more uncertain.

In what was a clear command, the orc pointed towards the pine trees while dragging one of the boars. She spoke some words into the elf's ear and he shot off into the woods. I might have imagined it, but the tree trunks looked like they parted out of his way. The pair of dwarves kicked at the ruined crops until the orc woman shouted at them. "Get a move on!" *That* was loud enough for us to hear.

The three of us remained mute for several minutes, staring at the scene of carnage and destruction. My mind was running at a hundred miles a minute, so I forced myself to take some breaths to calm down. As if having noticed my discomfort, Sam hit me with a <Health Bump> and the energizing mana helped clear my mind.

"What's the plan, Ron?" Sam asked.

"I was gonna ask you guys what you think," I replied, meeting both of their eyes.

"Best guess? Somehow fantasy creatures mutated on the surface just like every other wonky thing. Not only that, but they are also smart. I doubt these fields or those trees got planted by themselves," Daniela said, crossing her arms and huffing. Clearly, she thought that she had it all figured out.

"Could they be the sources of the humanoid tendrils?" Sam asked, then snapped his fingers as if a lightbulb had gone off. "Wait, what if those are humans?"

"They just up and started cosplaying?" Daniela retorted. "I don't think people would have that kind of time after Landfall."

"No, no. I mean what if they *are* humans? They just look that way because of their Attunements. Heck, look at us. We've already changed and we've not been on the surface that long."

"Then we follow them. It doesn't take a genius to know that tendril intended to kill them. We're going to need more information if we are going to try to interact with them. You two know more than anyone that I would love for them to just be changed humans, but we can't risk it," I said. I was already straining my eyes to search after the path they might have left and where we might follow out of sight.

"You mean like how you interacted with those <Stone Spikes>?" Daniela said, cocking an eyebrow.

"Well, the tendrils are technically our enemies. The boar was gonna get them, and I couldn't just let them die like that…" When she and Sam gave me wide smiles, I knew they were teasing me. *Always the gullible one.* "Hilarious, yeah, yeah. Har har. On a more serious note, Danny, do you think you can trail them without being spotted?"

"Can I spit fire?" she asked, casting a look towards the trees in mock disinterest.

"Can you?" Sam and I both asked in unison.

"Idiots, I tell yah." She shook her head. "I sure do hope those are humans so I can finally stop having to deal with you numbnuts. One has more plants than sense, and the other more rocks than brain. Maybe that lovely tusked lady will want a new friend. Yes, I will follow. Keep you posted on the comm-plant."

"The what?" both Sam and I asked, confused. In unison again.

"The comms. On the implant. The comm-plant."

"We'll work on that one. Go, get going. Take Anthony. I think he's been *antsy* to run loose a bit."

Her voice echoed in my head as she huffed and sprinted down the trees. "And you thought I was the cringe one with the ant puns." All she had to do was give our Fire Ant companion a wave and he followed. The two faded from view shortly.

"What's next for us?" Sam asked, turning from me to Blobby.

The slime had been silent and on good behavior the entire trip over. However, it was currently slapping its appendage against the ruin as if trying to eat the broken concrete. I tossed him a rock chunk from the ruined wall, and the slime wobbled after it like a dog playing fetch. Except it wasn't a dog, or a stick, and the rock disappeared into its gelatinous body.

"We'll follow slowly, but I'll prepare a small shelter for us here just in case. As good a place as any right now."

I matched words to action as <Earthen Barrier> sealed one of the damaged walls and I cast three more back-to-back to box off one of the corners of the building. After reaching Quotient 4, my spikes rose to seven feet with their regular cast and my barriers now rose up almost two feet. It wasn't a terribly big improvement, but the cost had remained the same. The backlash of the casting also affected me less than when we'd first come to the surface.

Sam and I offloaded most of our loot and supplies into one of our bags. Daniela hadn't bothered to take her stuff when she started tracking the potential humans. We had just enough for two days and enough water for the day. Traveling light was essential if we were going to be pursuing the group.

Less than five minutes after we'd begun our eastern trek parallel to the road, we heard Daniela's voice through the comm. "Nothing dangerous as of yet, but you two are going to want to see this. I just… Get here, please."

Her voice had a pleading tone to it. Sam and I looked at each other before we sprinted through the trees. With our enhanced attributes, we made short work of the mile and a half ahead of us. Anthony was there to lead us the last stretch through a thick series of trees and another small field of peanuts and cabbage. Daniela was crouched just behind a dilapidated building and I could just barely see the outline of another field beyond. Even through the trees, I could tell it was much larger than even the one we had just left.

She didn't say anything. Her tanned skin was a shade lighter and even the red accent of her fire gills had gone from maroon to a faded pink. The brunette pointed to the other side of the building. I didn't bother to pause and crept up to the edge of the building. Sam was close on my heels as we peered beyond.

Civilization.

In every sense of the word, that was what we encountered. The sprawling field before us was being tended to by a number of humanoids. Not humanoids in the faceless, four limbs and a head sense of the tendrils. Actual humanoids. Bulky, towering individuals carried heavy loads while dwarves pulled carts through the rows. Two of the strange-colored, sharp-eared people argued amidst crates of potatoes being loaded into the carts. A variety of orcs and the other races mingled up and down the road.

Said road led to what had to be a palisade. The trees that had surely been cleared for the farm stood vertically out of the ground to form a wall that stretched north and south out of sight. Even from half a mile away, I could see figures moving steadily along the upper part of the wall. While tracing the pointed log tips of the palisade, I came upon the gate. Unsurprisingly, it lined up with the road we'd been skirting through our trip. Roughly wrought steel and metal sheets that vaguely resembled car doors hung from the gate's frame.

I was at a loss for words. Just out and about in front of the walls were more than two dozen people. More people than could reasonably fit anywhere other than the greenhouse floor or the mess hall. Sure, most didn't actually look *human*, but now I was fairly certain Sam's hypothesis was right on the money. On my second pass, I even spotted a few older-looking people with mostly human features. At a distance, it was hard to tell, but something told me they were people like the Bunkerites. Born before Landfall.

A pulse of energy invisible to the naked eye flickered through my body. It didn't leave the tingly sensation I was familiar with, and instead felt like I'd pushed my body through an inflating soap bubble, but I recognized it. It was the area of influence of a Metier Entity Cluster.

Not worrying about possibly being spotted, I clambered up

the nearest tree. Sam and Danny whispered angry warnings about me being spotted. Danny even tried to jump and pull me by the ankle, but I had already snagged the next branch. The western part of a city sprawled out before me. Beyond the patched rooftops and sporadic trees beyond the wall was something that sent a chill down my spine. Not in fear, but in surprise and amazement.

A crystal larger than anything I'd seen outside of simulations towered in the distance.It was a near identical copy of the Entity back at the camp, just magnified to insane proportions. Unlike what I'd expected, there wasn't a ginormous crater in its wake. Whatever the reason for that, I had no idea. What ran through my head were all the possibilities a behemoth of that size would open for us. The Entity's mention of categories based on size suddenly made a whole lot of sense.

When the pulse of the crystal's influence flowed through me again, it almost threw me off the tree. That one had packed a wallop, and that one *had* been felt by my friends below.

"Ronan, what the hell is going on?" Sam asked, forgoing whispering for the sake of answers.

The answer came without needing me to provide it. A primal string of roars echoed across the farmland, and the loud ding of a warning bell caused all of the people outside of the city walls to freeze. That was when the monsters appeared. Dozens of twisted animals and a sprinkling of humanoids tore out of the woods after the people in the open. My heart clenched as I saw how deeply outnumbered they were. However, that wasn't the only thing that clenched.

Inadvertently, I'd channeled mana into my shield and a surge of strength caused me to crush the branch I'd been holding in my left hand. It was something I would've never dreamt myself capable of doing. With what added up to 1.62 times the strength of an average human, it wasn't impossible.

I could already see the people fleeing, and many that would not be able to make it. A pair of younger teens with short orc tusks lugged an older gentleman away from where he'd been weeding. The man struggled after them, but it was clear they wouldn't make it. A blue wolfhound and what had to be a younger version of the earth-attuned deer we'd spotted on our first trip were giving chase. Many more were already pouncing on the cart full of potatoes as the men hid under it and swatted at a pair of corrupted wind squirrels.

The tree swayed as I couldn't take the sight any more. Instead of saying anything, Samuel handed me my pickaxe. The fire burning in his and Danny's eyes was something I'd seldom seen, but I knew what it meant. Arguing would be pointless, and they would be following me post haste.

A brief series of commands to Blobby and Anthony had the two creatures rushing to intercept the trapped men while the three of us booked it straight into the path of the two Dreg-twisted creatures.

CHAPTER THIRTY-THREE

Missing Tribute

"<Earthen Barrier>!"

Two empowered casts of the skill ripped through my mana pool. Each hoisted vegetable and soil alike two feet up in front of each of the attacking creatures. The wolfhound tried to react in time, but only managed to get its front paws over the mound. It left a trail of frost in its wake as it tumbled and tried to catch itself. The earth-attuned deer cleared the hurdle with no issue at all. Thankfully, it gave me enough time to superimpose myself between its wickedly sharp antlers and the orc teens. The impact pushed me back a full five feet. I was sure if the rows of vegetables hadn't caught on my boots, I would have been pushed further.

As the momentum died, my shield let out a ripple of heat. The deer backpedaled long enough for me to disengage the top prongs of my H-shield. With my arm free, I let loose a pair of <Stone Spikes> into the creature's neck. Its head thrashed about, but I caught its attempts to gore me on my shield.

"Daniela, get the—" I started to shout before I saw the woman slice clear through the wolfhound's head without pause. "Cart. Go! Sam, defensive <Vine Whips>!"

I gagged as some of the deer's blood got in my mouth, but the creature stopped struggling when I managed to impale it one last time with my pickaxe. When I took a step back, the madness around me finally clicked into place.

Danny was flying down one of the rows. Her wisp was already ripping small blasts of fire across the space. The men under the cart had apparently been emboldened by the charging brunette telling them she was coming and were lobbing some of their scattered potatoes at the squirrels.

A smattering of people were rushing out of the gate and leading the farmers back into town. I recognized the orc woman as her fiery hair slapped a squirrel out of the air. A series of commands spilled out of her mouth to the varied people around her.

When a vine as thick as my leg slapped a squirrel out of the air above me, my drifting eyes focused.

"Ronan, get your head in the game!" Sam shouted, superimposing himself in the way of a fireball aimed at the orc teens. Human tendrils had reached the fight and brought friends.

My stomach really didn't like it when I cast magic close together, but I didn't care what it thought. Instead, I double cast a V-shaped fortification right in the middle of the field to help cover the teens and Sam. The life mage had already hit himself with a <Health Bump> to mitigate the burns of the fireball.

The sharp crack of a rifle took down one of the blue humanoids before they lobbed an ice attack at the defenders. Not to be outdone, I provided some defenses for them as well. Six half-powered <Stone Spikes> flanked the road. One of them even managed to impale a Dreg ant that hadn't been quick enough to get out of the way.

The orc woman spotted my skill and gave me a deliberate look as the spell chain faded and I coiled into the fetal position. My mana pool hovered in the tens, and the pain had taken me out of the fight momentarily.

Thankfully, Sam had enough presence of mind on the farm-turned-battlefield to save me from a sweeping squirrel. Vines wrapped around my ankle and dragged me roughly out of the speedy rodent's path.

"Get it together, Ron! You three, make sure he stands up. He'll take it from there."

I'd never heard Sam so commanding, but it served its purpose. The three men, mostly the younger orcs, helped me to my feet. I was still suffering from the casting backlash. A deep breath helped some, but I knew I'd be aching for a while.

The teens received a sharp nod from me and I leaned against my makeshift defenses.

"Danny, Blobby, and Anthony are pinned at the cart. The people from the town are holding at your spike defenses but there are too many humanoids on that side. I've been able to slap away the animal tendrils, but I can see more in the woods. They are holding back."

"Where the heck did all of these things come from? We should have seen a force this large heading this way." My mind was racing as I watched Daniela lob two condensed <Flame Blasts> into a humanoid fire tendril. The attack didn't seem to bother the creature overmuch, but it caused its own attack to fly wide.

The pink man from before threw his hands out to sprout wood supports between my spikes. I watched him swoon before one of the dwarves held him steady.

"Sam, we need to get together with them."

"Are you sure that is a good idea?" he asked. A whip crack marked the blond's control of his skill as it smacked another deer away. The top chunk of his vine burst into green plant goo, but he kept it poised to strike. The assorted animal tendrils eyed our fortification warily without approaching.

"You can trust the Wild Guard. They would never betray you!" one of the teens said. His voice cracked but he met my eyes when I turned. I weighed the risks and came up short on many options. With less than fifteen defenders between us and this 'Wild Guard,' we would be hard-pressed to deal with the tendrils as it stood.

"You two, hold Gramps there tight. Sam, what's your range on the vines?"

"With them getting more expensive, I say about twenty feet before they tap me out of mana." Another whip crack smacked an overeager tortoise, forcing it into its defensive shell.

"Shit. Here, you two hold onto this shield and put it between you if something throws magic at you," I said.I slid my arm out of the enarmes and slapped it into the closest teen's hands. "Cut the vines off, Sam. If something else jumps at you, snag it but keep moving."

"What about you?" he asked, his eyes drifting from his vines to me.

I barely heard his question as I cast my newest skill in combat for the first time. <Earth Shell> flowed out of the pores on my left arm even as I flinched from the pain in my abdomen. With it positively entombed, I yelled at the group to move before I could pay much more attention to my near empty mana.

Sam dropped his arms and slapped me on the back of the neck before turning. A tingling surged through my body, as if someone had dumped choco-coffee beans straight in my bloodstream. My senses sharpened for the moment as I watched my friend.

The blond helped the teens move the older gentleman. His vines thudded against the ground as his control over them faded. The teen who I'd given the shield held it up with a steady hand, glaring hatred in the tendrils' direction. Surprising no one, the creatures charged to the attack.

"On me!" I roared in their faces. Moving with my left arm locked wasn't the most convenient or comfortable thing, but when it smacked the deer in the head, I felt pretty good. The creature was nowhere near dead, but it was stunned enough to leave my friend alone.

A second after, the tortoise got the courage to tilt and roll its crystalline bulk in my direction. From experience, I knew that was less than great. I swung with the widened chisel end of my pick into the ground in front of me. The reptile hit the tool-turned-spike trap on the head and pushed me back as I attempted to arrest its momentum. The muscles in my legs strained even more than with the deer. I was ready to pop a blood vessel.

The creature's momentum plowed a new row diagonally across the field until it stopped. Two ants scurried past me, one the dull red of a Fire Ant and the other a midnight black I wasn't familiar with. I was able to react fast enough to hit the Fire Ant with a kick before the tortoise wanted some more attention.

A crystal the size of my fist ejected itself from its shell and punched most of the way through my vest. I growled in frustration just to ignore the pain, hot blood dripping down my side.

Hoping that Sam could deal with the two ants, I planted my feet and punched the tortoise back a foot. Some of my earthen armor crumbled, but it had been worth it. The brief reprieve gave me enough time to extract my embedded pick from the tortoise and deliver a devastating horizontal blow into its exposed underside.

My perception practically screamed at me. All I had time to do was put my arm between me and a deer's crystal rack.

My pickaxe flew from my grip and I tumbled through a cabbage patch. My shell crumbled to dust, but not before I managed to smack myself in the face with it. The iron taste of blood bloomed in my mouth as I tried to get my bearings. That instantly failed as rough green hands pulled me back before the two dwarves blocked off the creatures. Each was kicking the dirt at their feet to pepper semi-compressed soil at the creatures that had given chase.

The deer used its antlers to hoist a section of the ground like a shovel scoop, nullifying the attacks but failing to let it advance. The sharp crack of gunfire followed by a pained wail told me something else had been hit.

"Who in the hell are you, and what are you doing here?"

The person whose hands had dragged me away dropped me unceremoniously on the ground.

"Can… we go with friend…and figure it out from there?" I managed. My head was still ringing and the world hadn't stopped spinning.

"Please, a moment." Sam's sweat-covered face appeared in my vision before he slapped me on the face. Relief flowed through me and my thoughts sharpened. I still felt like someone had thrown me in a dull-bladed blender, but at least I could string thoughts together.

"What kind of healing is that?" the pink colored man asked, leaning over Sam's shoulder to watch me. Before we said anything, I wanted to discuss with my friends. Our poor attempt at surveillance now had us tangled up in a pseudo-standoff with tendrils and little to no explanation for the surface people.

"Maybe questions after we don't have murderous animals on the prowl," I said, taking my friend's hand to get on my feet.

"You better believe there will be some questions, squirt," the orc woman said. From up close, I realized just how much more intimidating she was. And at least a full head taller than me. All I could do was offer a weak nod in return.

"What's the status? Do you guys know what's going on?" I asked, trying to get my thoughts back in order.

"Those blasted tendrils said we needed to up tribute. When I told them that wasn't possible, they responded less than positively. Based on what I've seen, you had a hand in us making it back at all," the orc woman said. "I'm Sarah. We appreciate the assist."

The woman was halfway to shaking my hand when she snapped away. Her fiery hair formed in a moment and slapped a squirrel from the air. The attack drew my attention back to the field and the unusual level of intelligence the animals were showcasing. It was a mixture of their primal instincts, rolled with a hefty dose of aggression and bound within a previously unseen discipline.

It was the worst kind of standoff.

Now that we'd vacated my V-walls, the deer and two wolfhounds hunkered down there. One humanoid blurred across the farm fields before leaping into a roll behind my own fortification. The rest hovered amidst the trees with a smattering of creatures. I could have sworn I saw another boar, a rabbit, and another tortoise slinking in the shadows. My eyes lingered on the expressionless humans tendrils as they watched Danny's charges. Smoldering squirrel bodies lay at her feet.

"Can you two do that large skill you did before?" I asked, watching my own mana pool creep upwards.

"Yeah, kid, but it's not got much range and it takes time," the dwarf on the right said.

"Okay. First, we aren't children or squirts. If we are going to follow through, we need to be on the same page. The only thing we need to do is get to the cart and retrieve the others, then we can back up into the town."

"Problem, Mr. Not-a-Child. Those are all ranged tendrils. They'll cut you down before you get anywhere," the pink-colored man said. The other people in the group, an orc man and someone who looked vaguely reptilian, nodded at the man's words.

"Give me a distraction and I'll get them out," I said.

"Fine, but you're paying for Gallow's brew. The heartburn this is gonna give us after twice in one day..." the left dwarf said.

Him and the very similar dwarf clasped hands. The large spell chain wobbled around them. Now that I was only a few feet away, I could tell it was the primal version I'd seen on animals and not the crisp patterned ones of my friends and I.

My mana ticked past the fifty percent mark and I retrieved my shield from the teen. He didn't look like he wanted me to take it, but he didn't resist when I did. *These people don't have more defenses? How have they survived so long?*

The simple answer was the 'Wild Guard,' but I had a sneaking suspicion there was more to it.

Regardless, mana flowed through my pickaxe as I shaped a small crystal umbrella at its head.

"<Adrenal Surge>," Sam said, slapping me in the back of the head once again. The adrenaline boost flowed through me. His skill use explained how I managed to survive holding the creatures off.

"Thanks. If you've recovered enough, throw some heals at the injured and slap some tendrils."

Sam struck a mock salute and made his way over to the older gentleman as well as some of the others who'd sought shelter with the Guard.

I watched as the two men unleashed rock hail once again. Their complaints didn't even wait for the skill to land. With stone hail falling down in a wide area around the cart, I clambered over our defenses.

The response to the attack and my subsequent approach was immediate and intense. A lobbed fireball splashed against my H-shield while I batted a crystal shard from one of the tortoises out of range. I made note of the range on the creature's attack but pushed forward. Another fireball went way off course as the humanoid tendril got hit in the chest by the rock hail.

An icicle that had no business existing in Florida materialized in front of me. Instead of trying to dodge, I braced myself behind my shield and forced the attack to skim off the chitin. Since the attack wasn't braced against the ground like my own pointy-stabby skill, it dropped to the ground half-melted. The heat pulse from my shield had liquefied the surface faster than I thought possible.

The barrage that dealt with the mounds created by the rock hail gave me just enough cover to make it to Daniela. Blobby jiggled in joy at my appearance. I patted the slime gently on its absent head before focusing on my friend.

"Why haven't you guys retreated?" I asked, crouching behind the cart as another icicle tried to take my eye out.

"The cart, sir. We need these potatoes for the town. We

can't just leave it to the tendrils!" one of the odd-colored people said. He sounded younger than I would have expected for his size.

I gave Danny a look and she gave me a quick summary rolling her eyes all the while. "Bad guys take food from good guys. Good guys no have enough food. Bad guys go rarrr."

"You can be a real pain, you know?"

"Redeeming quality," she replied. She flicked her hand in the air and a <Flame Blast> leapt from her hand. It wasn't her condensed ones with more precision but a weak splash that detonated three fire attacks sent by the human tendrils. "And this is what I've been dealing with. Blobby has taken on the rock projectiles and Anthony is watching for icicles to melt. Don't know how we can retreat while we are surrounded like this."

A frown deepened as I considered what we should do. "Is there no one else in the town that can help?" I asked the two men.

"The other Wild Guards are out hunting and one is on expedition duty. We've never been attacked like this!" the same man answered. He had a potato in a death grip, which told me just about how well he was dealing with the stress of combat.

My eyes roved across the space until they landed back on the rock hail. I eyed my mana pool and the distance I'd covered before making my decision.

The slight static of the comm-plant buzzed in my ear as I contacted Sam. "Don't react. Pretend I am signaling you to do exactly as I say." While communicating via the implant, I pantomimed rain with my fingers then pointed at the rock hail and spun my hands in a circle.

"Tell those two grouches I need another hail. Plain and simple."

Sam immediately turned and relayed my message. The complaining was loud enough that we heard it from the cart, but they complied. Less than a minute later, condensed earth was pelting down around us.

"I want you two to pull as hard as you can. We'll provide

cover from anything that approaches," I said to the villagers. They barely nodded, but took positions opposite the cart.

With a flick of my wrist and a twist of my entrails, I raised an <Earthen Barrier> to fill in the gaps the hail hadn't. Earth rose out of the ground as I pushed on the cart to move it. A moment later, the odd-colored men tugged and the thing lurched forward slow but steady. Using the last of my mana, I dropped two half-powered <Stone Spikes> as a minute amount of cover from the rear. And it immediately proved useful.

Our actions were obvious for the tendrils to see. Their attack surged. An icicle that Anthony wasn't fast enough to melt whizzed by me and Daniela grunted with each <Flame Blast> she used. The sweat that covered her brow steamed as the heat of her body rose with each attack. I even noticed the gills flare with each of her breaths.

When the road inclined a bit, I had to brace the wooden construct with my back and I watched as the tendrils attacked. After having lost their surprise advantage, and a few of their number, the humanoid tendrils remained near the back to lob magic while they let some of the animals loose. Several shapes were still watching from the tree line and it worried me that they hadn't attacked. However, we managed to make it back to the Wild Guard without any crazy happenings.

The two potato men slumped to the ground with the other civilians. Daniela joined them on the ground as she gulped air from both her mouth and gills. Steam was rising off her body in droves. She spotted me watching. "Close to tapping out my mana."

"We'll handle the rest. The others should be in position by now," the orc woman said. She wasn't looking at our group, but instead focused on the animals who'd stopped their advance. They were reversing their steps when a barrage of wind threw one of the boars onto its side. What looked like moss clung to the creatures before blooming. Like green silly string bombs, the moss crawled all over them. Squeals, yowls, and angry chitters echoed from around them as the tendrils struggled against the growing mound of vegetation.

Just as they were freeing themselves or rolling out of the wind, a gunshot snapped through the clearing. Each shot took one of the creatures down, leaving several bodies strewn about the farm fields. When I managed to rip my eyes away from the sight, I followed the origin of the wind to see three women and a man leaning over the palisade. The man held a rifle slung over his shoulder while one of the women towered over him. She also had the pointed ears, but only the upward point. The second woman was blue, and the last I could only describe as a satyr. As I watched, the man put a conical device to his mouth.

"Surrender and you will not be harmed," he said in a hollow tone. I couldn't tell if it was his voice or because he was using the megaphone.

The Wild Guard around me tensed and I followed their gaze to a figure striding out of the woods. The palm-winged humanoid stared us down from several hundred feet away, which was impressive. Goosebumps crawled up and down my arms as it included me in its piercing gaze before addressing us.

"Perfection does not subject itself to mediocracy. Rebellion does not become you, town of Wildwood. You will pay for your insolence." Without another word, the tendril turned around and disappeared into the woods. Its other Dreg-corrupted brethren followed after. Trails of fire, splotches of frost, and churned earth marked their passage.

No one in our group moved. I wasn't in much of a shape to fight anything, but I would certainly give it hell. However, when clearly nothing was going to attack, the orc woman struck a conversation with the man on the wall. Almost as if it was deliberate, the elf in their group kept her hands moving slowly and air buffeted around them. My increased perception failed to catch anything they said, their words snatched away by the wind.

With a start, I remembered that I hadn't seen anything come from the direction of my makeshift fortification. The sight that greeted me was not what I expected. A dissipating mist clung like a blanket to my <Earthen Barriers>. Something tall and azure flashed within the mist, but the next blink it was gone. The icy air evaporated under the heat of the sun. In its wake were the wind human tendril, the deer, and two wolfhounds. All four dead.

Before I got a chance to ask about the strange occurrence, the orc woman had returned. Her finger wagged in my face. Normally I would have focused on the appendage commanding my attention, but my peripheral let me watch her fellow Wild Guard flank around my friends. It was an attempt to intimidate if I'd ever seen one. The slight smile I'd allowed myself after the victory slipped into a flat line.

"You have some questions to answer. First and foremost is: why do you look like the old humans?"

"I don't believe we owe you any kind of explanation," I said shortly, drawing myself up. It was enough to look the orc woman in the eye, which clearly she wasn't totally used to; she took a step back.

"Are you somehow connected to the tendril demands? Why did you intervene?" Sarah pressed.

"Oy! Boar mouth!" Daniela shouted as she shoved her way to me. The two people she'd passed between flinched, as if they were ready to react to an attack only for her surge into the orc's face. "We just saved your—"

"Enough," I said, placing my hand on her shoulder. Daniela flinched, glaring at me and ready to shoot an insult at me just for stopping her, but I gave her a meaningful look while glancing behind her. She grimaced, but retreated a step to cover Samuel as the other fighters circled closer. "We intervened to help. We know nothing else."

The orc glared at our group, her arms crossed in an attempt to be casual. When I didn't back down, she turned to the man who'd shot from the wall. Once again they exchanged words, but I failed to catch any of them. The orc woman looked over her shoulder before entering the walls without another word.

"Alright, we aren't going to stand here twiddling our thumbs. Come on," I said, half-turning to walk in the direction we'd come. My hunch proved unfortunately correct. The gunslingers raised their weapons, and the other fighters dropped ever so slightly into a fighting form.

"You three ain't going nowhere until we are good and ready," the seeming leader of the gunslingers said.

I hoped that our improved regeneration helped rebuild enamel because I ground my teeth loud enough to see the man grimace. Yet, his gun remained in place. I sent a quick message through our comms when I saw the cordoned area around us had been fully established. "Don't say anything, and don't use the implants. I don't like what's going on, and there is no sense making people with their finger on the trigger twitchy."

"I bet we could charge them," Daniela growled in our call.

Following my first suggestion, Sam stepped forward to pretend to check Daniela for injuries. It wasn't entirely unwarranted, but the man's use of his mana seemed to cause the group around us to tense. *Good.*

All actions had consequences. While our chance to meet the town's inhabitants on our own terms had been taken, and our welcome was less than auspicious, I would be damned if we came across as meek. So, I set my legs and met the stare of anyone that dared to hold it.

If decades in the Bunker couldn't break me, a standoff with the first of humanity I encountered wouldn't either.

EPILOGUE

Massive pillars of stone rose up out of the ground before crumbling and sinking out of view. The roiling sands pushed and liquified the rock around a central, unmoving crystal. A mud brown light flickered over the entirety of the grainy ocean. Some might have mistaken it for moonlight, but tonight was a new moon. The jagged, unnatural mountain of glowing glass illuminated a half mile of limestone desert.

On his knees, face pressed directly onto the crystal platform, was a man that would have been unremarkable if not for the distinct lack of fleshy limbs.

Ever-shifting muscles of sand bound the man's flesh, blood, hands, feet, and head together as the earth mana flowed out of the rocky maelstrom around him and into his body. His face was flat as he waited for a response from the creature within the crystal. As he had done countless times already.

"My brethren have awakened. Throughout this pitiful world, inhabitants seek to embrace real power, yet they do not understand that they play with the wrong set of dice. Your work has pleased me. It appears the time to reap what you have sown is upon us."

A path of semisolid rock surged out of the ground. Instead of falling back into the roiling mass of the creature's influence, it provided a miniscule reprieve. The man, eyes glinting with umber fire, retreated away from the crystal without a word. Numerous fossorial creatures parted out of his way as he vanished down a worn road. He knew there was work to do, even after his endless years of toiling. Two creatures that answered to the Dreg split off from the throng.

They shadowed the man step by step, mile after mile, until he stood on a cliff looking down upon a town. He'd been to this city twice before. Once, when life was simple. The other, when he'd begun weaving his will into its residents. He didn't know if the seeds he'd scattered in his wake would be sufficient, but the only fuel he had at that point was hope and rage. With a sandy huff, the man approached the inferior crystal within range of the city.

The words were acid on his tongue, but he knew that anything else would have spawned hells the world wasn't ready for. He'd seen the creatures hidden beyond reach, and the world was far from ready. Yet, as he spoke, he coated himself in another layer of determination. Yet another layer of responsibility.

"Demand the tributes. The Aberrant seek action."

The crystal wailed and the man had to pull his sand grain bound limbs tight to avoid being blown away. The wails echoed through the forest around him and out into the world beyond their audible range. His dark-rimmed eyes watched the pulse extend beyond even the places he'd been. He needed to remember, if not him then another. The Dreg stirred like it never had before.

ABOUT FRANK G. ALBELO

Frank is a Civil Engineer graduate who rediscovered his passion for writing. The twenty-something year old is happily married and has a toddler who is a cute, but huge, troublemaker. Originally born in Cuba, Frank moved to Costa Rica at a young age and then to Miami, Florida giving him a wonderfully diverse view of the world to draw on for the worlds he creates.

He has been writing stories since he was young and reading them way before that. He hopes to continue to write tales and create wondrous systems to share them with readers. Some of Frank's other hobbies include Magic the Gathering, video gaming, and bugging his wife about buying new bookshelves to accommodate the books that seem to magically appear in their home.

Connect with Frank G. Albelo:
Patreon.com/Falbelo
Facebook.com/FAlbeloWriter
Discord.gg/A6srSxk

ABOUT MOUNTAINDALE PRESS

Dakota and Danielle Krout, a husband and wife team, strive to create as well as publish excellent fantasy and science fiction novels. Self-publishing *The Divine Dungeon: Dungeon Born* in 2016 transformed their careers from Dakota's military and programming background and Danielle's Ph.D. in pharmacology to President and CEO, respectively, of a small press. Their goal is to share their success with other authors and provide captivating fiction to readers with the purpose of solidifying Mountaindale Press as the place 'Where Fantasy Transforms Reality.'

Connect with Mountaindale Press:
MountaindalePress.com
Facebook.com/MountaindalePress
Twitter.com/_Mountaindale
Instagram.com/MountaindalePress

MOUNTAINDALE PRESS TITLES
GameLit and LitRPG

The Completionist Chronicles,
The Divine Dungeon,
Full Murderhobo, and
Year of the Sword by Dakota Krout

Metier Apocalypse by Frank G. Albelo

Arcana Unlocked by Gregory Blackburn

A Touch of Power by Jay Boyce

Red Mage and
Farming Livia by Xander Boyce

Space Seasons by Dawn Chapman

Ether Collapse and
Ether Flows by Ryan DeBruyn

Dr. Druid by Maxwell Farmer

Bloodgames by Christian J. Gilliland

Unbound by Nicoli Gonnella

Threads of Fate by Michael Head